Buzzards of Bochimville

A Novel

Fonnette Bullard Harris

This book is a work of fiction. The characters, incidents, and dialogues are products of the author's imagination and are not to be construed as real. Any resemblance to actual events or persons, living or dead, is entirely coincidental.

Buzzards of Bochimville
Copyright ©2009 by Fonnette Bullard Harris
Published by Soaring Press, LLC

ISBN-10: 0-9823617-0-X
ISBN-13: 978-0-9823617-0-2

Library of Congress Control Number: 2009920115

Editing by Callie C. Brown
Cover Design and artwork: Robert Harris and Samuel Parker
Printed in the United States of America

To Robert

For his willingness to soar with the Buzzards

ক্তক্তক্তক্তক্তক্ত

Self-sufficiency is only the illusion of the ego. It is friendship that makes us whole.
-Novalis

In appreciation of treasured friendships

Elaine McWhorter, Jacque Bowen, Jean Stansell, Gerry Wright,
and Freeman Barber

ক্তক্তক্তক্তক্তক্ত

CHAPTER ONE

Ewell Moody

Ewell Moody struggled to remove the body of Bochimville's latest victim from the back of his pickup truck. Slightly inebriated and drenched by the heavy downpour, he removed his pants from around his ankles and threw them over the rail of the loading dock. The body, wrapped in two garbage bags and tied in the middle with Moody's suspenders, slid off the tailgate and landed face down in a patch of kudzu.

❧❧❧❧❧❧❧

The morning my troubles began big time and eventually forced me to make a quick exit from the town of my birth, I did not feel the discomfort from the cold as Porter snuggled on my pillow and Maggie and Audrey warmed my stomach with their soft, silky fur. In a deep, peaceful sleep, I resented the intrusion when Stump Dupree, my embalmer, Boy Friday, and life partner, as we have been together since birth, knocked, opened the door, and walked into my apartment.

As I slowly opened one eye and peered around my cat's sleeping body, I saw him moving towards me with my pants draped over his arm and my shoes in his right hand. Delilah, my pit bull, followed closely at his heels.

"My Lord, Ewell," I heard him say, "this place is colder than the naked corpse we dug out of a North Georgia blizzard." He yanked the quilt from my bed and slung snarling cats in three directions.

"Don't you know it's dangerous to waken me suddenly?" I asked, instantly alert from the brutal cold. "It could prevent my soul from returning to my body should it be on a spiritual excursion."

"Still reading that Buddha crap, I see."

He flipped off the window air conditioner, threw my pants and shoes in the fireplace, and opened the blinds. I placed a pillow over my face and peeked out into the room.

"Turn off the damn spotlight," I yelled. "You trying to blind me?"

"There's no light on, Ewell," he said. "That's the morning sun. The rest of the world is out working for a living while you're curled up in bed deader than a stiff on my slab. Delilah, leave the cats alone. If you've got the urge to kill, go outside and do it, but don't bring it back in here. This place is full."

I heard Stump open the door to put the dog out and then walk back to my bed. I could feel him standing beside me. I lifted the pillow and looked up at him. "Have you never seen a naked body that's breathing?" I asked. "Give me my covers. I'm cold."

Stump turned on the lamp beside my bed and held it close enough to singe the hairs on my butt, but the warmth felt so good I didn't complain.

"What's that rash all over your body?" he asked.

"It's probably goose bumps. I'm freezing my ass off since you took my quilt."

"They're not goose bumps," he said as he took a straw from his mouth and began poking me in the back. "You been flopping around on an ant hill? Sit up."

Like a well-trained old dog, I sat up.

"Now get up," he demanded as if he were my mama. "The day is half spent, and you're still sacked-out. A couple of old ladies have been waiting all morning to see you," he explained as if I would become emotional and break out in hives over his pronouncement. "Anybody who hates work as much as you do ought to preach or politick for a living. Besides that, Grandpa taught you better manners than to leave folks like them old gals down yonder without as much as a howdy or a cup of coffee. Even you know that's no way to do business."

2

"Jeeeezus," I mumbled.

"Better call on somebody else since Jesus ain't down there. Just two old gals that claim you've got their dead sister, and they've been sitting in the hall since daybreak waiting for you to get your butt in gear and tell them what to do with her."

I began scratching my chest with both hands. "Mercy," I said, "I've got poison ivy."

"Where did you get it? Have you been sitting in the woods naked?"

"Guess I fell in it last night when I dropped the old lady," I explained as I reached under the bed and picked up a large jar of Vicks. I opened it, held it close to my nose, and took a deep breath. "That's the only time I remember being in weeds, and I haven't been in the woods naked, not lately anyhow." I reached for my quilt, but Stump snatched it and threw it across the room.

"Come on, Ewell, get yourself together. I've seen stiffs more alert than you."

"You don't have to be nasty. Maybe I'm not up early enough to please you, but I didn't go to bed until four o'clock. While you were snoozing in dreamland, I was running from the sheriff with a soggy stiff on my back."

"Who passed? Or do you remember? I didn't recognize the old gals downstairs, and they didn't bother to introduce themselves. People assume old lady Death keeps us informed of her next victim, or we're supposed to recognize every face in this county, dead or alive."

"The old maid died."

"Which one? The town is full of them. Can't you give me a little hint, or do I have to look at her and play identify the stiff? Put down that jar. You've snorted enough of that stuff."

"The one with the purple Edsel," I said as I placed the jar of Vicks under the bed. "Hand me the robe on top that cage. Will you, please? My buns feel like I slept with my backside on the wall of an igloo."

"Lord, Ewell," he said as he threw me the robe, "you've got to get rid of these old magazines. One spark and this place would go up like a Roman candle. Who did you say the old gal is?"

"Logan, Emma, Maude, hell, I don't know. Have you had breakfast?"

"Erma, Erma Mae Logan?" he asked, real excited as if I had announced the death of a rich old broad whose passing would fill our coffers with gold. "You mean the one-legged old maid who spent her summers sitting in a swing reading to a sheep?"

"What do you mean one-legged?" I asked while looking for the sash to keep my robe closed before my body turned purple.

"In her younger days, she had the reputation of fornicating with a guy in her pa's corncrib. One night he dropped an ash in a pile of shucks and set the place on fire. While trying to escape the flames, she fell through a hole in the floor and ripped her leg to shreds. Doctors amputated to stop the blood poison and gangrene. What's the matter, Ewell? You look a little gaunt."

"That explains it."

"What?"

"I was pulling on her feet to get her out of the truck when the bag split and one of her legs came off. It scared me so bad I fell off the truck backwards. I thought I had been in this business long enough for nothing to bother me. Guess I was wrong."

"How much had you drunk up to that time?"

"Not enough." On top the dresser I found a snap clothespin I used to fasten my robe. "You want an egg?"

"Yeah, fry me a couple over light, but don't fry them in Vicks. Why in the world did the sisters put her leg on after she died? About a year ago Mama went to see her, and even back then she couldn't get out of bed to pee. Surely she didn't sleep in the thing."

"Don't ask me why fools do crazy things. Hand me that can of Crisco on the mantle. When I got there, they had the old gal fully dressed and spread out on the bed with an open book across her chest and a quarter on each eyeball. Sister Tweedledump sat in a chair by the bed sniffing and hiccupping while sister Tweedleplump paced back and forth across the room beating the floor with her cane. She kept mumbling something, and I never figured out if she was talking to me or a specter that only she could see. Dig around in the barrel over there and find me an onion that's not sprouted. Every time she passed a big old mirror, she'd look at herself, smack her lips, and say something. She started hyperventilating and farting at such a rate I thought she'd pass out."

I took a deep breath and paused for a few seconds before continuing my narrative.

"You're not going to believe this next part," I assured him.

"Try me."

4

"In the corner of the room lay a big, dirty old black sheep moaning like a wolf caught in a trap, and I am not making this up."

Stump laughed. "I know you're not. The old maid had a pet sheep named Crowie that went everywhere she went. The story goes that she found the lamb in the woods off Crow Road shortly after Springer Yates, her lover, died. She was convinced he had reincarnated in the animal. It is a rather eerie story, for to my knowledge there is not another sheep, especially a black one, in the entire county."

"There is one thing about the dead gal that really interested me, other than the sheep," I said, "and that is her unique taste in reading. In her room were more books than in the entire Bochimville library. I mean deep stuff—stuff that most folks in this semi-literate county have never heard of. She must have been reading *The Portable Nietzsche* when she departed, as a copy lay open on her chest. I looked around at other titles and authors while I bagged the old gal, and she obviously kept company with the best. Scott, Kipling, Dostoyevsky, Rumi and Gibran were just a few that I saw. She must have been a damn feminist since one whole wall contained books by women authors such as Eliot, Wharton, Cather, Stowe, Woolf and Buck. I'd give all I own, which isn't much, to have the old gal's books, but I'm sure that's only wishful thinking. Her bed was placed in the middle of the room, and handmade, rough shelves filled with books covered all four walls. If the rest of the family has the mentality the Doofus sisters seem to have, they'll probably use the books for kindling."

"Don't think so. The old maid's sister, one of the ones waiting downstairs, has a really smart granddaughter named Sophia. I hear she is one brilliant gal, so she'll probably get them. However, let's keep them in mind, and if the family needs financial help in burying the old girl maybe you can get her books, and she can have our best pauper's box. We'll even throw in a couple of *Readers' Digest* condensed books to keep her company during her dirt nap on the worm farm."

"I got so caught up looking at the books, I almost dropped the old gal off the bed. I know one thing, when I'm around monkeys like the two sisters that are still breathing, I have no doubt Darwin was right when he said we descended from baboons. I didn't know the dead woman. Who is she?"

"Her name is Erma Mae Logan, and I know you've seen her in the summertime sitting in her sister's yard wearing nothing but a petticoat while reading a book to the old sheep. In the winter she wore a coat that looked like it was made from field mice pelts, and when it rained she covered her head with a clear plastic pocketbook. When she walked in town or rode in her wheelchair, the sheep walked with her on a leash. She and Mama hung out together for years until she got terminally ill and became a recluse."

> *Erma had a little sheep*
> *Its fleece was black as smut*
> *And everywhere that Erma went*
> *The sheep was up her butt.*

"Okay, okay, I know you're in a bad mood, but try showing a little respect."

"I still don't remember her," I said, with utmost sincerity, since my poetry always sends him into orbit, "but that's not important. Keep away from my owl," I yelled as he poked it with the straw he took from his mouth.

"Ewell, you shouldn't have formaldehyde in the middle of your eating table. You'll go into a self-induced coma if you don't stop snorting so much of this stuff. That old lady didn't own an urn to spit in."

"Then you can see why I didn't jump out of my warm bed and rush downstairs to greet them old gals. When this day is over, we'll be no closer to getting ourselves out of the red than we were two years ago. Why can't somebody with money die?" I hit the side of the table with a can of biscuits to split it open, and a few fell on the floor. Stump gathered up the little dough balls and after picking off the hairs, laid them on the baking sheet. I placed a pot of cold coffee on the gas burner and began cursing Grandpa.

"Don't start on him," Stump begged. "Every time you have a problem, Grandpa Maslow gets the blame."

"Why shouldn't he get the blame? He's the one responsible for my being in this damn dismal trade. Since the day I began wearing long pants, I heard him say the same thing a dozen times a week: 'Now, Ewell, you learn the funeral business real good. One day you'll take over for me, and the time will come when you'll get everything I've got.' It's not difficult to understand why my old man and Uncle Delray were drunks and died in the nut house. They couldn't deal with Grandpa shoving corpses up their asses." I spread the biscuits in the middle of the baking sheet and placed them in the oven. "And just in case you haven't noticed my mental condition, I could play any role in *One Flew Over the Cuckoo's Nest* without a script. Because of Grandpa, my own mother left me when I was only four years old. When I think about her, I wish to hell the town idiot had whacked Grandpa on the head a lot sooner, and then perhaps this family could have had a different life."

"I know all that stuff about Grandpa," Stump reminded me. "Every time you get pissed, you tell it to me. You seem to have forgotten that I was supported all my life and even went to college on Grandpa Maslow's money the same as you did."

"Only because he slept with your mama for twenty years," I snarled. "But after all, he was doing his Christian duty taking care of widows and orphans. Take that cotton ball out of my owl's beak, and keep your frigging hands off my dead things. When you start talking, you don't pay attention to what you're doing or what you're doing it to. NOW PUT IT DOWN, DAMN IT!"

"Okay, okay, sorry," he said. "I forgot you don't share your toys with others."

I ignored his remark, but he kept bumping his gums.

"Your grandpa gave me the name Stump because he considered me dumb as one, and I don't even hate him for that."

"Any fool that allows a crow to peck his eye out is dumb as a stump," I said, "so for once I have to agree with the old man."

"Okay, okay, let's not go there," Stump begged. "Grandpa was good to both of us, so you shouldn't curse him so much. Does she still have that old Edsel?"

"Grandpa never owned an Edsel."

"I said she, the Logan woman. Ewell, get your brain in gear."

"Who?" I asked. "I haven't a clue who or what you're talking about. Can't you stay on the subject?"

"Good Lord, Ewell, do I need to run an IV of Vicks and coffee into your veins?"

"Oh, yeah, I remember," I said as my mind jumped back into gear. "I saw it this morning parked beside her sister's house with a spotlight shining on it. The tires are flat as frog farts, the windshield is broken, and it seems to be covered with crow dung or some related substance. Other than that, it ought to be a collector's dream. You want a sausage?"

"A couple. Maybe we can get the title, clean it up, and pawn it off on an old car collector in Atlanta. Might be worth a few bucks or at least the price of a pauper's box."

"Maybe so, but don't count on it being our ride to Bounty."

"Where did you put her?" he asked. "She's not in the fridge. Are we playing your little game of hide and seek the stiff?"

"In the kudzu at the end of the loading dock," I said. "See if there's a jar of prunes behind that stack of *Poets and Writers.*"

"What do you mean in the kudzu?" he asked as if I had not explained myself. Before I could answer, he made a few snide remarks about my housekeeping. "You need to make a trip to the Laundromat, Ewell. Your fireplace is running over."

I ignored his remarks and went on with my tale.

"After her leg came off, I got back in the truck and tried to push her out. The sheep shit on my shoes caused me to slip and knock her off into the kudzu. I fell on top of her, and when I finally got up, I felt like a snake slithering on a wet rock. I left her there."

"Damn it, Ewell, you mean that old lady is still laying out back on the ground? The lid on this jar of prunes is filthy. Wipe it off before you open it. I don't want grave dirt and feathers in my prunes. Do you know how hot it is out there?" he asked, but didn't give me time to answer. "It's eighty degrees, and not even noon. Why didn't you pull her out?"

"I was pissed," I said. "Hand me a paper sack to drain these eggs on."

"Pissed about what?"

"Because the old gal died on Wednesday," I said, knowing my answer would set him off. "I knew my day was ruined when I got the call at four in the morning."

"Will you never get it through you head that folks die on Wednesdays, and it makes no difference that it's supposed to be your afternoon off?"

"When a body dies on a Wednesday, it messes up my entire day. You just watch. It will take them old ladies down yonder all day to make the arrangements, and then the whole family will be back tonight yelling and hollering until the wee hours, and I won't have a minute to myself. When a body is inconsiderate enough to die on

Wednesday, somebody ought to throw a quilt over it and leave it there until Thursday morning. Not a damn thing is going to happen to it before I get there. People act like the dead need to be put in a box the second they drop or evil spirits will swarm out of the wall like termites and descend upon the living. I realize that death is like sleep. It comes when it comes, and we can't do a damn thing about it. Even Sandburg asked,

How do you bid death hold off?

I'm not necessarily asking that they don't die on a Wednesday, even though it would be nice if they didn't. I'm just saying don't plan to have anything done with the body until Thursday. Stop scraping my owl wing with that brain spoon. I'll never be able to fluff up the feathers the way you're treating it."

He laid the owl wing on the table, then opened the refrigerator and started moving things around as if hunting for something.

"You got any buttermilk?"

"Behind the big box, and the coffee is ready if you want some."

"What's in the box?"

"A coon. People do without everything else in this town from Wednesday noon until Thursday morning at nine o'clock. If you don't believe me, try getting in touch with a preacher or a doctor or buying a loaf of bread or a fifth of whiskey on a Wednesday afternoon and see what you get. Let a cottonmouth clamp your big toe at five minutes past twelve, and ask the Health Center to open and give you a shot of antivenin.

"The only fools that work on Wednesday afternoon in this god-forsaken town are that moonshine sipping sheriff and me. As soon as that pious bunch of Baptists crawl up their bell tower and begin playing those ghastly hymns at noon to remind us of our sins and warn us of judgment day, this whole damn town folds up. A couple of Wednesdays ago, I called Doc Frank at two minutes past twelve and asked him to come and sign the death certificate on Gary Draper. 'Ewell,' he said, 'if you say he's dead, he's dead. You know more about the dead than I could ever hope to learn, and you can sign my name might near good as I can. I ain't got time to run over there and examine no damn stiff. I'm playing croquet at the camp for the unencumbered this afternoon, so handle it.' Then he hung up."

"Ewell, you need to clean out this refrigerator," Stump said. "It looks like a zoo morgue in here, mercy." He stirred a couple of teaspoons of baking soda into a cup of buttermilk and kept on talking. "Okay, so you don't get Wednesday afternoons off like everybody else, but when a soul departs at an inconvenient time for you, it doesn't give you permission to leave the body in the yard all night. What if the sisters had seen her laying there when they came this morning?"

"There's no way they could have seen the old gal. She's under the pickup."

"What the hell is she doing under the pickup?"

"Laying there, I hope. When she fell in the kudzu, I backed the truck over her.

> *The old maid who died in her sleep*
> *Read Nietzsche to Crowie her sheep.*
> *She had a wooden leg, the color of egg.*
> *The old maid who died in her sleep."*
> - Ewell Moody

CHAPTER TWO

Ewell Moody

Stump's response to my limerick regarding the old maid spending the night under the truck convinced me that some folks don't have a sense of humor or an appreciation for creativity.

"That's not cute, Ewell," he snarled. "Cut the crap. We could get in serious trouble leaving a corpse in the yard overnight."

"I was lucky to get her covered. You try backing a truck over a body in knee-deep kudzu on a rainy night by the light of a bug-zapper and see how good a job you do. Plus, I was in a hurry to hide the truck since I thought the sheriff was on my ass. You want cheese on your biscuits?"

"Yeah, and I'd like a wedge for my coffee. I'll probably need it to kill the taste. Why did you haul the old gal in the pickup?"

"Virgil took the hearse to Atlanta," I explained. "He left me no other choice." I sliced a small wedge of cheese and handed it to Angel to keep her from squawking her head off.

"Jeeeezus, man," the bird screeched as Audrey tried to jump on the perch for the cheese. I tapped the cat on the head with a fork, broke several eggs in a bowl, stirred them, and sat the bowl on the floor.

"Why can't Virgil drive his own car when he goes to Atlanta to whore around?" Stump asked. "I've never understood why we have to furnish him transportation. He acts like we run a limo service around here." He poured a mug of coffee and added several lumps of sugar and a wedge of cheese. "Mercy, Ewell, this stuff will grow fungus on my tongue. You got any Coffee-mate? Your cream has hairs of an unidentified creature floating in it."

"Damn, you're hard to please," I said. "This ain't a restaurant. You'll find some under the sink. I think. You know preachers. They want to go fornicating in the big city, but they're scared they'll be recognized. Virgil figures if he drives a hearse from a small town to a titty bar nobody will suspect he's a preacher."

"Did you do something to the old lady?" he asked as he opened a fresh jar of Coffee-mate and stirred a spoonful into his coffee. "Have you been running around town naked?"

"You know the only places I go naked are here and down at the camp," I explained. "I thought we discussed this earlier? Sometimes you really piss me off. You've got me so upset with your questioning that I used the spatula to scratch my rash. I can't do a damn thing to change my past, and neither the gods nor saints can give me a clean slate, so why don't you leave it be?"

"With a past like yours, I can't help being concerned. If you didn't do anything to the old lady, why were your pants hanging over the rail of the loading dock, your shoes at the back door, and why was the sheriff after you?"

"Jeeeezus, you don't let up, do you? I told you earlier that Virgil took the hearse to Atlanta with my stuff in it, and the wagon has a flat tire. I didn't have a gurney or a body bag, so what was I to do? Besides that, it was raining. I couldn't just wrap a sheet around the old gal, so I put her in a couple of garbage bags and used my suspenders to tie the bags together. Every time I took a step my pants fell around my ankles, so when I got back here I took them off. You should have seen me trying to get out of that old lady's house holding the stiff on my back with one hand and my pants up with the other. And to add to my wretched state, outside their door I stepped in a pile of wet sheep shit. Turn that air back on before I swelter to death." I took off my robe and threw it across the room. "After the kind of night I've had, your questioning and this damn itchy rash is a crappy way to start a day."

"Calm down," Stump said, "there is no need to get all hot and bothered. I just don't want you getting in trouble with nobody dead or alive. Are you telling me that you bagged a corpse with garbage bags and did it in the presence of her family? Then, you threw her over your shoulder like a bag of salt while you held up your pants with one hand? Then, you tossed her in the back of your pickup truck in a rain storm?"

"That's what I'm telling you. The sisters wouldn't leave the room. They hovered in my face and watched every move I made. They even followed me out to the truck with the old sheep walking behind."

"I wish I had a recording of that scene," Stump said, then went into a laughing fit.

"I don't see what's so damn funny."

"Why was the sheriff after you?" he asked when he finally stopped laughing.

"I ran a red light."

"Jeeeezus, Ewell."

"Don't Jesus me. One traffic light in this Podunk town, and no matter which way I'm heading, it's stuck on red. I sat at that damn light so long I could see the old gal in the back about to float over the sides. I goosed it and took off. Course, there sits Driscoll in the yard of Lulu's Pub."

"Did he get you?"

"Course not. I turned off my lights and zoomed into the fog before he cranked up. By the time the chase ended, he thought he was on Thunder Road."

"Take my word, Ewell, it's just a matter of time before Driscoll locks your butt in the slammer for good. He knows you're driving with a suspended license. Come over here and let me put this paste on your rash. You're about to scratch yourself raw."

"No time for that. I've got to eat breakfast. The Burger King closes at noon on Wednesday, so I probably won't get another bite until tomorrow morning."

"Breakfast can wait. The eggs need to drain a little longer on the paper bag, seeing as how you've got enough Crisco on them to fry a pit bull."

"Keep that stuff away from me," I said, as he came towards me with a wadded up dishtowel and a cup of gook.

"It's a paste of buttermilk and soda. You saw me mix it. I need to put some on your butt so bend over. Mercy, Ewell, your rear is raw as goat's liver. It's for sure you're not going to sit down for any length of time without fidgeting, and for goodness sakes don't scratch your crotch when you're talking to the women."

13

"It's my crotch. I'll scratch if it itches. Stop pushing on my neck. I'm bent over so far now my head almost touches the floor. I'm probably going to faint with my blood running to one place. Will you take care of the old ladies for me?" I begged.

"You know I don't do that kind of stuff, and if I did, I don't have time. I've got to get Miss Erma out from under the truck and do heaven knows what to her."

"She can wait. She probably won't bring us any money, so why should we do her any favors? Besides that, I'm sure the two waiting in the hall have a hankering to put their dear departed sister away in the Finest Funeral Fashion Funds can Furnish like old Feinstein in Atlanta does. And like every other tightfisted miser in this town, they'll probably expect me to do it free. My nerves are not up to dealing with them right now."

"The only thing I can do for your nerves is get you a fresh jar of Vicks and a new bottle of Jim Beam. Money or no money, we've got to bury the old lady. Raise your arms and let me do your pits. Did you call Feinstein about borrowing a few caskets until we get money ahead for floor planning?"

"Yeah, and he laughed. How long does it take this stuff to dry?" I asked, standing with my arms over my head and my legs spread apart.

"It'll dry in a minute. Don't be so impatient. You can stand that way a little longer."

"That's easy for you to say."

He threw the dishrag in the bowl with the owl and splashed formaldehyde on the table and didn't even notice. He just went on whining.

"I didn't figure he would loan us anything," he said like he was about to cry. "We'll never make a dime until we get a stiff worth something. Our inventory consists of four pauper's boxes and a used casket that has already held four stiffs."

"Yeah, every time we take somebody out of that expensive box and plant them in the ground, the words of old T. S. keep ringing in my ears, and I feel like I am supposed to answer him.

That corpse you planted last year in your garden.
Has it begun to sprout? Will it bloom this year?"

"Yep," he agreed. "One of these days it will sprout and bloom and our asses will be like tall grass, with somebody waiting to mow us."

He picked up his eggs and sausage with the spatula and placed them on a plate beside two biscuits and a serving of prunes. I didn't remind him I had scratched with the spatula. I thought, what the hell, there are things worse than poison ivy on the tongue.

"Life ain't fair," he whined. "Curley Feinstein gushes with rich corpses while the ones that fall our way can't afford a burlap shroud. If we could snatch one good client from his establishment, we'd have enough to get our asses out of debt and perhaps a small place in the sun. Can you imagine how much he gets for planting one Buckhead matron? The rings on the fingers and crowns on the teeth of just one of his corpses is worth more than we make in a year. I've thought about robbing a few of his graves."

"Don't temp me, or I might be heading to Atlanta one dark night with a black shovel in the back of my pickup. Talking about a place in the sun, all I want is a small hunk of cash to get that whore-mongering preacher off my butt. Then perhaps I can have a little place where I can read my books, write a few verses, and even have a schooner to chase a whale or two. Hell, I just want to live a little so when my time comes to nap on your slab, I can croon with old blue eyes that I did it '*My way*.'"

"I told you two years ago when you borrowed money from Virgil Jordan you were making a mistake. I knew he would own your body and soul before we got it paid back, and now the scoundrel runs the joint. We don't have an opinion about a bloody thing around here, and every time we remind him the place is still ours, he gets sore as a boil on our butt and threatens to call in the loan. I agree with you, if we could make enough to pay him off I'd be content as an old coon in a tree above a hound dog he had out-smarted."

"I didn't have any choice but to deal with Virgil. His was the only game I could play in. The boys at the camp were planning to pour concrete in my life jacket and take me water skiing."

"This has been discussed a million times already, Ewell, but I'll say it again. Any fool that plays poker naked ought to know he has no place to hide cards, and if he cheats he deserves what he gets."

"Okay, okay, let's not get into that. So I made a mistake. At the time, I simply forgot my ass didn't have pockets, but as I was saying, I guess what I want more than paying off Virgil is to be rid of folks like those old ladies downstairs. I'm so tired of sucking up to people in the hopes they'll pay me for burying their dead I could gag. I'm tired of living like the Vice President of the United States or a flock of buzzards. Has it ever occurred to you that the only way we put bread on our tables is at the expense of some poor sucker exhaling his last breath? Any fool that would go into this business without being pushed hasn't got a rope long enough to wet his bucket. What man in his right mind would choose to make his living conducting funerals where folks sit around yelling, braying like a drove of wild jack asses, and babbling out of their frigging minds? I am sick of living with old lady Death looking over my shoulder all the damn time. She's everywhere I turn and has been all my life. She's in my bed and my clothes, and sometimes I try to scratch her out of my head."

"Is that why you are always scratching? I thought you had fleas. I'm glad to know it is just old lady Death. One is about as hard to get rid of as the other."

"Cute, cute."

"I know what you're talking about, Ewell, but right now we've got no choice but to hang in there, and maybe one of these days our golden casket will come rolling through the door. Can I have the last biscuit to sop up my prune juice?"

"Help yourself. The only gold we'll ever see in a casket will be in somebody's tooth," I reminded him.

"Maybe it'll be a big tooth."

"Yeah, sure, or one day the old fable will come true, and the buzzards will return to Bochimville shitting miracles and one will land on our head. The only thing that keeps me going is the hope that one day I'll have a little schooner and float off into the cool blue ocean never to be seen or heard from again by the fools in this frigging town. Like the poet Masefield said,

> *I must go down to the seas again,*
> *for the call of the running tide*
> *Is a wild call and a clear call*
> *that may not be denied."*

"Yeah, Ewell, I know you hanker for a boat and a body of water to float it in like some men crave a good whore to make them feel like a man, but you need to get yourself together. For starters, stop lining up prune pits around the side of your plate. Mercy, you're nuts. Take care of them old gals downstairs, and think about it this way. Miss Erma Mae Logan is the only person in this town with a tree and a bridge named for her. If that's not enough to make you take notice, let me remind you that she's the one person responsible for getting the nudist camp in this county and the only one I know arrested for horse rustling. With her track record for accomplishing weird and unusual things, she just might have a mouth full of gold chompers. Or, like you said, it could be the day the buzzards return to this old roost bringing us the luck of the century. At least remember Grandpa Maslow's slogan: 'In this dismal trade, expect anything, anytime from anybody. Be ready to grab what you can, smile a lot, and don't bury anything you can use unless you plan to dig it up later.'"

CHAPTER THREE

Ewell Moody

As I stepped out of my apartment and into the hallway leading to the funeral parlor, I looked around to see if anyone was lurking beneath the stairwell listening to me. Talking out loud to myself is one of the many reasons the empty-headed bozos consider me the town dingbat with tendencies to live on the dark side. But if I didn't converse with myself on a regular basis, I would be nuttier than I already am, as it is a well-established fact that humans must converse often with their own kind to remain mentally and emotionally fit.

The grandfather clock at the top of the stairwell announced the noon hour by chiming thirteen times.

"Shit," I said softly, continuing the dialogue with myself. "That fool clock is still screwed up. Like everything that belonged to Grandpa, it loves to pester the pee out of me. Now that I think about it, yesterday it ran two hours behind, so I guess I should be grateful for small favors.

"When I take an inventory of my life up to this point, there is no doubt the statement my life is no more than '*A tale told by an Idiot*' had to be written about me, and at the moment I can't recall who said it, wrote it, or whatever.

"When I look at my life from a religious standpoint, I am reminded the Buddha teaches that our lives are retributions of karma while the Christians yell all that happens to us is the will of God. So no matter how I look at it, both God and the Buddha are after my ass, so I'm screwed.

"I often think of what I could have been if Grandpa had allowed me to do my own thing regardless of how deviant from his definition of acceptable behavior I chose to be. What, may I ask, is wrong with reading for hours while sitting naked in the woods or floating around in a boat fishing without a hook? Does my early childhood choice of not wanting to be joined at the hip to a curly-haired, peony-lipped giggling female make me unacceptable? I know I could have been a poet had Grandpa not raided my room monthly and destroyed my verses. I could have been another Thoreau had I an Emerson to run to. I often find myself wishing I had followed my mother's example and left when the going was good. If only she had taken me with her, but at least she *followed her bliss* as Jo Campbell recommends. Oh well, one must not dwell on the past but live in the moment. I often wish the damn moments weren't so long." At least my one-way dialogues helped clear my mind and prepare me for the next moment.

I hated like hell to leave the safety of my little apartment and face the corpulent sisters patiently waiting for me to relieve them of the awesome task of laying to rest their dearly departed. I would never have left my little haven if Stump had not shoved me out the door after dusting the cat hairs off my second best suit, removing the prune juice stain from my red polyester tie, sewing a button on my cleanest white shirt, and washing the sheep shit from my shoes.

He also took several minutes to brief me on the names of the quick and the dead by writing the name of the defunct one in my right palm and the names of the breathing sisters in my left palm. I suppose some folks think I have a memory problem, as I can recite hundreds of poems but can't remember the name of a dead old maid, or any name, but what the hell. If you think about it, how many people do I meet whose names are worth remembering? Perhaps that is an indication that I have my priorities in order and not that I suffer from a mental disorder.

To make my day even more stressful, I had to enter the office occupied by Lucinda Faye Green, a cousin on my mother's side. The whey-faced girl with frizzy blonde hair had no redeeming qualities that I could detect. She was thin as a communion wafer, never smiled, and smelled like a drugstore cosmetic counter. I kept her on because she worked cheap and saw no difference in working with the dead than the living. I often went for weeks without paying her, and the empty-headed ninny never noticed. The insipid girl's one goal in life is to find a man. If the day comes that my golden casket rolls in the door filled with shinning teeth, after Virgil Jordan, she is the next one booted out the door.

"Where are the Logan women?" I asked as I entered the oppressive office.

"Who?"

"The Logan women!" I screamed. "If you'd stop smacking that wad of gum, you might hear something sometimes. Turn on the damn air. It's hot enough in here to give a desert rat a heat stroke."

"I ain't hot, and I can hear just fine," she said. "Are you referring to the pudgy pair down the hall or the stiff one Stump raked out from under the pickup?" She blew a bubble, popped it, and then sucked the gum back into her mouth. In front of her face she held up her right hand with the fingers spread apart to inspect the purple polish freshly applied to her long, store-bought nails.

"Smart-mouth wench," I mumbled loud enough for her to hear, but she didn't understand. Like most females, I found her dense and useless as prune pits. Damn broads cause as much trouble dead as they do alive, and I bet I'll not get enough from this old maid's funeral to keep the gravediggers in booze. She didn't own a damn thing but an ancient sheep and a purple Edsel with a body so rusty you couldn't open the doors with a crowbar. If we take it as payment towards the old gal's funeral, we probably couldn't give it away, and the damn sheep is too tough to eat and too ugly to stuff. Mercy, I dread dickering with these old broads. I had rather be a blubber hunter living off my catch than sucking up to folks like these. If the opportunity presented itself, I would trade this present life for an orange robe and spend the rest of my days meditating with Buddhist monks in Mammoth Cave. Still grumbling and mumbling, I suddenly found myself in front of the women.

"Good morning, ladies," I said, shifting from one foot to the other, a habit Stump had tried for years to make me break. "So sorry to keep you waiting," I lied, "but we've had an extremely busy morning." I lied again. "With the way folks are passing, one would think the scourge had returned." I addressed my remarks to the Alpha of the pack, or at least I assumed as much since she was obviously breathing. The other one left me wondering if perhaps she should join her sister in the kudzu.

I quickly consulted my left hand before speaking. "Are you Mrs. Gooch?" I asked the more alert one, a woman about the size of a small church, in her late sixties with large breasts that hung almost to her waist. Her short, thick gray hair parted on one side was held back from her face with a hairpin, and the heavy coating of face powder gave her a ghostlike appearance. Before she spoke, she shifted to the edge of the bench and licked her lips. I wasn't sure of her intent.

"You mean somebody besides Erma passed last night?" she asked. "Goodness gracious, I should have knowed with the moon in the last quarter and the sign in the groin a whole lot of folks would pass. Them two together stop a lot of folks in their tracks. With Sister sick, reckon I forgot the signs of the time. Before we leave, Mr. Moody, you tell us who passed. We want to show our respect so folks will do the same to us now that Sister is gone."

"You may check the registry for the names of the deceased," I suggested, knowing she would find the damn thing blank. "But now, please allow me to offer my condolence in the loss of your dear one."

"Thank you, Mr. Moody, and we do appreciate you coming to get her so late in the night or early in the morning, whichever it was. Hope it wasn't no bother to you. We know she didn't pass at a very convenient time, but Erma never was good about taking other folk's feelings into consideration before she done something. She had a habit of deciding to do something on the spur of the moment and then just up and done it. Passing weren't no different. She ought to have been dead years ago, but she just wouldn't give up her ghost, so to speak."

"It was no bother to come in the wee hours of the morning, Mrs. Gooch. After all, that is why my humble establishment is on call twenty-four hours a day, seven days a week, fifty-two weeks of the year, and I seldom get Wednesday afternoon off like most folks in this town." I got so emotional when I mentioned Wednesdays that I wiggled my tongue in the gap between my front teeth and created a low whistle. The old gal looked at me kind of wild-eyed. I smiled like a body caught farting in public. By now my itching had become so severe I twisted around as if warming-up for Saint Vitus' dance.

"Where is Sister now?" Mrs. Gooch asked, with her right hand down the neck of her dress. After rummaging around she brought out a strap that had apparently slipped off her fat old shoulder.

I leaned towards the women, cleared my throat, and then spoke softly in my best funeral-trained voice. "Your dear sister is reposing in the preparation room while we endeavor to make her ready for her departure from this life. She is at perfect rest."

"We need to talk to you about what we want done with Erma," the sleeping one said, speaking for the first time.

"Yes," I agreed. "You do need to select a service."

Like her sister, Mildred Roper leaned towards the fleshy type, but not near as plump as Mrs. Gooch. Her short hair stuck to her head and around her face like moss clings to a tree after a heavy rain. Around her blue, bloodshot eyes were deep, dark circles, probably from nights of interrupted sleep. I felt a touch of empathy for the old gal. Life had not been easy for her. Her unshaven, pear-shaped legs were dark and lumpy with varicose veins. She wore thin canvas slip-on shoes, and the black socks rolled over her ankles reminded me of an old tire around a stump.

She began rummaging in her large purple plastic purse and brought out a stack of papers. After slowly looking at each sheet, she handed me a wrinkled piece of yellow tablet paper so nasty it could have been part of a leper's shroud. I was less than anxious to hold it in my hands.

"One time my sister wrote this and put it in her Bible," she said. "It tells how she wanted things done at her passing. She didn't want no casket, no funeral, no preacher, nothing at all."

Well, hell, I thought. Why bother me? Had I known her wishes earlier, I could have left her in the kudzu, but now let's load the old gal up and take her to the city dump and be done with it. Before I had time to unfold the paper, Mrs. Gooch snorted like an irate bull.

"We ain't doing what's on that piece of paper, and there is no need in talking about it. You're just wasting Mr. Moody's time."

"But it's what Erma wanted," came the rebuttal.

"But it ain't Christian, and on top of that it ain't even decent." She gripped her walking cane, raised it, and then struck it hard on the floor barely missing my right foot.

"Mercy," I mumbled and stepped back, afraid of being hit.

Mrs. Roper began to cry. Her hands trembled, and her entire

body seemed to shake as she tried to speak. "I don't see nothing unchristian about not wanting to waste money on something that's turning back to dust."

How true, how true, I thought, unless it's going to put coins in my coffer.

"Well, I think it's a sin and mighty unchristian to put one's own flesh and blood away like white trash, and that's just what you're wanting to do. There is no way in this wide world that I'm going to let you do that to my sister." With her right hand, the old gal vigorously rubbed her left elbow, and her left eye began to twitch. "Besides that, I ain't going to let you do something that'll bring shame on this family. I have never heard tell of such in all my life."

"I just want her put away like she asked us to do," Mrs. Roper said, still crying softly. "She didn't want money from her insurance policy spent on a funeral. She made a list of people she wanted the money divided among."

Insurance policy? Money? Was I truly hearing words that were poetry to my ears? Since the old gal had a list of folks for the money to be divided between, I postulated it must be a good size policy. Things were looking up. Perhaps the buzzards were returning to Bochimville today, so I quickly became mentally alert and paid closer attention to their bickering.

"I've seen that list, and it's a disgrace whose names are on it," Mrs. Gooch continued to rant. "The first one is that poor little feeble-minded boy that belongs to the woman Hoover lives with. What in the world is he going to do with money? He can't talk and still pees in his britches even though he's nine years old. Another name that don't have no business being there is the woman that helped you take care of Erma, and that is a disgrace. You know what she is. Erma even wanted money put aside for the Estes twins to go to college on when they finish high school, but I'm telling you we ain't giving money to white trash no matter how smart Erma thought them two little gals are. The thing that puts my teeth on edge is her putting the name of that old black goat on there. So it followed her around like a dog and she loved it better than anything in the world, it still don't need no money. Sides that, I think we ought to barbecue it. Not one dime did she set aside for the church, me, my kids, or my grandkids. She was selfish, and I shouldn't even care how she's put away, but I do. That's my way. I can't help being the caring person that I am.

Guess I was born that-a-way, but it sure don't run in the family."

My, my, what a good soul, I thought. I felt sure we would hear a voice from the open sky saying, *my daughter in whom I am well pleased, hear ye, hear ye.* I wanted to get on to the insurance policy, but between the two I couldn't get in a word.

"She felt the money would help the folks on her list, and she didn't want it wasted on a funeral. She put her pet sheep on there just to needle you, Gladys. You know Erma wasn't serious about setting aside money for a sheep. Sides that, she knew me and Sophia would take care of Crowie. He's not a goat, but a sheep, and we are not going to cook him."

"Call it whatever you want, but it's just plain nasty," Mrs. Gooch said as she sat on the edge of the bench waving her cane in the air. "I've tried to live a God-fearing, Christian life, and I'm going to keep right on living the same way by seeing that my sister gets a nice, decent funeral. And only over my dead body is family money going to be spent on white trash, colored, the feeble-minded, and a black goat. I'm telling you right now, I'm going to see that she gets a funeral our family and friends will enjoy coming to and one they'll talk about for years to come. I mean what I'm saying, and I don't care if it takes every penny we get from that old policy. After all, that's what it's for."

Amen, amen, I said silently. I got so excited at the thought of the old gal actually having an urn to piss in, the sweat begin to flow down my back causing my rash to itch like hell. As discreetly as possible, I scratched while remembering where Stump told me not to put my hands. I realized I was smiling but they didn't notice.

"It's her money, and we ought to do what she wanted," Mrs. Roper said to her sister.

"It might have been her money once but it ain't no more, and she can't take it with her, unless you plan to sew pockets in her shroud. That's the way I see it, and any sensible person would agree with me," she said looking up at me as if seeking my approval.

"I understand, Mrs. Gooch," I said, "and I certainly agree with you." After all, she was in favor of using the insurance money for a big, tacky, expensive funeral, so how could I not agree? "Tell me about your insurance policy. Do you have it with you?"

Damn, I was excited. Then, I thought it's probably one of those puny funeral policies with a face value of $250.00 that the poor fool paid on for forty years. I wiped the sweat from my forehead and tried to scratch discreetly. I excitedly watched as Mrs. Roper opened her handbag and once more sifted through a stack of papers.

"Here it is," she said after what seemed forever.

Like a fool on television removing a card from the envelope to see who wins an Oscar, I carefully removed the document from its original cover and unfolded it to reveal the face value. At that precise moment I'm sure my eyes jumped from their sockets like a jack-in-the-box. My hands began to shake like I had palsy. Then I realized I was running my hand up and down my fly.

"Do you think there'll be enough money in that old policy for us to properly put sister away?" Mrs. Gooch asked.

Properly? This is enough to properly put the whole town away like the Chicago Racketeers used to do, I said silently. Even Al Capone didn't have this much spent on him when he passed. It's a happy day in old Bochimville. Mercy me. At that precise moment, I felt sure I heard the flutter of buzzard wings.

"We can use it all," Mrs. Gooch assured me. "When our parents passed on, Erma changed the policy to be paid to us. Course she does have that little old attachment saying how she wants it divided, but that ain't worth a hill of pumpkin seeds."

"I see, I see," I tried to assure her. "Talk about gold teeth," I smiled and realized I was talking out loud.

"Beg your pardon, Mr. Moody. What about Sister's teeth? She had a plate, upper and lower. She didn't have them on when you picked her up this morning, but we can bring them over when you get ready to close her mouth, and we do want her mouth closed. Everybody in this county will probably want her jaws wired shut cause she kept a ruckus going all the time until she got sick. If you like teeth, it might be nice to have her kind of smiling, not too wide, maybe like this. She didn't have no gold in them, but if you want them gold you can paint one of her front ones. Whatever."

Merciful days, I looked down at the old gal, and she was smiling like a Cheshire cat. "What were you saying?" I asked, trying to get back on the subject.

"We was talking about Sister's teeth."

"Before that."

"I was saying that when you hear what we're supposed to do now that Sister has passed, I know you'll agree we shouldn't do it. She wanted us to strip her naked soon as she breathed her last breath and stick her in the corncrib on top a pile of shucks and set fire—"

"That's not the way it's done, Gladys," Mrs. Roper interrupted. "Erma said those things just to get you upset. You know our sister didn't intend for us to do anything like that. We're supposed to pay Mr. Moody a small sum of Erma's money to burn her in his furnace, and then we'll put her ashes in the old well like she asked us to. It's called cremating."

Burning just went sky high, I said silently and made a little clicking noise with my tongue to celebrate the lovely idea. With this kind of money we can have the old lady burning for a week, and I can still walk away with my pockets bulging. The Indians in the county would love the fire. Be like old times. Maybe roast a few marshmallows and melt some Hershey bars.

"Call it whatever fancy name you like, Millie, but it all comes out the same. You must think I've got the mind of a Betsy bug. You know good and well Mr. Moody ain't got no oven big enough to cook a full-grown woman in, and if he did, she'd come out looking like a hog that had been baked for a couple of days. Then I guess you'll want to stuff a sweet tater in her mouth. My word, Millie, you know the rest of the family ain't about to go for something like that."

It would be different to say the least, I giggled silently.

"It's none of their business. We're her only living sisters and she trusted us to do what she wanted done, and I say we ought to do it. He's not going to put her in the oven. I said furnace. It's made especially for cremating."

"Just suppose I give in and let Mr. Moody put her in his oven, who do you think is going to take her out after she's cooked and throw her in the well?" The old gal stuck her hand down the front of her dress and gave her boobs a good scratching. I felt envious.

"I already told you it's not an oven but a furnace which gets so hot it turns the body into a small amount of ashes. Erma discussed it with me lots of times. You know how Erma felt about funerals. She didn't believe in them."

"What in the world would our friends think if they walked up to Erma's coffin and the only thing in there was a pile of ashes? My word."

How this poor ignorant woman had lived so long without a brain cell in her head was beyond my comprehension.

"Ladies, ladies," I said, trying to break up their useless dialogue. I had heard enough of Gooch's ignorant babble and was anxious to determine if the policy was in force, and if so, to begin making plans to roll the lovely dough into my coffers. If I couldn't get it all, even a small portion would pull my ox out of the ditch.

"There won't be a coffin, Gladys," Mrs. Roper said, as she reached up and took the paper from me and handed it to her sister. "Read this paper, and you'll see that Erma didn't want one." I was beginning to feel like the invisible man as they continued to ignore me.

"How in the name of common sense is Brother Jordan going to preach a funeral when there ain't nothing to preach to or about?"

Brother Jordan? Did I hear them say Brother Jordan? How wonderful. Things were looking better with each new revelation. Thank God they were not Episcopalians. Those people are so cheap they throw a damn quilt over the casket instead of buying flowers. The Catholics are even cheaper. They glue a cross to the coffin top, which is even tackier. If I had my preference, I'd bury only Presbyterians. They spend the most money for the shortest, quietest, and most dignified funerals. But for big bucks like this, I will gladly tolerate the loud, obnoxious, ignorant Baptists, which they are, if they belong to Jordan's flock. The old gals continued with their argument, but things were sounding better all the time. Hallelujah, mine is the glory or soon will be.

"I've never in my life been to a funeral when the body was in a tea cup sitting on the pulpit or floating around in a well someplace way over yonder," the old Gooch gal rattled on.

"Gladys, I don't know what else to say to you. I've explained it the best I know how, and right now, I'm too tired to fight, but one way or another, I'm going to do what Erma wanted, so you might as well face it."

Mercy, I quickly realized I had better do something about these old gals and do it quick. I could see that beautiful green stuff drifting out of my hands. My collar began irritating my rash so bad I grimaced and pulled it away from my neck.

"Ladies, ladies," I said a little too loud, "since you mentioned Brother Jordan, I assume you are members of his flock. Is that correct?"

"Our families have been members of the Rock Church that Loves Jesus since the day it opened its doors," Mrs. Gooch explained.

Hallelujah! "Does he know of your sister's passing?"

"We tried to call him this morning before we left home, but his phone was busy. We had the operator check it. She said it was off the hook."

That damn hypocritical bastard, I silently cursed. He knows the old gal is dead and thinks the family is penniless, so he is not going to bother with them until he has to. That's Virgil. No money, no preacher. He's probably still in bed sobering up from his night in Atlanta that began with dinner at a Mexican restaurant and continued with titty bar hopping until dawn.

"I know Brother Jordan would want to know of Miss Eunice's, Emma's, your dear sister's passing," I lied. "Let's go down to the Grief Room where you ladies can be more comfortable, and I'll call him." Won't he be surprised? I placed my hand on Mrs. Gooch's arm and helped her up. "Please follow me," I said and silently composed a little ditty to celebrate the lovely moment.

> *If you ain't got no money*
> *Don't call that preacher man*
> *Cause he ain't got no time for you*
> *And will ax you from his clan.*
>
> *But if your pockets jingle*
> *And you pad his greedy palm*
> *Then when you dial his number*
> *He'll come like a healing balm.*
>
> -Ewell Moody

CHAPTER FOUR

Ewell Moody

Slowly and silently I led the way down the long, dismal hall to the door of the Grief Room while giving the situation a great deal of thought. The Roper woman could give us some problems with her cremating ideas, and I could never charge enough to justify billing for the entire policy by burning the old gal. It's going to be a big enough challenge getting all the loot, and staying out of jail, by just having a funeral. Maybe they would like to have a barbecue, a raffle, or something more than the ordinary funeral. Something to run up expenses and justify my bill. Mercy, life is one challenge after another.

I've got to get Jordan to change the old gal's mind about cremating and come up with ideas to justify the cost of whatever they decide to do and what we can safely charge. We may even have to make her a gold plate. I am not concerned about the Gooch gal. The money doesn't mean jack shit to her, seeing as how all she wants is a big funeral. Well, we can provide that. Mercy, what a task I have before me, but what the hell, I'll just dump it on Virgil. I smiled at the thought. He thinks he owns the joint, so let's see how he handles this one. I opened the door to the Grief Room, and what I heard caused my teeth to clench so tight I felt my bicuspids loosen. The recorded music continued to ask over and over, "Shall we gather? Shall we gather? Shall we gather?" Merciful hell, where is Lucinda Faye? That fool girl must be deaf as a plank. The veins in my neck were swelling so quickly, I felt sure they were about to explode.

"Ladies," I said, through my anger and clenched teeth, "please have a seat. There seems to be a small problem with the music. I'll be right back."

In the front office, I found Lucinda Faye standing at her desk with one bare foot in the chair and cotton balls between her toes. She was painting her toenails while balancing the phone on her shoulder, chewing gum, and talking. I had an overwhelming urge to kill.

"Get off the damn phone," I said, "and do something about that infernal music. Are you stone deaf?"

"What's wrong with it? I don't hear nothing."

"If you don't hear that 'Shall we gather? Shall we gather? Shall we gather?' then you're deaf as a frigging tree. Just shut the thing off. Mercy damn." I turned and left the office.

In the Grief Room, the ladies were sitting on separate ends of the sofa like a couple of walruses. Mrs. Roper clutched the purple purse to her bosom and gazed across the room with vacant eyes. I quickly removed a roll of twine, a Sears Catalog, and a box of glass eyes from the Queen Anne chair and placed them on the table. I dusted the seat of the chair with the palm of my hand before sitting down. The room was a mess—not the type of place to entertain a family rolling in money and planning the funeral of the decade.

"I'm truly sorry about that little problem with the music," I said. "Now if you ladies will relax, I'll go back to the office and call Brother Jordan and send Lucinda Faye in with coffee. If there is anything you need, please inform her, as we wish to provide succor in your time of sadness."

I stepped out into the hall still clutching the policy like a kid with a prized toy. When the door closed behind me, I threw my arms in the air, shouted silently, and then pranced like a bantam rooster in the pen with a hundred hens. Oh, Lord, I felt good. Then I thought, hell, I hope I ain't about to get my balloon pricked or fixing to wake up from another grizzly nightmare like I've been having lately where I'm sitting behind bars while my establishment is being run by a bunch of debauchers.

I entered the front office yelling for Lucinda Faye to get off the phone. "You've got work to do," I said as I reached across the desk and took the receiver from her and placed it in the cradle. "Wash Grandma's cups, and take a pot of coffee to the Grief Room for the Logan women. If you don't have any made, get some from Stump. When you take the coffee to the Grief Room, stay with the old ladies until I get back, and for goodness sakes, try to carry on a conversation. I know it's might near impossible to do without a phone attached to your ear, but try it."

"Your little turned-up nose must have uncovered a big wad of green stuff if you're serving coffee in Grandma Moody's china," she said in a sarcastic tone. "Next thing we know, you'll be using big words and having Stump trim the hairs on your mole, and when he does, please have him kill the fungus growing out of your ears and nose holes. It has grown a little thick since the last expensive funeral."

I ignored her comments and began thumbing through the telephone directory for the number of the Life Insurance Company of Georgia. While I waited to be connected to the appropriate department, I bounced from one foot to the other and spoke softly.

"This is too good to be true. I know they are going to tell me the policy lapsed ten years ago, or it's one she bought out of a coin machine at the fair ground. Mercy, hurry up." When the lady asked for the policy number, I had to repeat it three times before getting it correct. I felt like the town dullard. With the conversation complete and assurance that the policy was in force, I walked into the small room where Lucinda Faye made a pretense of washing the cups.

"I don't want a half-ass job," I said. "Get the muck off of them, and for goodness sakes empty out the roach droppings. Before you take the coffee to the Grief Room, call Virgil and tell him to get over here quick. I need help. If his line is busy, tell Stump to run over and bring him back. If Louella has a cake, tell him to bring a few pieces to serve with the coffee."

"What do you want with Virgil? You need to take a leak and need his permission?"

"Just do what I tell you to do," I said as I went into my office and closed the door. I opened the drawer to my file cabinet and said hello to my friend Jim Beam. "Lord above," I mumbled, "this calls for a celebration. I wish I had time to tell Stump, but he'll have to wait."

About that time, some fool began pounding on my door. I yanked it open, and there stood Amos and Modean Quackenbush as if stepping out of a scene from *The Grapes of Wrath*. "Good Morning," I said.

"We're real sorry to be a bother to you, Mr. Moody," Modean apologized in a slow, grating voice that took twice as long to say a sentence as it would have a normal person. "We just heard that Miss Erma Mae Logan passed on this morning, Mr. Moody, and we want to visit a spell with her."

"Miss Logan is not receiving guests at the present time," I explained. "If you'll come back later this afternoon or tonight, I know the family will be happy to see you." I stepped back into my office and started to close the door, as Jim was waiting, but she started talking again.

"Do you know what it was that caused her to pass on?" She asked.

Hell, I had no idea what killed the old gal. Folks seem to think the undertaker is a combination of God, old Damsel Death, and the coroner.

"She died of cancer," I said in my most pitiful tone in the hopes of ending the conversation.

"That cancer can shore get you fast," Amos added.

"Yes, it certainly can. Now, if you'll excuse me, I'm busy making arrangements for Miss Lumpkin, Lugar, ugh, the dear lady's funeral."

"Do you know when it will be at?"

"No, but later today I'll be able to tell you everything," I tried to explain. "Here comes Brother Jordan to help with the arrangements. I must go." I stepped back into my office and cleared the way for Jordan as he pranced up the hall like a duck in heat.

> *Money is not everything they say.*
> *But it's good enough for me*
> *If it gets my butt out of a rut*
> *So happy I will be.*
>
> – Ewell Moody

CHAPTER FIVE

Ewell Moody

"This better be good, Ewell," Virgil Jordan said as he entered my office and slammed the door. "What the hell is so important about an old maid dying that you have to get me over here before I've had time to take care of my three S's. Old maids die in this town all the time, and you've never gotten excited before.

"What are you grinning about? The gap in your teeth looks wide enough to floss with a water hose when you smirk like that. Whatever it is, make it snappy. I have things to do. Just because you seldom work for a living doesn't mean the rest of us follow your example. I was up all night with important church business, and I knew the old maid died in the early morning hours, but so what? She never put a penny in my offering plate while she lived, and I doubt she'll put anything in there now that she's napping with worms."

"Take a look at this," I said, handing him the policy then waiting for his reaction to the face value. His hawk nose lit up brighter that Rudolph's, and his Prince of Wales ears twitched so fast I thought he would take off like Dumbo. I crossed my arms in front of my chest and smirked as I watched him lick his lips and flip the pages of the policy. Reality soon took over.

"I'll be a cock-eyed heathen," he said. "Who would believe the queen of loons was worth this kind of money? It's a wonder the policy is not eat-up with fungus. How did she plan to use the loot? Have you called The Life of Georgia? Are the premiums paid up to date? Who is the beneficiary? Is it signed over to us? Damn it, Ewell, take your hand off your crotch and wipe that fool grin off your face."

"Sorry, guess I was enjoying myself so much I forgot my manners. The lady at The Life of Georgia said the policy is in full force," I explained. "I talked with her myself. She said the old gal had never missed a premium payment, and the last one was paid three days before she died. The beneficiaries are her two sisters."

"Okay, so the old gal has money, but why the urgency in making me come here? You could have told me on the phone."

"We've got a problem that I'm not sure I can handle."

"That figures. Do you have a calculator?" He asked as he opened my desk drawer and began moving things around.

"There's a little one in the left bottom drawer under the box of prunes," I said. "The sisters are in the Grief Room ready to make funeral arrangements. The Gooch woman and her sister, what's her name?" I asked, as I had forgotten it was written on my palm.

"Roper, Mildred Roper."

"Roper, that's it, Roper. The Gooch woman wants to have a big, tacky, expensive funeral with everybody in the county coming."

"I got no problem with that. Sounds good to me, and with this kind of money I assume you are going to put the old maid in the mahogany box. Who's knocking on the damn door? Open it," he said as he sat down in my chair and spread the policy on the desk.

"Sorry to bother you again, Mr. Moody," Amos Quackenbush apologized when I opened my door. "Could my wife use your toilet?"

"Yes, she may," I said with a sigh. "It's down the hall on your left. You'll find a pan in the sink to fill the tank when you need to flush," I explained, then closed the door. I picked up the conversation with Jordan where we left off about the Gooch woman wanting a big funeral.

"It's not going to be that simple, Virgil. The Roper woman is hell-bent on cremating the old gal and doing God knows what with the cremains. They're butting horns like a couple of Billy goats over a nanny in heat, and I am not getting any closer to them than I have to. Merciful hell. Who is knocking on my door now?"

"What do you want?" I asked Lucinda Faye as she pushed me aside and walked into my office.

"Ray Attaway is on the phone and wants to know if you'll stuff his pig. It just died, and they're afraid to eat it, but he wants to keep it."

"Hell, no! I haven't got time to fool with no damn pig. Mercy."

36

"He said ask."

"You asked. Now get out, and close the door behind you. Where was I?"

"You were talking about the Roper woman wanting to burn the body," Virgil explained. "Have you got anything to drink?"

"Lucinda Faye made a fresh pot of coffee for the women."

"I mean something stronger. What's in the thermos?"

"Jim Beam."

"Pour me some," he demanded. "Preferably in a clean glass. Get on with what you were saying. I don't have all day. This thing has double indemnity. Could we say she got run over, accidentally shot herself, or drowned?"

"She was terminal and died in her bed, Virgil."

"What a shame. Could she have rolled out of bed and hit her head on something? Choked on her teeth or fell face down in the john and drown? Perhaps she fell off the back porch in a drunken stupor."

"The old gal died in her bed with her sister sitting beside her. It had been months since she got out of bed to pee. The only thing in her room is a bed, nightstand, and wall-to-wall bookshelves filled with a horde of books."

"Is an autopsy required since she died at home?" Virgil asked. "Are you friends with the coroner? Maybe we could pad his palm?"

"I tried that recently, remember? Lazarus Larson used to do that kind of stuff, but since he got saved he won't budge from the straight and narrow."

"Shit, I need to be more selective who I encourage to give up sinning. A chance like this doesn't come around but once in a lifetime, and it's a bloody damn shame not to get it all."

"It seems the old maid left instructions to be cremated immediately after she died, and the Lord only knows what she wanted done with her ashes. She specified no funeral, no preacher, nothing. Here, you'll have to drink out of this bud vase. It's all I can find. The Roper woman is determined to do what her sister wanted. Holy mother of Moses' brother, what now? Come in," I yelled in response to a knock on the door.

"Mr. Moody?"

"Yes, Mr. Quakerbrook?"

"I just want to thank you for letting my wife use your toilet."

"You're welcome."

"We got it flushed. When she goes to places like this, you know, round the dead, she gets the flux and has to go mighty quick."

"I understand, Mr. Crackerbrook, and she is welcome to go in my toilet anytime. Now please excuse me," I said politely and closed the door.

"Damn it, Ewell," Virgil said. "Be careful when you open that door. Somebody important might be standing on the other side, and there are a lot of folks I wouldn't want to see me sipping a snort, especially from a damn flower vase. Course what old man and old lady Crackerbox thinks don't amount to a pea hill. Neither one of them could drive a nail into a snow bank."

"I thought they were members of your flock."

"So what if they are? I've got a whole herd that ought to be locked up. Does this calculator work? How in the world that old lady paid these premiums is beyond me. Go on with your tale. So the Roper woman wants to carry out her dead sister's wishes? Is that your problem?"

"That's my problem. When we cremate we don't make a dime, and you know it. I want to sell them Croker's box. Mother of Judas, who is knocking on my damn, frigging door now? Come in," I screamed.

Wearing her usual dead pan expression, Lucinda Faye entered the office.

"Festus Belmont wants to know what to do with the buzzard."

"Does he have it with him?"

"Yep."

"Tell him to leave it on the loading dock, and close the damn door when you leave."

"That gal has the mind of an ass and probably acts like an ape in bed," Jordan said after Lucinda Faye closed the door.

"I wouldn't insult an ass by comparing her mind to its, and I don't know how she acts in bed. Furthermore, I've no intentions of finding out."

"Maybe you ought to, Ewell. You might like it for a change." Jordan held the vase to his lips and drained its contents. "What have you had in this thing?" he asked. "I'll probably catch the plague. Have you got a straw? I'm about to get my tongue hung in this tiny hole."

"No! I don't have a straw, and this is not a fast food joint, nor a damn bar, so stop fretting about catching something. You know nothing lives in alcohol."

"Good thing you've got a lot of it around here," he said. "Pour me another one. That old Logan gal paid more for premiums on this policy than I've paid on my house, and I can't figure how she did it. But there is one thing I do know about her, and that is she hated preachers more than anybody I ever met. If she knew I was going to get this money, she'd roll off your slab and crawl my ass." He grinned as he placed the calculator in my desk drawer, leaned back in my chair, and placed his hands behind his head. "So you want me to convince Sister Roper that cremation is a sin. Is that right?"

"I don't give a cat's ass what you convince her of as long as you persuade her to bury the old gal in the mahogany box." I picked up the thermos and took a small sip.

"Put that stuff down," Jordan yelled. "You've got to stop killing yourself one swig at a time. Furthermore, you've got a day's work ahead of you, and you're going to need all your faculties to deal with the old gal's family." He capped the thermos and placed it in my desk drawer. "Mildred Roper comes to church as faithful as the sun scorches the desert, and she thinks I sit on the right hand of the throne and rub shoulders with Jesus. That old gal is so righteous she lives with her head in the lap of God. She'll do anything I say, and she is so frazzled from taking care of her sister, she wouldn't be able to fight me if she wanted to. It won't be a problem changing her mind. The Gooch gal only comes to church for special events that include food, but she loves a good funeral better than a buzzard loves a roadside dinner, so that money is as good as ours. That is if you don't do something stupid and lose it. With that much loot you can pay me what I'm due and still be in the black. As a favor for loaning you the money, you're to get me the title to the Logan woman's old Edsel."

"What do you want with that old pile of junk?"

"I've got a hunch of what it's worth, and I know a dealer in Atlanta that buys those things sight unseen."

"Lord, Virgil, if we get the money from the old gal's insurance policy it'll be the rip-off of the century. Surely you don't expect them to sign over that old car, too?"

"That's exactly what I expect them to do, and you had better make sure they do it. See who's knocking on the damn door."

"Ewell, I think it's a might hot on the loading dock for this bird," Festus Belmont said as I opened the door. He held a large dead buzzard by the feet.

"Yeah, yeah, guess you're right," I agreed. "Here, let me have it." I took the bird by the feet and pressed the body against my knee. I folded the wings with my hands and brought it through the door. "I appreciate it, Festus. I'll let you know when I'm finished with it."

"Good deal. Know you'll make it mighty pretty. Howdy, Virgil. See you Ewell." He then closed the door.

"What in the living hell is that?" Jordan asked as I lay the bird on the floor.

"A buzzard."

"I can see that, Ewell. What is this place? A funeral parlor for a zoo? The nincompoops that come in and out of here are crazier than the dolts locked up at Milledgeville. Lord, Ewell, you're impossible. I'm going home to spruce up a little, and when I get back we'll take care of the old gals. Call Sara Nell and have a wreath sent to the Roper house. Better send a big one. I'm telling you one more time, Ewell, this is the chance I've been waiting for. Blow this deal, and you'll be the next one occupying Croker's box and the first one covered with dirt. I mean it, Ewell."

"Okay, okay, I hear you. Mercy."

"And another thing, when I go in the Selection Room that casket had better be shining like the gold calf in the desert. Round up the boys and get them on it. Tell them to take special effort in polishing the scratch on the side, and tell them to vacuum out the inside. I don't want no damn grave dirt on the satin lining." He turned to leave.

"Okay, okay," I said, wiping the perspiration from my forehead and mumbling softly as I watched him leave the funeral parlor. "That lanky scoundrel ain't never happy. If he'd stop whoring around all night and gorging himself on beans and avocados, he wouldn't be hung up and touchy as hell. Lord above, I dread asking for that old car as part of the funeral deal. Those folks will think I'm crazy."

I took the thermos from my desk drawer and tried desperately to drain another drop, but it was empty.

I called Sara Nell about the flowers then put on my coat. I took a dog biscuit from the pocket and used it to scratch my badly irritated body as I stepped out in the hall and closed the door behind me. On the way to the Grief Room, I hesitated under the portrait of Grandpa, shot him a bird, and scowled in the old man's face. I swear to God he smiled at me. From the door of the surgery, Stump stepped out with his hands cupped in front of him.

"What have you got?" I asked.

"Cremains. Open the back door, please. I couldn't get all of Hojo Bottom's ashes in that fancy can you sold his widow. I'm throwing the overflow in the kudzu."

I opened the door and stepped aside as I grinned. "You better get busy and spruce up the old Logan gal, but be careful when you open her mouth. Her gold chompers might plummet out."

I walked on down the hall without explaining to Stump what had transpired since our talk earlier in the morning. I intentionally waited to tell him in the hopes that as the day went on I would have more good news to share with him. Whether the news was good or bad depended on Virgil Jordan's persuasive powers to change Mildred Roper's mind about cremation.

> *Sister Roper is kind and neat,*
> *No one she would ever cheat.*
> *She'll put up a fight to make things right*
> *But lose from lack of sleep.*
> -Ewell Moody

CHAPTER SIX

Mildred Roper

As I sat in the Grief Room with Gladys waiting for Mr. Moody to come back from his conversation with Brother Jordan, I looked around at its rundown condition. I remembered a well-kept funeral home when I came with Erma to plan the funeral for our older sister when Maslow, Ewell's grandpa, was alive. Now, the drab, depressing condition of the room made me want to get up and leave, but I knew I had to stay and fight Gladys to keep the promises I'd made Erma.

The room's only chairs looked like rejects from the Bochimville Dump. The Windsor had one leg shorter than the other three, a broken arm, and a sagging seat. From the age and condition of the Queen Anne, it could have belonged to its namesake. The decrepit old table under the window made me smile, for its claw feet looked as if they hurt as bad as mine did. A photo of a gray-haired lady in an ancient frame sat on the table near a brass lamp with a dented base, an ashtray filled with stale cigarette butts, a worn Gideon Bible, and a red clay pot of thirsty Wandering Jew.

A painting of a redheaded Jesus with protruding eyes and a pitiful expression on his chalky face decorated the far wall. As I sat there looking at Him, I wished I could be as ignorant of my surroundings as that poor, pathetic Christ seemed to be, but I could not shut out Gladys' constant chatter. She reminded me of a wound-up toy that never stopped, as she prattled to Lucinda Faye who didn't seem to hear a word she said and responded to Gladys by snapping her gum, swishing the pages of the Sears Catalog, and occasionally grunting.

"I understand you've been engaged a few times, Lucy Faye," Gladys said. "Did your mama and daddy frown on the boys you picked? I guess it's kind of hard to find a man that suits them, seeing as how your daddy is a preacher. Have you ever thought about courting Mr. Moody's boy, Stump? I hear he's a mighty fine fellow and probably makes a lot of money seeing as how the dead pay real well. Since both of you work here, it might be real handy."

"Gladys, for goodness sakes," I said, "Lucinda Faye can find a man without your help. Leave her alone."

"Millie, it never hurts to listen to suggestions from somebody else now and then, now, does it?" Gladys asked Lucinda Faye who appeared deaf. "You can't tell when it might be just the one you've been looking for. That Stump fellow is probably a good bit older than the boys you been courting, and your mama and daddy might be happier to see you go out with him. He's a mighty nice looking man, but kind of spooky with that black thing over his eye. He reminds me of somebody in the comics, but for the life of me I can't remember who it is. Him being older than you, might make him different from younger boys who don't seem to have nothing on their minds but sex, sipping beer, and gallivanting all over the county watching wrestling matches and racing pickup trucks in mud holes. I know your mama don't want you getting tied up with that kind of trash."

I was grateful to hear Gladys respond to a knock on the door.

Mr. Moody came into the Grief Room smiling and bowing like the British do when the Queen is near. I wondered what we had done to get royal treatment. Lucinda Faye threw the catalog to the floor and left the room in such a hurry she almost knocked Mr. Moody down.

"Ladies," he said, "please forgive me for leaving you at a time like this, but I know you'll be glad to learn that Pastor will be with you presently. He was detained at home with urgent church business but sends his blessings and heartfelt sympathy. He wants you to know he is with you in spirit."

"That's real good to know," Gladys said as she turned on the couch, lifted her cane, and pointed to the painting on the opposite wall. "Mr. Moody, who took that picture of Jesus hanging over yonder? For the life of me I never knowed he had fiery red hair and eyes that stuck out from his face like a couple of doorknobs. Is that your door he's knocking on? From the way he looks, I don't think he believes it's going to open. If I was you, Mr. Moody, I'd take him down and hang up somebody else."

"Mrs. Gooch, I agree the painting is not a very good representation of our Savior, but the artist is a dear friend, and for her sake we must keep it there. Come in," he said when somebody knocked softly on the door.

Neatly dressed in an expensive suit like he always wore, and I never understood how he could afford, Brother Jordan came into the room beaming with what I suppose some folks call self esteem and moving with the gait of a thoroughbred horse. Under his right arm he carried his large, black leather Bible.

Mr. Moody quickly lifted the Queen Anne chair and placed it near the couch then stepped back. Brother Jordan sat down and leaned towards me and Gladys like he had something important to say.

"My dear sisters in Christ," he began. "Words cannot express the sadness I felt today when I heard that one of the Lord's chosen vessels had broken. I can only imagine how your dear hearts must bleed because of this loss." He lifted Gladys' right hand and gently caressed it. I thought he was going to kiss it. "I know you are grieved with the passing of your loved one, but let us rejoice that she has gone this day to be with her Lord." He smiled. I don't know why, but he did. He smiled like folks do when they are in pain. I wondered if his hemorrhoids were acting up. "What a wonderful consolation it is at a time like this to have precious memories of her and to know that in the sweet bye and bye we will gather at the river where we will meet her on that beau-ti-ful shore. My dear sisters, you know our Lord promised us many mansions if we would serve him and that he would not depart from us in our time of need. Today is surely your time of need, and if you do what he wants you to do, he will keep you cupped in the palm of his sweet hand throughout eternity. But better still, he will walk by your side during the next few days until your dear departed one is laid safely to rest in the warm bosom of mother earth."

"Brother Jordan," I said, "I've got Sister's request here saying how she wanted things done when she passed away. I feel we ought to do what she wanted." I handed him Erma's instructions, which he handled like a fierce little animal about to spit in his eyes. He quickly handed it back to me without reading it.

"Sister Mildred, I would never tempt the Lord by failing to put away one of my sheep the way the Holy Book instructs."

"Oh, Brother Jordan," I said, real upset, "I sure don't want to tempt the Lord." I guess Mr. Moody had told him I wanted Erma cremated, for how else would he have known what was in her paper? I had no idea that cremating somebody was tempting the Lord, but then he was the preacher and I wasn't. I learned later that I knew more about the Word of God than he did.

"I know in your heart you don't want to tempt the Lord, Sister Mildred," he said as he squeezed my hand so hard it brought on my arthritis. He let go of my hand, opened his big Bible, and spread it across his knees like old people do a shawl to keep their legs warm. He began reading.

"In Corinthians, we find that one day a trumpet will blow, and in the twinkling of an eye the dead will spring from their graves, and the ones put away with the Lord's approval will be changed into a new and beautiful body, just like that."

He closed his Bible, snapped his fingers, stood, and looked heavenward. I assumed he was seeking divine approval. As long as he stood there, I didn't hear voices or see flashing lights. He soon started talking again. "You must remember one thing," he said softly as he reached for my hand again and gently rubbed it.

"Only the body that is put away with the approval of the Holy Ghost will be changed," he said and then paused for a long time. I guess he was waiting for me or Gladys to say something, but by now I didn't have a thing to say. I was still upset about him accusing me of tempting the Lord. He finally went on. "What I'm trying to tell you, dear sisters in the Lord, is that if a body is burned up it can't be changed, for it is destroyed. When a body is burned, and the ashes thrown in the wind or the river or just tossed aside, the body can't be put back together. You see, dear sisters in the Lord, when judgment morning comes, and it's coming soon," he shouted, shook his fist, then jumped from his seat in such a hurry I thought he planned to run from the room or jump out the window. He appeared to be having a fit like I'd seen folks have who live at Milledgeville. He didn't leave, but got himself calm and sat back down in his seat and began speaking softly again.

"On that morning, ashes for her legs could have blown over into Monroe County with her face ashes way down in Albany. The ashes for her feet could have floated all the way to Alabama or stuck along the banks of the Chattahoochee and been eaten by otters." He leaned his face near me and spoke in a whisper.

"There would be no way the Lord could get her back together again. He would have to pass her by. She would never again be with her dear sisters," he said in a trembling voice.

46

"Oh, Brother Jordan," Gladys said, real happy like, "that is exactly what I've been trying to tell Millie ever since Erma passed on."

She wiped her face and nose with the palm of her right hand and then rubbed her hands together. I looked in my purse for a tissue or handkerchief, but didn't have a thing. I knew she would start using the hem of her dress before long.

"But Brother Jordan," I said, still afraid of tempting the Lord with my words. "Don't you think we ought to consider a little bit of what Sister wanted?"

"Dear, dear Sister Gladys," he said, rubbing my hand again.

"I'm Mildred," I corrected him.

"Of course you are."

He suddenly dropped my hand, and with a sour look on his face turned towards Mr. Moody who was standing on one foot while scratching the back of his leg with the other foot. Mr. Moody was rolling something between his fingers that made an irritating noise. Brother Jordan seemed really annoyed, but soon got himself together and turned back to us and continued talking.

"Dear sisters," he said, but I could tell he was not happy with Mr. Moody. He nervously rolled the sides of his Bible to create a tube, and his hands were never still as he continued to talk. "To teach us that burial is such an important thing to do with our loved ones, the Lord took time out from His creating to bury His old chum Moses."

"Ohoooo, Brother Jordan, I didn't know that."

"Yes, yes, Sister Gladys, right up there on Mt. Nero the Lord Himself put Moses in the ground. The Lord came out of the sky and laid that old man's bones to rest in a way pleasing to Himself. The Lord could have burned that old man's body just like He did the shrub many years before, but He didn't. You know why?"

I was glad he didn't give us time to answer because I didn't know the answer, and there was no guessing what Gladys would have said.

"It was not the right thing to do. The Lord didn't want his beautiful servant burned up. No, dear ones, he gently laid the body of that good old soul to rest with all his parts together, right there in the sand on Mt. Nero, and when the Lord returns he will find Moses just like he left him."

"Oh, Brother Jordan, that story is so sweet," Gladys said like she had never heard the story of Moses before in her life.

"That's not all, Sister Gladys. The Lord gives many more

instructions in the Holy Book about how to bury our dear ones. All we need do is listen." He sat in the Queen Anne chair and spread his Bible open across his knees again like he was going to read to us forever. "We read in Genesis that when Joseph died in Egypt, his sons embalmed him and put him in a coffin. They hauled that old man all over creation just to get him to the land of Canaan where he was to be buried. Now, dear sisters, wouldn't it have been a lot easier on everybody if they had burned him to nothing but a little jar of ashes to haul across the desert? Of course it would have, but they didn't do it. You know why? Because it would have been a sin. A SIN!" Jordan shouted so loud that it scared me for a second. I jumped. He jerked his Bible off his lap, wadded it up, and raised it towards the ceiling.

"The Lord didn't take to burning bodies," he yelled, "and I'm here to tell you that he isn't going to be happy with nobody that burns bodies today."

"But, Brother Jordan," I said, trying to get a word in on Erma's behalf. "They burned the bodies of King Saul and his sons when they were killed in battle." In the middle of my sentence, Mr. Moody dropped something and it rolled across the floor.

"But, but, ugh, dear sister," Brother Jordan said, a little rattled from my statement. "King, King, ugh, King Saul and his sons were wicked men and deserved to be cast into outer darkness where there will be gnashing of teeth throughout eternity, but your sister was a good lady and deserves a happy parting from this earth to start again somewhere else. It should be with a sense of joy that you, her family, and me, her preacher, make every effort to see that she gets a real Christian send off. You should be willing to sacrifice until it hurts, just for her."

"That's what we want to do," Gladys agreed, "but Brother Jordan, all we've got is Sister's life insurance policy. You see, she didn't have no savings or nothing worth anything."

"My sister didn't want her money spent on a funeral," I said, knowing nobody was listening to me. "She wanted the money from her insurance policy used to help somebody else."

"Don't let your meager funds worry you none," Brother Jordan said to Gladys, ignoring what I said. "Like I told you, it's the responsibility of all of us to see that she gets put away real nice. Mr. Moody here will help you make the right decisions and keep the price within your limited budget."

"I'll be glad to do that," Mr. Moody said. With his hands in front of him, he bent over like a Chinaman bowing to his emperor. I didn't understand all the bowing he was doing. He seemed nervous about something. "Since Pastor is here with us," he said, "why don't we make the arrangements now so he can help us?"

It really upset me when I saw Mr. Moody look at Brother Jordan and wink and Brother Jordan look back with a smirk. I was beginning to think Erma had been justified in hating preachers as much as she did. I guess Erma saw things that I couldn't or didn't want to see. Did they think me blind? Or did they just not care? I felt as if they were making fun of me and the whole situation.

"Oh, Brother Jordan," Gladys said, "will you help us, please? We just don't know how to do things on our own."

"Of course I'll help you," Brother Jordan replied, gently laying his hand on Gladys' arm. "Let's go into the Selection Room and see if we can't find the perfect crate, ugh, I mean coffin for your dear, departed sister."

As I slowly walked behind Brother Jordan to the Selection Room, I had a strong feeling that I was following someone who was deliberately leading me down the wrong path, and at that moment I felt I would never be on the right path again. O Lord, I silently prayed, deliver me from the violent that plot and stir up trouble all day long. Their words sting like poisonous snakes. Keep me out of their power, for they are plotting against me.

CHAPTER SEVEN

Mildred Roper

As we walked down the hall to another room, I sensed that Brother Jordan resented having to help us, and he seemed impatient with me for walking so slow, but I had to hold onto the wall to keep from falling over.

When we entered the room, I noticed a mule's head hanging on the wall with its lips pulled back like it was smiling. If I had not been so tired and frustrated, I would have found it funny. I watched Mr. Moody flip a switch on the floor and heard the grinding sound of a struggling motor. He then pushed on a large, black-draped platform that held a mahogany casket shining as bright as a Christmas tree. It swirled around like a kid on a merry-go-round, and the bright lights from the ceiling cast a nice glow from all four directions and made the coffin gleam like burnished gold. Somebody had recently spent a lot of time polishing the box, as I could smell the furniture polish. When it had made a complete turn, Mr. Moody flipped the switch again, and Brother Jordan stepped up on the platform as if ready to perform. He opened the lid of the casket and rubbed his hand on the lining.

"Brother Jordan," I said as loud as I could in my tired condition, "Sister didn't want no casket. She said they cost too much."

"Dear ones," he said, ignoring every word I said and not looking in my direction. I know I spoke out loud because I heard myself and felt my mouth move. All three of them were acting like I was invisible and couldn't be heard. "This superb masterpiece," he said, "makes the families of the departed feel so good when they lay their loved ones to rest in this marvelous work of art. This casket, I mean one just like it, has been used many times in our community by the best of our residents."

I felt a lump as big as a wad of cotton in my throat and a taste as bitter as gall fill my mouth when I realized my own pastor had deliberately ignored my remark. I swallowed my bitterness and brushed tears from my face. I knew I was alone in my battle for Erma. What could I do? Who could I turn to? I needed the one member of my family I could always count on for help, and she was gone from me forever. At least that's what I thought at the moment. Later, I began to think differently.

"Now, dear ones," I heard Brother Jordan say, "I want you to feel the softness of this mattress. Me and you both know how important it is to sleep on something real comfy. Don't we?" He paused and smiled. "We would never think about putting a loved one away on a rigid mattress for all eternity. Would we? This mattress will hold your dear sister in a restful position as if it were part of her backbone until Jesus returns and pulls her dear body from the grave." Brother Jordan lifted one of the handles in his hand and held it like a baby holding a rattle as he continued speaking.

"Dear sisters, I now call your attention to these superbly crafted handles that are cast of the purest bronze to perfectly fit the hand of each pallbearer so there will be no danger of the casket slipping from his hand when he lifts the lovely body of your dear one up and down the church steps and out to the graveyard. When you place that sweet, departed soul in this casket, she will be as safe and secure as the rock of ages."

"Will it keep out worms, Brother Jordan?"

"Yes, yes, Sister Gladys, it is worm proof."

"And termite proof," Mr. Moody added.

"That's good to know. I sure don't want Sister eat up by worms or termites chewing on her wooden leg."

"It's also waterproof," Mr. Moody mumbled.

"I'm real glad to know that. I would hate for it to fill up with water. Erma might drown."

"Erma is dead, Gladys," I said, with my words falling on deaf ears. "She can't drown." Erma often said Gladys was slightly unhinged, but today she didn't seem hinged at all. She was in bliss and only heard and saw what pleased her.

"Sister Gladys," Brother Jordan said, "it is comforting to know that when our Lord returns to earth and snaps his fingers over your dear sister's grave, this casket will rise up out of the ground, and when Jesus pops the top, your loved one will look just like she'll look the day of her funeral when Brother Moody closes the lid and tightens the screws."

"Will she smell the same as she does today?"

"Yes, yes, Sister Gladys. Hallelujah, nothing will have changed. Amen."

"That's plumb wonderful."

I wanted to say something, but knew I would be ignored. So, I just shook my head and sighed.

"Now, dear ones, as a final touch please look at the nature scene in the lid."

"Oh, how pretty," Gladys said, and with the aid of her cane climbed onto the platform. "Look at them sweet little birds flying around everywhere. My, my, won't our friends be flabbergasted when they see what we've bought for Erma? Millie, you ought to come up and look at this."

"Your friends will be dazzled beyond words," Brother Jordan agreed. "Now, for the fabric—"

Gladys was so excited she interrupted Brother Jordan and said, "I do believe there's a little fox poking its head out of the hole."

"Yes, Sister Gladys, but as I was saying, this material is fine enough for the robes of kings and queens and will be perfect to caress Sister Er...Eunice, ugh."

"Erma Mae," I said. I couldn't believe Brother Jordan had forgotten Sister's name so soon.

"Yes, yes, Sister Erma Mae. I'm sure you will agree this fabric will be perfect to wrap around Sister Erma Mae on her eternal sojourn in the grave." He stepped away from the casket and came over to me. Looking me in the eyes, he said, "Sister Roper, when you lay your loved one to rest in this enchanting vessel, you are saying to the world that nothing was too good for her. You are saying that you were willing to sacrifice all, if necessary, to see her leave this world in a manner in which she would have been able to live if she had not given everything she had to her family and others."

"You know, Brother Jordan," Gladys piped in before I could speak, "this fabric is so soft to touch and the picture in the lid so sweet it's enough to make folks want to be buried in it before they die. Brother Jordan, do you agree?" Gladys asked like a fool.

"Yes, yes, Sister Gladys," he answered like a fool.

I turned away from both of them and looked at Mr. Moody, still scratching the back of his left leg with the toe of his right shoe. He reminded me of an old hound dog covered in fleas and ticks. He put his foot down on a marble or something he had been rolling around in his hand, slipped, and hit the floor switch. It caused the casket to suddenly start turning, and at a faster rate than before. Brother Jordan fell off the platform and knocked over a stack of cardboard caskets near the wall. Gladys grabbed the side of the casket as the lid closed on her fingers. From the way she screamed, I assumed she was hurt.

"Goddamnit, Ewell," I heard Brother Jordan yell as he got up from the floor, brushed off his suit, and hurried onto the platform. "Are you all right, Sister Gladys?" he asked as he lifted the casket lid off her hand.

"I don't rightly know, Brother Jordan. My hand feels a little crushed." She rubbed her left hand with her right one as tears welled up in her eyes. "That lid is mighty heavy, but you know, Brother Jordan, that cloth is real soft, just like you said it was. I know Erma will love to snuggle in it."

I watched the whole scene in amazement and then walked to the other side of the room and sat down in a folding chair close to where Mr. Moody was standing. I remembered a book on Erma's shelf titled *A Ship of Fools* and often meant to ask what it was about. I'll bet its characters were just like these three. I looked at Mr. Moody and said, as if talking to myself,

"Serves them right. I'm beginning to believe Erma is here, just like she said she'd be." He looked at me and smiled, as if he agreed with me.

Brother Jordan stepped down from the platform with his right hand holding Gladys' arm. He wiped his forehead with a clean linen handkerchief and then spoke to Mr. Moody.

"Since Sister Gladys has assured me she is alright, I want you to take the ladies to your office and make the final arrangements. These dear souls need to go home and rest." He took my rough hands in his preacher-soft ones and gently caressed them. "Dear Sister, I assure you that you are making the right decision by providing your loved one with the finest perpetual care money can buy, and I know the Lord will bless you real good. Let's pray."

"No, Brother Jordan," I said, "the right decision has not been made. My dead sister's wishes have not even been considered, and I know the Lord will not bless me for this. To be honest, I'm afraid of what He will do to me if I let this happen to her, for I believe it is a sin to spend money on a funeral except for the essential things needed to put one away. You and I both know Erma doesn't need this casket or one like it."

He dropped my hands as if they had burned him and in a loud voice said, "Let's pray. Oh, Lord, I thank you for giving me divine wisdom this day to advise these dear souls on the right thing to do in their time of loss."

I did not close my eyes while he prayed, but watched as he crossed his arms in front of him, raised the cuff of his shirt, and glanced at his watch. When he saw me watching, he began talking faster.

"Because of their unselfish sacrifice for the sake of their dear sister, please keep them safe from the devil's force and reserve them a place on the right hand of Jeeeezus throughout eternity. Amen."

"Brother Jordan?"

"Yes, Sister Mildred."

"What about those caskets over there?" I asked and pointed to the cheap ones he had knocked over.

"What about them?"

"Wouldn't they be cheaper than the fancy one up there on the stage?"

"Sister Mildred, I would be ashamed to stand in the pulpit and preach your sister's funeral if she was laid out in one of them crates."

"Then why does Mr. Moody have them in here?"

"They're for people who don't care how they put away their loved ones," Gladys piped in with words of warped wisdom. "Ain't that right, Brother Jordan?"

"Yes, yes, Sister Gladys, that is right. Now, dear ones, I must leave you as other members of my flock are in need of their shepherd. Brother Moody here will take care of you," he said, then squeezed Mr. Moody's arm. "I'll come by your home this afternoon to pray with you again and finalize my part in the funeral plans." Jordan talked hurriedly as he headed for the door like he didn't want us to speak another word. Mr. Moody followed him and seemed anxious to get out also. They behaved like we had a dirty disease and might infect them if they didn't get away immediately.

"If you ladies will excuse me for one moment," Mr. Moody said, "I'll be right back. I need a word with Pastor."

With the men out of the room, I continued sitting in the chair near the wall. Gladys walked around the casket, poking it with her cane like she was examining a cow for sale.

"I'll tell you one thing, Millie," she said, "folks in this town are going to know the Logan family has money. For once in our lives we are going to be noticed. This is the finest casket I ever saw anybody laid out in, including Elmo Croker or any of them highfalutin Presbyterians that put their folks away a little better than anybody else. Erma couldn't afford to live, but she sure can afford to die, and she's going to do it in style. Even Erma would be proud of what we're doing for her, no matter how much she used to carry on about hating funerals."

"No, Gladys, Erma would never be proud of what you're doing," I said, "and you know it. As a matter of fact, while you and Brother Jordan were making fools of yourselves, I felt Erma's presence in this room. I know she's upset, and you had better watch out."

"Now, Millie, damn it! Don't you start that!" Gladys raised her cane above her head and came down with a loud bang on the back of a metal chair. "You're just trying to scare me. I know Erma used to swear that when she died, if her family didn't go by what she wrote on that paper you've got in your pocketbook, she would come back and haunt us. I don't believe in that kind of stuff, so you stop it."

"If you don't believe in it, Gladys, why are you so upset, and what made the casket lid fall on your fingers? I think that was Erma's way of getting our attention."

"I don't want to hear no more about Erma being here. Nobody has ever come back from the dead and you know it."

"Jesus did," I reminded her, "and the Witch of Endor brought

Samuel back for Saul, so why can't Erma come back for me to right the wrong that is being done to this family?"

"Enough of this nonsense," she said. "I've got to pee. I shouldn't have drunk that whole pot of coffee Lucy Faye brought in the Grief Room, but I had to drink it to wash down the cake that was stale as a rock. If I'm not back by the time Mr. Moody is, y'all better wait. Don't do no planning without me. This is my big day, and I plan to enjoy every minute of it."

Yes, Gladys, I thought, enjoy yourself while you can. Right now I'm too tired to fight, and I don't have a living soul on my side, but that will change. I'm sure you feel that what you're doing is right, for *the way of a fool is always right in her own eyes.*

CHAPTER EIGHT

Ewell Moody

When I saw the look of disgust on the preacher's face, I knew he was pissed because I had left the old ladies alone and followed him into the hall. When he looked at me with his fists clinched and teeth locked, I felt about three years old with pee running down my leg.

"I need to talk to you for a minute," I said, a little sheepishly.

"That comes as no surprise. At times you act like you're about six years old and feebleminded. You have got to get yourself together, Ewell. You have important things to do today, and I've already told you you're going to need what little faculties you have to get everything done. First of all, get that damn policy signed over to us as quick as possible. I don't care how you do it, just do it. The Gooch gal won't give you any problems, seeing as how she doesn't have her marbles in a circle, and even if she did, she is so determined to have a big funeral she'd wear a mule collar and sit on the coffin naked if she thought it would impress the town and make the Logan clan look important. I am a mite concerned about the Roper gal. If she weren't so tired she'd be causing more hell than John saw. She and that dead sister were close as the toes on a foot, and I know she is hell-bent on doing whatever is written on that nasty, urine-tinted paper she hauls around in that tacky, old purple plastic purse. Another thing, she is a lot smarter than she appears. She is not the dumb broad her sister is, and right now the only thing in our favor is her worn out condition. She is so exhausted from taking care of her sister, I expect her to fall on her face any minute. Make sure we have that money locked up before her nephew, Hoover Murdock, and her daughter, Joan Joiner, hit town. They are a mean pack, and Mildred Roper has a granddaughter whose mouth is as loud as the blowhole of a whale. She loves her grandma and is just like the dead old maid. That gal is a pecker hating, bra burning, sandal wearing, woolly leg feminist and a real intellect. There is no telling what kind of trouble will start brewing when the family gets here. Take the old gals in your office and have them start signing. If they squabble about anything, tell them the law requires it. Don't give them any choices, and for God's sake put that policy in the safe. Some of the relatives may not know the face value, and we sure as hell don't want them finding out now. It is obvious the old Gooch gal hasn't a clue as to what the policy is worth, and you had damn well better keep it that way because she would tell the whole frigging town and how would that make us look? Ewell, I'm telling you one more time, and I mean it. If you blow this, you'll be the next animal mounted and hung on a wall."

"Okay, okay, Jesus."

"You better call on somebody that knows you. You don't exactly play in Jesus' ballpark, and while we're discussing your behavior, there was no excuse for what you did in there. You could have broken the old gal's neck, and then where in the hell would we be? A lawsuit on our hands. Keep your big feet where they belong and get rid of those glass eyes, marbles, or whatever the hell you're always rolling across the floor or rubbing together in your hands. Straighten up or you will be seriously calling on Jesus, and I doubt he will come to your rescue. Another thing, I told you a month ago to clean up that Selection Room. One day we might have a family of some importance come in here, and I'd be ashamed for them to see all that junk. If I've told you once, I've told you a hundred times to get that mule's head off the wall. I am sick and tired of trying to sell a casket with a bug eyed ass looking over my shoulder."

"Okay, okay," you art-hating bastard, I wanted to say. Your shallow mind doesn't appreciate creativity.

"Get Moss and Angus to move the pauper's boxes to the storage room."

"There's no room in there. They'll have to go to the barn."

Jordan almost knocked me down getting to the storage room where he yanked open the door. "I'll be a damn frigging infidel," he said. "You mean to tell me that mule's head is still attached to its body? And what in the hell is all this other junk?"

"You get upset over the least little things," I said. On a high platform in the storage room, I had Grandpa's mule mounted, and the head stuck through a hole in the wall between the storage room and the Selection Room. I thought it rather inventive of me to do it that way. On the mule's rear, I had preserved a large horsefly in plastic with its wings proudly spread like it was about to take off.

"Reba is a work of art," I tried to explain about the mule. "I am not getting rid of her."

"A work of art my ass."

In the room were a few stuffed animals of assorted sizes, and I'll admit some were a little scarred from insects and moth damage, but what the hell, they were mine. An old plow leaned against the wall alongside a couple of shovels, a watering trough, a harness, a hoe, and the front bumper from a 1934 Cadillac hearse. None of it was new, but it was stuff that might come in handy someday, and I couldn't understand Jordan getting so upset over a few keepsakes.

"Jesus Christ! What in the name of common sense are you doing with all this junk?" he asked.

"Lower your voice, Virgil," I said. "The old gals might hear you."

He clamped his teeth together and began to speak in a whisper. "Get them damn moth-eaten critters out of here and burn them. I have never seen such a mixture of stuffed shit in all my life." He slapped the mule on the rear causing it to turn slightly.

"Virgil, I can't burn that mule. That's Reba. I rode her when I was a kid, and she was Grandpa's favorite farm animal and for years stood in his front office."

"I don't give a squatting cat's ass if it was his favorite whore and he screwed her on his desk. Get rid of it. NOW! What happened to the plastic head of Jesus the Presbyterian preacher's wife made? I gave it to you to put on a stand in the Selection Room."

"Delilah chewed off its nose."

"Then what happened to the picture she gave us of the Lord and his buddies sitting around the table eating? I know I told you to hang it in there."

"Well," I mumbled, twitching my neck and trying not to scratch, as I knew that would upset him more than my answer to his question was about to do. "Stump splashed embalming fluid on it and smeared the paint. The Disciples look like their ears are bleeding."

"All I've got working around this place is a bunch of damn dolts," he said, then turned and hurried down the hall. "Another thing," he said as he stopped and motioned for me to come closer. "Don't forget the title to that old Edsel. I'm sure they don't have it with them, but remind them to bring it tonight to the viewing. I know you think you've panned a little gold and will be rid of me soon. Well, you are not rid of me yet, and until I'm paid off, lock, stock, and barrel, I'm going to be around giving orders, so straighten up."

"Okay, okay."

"Another thing, why are you always scratching? Have you got fleas? You've got to stop sleeping with that nasty pit bull and those flea infested cats. Lord, Ewell, you act worse than a hog trying to rub caked-up slop off its hide."

He turned to leave, and then stopped again as he spoke. "To be on the safe side, call J. R. and tell that shyster if anybody from the Logan family comes seeking his advice on how to get the old lady's money back, tell them they don't have a leg to stand on. Another thing, you have got to get both of them to sign the release to turn the proceeds over to us. Old lady Gooch will sign anything, but the Roper gal will not sign a damn thing without a little persuasion. You might need to dope her coffee or whack her on the head, but do whatever it takes."

"If I call J. R., you know we'll have to pay him. That bastard won't say good morning on the street without charging for it."

"I know that, Ewell, but we can afford him if we get this money, and we better get it or you'll be sleeping in a pauper's box."

As I watched Virgil Jordan hurry down the hall, thankful he was finally leaving, I spent a little time with my thoughts. If ever the devil lived inside a person's soul, he definitely lived in Virgil Jordan's, for every time I was in his presence I could see his black shadow wrapped around him like an evil shroud. I could only guess the horrors that lurked in the mind of that speck of a human. When I observed his actions, I understood why intelligent people hated preachers, as he wouldn't survive a minute among people who had half sense. I vowed at that moment it would be the last time that cad gave me orders about anything. I would suck up to them old gals as much as it took to get the insurance money and get him out of my face for good. One thing for sure, I was not going to burn Reba even if I had to hide her in my bed. Mercy. What a life. I straightened my tie, wiped my face and hands on my handkerchief, and slowly walked across the hall. I softly knocked, then opened the door to the Selection Room.

> *Entering the door to the Selection Room,*
> *Was a lot like entering hell,*
> *For the way I dealt with those two old broads*
> *Helped pave my way to jail.*
>
> - Ewell Moody

CHAPTER NINE

Ewell Moody

"Oh, Mr. Moody," the Gooch woman exclaimed when I entered the Selection Room following my excruciating ordeal with Jordan. "While we were waiting for you to finish talking to Brother Jordan, your mule suddenly said his name was Jesus Christ. In a few minutes he turned his head and looked at us. I swear, Mr. Moody, it really happened. Since Jesus spoke to us through your mule, I take it as a sign we're doing the right thing for Erma."

"Yes, yes, Mrs. Gooch," I assured her. "I'm sure the Lord used Reba to tell you that you are doing his will. Now if you ladies will follow me to my office, we will quickly take care of everything so you can go home and rest."

Still shaky from my ordeal with Jordan, I led the ladies down the hall with Mrs. Roper leaning against the wall for support. In her fatigued state, I felt sure she would most likely be on the slab with her sister before this day ended. I was in no hurry to give her assistance, as I feared that if she did go down she would take me with her. I opened the door to my office and stepped aside for them to enter.

"Mr. Moody," Mrs. Gooch said, "there's a buzzard sleeping on your floor."

"Yes, Mrs. Gooch, there is. I promised to stuff it for a friend." From the back of my chair I took an old, bloody lab coat and threw it over the large vulture.

"You're going to stuff it like a turkey?"

"No, no, I'll preserve it."

"You're going to make preserves out of it?"

"No, no," I said, shaking my head as if I had water on the brain. I started to explain what I planned to do with Festus Belmont's buzzard, but decided it was hopeless for the old gal to understand. "Ladies, please have a seat," I said.

The armchairs in my office were almost too small for the women, especially Mrs. Gooch, and I watched with concern as they twisted and turned until able to seat themselves in a presentable fashion.

"Now, ladies," I began, "let's start at the beginning." From the bottom drawer of my file cabinet I removed several forms and spread them on my desk. With my left hand I picked up a leaky ballpoint pen. "I assume you want the funeral at the Rock Church that Loves Jesus."

"We sure do."

"No, we don't," Mrs. Roper corrected her sister. "Erma didn't want to be hauled from one place to another after she passed away. I gave up not having her cremated, so can't we do something she wanted? She didn't like the church and never in her lifetime entered its doors, so why take her in it when she's dead?"

Mrs. Gooch crossed her arms over her stomach and glared at her sister. She reminded me of a sumo wrestler preparing to use her opponent for a trampoline.

"You know we're going to have a big crowd, and the funeral parlor ain't big enough to hold everybody that will come."

"You just want to show off, and I can't imagine anybody but family coming to Erma's funeral since she has been out of sight for so long."

"Ladies, if I might say a word," I said in an effort to maintain peace and move the ordeal on. "I don't mean to take sides, but we do have a lovely chapel that seats almost as many as the Rock Church that Loves Jesus," and the good thing, I thought, I could justify it on the bill, but if they had it at the church I could only charge the gas mileage from here to the church, which unfortunately is less than a mile.

"Alright, alright, we'll have it in the funeral parlor," the Gooch gal reluctantly agreed, "but I don't like it, and the rest of the family ain't going to either."

"What kind of blanket do you want on the coffin?" I asked in an effort to change the subject. I made no mention of a casket, as I assumed they would buy the mahogany box. I resented having to take care of flowers, but if I didn't, and they bought from someone other than Sara Nell, Jordan would have my ass since his wife was part owner of the flower shop.

"What do you mean blanket?" Crazy Gooch asked. "I thought it had a lid. The thing that hit me on the fingers sure didn't feel like no blanket. Look at my hand, Mr. Moody. It's swelling. By morning I'll not be able to wiggle my fingers."

"Gladys, he's talking about flowers," Mrs. Roper explained to the family imbecile, "but we don't want any. Erma didn't like funeral flowers. The smell made her sick."

"Well she ain't gonna be here to smell them, and we do want flowers," Mrs. Gooch said as she tilted her nose in the air as if encountering an unpleasant odor. "I like the kind that comes in pots so we can take them home after the funeral and sit them on the front porch till frost, and I want some plastic ones, so we can have some on hand to send to the next funeral."

"You can't sit a pot of flowers on top the coffin, Gladys, and I am not going to have plastic flowers at Erma's funeral no matter what you say."

"Mrs. Gooch," I said as the old gal banged her cane on the floor. "I suggest placing a spray of cut flowers, say roses, orchids, or carnations, on top the casket as they will lie flat, and you can suggest that close friends and family send bloomers in pots, if that is your desire."

At that precise moment I didn't give a cat's ass if she sit a pot of kudzu on top of the box.

Mrs. Roper began to cry. "We ought not to have flowers at all. I promised Erma this would never happen to her."

"You know our kin and friends will want to send flowers, and I ain't going to tell them they can't. In sad times people want to bring food and send flowers. I'm planning on folks bringing enough food so we don't have to cook again until frost, and if we suggest plastic flowers we'll use them for Erma and then stack them in the corncrib. We'll dust them off for the next funeral and not have to spend a dime. When I get home and start calling everybody, I'll tell them to bring plastic or real flowers in pots like you suggested, Mr. Moody. I also want some black roses like I saw at a funeral once. When the casket was put in the ground, folks stood around throwing black roses in the grave. It was so impressive and rich looking."

"That is not what Erma wanted," Mrs. Roper whined.

"Millie, you always could be mule headed. Why don't you forget about what Erma thought, said, and done. She ain't here no more, and she don't even count."

"Mrs. Roper," I said in an effort to keep down an argument, as if that was humanly possible. "After the funeral, why don't you take some of the flowers to the Last Light of Home for the Elderly and share them with your sister's friends?"

"She didn't have no friends in the nursing home," Mrs. Gooch said. "If you think about it, she didn't have no friends nowhere. She was peculiar as they come."

"Ladies, we must go on," I said quickly then wiped my ink-stained fingers on the leg of my pants and wiggled around in my chair to scratch. "We have a lot to do before this day is over. Let's talk about the proper attire for Sister Edsel."

"The proper what? For who?" Mrs. Gooch asked, and I realized what I had said. Talk about a Freudian slip. That was a biggie.

"Clothes for your sister, Sister Edith." Hell, I couldn't remember the old gal's name, and by now my sweaty palms were erased clean of all names.

"Erma, Erma Mae," Mrs. Gooch explained. "You can call her Erma, Mr. Moody."

"Good, now let's talk about clothes for your dear sister. We have a lovely selection of lingerie that we order from Eternal Undies by Rita that you may choose from."

"I want her buried in one of her own dresses," Mrs. Roper said, and I knew that would light a fresh spark under her portly sister.

"I want her in new stuff," Gooch bellowed. "We can't lay her out in that fancy casket in an old dress. That would be like putting old booze in new crocks like the Lord said not to do."

"New wine in old skins, Gladys."

"Whatever, but she's having new clothes."

"Did your sister have a favorite color?" I quickly broke in.

"Purple and orange."

"We ain't putting her in purple and orange," Goochie insisted. "I can't stand them colors on nothing except grapes and pumpkins. I like green and yellow with a touch of beige."

"You won't be wearing them, Gladys, so you don't have a say."

"Since the deceased is really asleep," I said, "perhaps you should consider a gown."

I didn't give a tinker's damn if they buried the old gal in purple and orange knickers. I just wanted to get on with it. I needed a drink and a good scratching.

"I agree with you, Mr. Moody," Sister Gooch crooned. "Sister should be wearing a pretty nightgown."

"People don't go out in public wearing a nightgown, Gladys, and you know everybody will be looking at her. We buried our other sisters in black dresses, and I see no reason we can't do the same for Erma."

"She don't have no black dress, and if she did, it would be old as sin. Mr. Moody," Sister Gooch continued speaking as she looked down at the buzzard near her feet. "I don't think that bird is dead. It just moved a foot."

I ignored the buzzard remark and looked at Mrs. Roper as she spoke.

"It makes no difference if her dress is old. It's going to be put in the ground. Erma had few new things when she was living, and she certainly wouldn't want anything new now that she's dead."

"Let's not start that again, Millie," Mrs. Gooch said. "Erma was strange. You've got to admit she was plumb freakish. She never got married, but spent her life meeting men in corncribs, barns, swamps, and the Lord only knows where else. She sat a week in the top of an old oak tree without coming down to bathe or pee to keep the county from cutting it down. Then a few years later she lay in a creek until she might near froze to death just to keep the county from allowing Mack Williams to build a subdivision that would fill up the creek. If that ain't strange, I don't know what is. She'd go off for days at a time without telling a soul where she was and when she'd be back or who she was with. If that ain't queer, I don't know what is. Mr. Moody, I think you ought to check on that bird. Erma never was right after she drunk that Nuks vomiting stuff when she was young. I seen her fall out of bed many nights and lay on the floor like she was dead. I guess you think it's plumb normal that she got her leg chopped off, too."

"She couldn't help that."

"Couldn't help it my foot," Mrs. Gooch said.

The old Gooch gal's mind bounced from subject to subject like a jungle monkey jumping from limb to limb. She was wound tight and on a roll. I lay my pen down and waited for her to run down, if that was possible.

"She didn't have no business in that corncrib with Springer Yates in the middle of the night. Lord only knows what was going on in there when it caught fire and she got her leg hung between two boards in the floor. The ambulance driver that hauled Erma to the hospital in Atlanta told Gurdy that she was stark naked when he picked her up. She told us later that her and Springer was shucking corn for his mule, and you know that was a fib. Springer would never have kept coming back to Erma if she did nothing but feed his mule, even if she did do it naked. My Lord, Millie, have some sense. You know what kind of reputation them Yates boys had, and Erma's wasn't too good either."

"Ladies, ladies," I said hoping not to hear another of Miss what's her name's escapades, even though it sounded like good writing material I could use later. "Why don't we forget about what Miss, Miss, your sister is going to wear for right now and talk about the funeral? When do you want it?"

"Day after tomorrow," Goochie gal said quickly.

"What's wrong with tomorrow?" Sister butted in.

"Mrs. Roper, we will not be able to have your sister ready for viewing before tonight. These things do take time."

Course after a few hours with these two, I was ready to load the old gal up and haul her somewhere quick and get on with it.

"I'm too tired to sit around for two days waiting to bury a sister that didn't want to be buried," Mrs. Roper said, "and all the family lives within a hundred miles of here and will be in tonight. We are going to bury her tomorrow, Mr. Moody, so do what you have to do, but get it done. Erma didn't want nobody looking at her in the first place. Embalm her— put her in the casket and get on with it. NOW."

Mercy, the old gal is pissed and may cause more trouble than we expected. I'd better get this load of dung on the road.

"I think we ought to bring her home and sit her in the living room like folks used to do. When I was a girl, folks took shifts sitting up, eating good food brought in by neighbors, popping corn, talking about the dead, and in the summer we made homemade ice cream. At some sitting-ups we even drunk clear liquor that was refreshing as drinking fresh churned buttermilk. We could stay awake for about two hours after drinking a gallon of that stuff, and it didn't make us blind, howl at the moon, or shoot nobody. I remember a sitting up when a snake-handling preacher brought his snakes. After we had drunk that clear liquor for a couple of hours, he passed them serpents around and nobody got bit. Good, hard liquor can shore improve one's faith. Sitting-ups are a lot of fun. I wish they hadn't gone out of style. Don't see why we don't bring them back in. This custom of not having one is plumb disrespectful."

Merciful hell, what in the name of Ahab's ass is this old bovine going to come up with next? "Mrs. Gooch," I said, "setting ups, as you call them, are no longer feasible." I'd seen human buzzards, but none like this old broad. All she wanted to do was eat, talk, and look at the dead. I silently promised that when I got Festus' buzzard stuffed, I would mount it on the old broad's mailbox.

"If you are not going to take Erma home, Mr. Moody," the old gal whined, "you have got to keep somebody with her all night to make sure the devil don't sneak in and steal her soul before we get dirt dumped on her tomorrow. If we take her home, we can take turns sitting up and save you the trouble. Course, now that I think about it, my sister was so sinful she probably didn't have a soul."

"Let's continue, please," I found myself begging. "I assume Brother Jordan will officiate. Is that correct?"

"He'll do what?"

"Preach, Mrs. Gooch, preach." Dealing with the old gal gave me power surges so strong I felt my underwear light up, and the heat caused my rash to itch like hell.

"We want our nephew to have a part too," Mrs. Gooch said.

"Is he a preacher?"

"Yes, and a mighty fine one. Since the finger of Jesus touched him a while back, he has never stopped preaching. He's the son of our sister Louise who has already passed. Mr. Moody, I think he wants to get up and walk out."

"Your nephew?"

"The buzzard. I believe it's trying to wiggle its wings a little. You sure it's dead?" She lifted the lab coat from the bird's head with the end of her cane, then nudged it in the side. "What killed it?" she asked.

"A pitchfork."

"It ate a pitchfork?"

"No, Mrs. Gooch, Festus Belmont stabbed it with one. Now, about your nephew, do you want him to have a short prayer, perhaps after the first song?"

"Oh, no! We want him to preach as much as Brother Jordan does."

Mrs. Roper spoke for the first time in several minutes in a voice so low I could hardly hear her. "Erma loved her nieces and nephews, but she wouldn't want Flynn preaching her funeral, and you know that. Flynn can't preach. He can hardly talk. Mr. Moody, could I have a glass of water?"

"Certainly, Mrs. Roper," I said, looking around for a clean paper cup. She drank the water and then, placing her hands on her stomach, her chin fell on her chest and she seemed to drift off to sleep.

> *With chin on her chest*
> *And hands in her lap*
> *Sister Roper settled in*
> *For a short, drooling nap.*
> - Ewell Moody

69

CHAPTER TEN

Ewell Moody

After Mrs. Roper drank her water and drifted off to sleep, I became concerned with her difficulty in breathing. She seemed to struggle for every breath, and I felt sorry for her. But hell, I couldn't get wimpy at a time when all my worldly goods consisted of a used casket, four pauper's boxes, a slobbering, flea infested pit bull, three spoiled cats, and a loudmouth parrot. Life goes on, and we have to grab whatever we can at whoever's expense we can grab it. I smacked my lips and continued.

"Since Mrs. Roper doesn't want your nephew to preach, I'll tell Brother Jordan you want a short service."

"Don't you dare do that," the Gooch gal yelled as she banged her cane on the floor. "Flynn is gonna preach, and him and Brother Jordan can say what the Lord lays on their hearts. It ain't gonna hurt nothing nor nobody. I'll call Flynn and tell him he's going to preach Erma's funeral. He'll be mighty proud to do it, whether she wanted him to or not. Brother Moody," Sister Gooch whispered as she nodded her head towards her sleeping sister, "Millie is about as out as a body can be without drinking moonshine, and she ain't gonna give us no more trouble. She's worn out from being up with Erma every night for the last few months, so let's just forget about what she said, did, or wanted, cause when she wakes up it will all be planned and she can't change a thing."

"Whatever you say, Mrs. Gooch, but please let's talk about music," I suggested. I moved the end of my pen up and down the inside of my legs, as the rash was giving me fits.

Mrs. Gooch turned in her chair and spoke softly into my face. "My son and his wife from Blueridge will do the sanging, and she'll play the piano."

"Their names?"

"They don't really live in the town of Blueridge. You see—"

"Their names, please, Mrs. Gooch," I begged.

"Leonard and Estelle McTyre."

"Thought he was your son?"

"Oh, he is. He's by my first husband who passed away when Leonard was just a little boy. Mr. Moody, did you think I'd been divorced? Mr. Moody, has it got teeth?"

"Do what?"

"The buzzard. Has it got teeth? It just opened its pecker like it's trying to bite something."

"I assure you, Mrs. Gooch, the buzzard does not have teeth."

At that moment, I wished the damn bird was alive, starving, and eager to devour a fat woman.

"Oh," she said. "What was I saying? Oh, yeah, I remember. If it don't have teeth, it's got white stuff hung in its gums. Leonard and Estelle sing with a gospel quartet, and they might be able to come down with them. I want you to hear my daughter-in-law play the piano. She plays with her ear, and she sangs with the Sweet Jesus Trio She sangs like an angel."

"That right?"

The old gal looked at her sister and then whispered to me. "If we keep Millie sleeping, me and you can plan the best and biggest funeral Bochimville's seen in many a year." She licked her lips and took a deep breath. "You know something, Mr. Moody? I am determined to give Erma a bigger and more expensive funeral than Lurlene Croker give Elmo. I want Erma's casket to be a lot nicer and cost more than Lurlene ever thought about. I understand y'all went all the way to Atlanta to buy that one for Elmo. Tell me, Mr. Moody, is the one in yonder nicer than the one he was put in? If it ain't, I want you to run up to Atlanta and get us a bigger and better one."

"Mrs. Gooch, I assure you, your sister's casket is much, much nicer than the one Elmo Croker is in today. I think it would be best if you and Miss Lurlene did not compare caskets." What will she come up with next? Damn, she makes me nervous.

"Where will your sister be buried?" I asked. "Where is the cemetery where the old bag, I mean, your dear sister will be laid to rest?"

"Oh," she smiled, never realizing I had made another slip of the lip. The expression on her face made me fear her answer. "The family graveyard in Dallas," she said. "You see, we got this big place up there that's on land which belonged to my pa's grandpa. It's mighty pretty, and we got relatives all over the place. When we get up there, I want to have another little service especially for them out under the big oaks."

"Mercy," I mumbled. "Then we must have the funeral early in the day. About eleven o'clock, so we'll have plenty of time to get to Paulding County." I twisted my neck around to scratch it on my collar, and I must have done something to upset the old gal.

"Is something wrong, Mr. Moody? You seem troubled."

"No, no, I was just thinking about the traffic that time of day. I don't mind it myself, but I hate for your relatives to have to drive so far in their bereaved condition."

"You're so thoughtful, Mr. Moody," she said sweetly as she placed her hand to the side of her mouth and whispered. "I'm really sorry Millie has given you so much trouble today, but she never could handle things the way I can. She has never knowed what is best for the family."

"That right? How about eleven o'clock?"

"Eleven o'clock?"

"For the service."

"Service?"

"The funeral, Mrs. Gooch. The funeral for your dead sister." Merciful days. I realized I was screaming at the old gal. I felt sure if this kept up, either me or her would surely blow an aneurysm. If she ends up on Stump's slab I won't get a dime of this lovely green stuff, and I'll have two pauper loons to bury. But if I end up on Stump's slab, well, so be it.

"You don't have to scream, Mr. Moody. I ain't deaf. I just don't want no funeral at night with the mosquitoes and lightning bugs flying around biting us."

"Lord, help us all," I heard myself begging. "No, no, Mrs. Gooch, eleven o'clock in the morning. You know, around the dinner hour."

"I don't think so, Mr. Moody. Most of the relatives won't get here until tonight, so I don't see how it can be before three o'clock in the afternoon. If we have it that late it will give us more time to play with Erma. You understand, Mr. Moody?"

"Sure, sure, I understand, and I'll need directions to the gravesite."

"Mr. Moody," she said as if she had just experienced a power surge to the brain. "I have this wonderful idea. Let's have the funeral at the church like I wanted it to start with," she whispered and tilted her head towards her sister. "Since Millie is sleeping she can't do nothing about it when it's too late."

"Whatever you say."

"That's what I say," she smiled. "It sure will be a lot nicer there, and let's change it to day after tomorrow. That will give us another day to show off Erma and allow folks more time to cook, so the food they bring will be better and more of it." She leaned back in her chair, sighed, and smacked her lips. "I knowed I'd get what I wanted. Erma thought she'd get the best of me with that little old note of hers, but she didn't. The Lord is surely on my side today. Don't you think so, Mr. Moody?"

"Yes, yes, Mrs. Gooch," I assured her. "I'm sure the Lord is on your side. Three o'clock at the church, Friday afternoon is when the funeral will be." I looked at Mrs. Roper in her completely exhausted state and another tinge of guilt hit me, but thankfully, it went away as fast as it occurred. The saliva oozed from the corner of her mouth and ran down her arm. She snored softly and occasionally made loud smacking noises but seemed to be breathing easier, and for that I was grateful. "Your sister seems a little tired," I said.

"Yes, she never has been strong like me," Sister Gooch boasted. "You see—"

Hell no, I didn't see, and I was not about to listen to another one of her tirades. "Mrs. Gooch," I responded as quickly and loudly as possible, "we need to discuss pallbearers. Do you know who you want for the job? They're the men who tote the casket," I tried to explain as simply as possible.

"Oh, yes, yes, I know who they should be. My son Leonard will be one."

"I thought he was singing?" Merciful days. Are there no other members of the Logan family except her brood?

"Oh, he is, but can't he do both? He enjoys a good funeral so much."

"It's a little unusual. It would be better if he came in with the preachers and sat up front with them, say, on the front row."

"Oh, I see," she drooled. "That would look real nice wouldn't it? And make Leonard as important as the preachers. Don't you think? Okay, let's use Ernest Junior. He's Millie's grandson, Ernest Head Jr., and I'd rather not use him, but I don't want to hurt my sister's feelings. He works at Pearl's Pink Piggy in town and smells like he has just come from a hog killing. Course I do love to eat pig. Maybe we could scrub him real good before the funeral and have him smelling better."

"Next name, please," I begged as I rubbed my legs together and twisted around in my chair to get a little relief to my itching butt.

"He tried to get in the army but couldn't pass some kind of test cause his feet weren't right. Too fat, too flat, and walked like a duck. Don't rightly know what it was. Army said they had never seen feet like his, and they couldn't make boots to fit him. They packed him up and sent him home. We call him E. J., which is short for Ernest Junior."

I had no idea who the crazy woman was talking about and sure as hell wasn't about to ask. I began wondering how much more I could endure before stripping naked and running through the door screaming and jumping headfirst into the kudzu where the old lady spent the night.

"The next name, please, please, Mrs. Gooch," I heard myself begging.

"The next what? Oh, I remember," she smiled. "My sister Pauline's oldest son, Luther, Luther Hightower will be one." She picked up a stapler from my desk and began turning it in her hands as she talked. "He lives in Milledgeville so his wife can be close to the hospital there. Do you know what kind of hospital is in Milledgeville, Mr. Moody?"

"Yes, I am aware of the type of hospital in Milledgeville, but I thought it closed years ago. Next name please."

"You know the woman is plumb goofy. Sometimes she goes for weeks without saying a word to a soul. One time we was down thataway and went by their house just to visit and you know she wouldn't say nothing to none of us. She just sit there batting gnats in front of her face, smoking them little brown cigars, and rubbing the back of a cat sitting on her lap. I thought she was going to set the cat on fire. Have you ever smelled burning cat hair, Mr. Moody?"

"No, Mrs. Gooch, I can't say I have." Lord above, if there is a God, He, She, or It is surely trying me today. "Next name please."

"When she goes to the hospital, she takes the cats with her. She's got at least fifteen or twenty. Her house smells like a slop jar without a lid, and she talks to people that ain't there. They're not only not there, but they sit on the couch beside her."

"Next name, please," I begged. I was getting a little annoyed with her flipping staples on my desk. Apparently it didn't occur to her that staples cost money. Oh, well, what the hell, I thought. When I get her signature in a few minutes, I can buy a whole truckload of staples. So flip away old gal.

"You know, Mr. Moody, didn't none of us have gnats in our faces. Her oldest daughter, Denise, is a lot like her. I guess someday they'll take her to the nuthouse and fry her brain like they done her mama's. Course I can't see where plugging things in her ears and turning on the juice helped her none. She still thinks she's got gnats in her face and keeps talking to folks that ain't there."

"We need more names, Mrs. Gooch."

"Sometimes you see her and she talks so nice. Then ten minutes later she won't say a word to a living soul. It's a shame, Mr. Moody, but I do think they got her brain too hot. Don't you?"

Sounds about as normal as anybody else in this deranged family, I thought. "I'm afraid I can't say, Mrs. Gooch, but I would appreciate another name."

"Luther is in the recapping business. He always tries to be a big shot."

"Who?"

"Luther, Luther Hightower. The one with the crazy wife that I said would be a pallbearer."

I had no idea who the old gal was talking about. "You want a woman to be a pallbearer?" I asked. By this time I didn't give a tinker's damn if she had King Kong toting the box.

"Oh, no, Luther will be the pallbearer, not his wife. I wouldn't want her near the dead because there ain't no telling what she might do. She can scare the blooming daylights out of the living. One day, me and her was sitting on the porch at the old home place and everything was real quiet. All of a sudden she looked at me kind of wild-eyed and said, 'Here he comes. Do you know him?' I asked who? I didn't see nobody. 'Don't you hear him whistling?' Then she jumped out of her chair and ran in the house and locked the door. I could hear her in the house screaming. 'He's come for me. He's come for me.' She wouldn't unlock the door, so I had to crawl in the dog's door. I got hung halfway in and halfway out and here comes Dugan. He thought I was after his food, and he might near broke my thighbone when he pushed me out of the way. When I finally got in the house, she was asleep on the bed with her tongue showing through her teeth, sort of like this."

"Godallmighty damn," I mumbled with my hand over my mouth. "Mrs. Gooch, who are the others?"

"Other what?"

"Pallbearers, men or women to tote the casket." I imagined that in this family one could find a few Amazon females capable of toting anything.

"Oh, yeah, let me see," she said as she gazed at the wall behind my back so long that I turned to see what had her intrigued.

"I guess we'll have to use Hoover," she said.

"Hoover who?"

"He's my dead sister Florence's boy."

"What is his last name?" I begged her to tell me before she went out again, but I was too late.

"He's an artist."

"That's nice, but does he have a last name?"

"I don't think he's much of an artist myself. All his pictures are silly little squares or circles stacked on top each other. They don't look like nothing I've ever seen in the real world. I like haystacks in the moonlight, with lightning bugs and pumpkins. Mildred's husband, Leland, says Hoover paints like a whore. Course, I ain't never seen a whore paint, so I wouldn't know."

"Mrs. Gooch what is his—"

"Most the time he don't use a paintbrush but a chainsaw. You ought to see what he does to a tree and calls it art. Lord, Mr. Moody, he'll whack on a tree stump for days, then rub and polish it for weeks. When he gets through, he'll haul if off to a show and expect somebody to buy it. You know, Mr. Moody, sooner or later some fool comes along and gives him money for it. Course he does have a whole yard full that nobody has bought. He has an eight-foot pink flamingo that I would love to have to sit in front of my doublewide. I tried to get him to lower the price, but he only laughed."

"Mrs. Gooch, we need to—"

"He never does real work. He lives with this woman that's got a kid with something wrong with it. It ain't got no kind of a neck. It has a flat nose, little bitty eyes, and ears that stick out from his head. He's the one whose name is on Erma's list to get some of our insurance money. He has this funny looking little—"

"Mrs. Gooch," I interrupted and spoke as loud as I dared without taking a chance on waking Mrs. Roper. "We need to get everything settled, now! What is his last name?"

"He come here with his mama when she moved in with Hoover. She does hair and nails. I hear she'll do toes. They say she does something else with wax. I don't rightly understand what it is. You know something else? They ain't married, and that means they're living in sin. Lord, Mr. Moody, I wouldn't tell this kind of family stuff to just anybody, but I know you'll not repeat it."

You got that right, sister, and I wish to hell I wasn't hearing it. But, I guess that's the price I pay for big bucks, I consoled myself.

"Mrs. Gooch, what in the name of...excuse me," I said. "Where is Hoover from?" I asked without any idea of his last name.

"Oh, he's from here," she said. "Another thing, Mr. Moody, the kid's thick tongue hangs out its mouth all the time. Kind of like this." She leaned across my desk and demonstrated. "The kid's name is Elton, but they call him Dodo," she explained as if I gave a shit.

"Mrs. Gooch," I pleaded and backed away from her face. "What is his last name?"

"McLoof."

"Hoover McLoof?"

"Oh, no! Murdock, Hoover Murdock, Dodo's name is McLoof," she explained. "You know, Mr. Moody, I'm not sure—"

Suddenly, she stopped talking and looked at her hand. "Oh, Mr. Moody, look what I just done to my finger. Oh, heavens above, and on the same hand the casket lid might near broke."

"Mercy," I said as I leaned over the desk to look at the staple in her thumb. "Did it go all the way through?"

"I don't see it on the other side," she said. "How are we going to get it out? I think I'm going to pass out, Mr. Moody."

Not if I can help it, you ain't. "Now, Mrs. Gooch, just lay your head over on the desk and relax and I'll get help. Don't try to stand up."

The next few minutes proved hectic, trying to keep one asleep and the other from fainting. Jeeeezus what next I found myself asking, knowing I would not get an answer. During times like this, if I were given a choice, I would always commune with the dead and not the damn living.

> *I love to commune with the dead*
> *It doesn't fill me with shivering dread*
> *They don't talk back when I give them a whack*
> *They just lie there smiling instead.*
>
> -Ewell Moody

CHAPTER ELEVEN

Ewell Moody

"Jeeeezus," I mumbled softly when I realized the Gooch gal had driven a staple through her thumb. I opened my desk drawer and shuffled things around in an effort to find a pair of pliers.

"Let me have your hand," I said. "This might hurt a little, but we have got to get the wire out." With considerable effort, I pulled the protruding staple from her tough old hide. It had to hurt like hell.

"Oh, Lord," she moaned, "I do believe I'm going to fall right down there next to that buzzard."

Oh, hell no, you're not, if I can prevent it, I thought. You land on that bird, and I'll never be able to fluff up its feathers. I took my foot and pushed the buzzard under the desk.

"Now, Mrs. Gooch," I said, "lay your head over on my desk and rest a moment. I'll be right back." I opened the door with a jerk and entered the hall screaming for Lucinda Faye.

"What's the matter with you?" she asked as she stepped out of the front office smacking her gum. "I'm not deaf."

"Wet some paper towels. The Gooch woman is about to pass out, and if she falls on the floor it'll take a damn crane to get her up." I hurried to the surgery for a bottle of iodine and returned to my office to find Lucinda Faye standing in the doorway popping gum and holding the dripping towels in her hand.

"What you want me to do with these?" she asked. I glared at her in disbelief.

"Wet her face, you idiot."

"Oh."

"Let me put some medicine on your finger, Mrs. Gooch," I said as

I lifted her hand and rubbed iodine on her bruised thumb. The damn thing had already turned black as a prune.

Lucinda Faye cracked her gum but did not speak as she stood beside Mrs. Gooch dabbing a dripping wet paper towel to the poor old gal's forehead. As the water ran down into her mouth she caught it with her tongue like a frog catching bugs.

"Oh, I'm so embarrassed," Mrs. Gooch whined. "I get excited when I talk and don't watch what I'm doing." She sat back in her chair and sucked her sore thumb.

"That's all right, Mrs. Gooch," I assured her, watching her suck off the iodine. "If you feel up to it, I think we should continue." I flipped through my papers as I spoke. "I believe we were discussing pallbearers."

I waited for Lucinda Faye to throw the towels in the trashcan, close the iodine bottle, and get the hell out of the room before I asked the next question.

"You know, Mr. Moody, that girl has about as much personality as a corn cob."

"I have to agree with you, Mrs. Gooch. She is not very friendly. As a matter of fact, I have known cockroaches with better dispositions. I believe we were discussing Hoover's last name. Is that right? I think you said, Murdock?"

"That's right, Mr. Moody, but I'm not sure we ought to use him."

"I beg your pardon," I said as I rolled over on one side of my buttocks and moved my pen up and down the other side. Not exactly acceptable behavior in mixed company, but I was about to die, and the old gal didn't seem to notice.

"He never wears shoes but them Indian things or sandals with socks. Nothing but Yankees wears sandals with socks. You know what I'm talking about?"

"Mrs. Gooch, I see no reason that should keep him from being a pallbearer."

"What if he wears them to the funeral?"

"Mrs. Gooch," I said, completely exasperated. "I don't think he would, but if he does, nobody is going to be looking at his feet. Please give me another name."

"I guess we can use Tillman Askew, my sister Louise's daughter Marty Lou's husband. He sells insurance to colored folks up in Atlanta. He's from Texas. You know, Mr. Moody, he totes a gun all the time." With the aid of her cane, Mrs. Gooch pulled herself up from the chair. "Is it alright if I stand up a bit?" she asked.

"Sure, but is something wrong?" I asked and stood trying to decide what I would do if she suddenly sprawled out on the floor. If she did, at least my buzzard was safe.

"Nothing is wrong," she said, "I just got a little tingle in my leg." She walked across the office a few times, and then sat back down. "Mr. Moody, I told you awhile back that the buzzard wasn't dead. It's done crawled under your desk. Do you reckon he'll bring it to the funeral?"

"Mrs. Gooch, I assure you the buzzard will not come to the funeral."

"No, no, I mean Tillman's gun. Do you reckon he'll bring it to Erma's funeral?"

Merciful God, I silently begged, please change my name to Uzzah and strike me dead. "Mrs. Gooch, if he wants to bring a machine gun and drive a tank to the funeral, I don't think you should concern yourself with it. The next name please."

"How old do they have to be?"

"To carry a machine gun or drive a tank?"

"Tote the coffin?"

"It doesn't matter. As long as they're strong enough to do their part."

"Then I want my grandson Russell to be one. His name is Russell Vinning. He's the son of my daughter, Bertha Jean, by my first husband. She's Leonard's whole sister. I raised him. His sorry daddy left my daughter when Russell was real little, and she couldn't take care of no baby without a husband so I took him for my own. He's real little for his age, but he's a mighty fine boy, Mr. Moody. You won't believe what they caught his daddy doing."

"That right?" Frankly, old gal, I don't give a cat's fanny, and please, please be merciful and don't tell me.

"They caught him in a railroad car with a couple of...Mr. Moody, I don't believe I can tell you what he done."

Thank you, God. "Another name, please, Mrs. Gooch."

"I swear I ain't never heard tell of nobody doing like that in all my born days. Tillman's got a boy name Dale."

"That's fine. What is Tillman's last name?" I asked then ran my pen down the page in search of Askew. "Here it is," I said. "How old is Dale?" Mrs. Roper smacking her lips and making soft moaning sounds interrupted us.

"We better talk a little quieter," I whispered. "We don't want to waken your sister. She surely needs her rest." Most of all I didn't want to get in the middle of another Logan family brawl.

"I don't see how a mama could name a boy Dale. Don't you think it's girlish, Mr. Moody?"

"How old is Dale?"

"When I hear the name Dale, my mind sees a fat girl riding a mule, playing a git-tar, and singing sad songs like in the picture show."

Merciful hell, I grumbled silently. I don't care how old he is. If I get there and find out he is just five, it's not going to be my problem. I've had midgets tote coffins before. If she doesn't answer me, I can't sweat it. With as few brain cells as she apparently had, I didn't know it was possible for her to experience pain, but she kept squeezing and sucking her injured thumb like it hurt.

"Dale is real strong," she said, and I could tell by the far off look in her eyes she was off on another babbling rampage. "He might have a girlish name, but he's strong. He plays baseball for that school in Atlanta next to the eating place that has the best hot dogs in the world. They come smothered in chili or kraut or just about anything you might want on one. I wish I had one now. When a boy graduates from that school, he can get a job making all kinds of money. Do you know what school I'm talking about, Mr. Moody?"

"Georgia Tech," I said. "I think that about does it, Mrs. Gooch. The time and place of the service and the names of the pallbearers will be in the morning edition of the Atlanta paper and in next week's *Bochimville Runner*," I explained. I knew I should read back the list of pallbearers and get the names of the surviving relatives, but it would take another hour to do that with the deranged old heifer, and I wasn't going to waste anymore of my time, especially on what should have been my afternoon off. I needed to see my friend Jim Beam real bad. If anybody asked why I didn't get the information, I would say I thought the old maid was orphaned. I took a deep breath, cleared my throat, and then laid a few papers in front of her.

"Mrs. Gooch, I need your signature."

She took the pen from my hand, signed where I indicated, looked down at the floor, and with her cane reached under my desk and nudged the buzzard. I was amazed she signed everything I placed in front of her without comments or questions.

"One other thing, Mrs. Gooch," I said, hardly able to speak with my throat as dry and scratchy as if I had eaten a pinecone. I was sure my dilemma was brought on by severe guilt. "The insurance policy won't pay for everything, so I've filled out this form asking you to sign over Miss Edna, Edsi, Miss..."

"Erma."

"Yes, yes, Miss Erma's old Edsel," I said, embarrassed. "You know it's not worth much, but it will help defray the cost of her funeral. Tonight when you come to visit your sister, I would appreciate you bringing the title to the car."

"I understand, Mr. Moody. I ain't got no problem giving you that old piece of junk."

Her words were music to my ears, and I hoped the rest of the family would feel the same. But, somehow I had a feeling she was the only family member with a generous heart.

"You had better wake Mrs. Roper," I said. "She'll need to sign also."

Mrs. Gooch gently shook her sister's shoulders and called her name. "Millie, Millie, you need to wake up."

"Huh?" Mrs. Roper said as she woke with a little clacking of her tongue against her teeth and smacking her lips as if tasting something sweet. She dabbled at her eyes as she asked, "Did I go to sleep?"

"Yes, but that's all right, Mrs. Roper," I assured her. "We knew you were tired, so we let you rest." I laid the papers in front of her and placed a pen in her hand. "We do need your signature on these papers, so if you would be kind enough to sign near the X marks I would be so grateful." I found myself fearing some kind of divine intervention that would make her question what she was signing. I also kept expecting lightning to zap me.

When the pen fell from her hand three times, I should have taken it as a bad omen, but I silently thanked God, or whoever, that there was no shyster lawyer peering over my shoulder, for I literally held the pen in her hand forcing her to sign. The old gal didn't have a clue what she was doing, but then there were no witnesses so my ass was covered. When she finished the signing, she tried to stand but seemed unable to do so. She appeared about to faint. I hurried around the desk, took hold of her arm, and gently guided her back into her chair.

"You sit here, Mrs. Roper, until you feel better," I instructed her. "There is no hurry for you to leave."

I removed the papers from in front of her and placed them in my desk drawer, elated that the dreaded ordeal was over. But, I grumbled silently over the situation at hand. If she fell in the floor, I would have to call the damn fire department to get her up. My, Lord, what a morning.

"I feel alright now," Mrs. Roper assured me as she slowly pulled herself up from the chair.

"Are you sure?" I asked as I held her arm and led her to the door. "You go home and rest, and I'll call you this evening when your sister is ready to receive guests."

"Oh, Mr. Moody," Mrs. Gooch addressed me again before leaving the funeral parlor. "I need to ask you one more thing."

My, my, why am I not surprised? "Yes, Mrs. Gooch?" What now?

"Did Sister have on her leg this morning when you picked her up?"

"Yes, Mrs. Gooch, I assure you she had it on."

"Good, because I want Sister going to her grave with all her parts attached to her body, and Mr. Moody, you make sure you close her eyes good and tight. I don't want her putting the evil eye on nobody when they look at her laying in that nice casket."

"Yes, Mrs. Gooch, I will personally see that your dear sister's eyes are firmly shut."

When the women's car left the parking lot and entered the street, I hurried back to my office, removed several books from the shelves, and uncovered a new bottle of Jim Beam. Hugging my friend close to my bosom, I sat down in my desk chair and began enjoying the pleasure of my friend's company as I spoke out loud.

"Lord, what a day. It's only two o'clock, but it seems like it ought to be midnight." After consuming most of the contents in the bottle, I recapped it and placed it back in its hiding place. I pulled the buzzard out from under the desk, picked it up by the feet, and walked out of my office. I was now ready for a visit with Sister Eunice, Er...whoever to evaluate the situation and see what it would take to get her polished up for Elmo's box. It was definitely going to be a case of putting old booze in a new crock. I smiled, did a little soft-shoe to celebrate the occasion, and composed an appropriate verse that I gaily sang as I entered the surgery.

Old maid with a wooden leg
In a used mahogany box,
Will bring me funds to free my buns,
Or lock me away for life.

-Ewell Moody

84

CHAPTER TWELVE

Mildred Roper

The short nap in Mr. Moody's office seemed to renew my physical strength and mental powers enough to get me home, and with Gladys driving, I needed my mind alert and body awake.

In an effort to shut out Gladys' non-stop talking and help me stay alert, I looked out the car window at familiar places where Erma played an active part before her one-legged condition kept her home and cancer finally claimed her life. Places like Grumby's Movie House on the square across from the courthouse where Erma bought Saturday matinee tickets for her nieces and nephews and their friends. At the corner of Grand Wizard Circle and Stephenson Drive, I smiled at the sight of Yates Pest Control—the place for Erma's Saturday morning and late evening escapades.

It was there Erma chatted with Springer Yates and his boys about the roach and rat population in Bochimville, and the serious consideration of organizing a woman's KKK as well as other topics that made the town cringe. Remembering the bedlam my sister caused over so many of the topics, especially the pink sheets for the KKK, brought a smile to my tired old face.

The Godfrey Chiropractic Clinic, a remodeled butcher shop on Bochim Street, practically served as a second home for Erma, as she needed adjustments every week from the time she lost her leg until the morning Mr. Moody hauled her off in his pickup. When she could no longer go to the clinic, Doyle Godfrey came to the house to tune her crooked spine and help her adjust to a one-legged lifestyle.

The sight of the Eugene Talmadge Memorial Park brought more sweet memories of Erma. I remembered the ice cream suppers, cake walks, square dances, swimming meets, and kite flying contest Erma had an active part in organizing. I cherished the memory of the park dedication when Erma introduced the members of the Talmadge family, Georgia's most prominent 20th century political dynasty. How proud I was of my sister that day.

We drove slowly by the Maude Gower Nursing Home where Erma spent every Thursday following her retirement until her final illness ended her volunteer work. At the home she helped bathe the patients, read them the Bible, Sunday comics, the *Bochimville Runner, Watchtower,* or *Unity Magazine.* She shampooed their hair, made up their faces, trimmed their nails, and massaged their feet.

As my mind flowed with memories of Erma, I longed for a time of silence to deal with my thoughts, but being with Gladys was like being in a chicken coop. The racket never stopped. In my search for silence, I knew it was about as likely for the statue of William Joseph Hardee to come alive and gallop across the lawn of the courthouse as to expect Gladys to hush for thirty seconds. If she wasn't talking non-stop, she was humming a hymn I assumed she planned to use at the funeral, or she was blowing the horn and calling from the window to tell the town folk about Erma's death. Gladys would have made a wonderful Town Crier like in olden days.

"Lord above," she said, hitting the brakes and throwing me against the dash. "Here comes Allie Gibson out of Mason's Hardware store. I ain't seen her in a month of Sundays. Yoo whoooo, Allie," she called, "did you know Erma passed away this morning?"

"No, I sure didn't, but I know this town will certainly miss her," Allie said as she walked up to the car, reached in, and squeezed Gladys' arm. "How are you and Millie holding up?"

"Very well, under the circumstances," Gladys whined. "The funeral will be Friday afternoon at the church. Y'all be sure and come cause it's going to be a big one and mighty nice to boot. Better come early if you want a place to sit. You've got to see Erma's coffin. Not another one like it nowhere, and you wouldn't believe what it cost."

"Gladys, you've got to move," I said. "You're blocking the street." Several horns were blowing.

"Erma won't be ready until tonight, but y'all come on anytime. The family will be eating at Millie's house, and we expect a crowd of relatives. Tell everybody you see cause we want the whole town to know it," Gladys called as she slowly drove off. "Millie," she said, "when I'm talking to somebody out the car window, don't tell me to move on. I don't care if horns are blowing. The fools can wait. I've got something important to say and they don't. But more important, have you forgotten what good goose suck-a-hash Allie makes? We've got to get the word out, or we could end up feeding everybody ourselves."

"What do you mean the funeral will be Friday at the church?" I asked. "We agreed it would be Thursday at the funeral home."

"I'm going to stop at the post office," she said, ignoring my question. "I want to tell Letch Moon about Erma so he can pass the news on to everybody that comes in to buy stamps and money orders."

"There is no need for that, Gladys. Everybody that needs to know about Erma will find out. Besides that, we need to get home. We've got a lot to do before tonight." I knew if I had been speaking into the mouth of a Mason jar, my words would have been about as effective.

"There is nothing we can do until Erma is ready and we can go back to the funeral parlor, so I'm going to tell everybody I see. I want the town to know early."

With her mission at the post office completed, she drove up to the front of the Feed and Seed Store and blew her horn until Broadus Leach came out.

"What the hell is the matter with you, Gladys?" Broadus asked. "Is that old Studebaker on fire? I ain't never heard such a commotion. That racket could cause my seeds not to sprout."

"Just wanted to tell you and Kate that Erma passed away this morning, real early, and the funeral will be at the church Friday at 3:00."

"Know all about it, Gladys. Kate has been on the phone most of the morning planning meals to take to Mildred's house. How you doing, Miss Mildred?" he asked as he bent over and looked in the window. "Know you're probably worn out from all them years of taking care of your sister. You did a mighty fine job from what I saw. Hope you get some rest now. Mighty fine woman, Miss Erma Mae. She did a lot for this town in her day. Every time I look at that big old oak tree in the middle of the square, I think about Erma Mae and chuckle. I know the town—"

Before Broadus completed his sentence, and I had a chance to thank him for the nice things he said about Erma, Gladys stepped on the gas and left him standing on the street still talking to us.

"Gladys," I said, "you drove away before he finished what he was saying. That was not very kind of you. His arm was resting on the side of the car. You could have hurt him."

"I get tired of folks harping and hollering about what Erma did for this town and how proud the family ought to be of her. I'm not proud. I'm embarrassed about the things she did, especially that old tree. I wish lightning would strike it—a storm blow it down or insects eat it. And every time I pass that woods full of naked people, my teeth set on edge to think they wanted to name that place for her. Can you imagine the Logan name associated with a place where trashy folks run around naked as newborn birds? I heard her say time and again the only thing that kept her from joining them was that she never learned to play croquet, and her wooden leg wouldn't look good naked. It's embarrassing enough to have the Logan name on a tree and a bridge. My word."

"There is nothing wrong with Nature's Natural Covey of Complete Comfort," I argued. "Erma believed folks have the right to do as they please, as long as it don't harm nobody else. And Gladys, you can't say that those folks running around naked in the woods, behind a twelve foot wood fence, minding their own business have ever been a bother to you or anybody else."

"That ain't the point, Millie. It's bad enough Erma associated with folks like that, but to get her picture and the Logan name on the front page of the Atlanta paper because of what she did to persuade the county commissioners to allow them to build that place in this county is more than I can forgive her for."

"Did she ever ask for your forgiveness?"

"Lord, I hope none of them come to her funeral," she said, ignoring my question. "Can you imagine a couple of pews filled with white trash wearing nothing but shoes and funeral hats? My word."

I knew it useless to argue, so I let it drop. She drove to the other side of the square, parked the car near a yellow curb, and got out.

"Why are you stopping at the court house?" I asked.

"I'm going to tell Judge Darleen to inform everybody that comes in court today about Erma's passing, and I'm going in WRFA and have Radio Ralph announce it on the air and dedicate a hymn to her memory. I know Maureen in the solicitor's office would want to know it, too."

In front of the courthouse, I watched people coming and going and began wondering why they were there. I laughingly remembered the only trial I ever attended. The memory brought a smile to my face. It was the day Erma and Springer Yates were tried for horse rustling. Erma and Springer refused to have a lawyer and defended themselves. The courthouse was packed. The television and radio people came from Atlanta and the surrounding counties.

The memory of that day brought so much pleasure and peace that I lay my head back on the seat and placed my hands in my lap. I no longer cared where Gladys went or who she talked with. I also knew she would do as she pleased regardless of my feelings, so I soon fell asleep. I slept until we drove up to my house and I felt Gladys shaking me and heard her talking again.

"Millie, Millie," I heard her call as I felt her pushing on my shoulder. "You've got to wake up. We're home. Never seen nobody sleep as much as you do. Folks are going to think you've got dropsy. When I stopped around town, folks were plumb amazed that you could sit in the car snoring and slobbering all over yourself with Sister laying dead over yonder in Moody's funeral parlor. At times you seemed as lifeless as Erma. Come on down here, Leland," I heard her calling to my husband sitting on the front porch, "you need to help Millie out of the car."

Leland got up from his rocking chair, came down the steps, and opened my door. He took my right arm and helped me from the car.

"Lordy," he said, "y'all been gone long enough to come back with Erma's ashes cooled off and ready to set afloat in the well. Moody must have been mighty busy or slow as an addled turtle to take that long to get rid of one old lady's remains. Careful going up these steps, Millie," I heard him say. "You seem a little dizzy-headed."

"I'm alright," I assured him, "but what are you doing home this time of day?"

"Thought you might need a little help taking care of relatives, and besides that, weren't much going on at the mill. Too hot."

"I appreciate you coming home," I told him, "but I'm not too tired to take care of things around here." With him holding my arm, I slowly walked up the steps and sat down in a rocker near where he had been sitting when we drove up. Crowie came over and lay his head in my lap. I made a mental note to ask Leland to bathe him before tonight.

"You ain't tired my foot," Gladys said, following us up the steps. "You fell asleep while we was talking to Mr. Moody and didn't wake up for nothing, not even when I hurt my thumb. You sit over there drooling all over yourself worse than a kid cutting a tooth and might near fell out of your chair. I had to make the arrangements by myself. You snored and grunted something awful. I thought any minute you was going to start breaking wind. You embarrassed the life out of me."

"I couldn't help it," I said, fighting my tears. "I was up every night for the last month, and nobody but Leland offered to help me, and he couldn't stay up at night and work all day. Cassie helped during the days until she got down and couldn't do any more. Two days ago I had to send her home to rest. I need to call and see how she is doing and let her know about Erma. I'm so tired right now, Gladys, that I can hardly put one foot in front of the other."

"My word, Millie, don't start feeling sorry for yourself. I know you took care of Sister in her last days, and the family's mighty grateful to you. I know you're plumb worn out, but now is your chance to get some rest, so go on back yonder in your room and go to bed. While we're talking about Cassie, I need to say one thing. You make it clear that she can come to Erma's funeral, but she will have to sit in the back where she belongs. I know if Erma had her way she would have her on the front seat, but I'm in charge of this funeral, and any colored folks that show up are going to sit in the back where they're supposed to sit."

"Gladys," Leland said, and from the tone of his voice, I knew he was mad. "If my memory serves me right, Erma didn't want no funeral, but I'm sure if you got your foot in the door first there will be one, and we'll discuss it later, but right now I'm concerned about my wife. I want her to go in our cool bedroom and rest, and I'm going to sit right here and take care of anybody that comes, and if the telephone rings, I'll answer it. And while we are talking about Cassie, I've got a few things to say myself, and I suggest you listen. If that good woman is able and wants to come to Erma's funeral, if there is one, she can sit any damn place she desires even in the pulpit with Jordan, and nobody, especially you, had better not say a word against it. If you're afraid to sit in the church with her, then sit your racist butt in the parking lot, and for the sake of this family that would be the best place for you anyhow. Now, have I made myself clear?"

"Alright, I hear you. I told Millie I would stay and take care of things and call everybody while she sleeps. When she gets up, I'll go home and spruce up a bit."

"Gladys, go home now, spruce-up, then while you're there call everybody in the whole state so you won't be using my phone. I ain't a hankering for no great big phone bill next month. Better do your talking before you come back here, and I'll stay with Millie. I know you'll want to be back here tonight when the party gets going and the relatives start swarming out of the hills like a hive of bees on a honey looter."

"I am not going home now," she said and banged her cane on

the porch floor. "Somebody has got to be here to take care of the food that'll start coming in soon as the word gets out."

"Gladys," Leland said, and I could tell he was about fed up, so I sat back, rocked, and enjoyed the scene. "I know some folks think I'm not real bright, but it don't require much sense to take a pot of beans from somebody and stick it on the back of the stove or put a banana pudding in the refrigerator. Folks that come by this morning while y'all was gone, and I was in the garden, put their stuff in the kitchen. Don't looks like to me nobody is needed anyhow, and I can certainly take care of my own wife. Now, shoo, get out of here." He leaned over the porch banister and spit his tobacco juice into the Azaleas.

"Well, okay, but I'll be back shortly. It ain't gonna take me long to spruce up."

"I'm sure it won't, Gladys," Leland said. "I'm sure it won't, but please don't hurry, and I promise not to eat all the food before you return."

I was so glad to see Gladys finally leave, as I needed to talk to Leland about the morning. As I watched her hobble down the steps, mumbling to herself about the food not being properly taken care of with her away, I remembered a quote I read somewhere: *Most folks have no idea how many others are affected by their behavior and example.*

CHAPTER THIRTEEN

Mildred Roper

With Gladys off the porch, it seemed as quiet as midnight in a chicken house with no one cackling or crowing. I needed to enjoy the peace while it lasted, for as soon as she returned the racket and disturbance would start up again.

"Any phone calls?" I asked Leland

"A few. Sophia called. She'll be in tonight as soon as she finishes her exams. She left you a long, complicated message, but for the life of me I don't recall what she said. You know how that child is. Half the time I don't understand a word she utters."

"That's alright. I'll see her tonight."

"How did you come out with Moody? Did you get everything taken care of the way Erma wanted it? Has Moody already burned her up and dumped her ashes in the well like she asked? What's this about a funeral?"

"Didn't get a thing done like Erma wanted," I said. I wasn't sure I could talk about it, but knew I had to try. "I showed Mr. Moody Sister's request, and Gladys had a fit. She beat her cane on the floor and made all kinds of racket. Moody got Brother Jordan to come in and tell us how wrong it is to burn a body. He made me feel like the worst sinner on earth to even consider having it done. I was so tired and upset I went to sleep in Mr. Moody's office, and him and Gladys planned the whole thing. She's going to have a big funeral and bury Erma in the family graveyard in Dallas."

"I'll be damned. I knowed I should have stayed home and gone with you this morning. How much of Erma's policy money did Moody get?"

"Probably all of it."

"Did you ever look to see what it was worth?"

"No. It stayed all them years in her little box, and it never crossed my mind to look at it. She would remind me every now and then that it was there and tell me what she wanted done with it when she passed away. I feel so bad about letting her down."

"Millie, this is the first time in your life you've had to fight Gladys without Erma's help," Leland said, trying to console me. He took off his straw hat and used it to kill a bumblebee buzzing around our heads. "I shouldn't have called her this morning to be with you after Erma died and certainly not to go with you to the funeral home. I just didn't want you going by yourself in your worn out condition." He scraped the bee from the brim of his hat and threw it over the banister, then placed the hat on his lap. "I can see Gladys now, crying and carrying on like she loved Erma more than anything in the world, and she ain't even seen the woman in near on to ten years. Guess I had about forgotten that Gladys would do anything for a chance to plan or attend a big funeral. Lord, she'd ride twenty miles barebacked on a humpback mule just to go to one, even if she didn't know the corpse. I bet Erma is so damn mad right now that wherever she is, she's causing one hell of a ruckus."

"I wish I was more like Erma and could have done for her what she did for Mama and Poppa when they passed."

"Millie, you can't be somebody you ain't. Erma never expected you to do much in your worn out condition. Lord, you took care of her night and day for over ten years. There's a limit to what a body can do. When your parents passed, things got done Erma's way cause she knew how to handle Gladys."

"I remember Poppa saying lots of times that when he died he didn't want to be fitted in a suit of clothes he wouldn't wear when he was living, much less dead. He didn't want nobody painting his face like an old Indian getting ready for war or taking out his teeth and stuffing his jaws with cotton. He didn't want nobody scrubbing his hands until all the dirt he had accumulated in his lifetime of honest hard work was washed away. He didn't want no pennies on his eyes till they stayed shut cause he sure as hell wanted to see where he was going." It did me good to think about Mama and Poppa, but it didn't help when I realized that today was a repeat performance for Gladys. The only difference, back then Erma was alive and kept Gladys in line.

"I remember your poppa saying he didn't want to be parked in no damn church or funeral parlor so folks could come from everywhere just to see how he was dressed and take bets on how much the box he was laying in cost his family," Leland added.

"I heard him say more than once that he didn't want no jackleg preacher standing over him, spitting in the flowers and telling everybody what a good soul he was cause the whole county knew he'd been mean as hell and proud of it." I lay my head back in the chair and began to rock slowly. The sound of our voices and Crowie pressing his face on my hand kept me awake.

"I remember when you and Erma Mae begged Gladys, Florence, Pauline, and what's the other sister's name?"

"Louise."

"Yea, Louise. You and Erma Mae begged the four of them to give the old man the kind of funeral he wanted, but they would have no part of that. They crawled on their high horses and yelled it would disgrace the family and make people think them poor if they buried their poppa in a cheap coffin wearing an old suit. Your poor mama sided with you and Erma Mae, but the old gal had never had a word in anything, so she didn't really count."

"Lord, I'll never forget that morning. When Erma Mae felt she was losing the battle with the sisters, she picked up Poppa's shotgun and told me we were paying Maslow a visit. I never questioned what she was about to do, for all my life I would have followed her into hell had she led the way."

"What a woman," Leland laughed. "I wish I'd been with you. The whole town talked about that for years, and Maslow told it till the day he died."

"I watched as she walked up to Maslow and stuck the gun in his belly and warned him to carry out Poppa's funeral plans the way she was about to outline them, or she'd blow his remains all over Bochimville. She also told him he was not to listen to a damn word any of her sisters said. Maslow gently took the gun out of her hands, put his arm around her, and kissed her on top the head.

"'Erma Mae,' he said, 'I would never go against the wishes of a spunky little gal like you. You tell me what you want, and I'll see that it's done. You've always been one of my favorite women, and you probably would blow my insides to kingdom come if I didn't follow your orders.'"

"But it didn't hold a candle to the caper Erma pulled when your mama passed on," Leland said and chuckled. "Some folks are still standing around with their mouths hanging open about that one."

I also smiled at the memory. "If only I had a little of Erma's spunk, I wouldn't be sitting here crying over what happened this morning because it wouldn't have happened. But you know, Leland, today at the funeral parlor when I was trying to get a word in edgeways with Brother Jordan and Gladys, I got the warmest feeling that Erma was right there beside me trying to tell me something."

"I don't know much about life on the other side, but I know this much. If Erma can find a way to help you, she won't leave you alone to fight this battle with Gladys. Erma was a mighty smart woman. She read more damn books than anybody ever did. She could always figure out a way to beat her sisters, politicians, and preachers at their own games and leave them standing there wondering what happened. Go on in yonder and get some rest. You're going to need it when the kin folk start coming in and Gladys gets to acting up like you know she will. I got a mighty strong hunch we ain't heard the last from Erma Mae, and before this thing is over, you're going to be at peace with Erma's passing. Go on to bed, things will work out."

I did as he suggested and went to bed, for I learned a long time ago that *sleep is the only cure for a tired body and a weary mind.*

CHAPTER FOURTEEN

Mildred Roper

I awoke from my two-hour nap in a quiet and peaceful house with my physical and mental strength somewhat renewed. I attempted to enjoy the moment, for it was only the peace before the storm. A storm named Gladys that would bring more destruction and cause more strife to this family than a tornado could ever do to an Alabama trailer park.

I watched from the kitchen window as Gladys ambled to the house from the garden where she had been talking to Leland. She wore a yellow sleeveless cotton dress with pockets on each side and an embroidered duck across the front. Her big, out-of-style reading glasses hung around her neck on a worn leather bootstrap. I smiled when I thought of what Gladys had done to spruce herself up, as she called it. She smeared Vaseline on her lips, sprinkled her armpits with toilet water, and powdered her face until she looked like a ghost.

Gladys never believed in bathing. When we were children, Mama would often threaten to whip her if she didn't take a bath at least once a week, and now in adulthood she only bathes when forced to do so.

She was wearing a green plastic necklace with matching earrings, as she seldom went out in public without earrings. I sometimes thought she felt just having them on made her smell good, look nice, and have a good disposition. If that were true, I wish she had worn them to the funeral home this morning. As she walked up to the back door, I went in the laundry room.

"My word," I heard her say, loud enough to be talking to a room filled with people. "This place is too quiet for me. I better check on

Millie. The way she looked when I left here, I wouldn't be surprised if she's not as dead as Erma."

"You don't need to check on me," I said. "I'm right here, so don't start planning another funeral."

"I came by earlier, and Leland wouldn't let me in the house," she whined. "He told me you was still sleeping, and he didn't want me making no noise. I don't know what he thought I would do that would wake you up. He acted like I was going to yodel or dance in the middle of the kitchen table with bells on my heels. He wouldn't even let me in the kitchen to see if the food had been put up like it ought to have been. Your husband can be mighty rude sometimes, especially when he's bathing that big old goat like he was doing. He said he was getting it ready for company. Best way he could get it ready for company would be to put it on the grill."

"Gladys, will you please see who's at the back door?" I asked when I heard a tapping on the screen.

"Oh, Mollie Bea, do come in," Gladys said. "Let me take some of that stuff from you. My goodness that looks good. Nothing like your potato salad and baked beans with bacon on top. The grease makes them so juicy. Have a seat at the table, and let me put some of these things up that people brought while I was home sprucing up a little. Food is coming in mighty slow."

"How are you doing, Gladys?" Mollie Bea asked.

"Well as can be expected under the circumstances. You know how these sad times get you down."

When Gladys opened the door to invite in Mollie Bea, I went back to the laundry room and kept folding clothes. I was behind with my work since Erma had needed me almost full time the past few weeks. I left the door open because it was hot in the tiny room, and I could see the women and hear them talking. They had no idea I was there.

"So Erma Mae passed early this morning," Mollie Bea said as she took a seat at the kitchen table. She folded her hands neatly in her lap and looked around the room. She then lifted her nose as if sniffing the air. "You know," she said, "there's nothing like the smell of death. No doubt it has been in this house recently. It leaves sort of a worn out odor. Did she die easy or did she struggle? Knowing Erma Mae, I bet old lady Death pulled her out screaming and grabbing at the bedpost."

"According to Millie, it went real easy," Gladys said as she smacked her lips. "It seems she wanted some tater pie for supper, and of course Millie cooked her one. She loved tater pie better than anything put before her. Would you like a glass of ice tea?"

"I sure would."

"Anyway, as I was saying, she ate a piece of pie and went off to sleep. Early in the morning, she woke up complaining about a pain in her stomach. Millie pulled the covers back just as she broke wind. She died that quick," Gladys said, snapping her fingers in the air.

"My word, you mean she passed a big enough one to stop her heart?"

"Sounds that way. Don't it? Just like Elvis."

"That's a mighty good way to go. Hope I'll be that lucky. When people pass a lot of gas just as they die, do you reckon their soul comes out at the same time and place? Could that be the reason death leaves behind an odor? I've always wondered about that. Have you?"

"Can't say I have."

"Have you been to see Mr. Moody?"

"Me and Millie spent about three hours at the funeral home this morning, and you won't believe what went on there. You know how Millie has to have her way. Well, she put me through rough waters, and Erma ain't been dead a whole day. You'll never believe what I'm about to tell you, but it's the Lord's unflyblown truth. The tea is sweet, and here is lemon and mint leaves."

"I'll have the mint. Don't care for lemon. I like tea sweet. Sour stuff makes my bad valve quack a little faster."

"Does the quacking bother you much?"

"No, but it keeps George awake at night. He says it sounds like a big duck in my chest."

Gladys fixed her glass of tea and added a sprig of mint and a slice of lemon then stirred it with the forefinger of her left hand, a habit I hated.

"Would you like a wedge of this egg custard?" I heard her ask Mollie Bea as she held up the pan and read the name on the tape attached to the bottom of the pan.

"No, thank you. I've been fasting to cleanse my body after a bad case of shingles that round plumb around both my ankles. That sickness fills the body with poison, and I have to watch what I eat."

"As I was saying," Gladys continued, "you know Erma and Millie was always thick as two yolks in the same egg, and Erma would rather upset this family than take a bath when she was gamy even though she bathed might near every day. Can you believe that even after she died her and Millie tried to cause a ruckus in this family? Would you believe Erma wrote out her death wishes telling Mr. Moody to burn her up and throw whatever was left in the well at the old home place?"

"My word, I just quiver to think how the well would smell in about a week."

"It would ruin the water for months to come, and can you imagine drinking water from a well that's got your sister's parts floating around in it?"

"It puts my teeth on edge to think about it."

"It would be as bad as the time the cat drown in the well and we had cat hairs in the dipper for months. Mollie Bea, you ought to taste this custard," Gladys said. I could tell her mouth was full as she talked. "It taste worse than oatmeal without salt."

"Who brought it?"

"Elsie Thomas."

"She probably used duck eggs."

"I bet you're right. All they have on that old red dirt farm is ducks and guineas." I watched Gladys take the lid off a small black pot, dip out a spoonful of Brunswick stew, and put it in her mouth. "Hmmmmmm, this is plumb good," she said. "Some folks are such good cooks, and then there are some who can't separate an egg without getting yoke in the white. Gurdy will love this. I wish you would taste it. Mavis brought it while I was gone. It taste like the hog was shot this morning." Gladys opened a Mason jar of pickled okra and took out a pod with her fingers. I knew she would comment on its taste. "My goodness gracious," she scoffed, "Mollie Bea, you ought to taste these pickles. They're limp as a dishrag and taste about the same. Flora brought them."

"I ain't never knowed a one of them old maid Gray women that could cook a thing fit to eat."

"They never check the almanac for the right time to put things up, and I bet my bottom teeth she pickled this okra when the sign was in the bowels."

"Or the groin. That always makes stuff come out tough and limp."

"I'll leave them here for somebody else, but I'm going to take these other things home before the house fills up and folks start eating like it was free. Here, let me fill your tea glass."

"Gladys," I said as I stepped into the kitchen from the laundry room. "If you take food home, please bring the dishes back tomorrow and don't lose any of the labels. Sophia and Joan will send thank you notes to the people who brought the food. Hello Mollie Bea, how are you?" They seemed surprised that I was so close.

"I thought you was laying down again," Gladys said. "Me and Mollie Bea are discussing the funeral and trying to straighten the kitchen up a bit."

"Try not to overdo it, and if you have time could you please answer the door?" As I spoke, I walked into the dining room. "I would appreciate it if you would listen out for folks when they come, and don't make them stand outside banging on the door."

Gladys returned from the front of the house carrying a pan of chicken and dumplings and a pound cake.

"That was Janet Stansell at the front door," she said. "I don't know why she didn't come to the back like everybody else does. Guess she wanted to make me walk a little further. Now Mollie Bea, I know this cake is right out of the oven, for it is still warm. But for the life of me, I can't figure out why she didn't bring one of her carrot cakes. Nobody in this town has ever died that the family didn't get one. I know her ankles are swollen big as elephant toes, but it wouldn't have taken her much longer to grate a few carrots and stack four layers together with a little icing than it did for her to stand up and bake this pound cake. She wanted to come in, but when I looked through her plastic cake cover and saw it weren't no carrot cake, I told her nicely that we weren't ready for visitors and she'd have to come back later. I started to say, if you want to come in, come back with a carrot cake."

"I don't blame you. She always has been the inconsiderate type. You know she's got a bad heart, and they might have to replace it. Every time you see her, she's real winded and acts like she's going to smother to death."

"Gladys," I said, "I don't like you treating her like that. No matter who comes to this house they are invited in, and I don't care if they bring the fatted calf, a bucket of purple cabbage, or absolutely nothing. Don't you turn nobody away from my door, and I mean what I'm saying. I'll call her and apologize for your meanness."

I knew Gladys turned a deaf ear to what I said as I watched her place a bowl of stew, half pone of cornbread, a carton of buttermilk, and a saucer of sliced onions and fresh tomatoes on the kitchen table. She then turned to Mollie Bea and started talking again.

"I wish you would join me for a little bite, Mollie Bea, but I understand you wanting to clean out your body after them shingles. Can you at least eat a slice of this warm pound cake? As I was saying, before we was interrupted with Millie's orders, she really showed herself at the funeral home this morning."

Over the years when Erma wanted something really bad, she

would say, *My Kingdom for a horse, My Kingdom for a horse.* I suppose it was a saying of somebody famous, but I never knew who said it. Right now, if I had a kingdom I would give it for a moment of silence. I knew the next few days were going to be rough, but the worst part would be Gladys' non-stop talking.

"Millie harped and hollered about having Erma burned up in the most unchristian way I ever heard of," Gladys explained to her guest. "That is, until Mr. Moody got Brother Jordan to come and show her the error of her ways. When Brother Jordan finished talking to us and left the funeral home, me and Millie went to Mr. Moody's office to plan the funeral. The second she sat down, she dropped off to sleep like she had swallowed a dose of paregoric. If that ain't proof the Lord is on my side I don't know what is. She just sit there snoring and slobbering all over herself. I kept expecting her to start passing gas, but that was alright, cause while she slept and slobbered me and Mr. Moody planned the best funeral you'll ever come to. Would you like another piece of cake?"

"No, but I would like a saucer of chicken and dumplings. They smell so good."

"Gladys," I called from the dining room, "please answer the phone."

"Get all the chicken you want," she said to Mollie Bea. "Let me see who this is. It seems I have to do everything."

"Hello—no this is Mrs. Gooch. I see. I'll tell her. I'm sure somebody will be right down."

"Who was it?" I asked.

"Mr. Moody is ready to set Erma's mouth and needs her teeth."

"You'll find them in a glass beside her bed. Put them in a plastic bag, and I'll get Leland to take them down there."

"Millie, my Lord above," she said as she hit the side of the table with a dishtowel. "You know good and well I am not going in that room and touch anything that belonged to Erma's body. Lord, I'd be plumb terrified. Let Leland do it."

"What do you think could possibly bother you in that room, Gladys? But never mind. I'll do it myself."

I wrapped the teeth in aluminum foil for Leland to take to the funeral parlor. I then returned to the laundry room and began filling the washer.

"Why do you reckon Erma wrote such an outlandish request about what she wanted done when she died?" I heard Mollie Bea ask Gladys. "You think she might have been a little bit touched in the head? Looks like after she was in that fire with Springer Yates, she wouldn't want no more flames near her body whether she was dead or alive. I don't understand her."

"I don't know what made Erma write such foolishness. She always tried to be so uppity and do things different from everybody else. Look what she did when Mama and Poppa died. Lord, I was determined that we weren't going through something like that again, but that's not important right now. As I was about to say, I'm here to tell you them highfalutin Presbyterians that haul their dead to Atlanta ain't never seen a better funeral than what I got planned for Erma, and I'll tell you another thing, Lurlene Croker will have to stop telling everybody that the biggest funeral this town ever saw was when she buried Elmo. Mr. Moody told me, himself, that the box Elmo is laying in at this minute don't even compare with the one we got for Erma. There's somebody at the door. Get you some more dumplings if you want them, and let me see who it is. I hope they're bringing something good and different."

"I've had enough dumplings," Mollie Bea answered Gladys, "but I will have a cup of stew."

Gladys made a quick trip to the front door and returned to the kitchen with several containers of food. She placed them on the cabinet and made two more trips to the front of the house for more dishes she had left on a table in the hallway.

"That was some of the women from the church bringing more food," she said. "You know, Mollie Bea, I been thinking. If we had burned Erma's body like her and Millie wanted us to, and not had a funeral, folks might not have brought food. Folks didn't bring much of nothing when Mama passed. They were so stunned over what Erma did they didn't know what to do, but I'll tell you one thing, before this funeral is over, I plan to have enough food to last till frost."

"And you be sure to take home all you can and put it in your freezer cause you're entitled to it the same as anybody else. After all, it's your sister that passed away the same as Mildred's."

"Look at this stuff, Mollie Bea," Gladys said as she removed covers and lids from the dishes. "Can you imagine how many chickens lost their gizzards to fill this platter? Lord, there ain't nothing Gurdy loves better than fried chicken gizzards with a little chow-chow on the side."

"Gladys," I said as I came into the kitchen from the dining room. "I need help cleaning Erma's room. Please take the sheets off her bed and bring them to the laundry room along with her dirty clothes and towels. We need to put some of her books in boxes and straighten up her room. Somebody will need to sleep in there tonight."

"Millie, for goodness sakes, I told you earlier that I am not going in that room when Sister ain't been dead a whole day. I don't know what's in there, and I don't intend to find out. Wait and let Joan help you clean it up. You know Sophia will want the books. Let her box them up, and I'll take care of the kitchen. Sides that, who in tarnation is going to sleep in there tonight when Erma was still breathing and breaking wind in that bed no more than a few hours ago? My word, Millie, course on the other hand, Sophia is crazy enough to sleep in there. If she had been here, she probably would have gotten in the bed with Erma after she died. Let her clean it up."

"This homemade macaroni and cheese is mighty creamy, and the fried chicken is crisp like it ought to be," Mollie Bea said. "I think I'll eat a pulley bone."

"Help yourself. This pot of corn beef and cabbage smells mighty good, too. I think I'll have a bite of it. Millie don't you want a little something to eat?"

"No, but I would appreciate y'all leaving something for supper tonight. I know we'll have a crowd to feed."

Gladys reminded me of a rat in a cute movie I watched with Erma a few months back. The movie was *Charlotte's Web*. The rat was always eating and never thought about nobody but himself. At the time we watched it, Erma said the rat should have been named Gladys.

"I don't believe nobody ever died that their kitchen didn't get filled with deviled eggs," Mollie Bea said. "I bet there are four dozen on this tray, and that's one funeral dish I can do without."

"I love deviled eggs," Gladys said, with her mouth so full she could hardly speak. "Put three or four on my plate. As I was saying before the women came, we got everything taken care of with Mr. Moody. Brother Jordan will be here this afternoon, and I'm going to tell him what I want him and Flynn to do."

"Who's Flynn?" Mollie Bea asked between bites of pecan pie and rice pudding. I would love to hear her definition of fasting.

"He's Louise's boy. I know you remember him."

"Is he the tall one with red hair and front teeth that stick out?"

"They don't stick out like they did when he was a kid. He lost one in a jail fight, and the other one got pushed back. I know Flynn don't have a real good reputation for being in jail, but it was good for him to be there. He got saved just before he went in, and in jail he practiced his preaching when he could. Now that he's out, I'm going to let him preach Erma's funeral."

Leland came in from the garden with a bucket filled with butter beans and a basket of tomatoes and eggs and placed them on the countertop.

"Gladys," he said, "how about y'all shelling these beans for supper tonight? Can't tell what kind a crowd might show up, and we want to be able to feed them. Here's a basket of tomatoes you'll need to wash and slice. Might even stew a few with peppers and onions, and you need to boil these guinea eggs and devil them."

"Put the stuff on the porch, Leland," Gladys told him. "If we have time, we'll get to it. We've got a lot to do before Brother Jordan gets here."

"I see how busy you are, and I sure hate to pull you away from the picnic you and Mollie Bea are having at my table, but Millie could use help in getting the house in order before the kin folks start dropping in."

"Soon as we get the funeral plans together, I'll help her in the house, but I've got to have everything ready by the time Brother Jordan gets here this afternoon. Planning a good funeral is a lot more important than getting this house clean. After all, it's just going to get messed up again when everybody shows up and starts eating."

"Leland," I called from the dining room where I was dusting the furniture. "What time do you have? Erma's clock seems to have stopped."

"Again? I set it this morning while y'all was gone to the funeral home and wound it tight as a sow's tail. That clock ain't stopped since the day Erma brought it home from Sears Roebuck." In his right hand he took his round silver watch out of his overall pocket and looked at it. "It's about half passed five," he said, then snapped it shut and returned it to his pocket.

"Well, it's stopped now," I told him.

"Then I'd be mighty concerned," Mollie Bea added. "When a clock won't run right after somebody's passing, it's a sure sign the soul of the dead is still roving round the house. Might mean Erma's upset about something. I told you when I came in I could smell death in here."

"Now, Mollie Bea, don't you start that," Gladys said as she picked up a potholder and hit the side of the table. "I don't believe in no such doings."

"It don't make no difference whether you believe it or not, Gladys.

It's the truth. When I was little my grandpa passed away mad with his brother for cheating him out of a right smart of money when they sold the sawmill. Every clock in our house stayed stopped until my great uncle paid Grandma her share, and that was might near six months later. Is there any chance Erma is mad or upset about something?"

"Erma was always mad or upset about something, and I don't see that it makes no difference now. Furthermore, we can live without that old clock. I always thought it ticked too loud and struck more times than it was supposed to."

Leland looked at me and winked but didn't say anything. He went outside to the garden, and I went back to the laundry room to load the dryer and put another load in the washer.

"Is Leonard and Estelle coming for the funeral?" Mollie Bea asked Gladys. "I think I'll taste that squash casserole and one of them fresh rolls. I can smell the yeast. Who brought this little churn of fermented peaches? I love to drink the juice."

"Me, too. Pour us both a cup full. What was your question? Oh, never mind, I remember. Course they'll be here. Do you have any suggestions as to what they ought to sing? Since you've got a daughter that sings a lot. This blackberry cobbler is mighty good. Try a little," she said as she spooned some onto Mollie Bea's plate. "I think "Beautiful Isle of Somewhere" is mighty fine. Course you should never have a funeral without "Precious Memories" and "Amazing Grace" as far as I'm concerned, because there ain't nothing that can lift the soul right up to heaven's gate like them two songs can unless it's "In the Sweet Bye and Bye." Pour me a little more of that peach juice. It sure hits the spot."

"It sure does. "I'll Fly Away" is a good one. Talking about lifting the soul right up to heaven's gate, a cup of this peach juice don't do a bad job of lifting. It makes me feel just like the Holy Spirit flowing through my body or sort of like that stuff they shoot you full of when a snake bites you. Have you tasted this roast?" Mollie Bea asked. "It's tough as a shoe."

"Sit it on the back of the stove. It'll get eat tonight when the teenagers start coming in." The conversation was interrupted with a loud burp from Gladys. "Excuse this pig," she said and continued talking. "I guess I'll let Brother Jordan pick the Bible reading unless you got any suggestions. I like them verses about the Lord having mansions waiting in the sky, but I don't find nothing comforting about laying down in a pasture while the Lord or nobody else pours oil on my head. Now, if He poured this peach juice that might be another thing. Merciful days, I don't know what's making me burp so."

Lord, give me the strength I need to survive the next few days, I found myself praying. I flipped out a bed sheet, draped it across the ironing board, and began ironing in an effort to shut out the criticizing, belching, and whining coming from the kitchen. It didn't help.

"I wish preachers would come up with something new to read and say ever once in a while," Mollie Bea said. "Funerals have a tendency to get real dull. I know what you mean about the burps, I've got a few myself. This ham is mighty good. Here, I'll put a slice on your plate."

"The preacher read a poem at my sister Pauline's funeral, and I'm going to have Flynn read it for Erma," Gladys announced. "I hear Queenie barking. It must be folks with more food. Goodness gracious I'm stuffed."

"It's Brother Jordan," I said as I stepped out of the laundry room and walked over to the kitchen window.

"Oh, my Lord, Mollie Bea, will you straighten up in here while I talk to him?" Gladys asked, then belched. At the sink she took out her teeth and rinsed them, washed her face with a damp paper towel, drank a handful of water, and brushed the crumbs from the front of her dress.

"You go on, Gladys," Mollie Bea said, "I'll take care of everything in here. When I finish I'll slip out the back door. Me and George will see you tonight at the funeral parlor."

"Y'all be there early. I can't wait for you to see Erma's casket. If it had headlights and a horn it would be prettier than anything Henry Ford ever thought about making."

I shook my head in disbelief as I watched Gladys pick up her cane, hook it over her arm, and hurriedly make her way to the living room, humming as she went.

Lord, pour out patience over me and make firm my steps for the enemy is surely in my camp.

CHAPTER FIFTEEN

Mildred Roper

As fast as Gladys could walk without the aid of her cane, she hurried to the living room loudly singing "Precious Memories" in a voice that had never held a tune. When she came in sight of Brother Jordan, she placed her cane on the floor and hobbled like a cripple.

"Ohoooo, Brother Jordan," she said, with a tremble in her voice, "I'm so glad to see you again."

Brother Jordan cupped Gladys' right hand in both of his as he spoke. "Sister Gladys," he said, "it is my prayer that the Lord will comfort you real good this day in your time of need."

"Thank you Brother Jordan," she whined. "I was sitting at the kitchen table discussing the Bible with Mollie Bea McWhorter and trying to plan Sister's funeral when I heard you come up." She placed her hand over her mouth and burped. "I am so glad you're here."

Leland, standing near the front door, looked at me and winked. We walked into the living room and took a seat across from Gladys and Brother Jordan.

"Well, now, I'm here to take the burden of planning the funeral off your weary shoulders," Jordan said, speaking to Gladys. "You just tell me what you want, and I your humble servant will attempt to carry it out."

"I do appreciate that," she said. "Could I get you a cup of coffee or a glass of ice tea?"

"Ice tea would be mighty fine," he said. "It's a real scorcher out there today, and I can't seem to get enough to drink."

He sat in the high back rocker near the couch with his legs crossed and his hands neatly folded in his lap. I couldn't help noticing him leaning towards the left in order to see himself in the large, gold-framed mirror on the wall.

"Millie," Gladys said to me, "would you mind getting the tea and me a cup of coffee? I need to start talking to Brother Jordan, and you know how slow I am with my cane."

"Yes, she would mind very much," Leland said. "This woman is about past going, and she needs all the rest she can get. You offered the drinks, Gladys, you get them."

"Well, don't y'all do no talking till I get back because I want a say in all the planning."

"Way I see it, Gladys, nobody but you has had a say in what's going on," Leland said, "but we'll sit here with our mouths zipped till you get back. You and Brother Jordan need to know that we don't like what's been done so far, and in time we're gonna need some answers."

Brother Jordan cleared his throat and looked down at his lap but did not respond to what Leland said. The three of us sat in an awkward silence until Gladys quickly returned from the kitchen carrying a tray with a glass of tea for Brother Jordan and a cup of coffee for herself.

"Would you like mint and lemon for your tea?" She asked.

"That would be fine."

Brother Jordan took a sip from his tea glass then sat it on the coffee table. "It's getting late in the day, Sister Gladys," he said. "We better start planning the service." He took a pad with a leather cover and a gold pen from his pocket and held them in his hands ready to write. "Other than my sermon, what would you like me to include in your dear sister's funeral?"

"My son Leonard and his wife Estelle are coming from Blueridge and are going to sing. Estelle will play the piano."

"Fine, Fine."

"Leonard is a preacher, too."

"Is that so? Does he have a church?"

"No, he'd rather serve the Lord with his singing," she said. Holding the cup with both hands like a baby with a training cup, she sipped her coffee. The spoon in the cup pressed against the middle of her nose as she drank.

"Does he plan to say a few words at the funeral?" Brother Jordan asked, still admiring himself in the mirror. I placed my hand on Leland's arm, and then nodded my head in Brother Jordan's direction as an indication for Leland to watch the preacher admire himself.

We giggled.

"No, but my nephew, Flynn Shockley, does," Gladys said. "He's the son of my sister Louise who has done passed." She moved to the edge of the sofa and leaned in Brother Jordan's direction as she talked. "He has a chicken farm in Covington. He's the one my grandson Russell drives a chicken truck for."

"Is he ordained?"

"Oh, no! Russell ain't never had no desire to preach."

"Gladys," I said, "he asked if Flynn is ordained."

"Oh, yes! They done that to him at the Circle of Light Primitive Baptist Church just outside Covington the night he heard the call."

"Does he have a church?"

"No, he don't have a church," Leland said, "and when you hear him talk, much less preach, you'll know why."

"You see, Brother Jordan," Gladys explained, "Flynn only found the Lord a short time back, and he ain't had time to get all this preaching stuff quite right just yet, but he is working at it, and working hard."

"Is that a fact?" Brother Jordan asked. "Then why don't we have your nephew pray a short prayer at the graveside? I think that will be plenty for a man new in the Lord's work."

"That boy can pray longer than any preacher ever thought about praying, and he don't say nothing worth hearing," Leland said. "You better keep him with his eyes open so you can tell him to sit down and shut up."

"I don't think he needs a part at all," I said.

"Well, he's going to. He's so full of the Lord right now that it would be a sin for him not to preach his aunt's funeral. I've got this poem the preacher read at my other sister's funeral, and I want him to read it for Erma," Gladys said as she reached in her pocket and brought out a wrinkled piece of paper and handed it to Brother Jordan. He held it like something nasty. He ignored a dried flower that fell out when he unfolded the paper and, after quickly skimming what was written on it, handed it back to Gladys. I got really mad when I realized Gladys had rummaged around in my room while I slept and had taken the poem out of my Bible without my permission.

"You see, Brother Jordan, Flynn has been real sinful most of his life, and—"

"You give the poem to your nephew," Brother Jordan interrupted. "After he reads it, we'll let him pray a short prayer."

"Flynn has been married three times and has six kids," Leland said. "He never pays the wives a cent, and I know his kids go hungry.

I don't give a cat's fanny if he is a relative, I don't want that lowlife hypocrite preaching Erma's funeral, especially since she didn't want a funeral to begin with."

"How many songs do you plan for your son and his wife to sing?" Brother Jordan asked, ignoring Leland's remark about Flynn.

"I know he's done bad things like stealing, bootlegging, and a lot of stuff I wouldn't want to bring up just now," Gladys whined, "but the Lord is forgiving, so shouldn't we be too? He even got caught learning some of his roosters how to—"

"Have you picked the songs, Sister Gladys?" Brother Jordan interrupted.

"He was out in the chicken house one night getting ready to go back to jail," she said before pausing to burp. "He kept hearing somebody call his name. At first he thought he had some sick chicken—"

"I see, now, Sister Gladys—"

"When he didn't find no ailing chickens, he decided he must have been chewing tobacco that had gone bad and was making him hear things. You know Brother Jordan, tobacco can make you do strange things if it's gone—"

"Sister Gladys, how many songs do you want sung? "There's Power in the Blood" is a good one."

"But it was the Lord, Brother Jordan, it was the Lord."

Jordan picked up his pen and started to write, then stopped. "I'm afraid I'm not familiar with that hymn, Sister Gladys."

"The Lord was right there in the chicken house, Brother Jordan, and I'm here to tell you there weren't no sick chickens or no bad tobacco. The Lord was right there amongst that chicken poop—"

"Do what?"

"It was the Lord, Brother Jordan, talking to Flynn."

"I think we should use "In the Sweet Bye and Bye." It's everybody's favorite."

"He reached right out from under that big rooster's wing and touched Flynn on the shoulder," she said, waving her arms in the air like a chicken flying.

As I had been ignored at the funeral home, I didn't say a word. I felt Brother Jordan deserved what he was getting from Gladys. After all, he encouraged her to buy the expensive casket and didn't listen to a word I tried to say. I looked at Leland. He shook his head and smiled. I knew he felt like they deserved each other.

"Would "Amazing Grace" be all right with you?" Brother Jordan asked as he leaned back in his chair to keep from getting hit by her hand.

"Flynn fell right down on that dirt floor among all that chicken sh...ugh mess and started praying, and he's been preaching and praying ever since, anywhere, anytime, to anybody. He got to preach a lot while in jail, but some prisoners didn't like him preaching, so he got into a lot of fights. Even fighting didn't stop him; he kept right on serving his Lord." Gladys leaned back on the couch like she was worn out, picked up her cup, and licked it down the side.

"Sister Gladys," Brother Jordan said as if completely exhausted from her performance, "a funeral is no place for a newly-converted man to preach. He doesn't have enough experience to know what to say."

"Well, Flynn is a mighty bright boy and can lean real quick. You just tell him what you want him to say, and he'll say it."

"Gladys," Leland said, "Virgil is trying to tell you that Flynn is not qualified to preach Erma's funeral, so let it alone."

Gladys seemed at the point of tears. "Maybe you're right," she said, "I'll tell Flynn to read the poem and pray a little bit." She curled her lip slightly and looked down at her lap. I was amazed that she had given in so easily. It worried me. Gladys always fought for what she wanted and never quit until she got it. Everybody was usually worn out by the time she won her battle. She had something in mind, and I wondered what it could be.

"Now, Sister Gladys, as I was saying, how many songs do you plan for your son and his wife to sing?"

"Three I guess," she said like she was pouting. "I'll wait till Leonard comes, and he can pick them out."

"That will be fine."

"If the quartet comes they'll—"

Brother Jordan flipped around in his chair like he had been shot. "What quartet?" He screamed.

"Leonard and Estelle are part of a quartet, and I told Leonard to see if they could come. If they can, we'll have to let them do at least two numbers. That's only good manners to ask them. Estelle and her sisters are the Sweet Jesus Trio, and they might come, too."

"Sister Gladys, I talked with Brother Moody before I came over here, and he said your sister is to be buried in Paulding County."

"What has that got to do with how many songs we have at her funeral?" Gladys asked. She took her napkin and wiped the perspiration from her forehead and upper lip.

"If the funeral is too long here, the people will not want to drive all the way to Paulding County to see your sister laid to rest."

"Way I see it," she said, "anybody that can't sit through a good funeral for my sister and then ride a few miles to see her buried can stay home to start with."

"Them few miles, as you call it, Gladys," Leland said, "happens to be one hundred miles each way."

"It don't matter how far it is. If they're friends, they will want to go."

"Sister Gladys," Jordan said as he stood up, "you let me or Brother Moody know your plans tonight at the funeral parlor." I was surprised he didn't pray. He seemed preoccupied and in a hurry to get away.

"Okay, Brother Jordan," she said with a whine in her voice as she began to gnaw her bottom lip like she does when she's mad. It bothered me greatly that she did not walk with him to the door. I had a feeling she planned revenge. When Gladys got mad, somebody ended up paying a price.

"Brother Leland, may the Lord bless you and you, too, Sister Mildred," Brother Jordan said as he as leaving.

As he shook my hand, I noticed him looking over my shoulder still admiring himself in the mirror. When he turned towards the door I almost jumped out of my skin at the sound of a loud crash. Glass flew all over the living room.

"Goddamn it," I heard the preacher say, and then he quickly placed his hand over his mouth.

"Merciful days, what happened to the mirror?" Leland asked. "Virgil, are you all right? Are you women hurt?"

"It might near hit Brother Jordan's foot," Gladys said, her voice shaking as she spoke.

"I guess the nail came loose," I said as I began picking up the pieces.

"That mirror wasn't hanging by no nail," Leland explained as he examined the steel cable that had held the mirror to the wall. "I hung it with a four inch bolt through a four by four beam. That's mighty funny. The cable is not broken, and the bolt is still in the wall. Mighty strange, mighty strange. Don't see how that could have happened, but strange things do every now and then."

"That was Erma's favorite gift from Springer," I said. "He gave it to her when she came home from the hospital after losing her leg. He wanted her to see that she was still pretty, even with a body part missing."

While Leland walked Brother Jordan to the car, I brought in a box from the back porch. Gladys talked softly as if speaking to herself while she helped me pick up the glass.

"I'll tell you right now, that Jordan gets to be mighty uppity sometimes. If he thinks he can tell me what kind of funeral to have for my own sister, he's got another thought coming. I'll tell Flynn to preach as long as he wants to, and Leonard and Estelle and everybody else can sing all day if they have a mind to do so. Just wait till Flynn starts playing his guitar and singing, and if the Sweet Jesus Trio comes, they can do a few numbers, too. This is one time I'm going to have a funeral like I want, and nobody is going to stop me. One good thing about it, Erma ain't around to interfere and do foolish things like she did when Poppa and Mama passed."

"Don't be so sure Erma is not around," I said. "How do you explain the mirror falling? What about the casket lid? A few minutes ago, I remembered how the papers you and Mr. Moody had me sign flew out of my hand at least twice." I was beginning to feel that maybe, just maybe, I wasn't alone in my fight with Gladys. I found assurance in the knowledge that only time would tell.

Gladys threw the glass she was holding into the box, turned, and glared at me as she spoke. "I've done told you to stop that kind of talk. You just want to spook me, but I mean stop it."

"I will if you explain why the mirror fell. The cable wasn't broken. The screw is still in the wall, and it fell mighty close to a person Erma despised."

Gladys lifted her cane and hit the side of the box that held the broken glass. "I told you to stop it. I know Erma was odd and folks at times believed she might be a witch, but I don't think she can do nothing to us now that she's dead. You're beginning to sound like that granddaughter of yours, and when she gets here tonight for the Lord's sake, my sake, and everybody else's sake don't bring any of this up, or she'll harp on it all night long."

"I don't intend to bring anything up when Sophia gets here. The child does her own thinking. But Gladys, I'm going to say this, and you might as well hear me out. I believe in the hereafter and in a powerful and just God, and as sure as I'm standing here, I believe Erma is still around and knows what happened today. She took pride in leaving that money to folks who needed it, and she did without to pay the premiums. Now nobody will get one penny, and Erma may not rest until the score is evened up. I don't know how she'll do it, but she will."

"That's hogwash, and you're not going to scare me. You just want to get me upset so I won't have a nice funeral for Erma. You hope I'll let you do something gosh awful like she did to Mama, but I'll tell you right now nothing like that is ever going to happen in this family as long as I'm in charge. And like I already said, for goodness sakes don't mention the mirror, casket lid, papers, or the clock tonight when the family gets here. They'll think you're crazy. Let's get this glass picked up. Mercy, what a day. I'm worn to a frazzle." She burped and passed gas as she continued talking. "All this stress is making me feel bloated."

As we worked to clean up the glass, I looked at the portrait of Erma gazing down from the beautiful gold frame given to her by Springer. She seemed to smile and assure me that all would be well if I could only live in the moment. I continued to work as Gladys ranted and raved about one thing or another. It never ceased to amaze me that Gladys felt she was right in every situation and on every subject, but then *none but a fool is always right.*

CHAPTER SIXTEEN

Mildred Roper

With Brother Jordan's visit over and the glass from the broken mirror picked up, I peeked in the kitchen and saw Gladys in a sulky mood, chewing her bottom lip and swatting flies with a potholder. For a change she was mumbling softly, so I tiptoed to my bedroom, lay down on the bed, and quickly drifted into a peaceful sleep filled with more pleasant dreams of Erma. I slept for about twenty minutes.

As I dressed, my mind continued to run wild with thoughts of the mirror episode, the stopped clock, the casket lid, and the flying papers. I kept asking myself if something out of the ordinary was going on. By the time I entered the kitchen, I felt like a new person compared to the morning, even though my mental faculties were far below normal and my body still tired.

I piddled around greeting relatives and spicing up the food by adding more hot sauce to the turnip greens, diluted cornstarch to the roast gravy, and bacon grease to the black eyed peas. Even though my activities were fairly mundane, I still felt the presence of my dead sister several times that day and was convinced of Erma's appearance in my dreams. Even after Leland told me later that the screw in the two by four had apparently worked its way out and caused the mirror to fall, I still wanted to believe that a supernatural power was at work. In my heart I had to believe Erma was trying to get in touch with me. If I sound crazy, so be it. Like most folks, I know nothing about the life beyond this one, and my feelings may be no more than wishful thinking, but it gave me renewed strength to deal with Gladys.

The kitchen in my large, old farmhouse seemed to sink with the weight of food brought in by neighbors and friends. Even though Gladys and Mollie Bea ate like fattening hogs all afternoon, the large amount they consumed was not missed. Gladys also sneaked home as much food as she could carry before the guests arrived.

With a few exceptions, such as Mollie Bea, most of the neighbors and friends who brought food extended their condolences, and then left with a promise to visit at the funeral parlor or attend the funeral.

The first of the family members to arrive was my daughter from Lithia Springs. I was pleased with Joan's arrival, but sensed that Gladys was less than happy when Joan appeared on the scene, for at most family gatherings, she and Gladys butt horns, and I felt this occasion would be no different. Joan, in her middle forties, tall and thin except for a protruding stomach, has been a heavy smoker since her teens much to my displeasure, but I managed to keep my thoughts about her nasty habit to myself. Since birth she seems to have talked non-stop and gets a great deal of pleasure in taking charge of funerals, weddings, and births. Joan, married to her third husband, Vernon Joiner, has one child by each of her former husbands.

Before I had an opportunity to visit with Joan, other family members arrived at the same time. Hoover Murdock, mine and Erma's favorite nephew, and a person Gladys disliked, arrived soon after Joan. Hoover, the artist son of my older sister Florence, dressed his thin frame in tight Jeans held to his slim waist by a wide belt fastened with an impressive buckle of two naked nymphs cavorting under a tree. He covered his long, thin hair with a short brimmed straw hat that had a band made of caps from Bud bottles. In the lobe of his left ear I noticed a small gold ladybug earring. I enjoyed the way Hoover dressed, even though most of the relatives, especially Gladys, found him offensive.

"Well, well, if it ain't my favorite cousin and aunts," Hoover said as he spoke to me and kissed my cheek. He then reached for Joan and held her in his arms as he kissed her for a long time on the lips. "I do hope that baby daughter of yours is arriving soon," he said to Joan when they got their breath back. "Family get-to-gathers are no fun without her input." He then turned to Gladys. "Aunt Glad," he said, "are you trying to ignore me? Turn around and let me see your sweet face." He put his hands on her shoulders and turned her towards him. "A woman's backside never gives me a thrill. Now, tell me, Aunt Glad, have you been running around all afternoon making mischief, telling tales, and gorging yourself on pig flesh?"

"I'm doing fine, Hoover," Gladys said, never looking at him as she spoke. "Yes, I have had a few bites to get me by till supper, since it has been a long, tiring day."

I felt so good having Hoover and Joan with me, for I knew my problems with Gladys would lessen, and whatever else happened, I would have somebody on my side.

As the relatives arrived, they filled their plates with the food on my kitchen table. The less friendly adults went into the dining room, and the younger children carried their plates to the front porch where they fed the family pets and engaged in food fights safe from the critical eyes of older siblings and parents. The teenagers and young adults preferred the homey atmosphere of the kitchen so they could be near Hoover, who could usually be found leaning against the side of the refrigerator ready to share a few bawdy tales guaranteed to create distress among their parents.

While removing covers from the bowls and pans and refilling the dishes on the table, I took time to greet neighbors as they arrived with food. Every time I uncovered a new dish, several relatives hurried over to see what was there even though the tables and cabinets were never empty. At times they even took the container from my hands to make sure they got the first helping. Their behavior got to be embarrassing, but I hoped my neighbors understood.

"Leland," I called from the kitchen to the back porch where I knew he would be with the men, "you need to find some coolers to put this food in. I can't get it all in the icebox, and I know there's going to be a lot more. Folks are so kind."

"Aunt Millie," Hoover said as he placed his hand on my shoulder, "I wouldn't fret none about having a place to put food. The way this crowd is indulging there won't be a crumb left for the cat, and if there is, Aunt Glad plans to haul it off in her little red wagon tied out front."

"Now, Hoover," I said, "you be nice. There's plenty here for anybody that wants it. We don't need to be ugly to one another about a few vittles."

The cabinets, as well as the kitchen and dining room tables, were filled with pots of braised short ribs, beef hash, vegetable soup, and fresh peas. Platters and bowls overflowed with rice stuffed peppers, pickled beets, sweet potato soufflé, sliced tomatoes, fried okra, deviled eggs, boiled corn on the cob, and green beans seasoned with fat back.

Leland looked over the table and said, "Chickens didn't have a chance in this town today. They've been fried, baked, and made into stews, salads, dumplings, and ways I don't even recognize. The pies stacked over there look like my pile of checkers on the corner of a board when I play with Gurdy, and some of them pies have crust glued together with stuff I've never seen or tasted. Mercy, folks are mighty good to us poor souls."

"Tell you what, Uncle Leland, far as I'm concerned you can have all the chicken in this kitchen."

"Now, Russell, what have you got against chickens?"

Russell Vinning, the grandson of Gladys and Gurdy, wore dirty Jeans, torn running shoes, a baseball cap with the bill turned backward, and a sweaty T-shirt with the imprint Chicken Pluckers do it with a feather. Russell had lived with Gladys and Gurdy since he was four. He was a sweet, kind boy only five feet tall, and Gladys favored him over her other grandchildren.

"I never had nothing against them suckers," Russell said, "until I started hauling them. You smell them mothers all day, especially when they're wet, and hear them begging not to have their heads lobed off as you drive up to a processing plant, you won't eat them either."

The chatter in the kitchen stopped when the phone rang and Leland took the receiver from the wall.

"This is Leland Roper. I don't know. Hold on and you can talk to my wife." He put his hand over the receiver, and then turned to me as he spoke. "It's Stump at the funeral parlor. He wants to know how to comb Erma's hair."

Before I could take the phone, Gladys reached across the table and jerked the receiver out of Leland's hand. "Hello," she said in a low, sad voice like she was about to cry. "This is Mrs. Gooch. We understand and that is perfectly alright. She wore her hair pulled straight back. Oh, how sweet of Mr. Moody to suggest a permanent wave. That would be real nice. No, no, you tell Mr. Moody we don't mind the added expense."

Comments on Gladys' phone conversation were heard from various members of the family gathered in the kitchen.

"Lord above, what are they going to think of next?"

"Man, you've got to be kidding."

"Are they really going to curl dead hair? That is gross."

"Can you imagine how it'll smell?"

"Like rotten pumpkins."

"How do you sit somebody up that's dead and put curlers in their hair?"

"You don't think she'll be ready by tonight?" I heard Gladys ask. "I see, but please call us no matter how late it is when you finish. We want to see her tonight. Bye, bye."

"Big Mama, please don't get sore at me," Russell said to Gladys, "but I can't come to the funeral. I've got to make a run every day this week."

"Russell, you know good and well Flynn will give you time off to come to your great aunt's funeral. Besides that, you're going to be a pallbearer, and Flynn is going to preach."

"If that red headed peckerwood is going to preach," Hoover said, "we might as well plan to stay until the crickets start chirping. That simpleton ain't never known when to shut his mouth." He looked at me and smiled.

"Big Mama, there ain't no way I can do it," Russell whined.

"Sure there is." Gladys assured him. "You can park your truck at the church."

"Russell, my boy," Hoover said, pausing for a sip of Bud, "just bring them cluckers to the funeral. They'll fit in fine with this crowd, and if they decide to cackle a little, nobody will notice."

"Big Mama, have you ever smelled a truckload of chickens?"

"Ain't gonna be nobody sniffing chickens at Erma's funeral," Gladys said, "so bring them on."

"You know how dirty I get driving that truck."

"You can take your clean clothes to the funeral home or the church. Mr. Moody will find you a place to change."

"Who else is going to be one?"

"One what?" Gladys asked as she inserted a boiled egg in her mouth.

"Casket toter."

I waited to hear Gladys' answer, as I was asleep when she made the selection in Moody's office earlier in the day. Gladys poured a cup of coffee, cut a wedge of chocolate pound cake, and topped it with several spoons of banana pudding before she answered.

"Hoover is going to be one."

"Course I am," Hoover said. I could tell he was not happy about it. "I've helped haul every dead body since I was knee-high to a gofer, and I don't mind doing it for Aunt Erm, but every now and then it would be nice if somebody asked me if I would instead of telling me I'm going to."

"Hoover, you've got no respect for nobody," Gladys whined.

"I've got plenty of respect, Aunt Glad, and there is nobody I respected more than Aunt Erm, but I don't recall her asking me to be her pallbearer. If she had, I would have said yes."

"Don't see why the funeral home can't furnish men to tote the coffins," Gurdy said. "They get enough money for what little they do."

Gladys' husband, Gurdy, was a tall, lean man in his late seventies who usually dressed in bib overalls, a dark blue work shirt, and a straw hat for almost every occasion. From the bib of his overalls could be seen the chain of his pocket watch and the string from his bag of smoking tobacco. He wore steel-toed plow shoes and heavy wool socks year around. On occasions, such as funerals, when Gladys made him dress up, he put on a clean work shirt buttoned up to his throat and his black dress coat. In his hand, he carried a felt hat.

"I agree, Gurdy," Leland said, "seeing as how the funeral home gets one heck of a lot for what little they do, seems only fitting they furnish somebody to tote the coffin."

"Since we're talking about money," Joan said, "how is this funeral being paid for?" Joan had been eating in the dining room with the other guests and entered the kitchen about the time the money subject came up.

I looked at Gladys and waited for her to speak. I wanted to see how she would explain what she had done to Erma and how she had spent family money.

With her mouth filled with pudding, Gladys seemed anxious to speak. "Erma had an insurance policy that's going to take care of everything."

"Bet it ain't big enough to pay for more than a pine box and a flour sack dress," E. J. said.

"Must be a lot more than that," Hoover answered. "They ain't curling her hair for nothing." He cleaned his nails with the blade of his pocketknife as he spoke. "How much did she have?" he asked Gladys.

Gladys placed a fork filled with cake in her mouth before she answered.

"She had enough to leave this world in style, and that's how it's going to be."

"It's a shame," I said softly, more or less to myself.

"What's a shame, Mama?" Joan asked as she came over and laid her hand on my shoulder.

"What her funeral is going to cost."

"I thought she was to be cremated."

"She was, but she's not."

"Why not?" Joan asked. "If I remember correctly, she wrote her request and put it in her Bible, and I heard her say lots of times that she wanted to be burned and her ashes dumped in the well at the old home place. If that is not going to happen, I want to know why the hell not?"

"Oh, boy, the fun is about to begin, and I feel so lucky to have a front row seat," E.J. added as he placed a slice of ham on a biscuit and poured a glass of lemonade from a cardboard carton.

"It ain't Christian to burn bodies," Gladys said as she wiped her mouth with a wadded napkin, "and I ain't about to let no sister of mine be burned up like white trash, unchristian folks do."

"Especially a sister you loved so much."

"Joan," Gladys answered, "I did love my sister, and she's going to have a funeral that is right, proper, and fitting for a Logan."

"You mean what is right, proper, and fitting according to you," Joan said. "While we are on the subject of how much you loved your sister, all I can say is you sure have an odd way of expressing it. If I recall, you had not seen nor spoken to Aunt Erm in over ten years. To put it bluntly, you couldn't have picked her out of a line-up of twelve if eleven of them had been red-headed, bucktoothed, naked Eskimos."

"I couldn't help it if she was hard to get along with," Gladys said. "Besides that, I just couldn't bring myself to come around her after what she did when Mama passed."

"Hard to get along with, my ass," Joan said. "Aunt Erm could get along with anybody that treated her half decent."

"Now, now, Joanie," said Tillman, one of Gladys' chosen pallbearers. "There is no need for that kind of language in front of the children."

"Back off, Tillman," Joan said, "or I'll take that big iron off your hip and blow the crap out of you. Furthermore, you are not a member of this family. You just married into it, so it's none of your damn business."

Leland began choking, and Hoover slapped him on the back until he was able to speak again. "I'll be dad blamed," Leland said. "You folks have got me so upset with your infernal bickering, I done swallowed half a plug of Brown Mule, and that stuff is too expensive to waste. Come on, Gurdy, let's go on the back porch where we can have some peace and quiet and play checkers."

"Suits me. These relatives is getting on my nerves so bad I need a short snort from your jug."

"Yeah, reckon my nerves could use a little settling now that you mention it."

"You'll have to get a fresh jug from the cellar," I whispered to Leland. "The one on the porch is empty."

"How much did you spend for the funeral?" Joan asked Gladys.

"It was her money," Gladys answered as she began drying the silverware I had washed and placed in the sink.

"It was until she died, and then Mama should have been in charge of it after Aunt Erm's death. What happened to the list of people she wanted the money divided between?"

"The policy said it was to be paid to her sisters."

"That doesn't give you anymore privileges than it gave Mama."

"Mr. Moody said it did because I'm the oldest."

"Moody's butt," Joan said. "What does that blitzed eunuch know about the law, or anything else for that matter, except dead animals and cheap liquor? Have you forgotten who took care of Aunt Erm all the years she was sick and who she lived with when she was well?"

"I can't help it if she was sick in the head and didn't know how she was treating her family," Gladys answered with trembling voice. "She wouldn't let nobody come around her but Millie."

"Aunt Glad," Joan said as she glared at Gladys, "let me make one thing clear. In my presence, you had better never say Aunt Erm was sick in the head, or I'll not be responsible for what I'll do to you. I was around Aunt Erm one hell of a lot, and she never refused to be nice to anybody whether or not they were nice to her. The way I see it, if anybody in this family is nuts, it's Y.O.U."

"Now, Joan," my niece, Marty Lou, said as she placed her hand on Joan's arm. "You just told my husband to butt out of family politics, but I am part of this family, and I say it's not worth getting the family upset over a little money spent on a funeral."

"Leave her alone," Hoover said. "She's doing a damn good job, so butt out." He did not look up from his nail cleaning as he spoke.

"Go to hell, Hoover," Marty Lou answered.

"I probably will, but unfortunately I'll still have to put up with most of my relatives when I get there."

"Joan," the cousin continued, "my mother was Aunt Erm's sister the same as Aunt Millie. If Mama was alive she would want Aunt Erm put away nicely."

"Put away nicely," Joan said, mimicking her cousin. "Doesn't anybody in this family but Mama give a tinker's damn about what

Aunt Erm wanted?"

"People have no right to say what ought to be done with them after they pass," Gladys said. "The closest living relatives ought to decide."

"Right from the drunken mouth of he who plants the dead and fleeces the living," Hoover added.

"I'll bet that egg sucking preacher had something to do with it, too," Joan added.

"You can bet your ever-loving ass that when Moody and Jordan found out about the insurance money, they moved in like ghouls."

"Don't y'all talk about Brother Jordan and Mr. Moody that way," Gladys said, with a whine in her voice. "They are fine men."

"If they are fine men, this world is in mighty deep crap." Hoover added. "That preacher would steal from his own collection plate if he didn't have deacons watching him, and you know damn well Moody would steal anything, even a gold tooth from a corpse. So if you think, dear Aunt, that those two are not out to skin this family, you are barking up a coon-less tree, and somehow I am going to prove it."

"I forgot what the face value of her policy was," Joan said, "but I know it was a hell of a lot. How much did Moody take us for?"

"We don't know yet."

"You might not know, but Moody sure does," Russell added. "You can bet your bottom dollar he'll get every penny before it's over." As he spoke, he sliced an onion on a plate filled with black-eyed peas, boiled cabbage, and a wedge of chocolate cake.

"He'll probably make you throw in her old Edsel just for good measure."

"I'd like to have that thing myself," Russell said.

"I don't recommend holding your breath until you drive off in it," Hoover suggested. "You know damn well Moody and Jordan will find a way to get it, but it's going to be over my dead body. I promise you that."

"Mr. Moody said he needed the title to that old car to pay what the insurance policy will not pay," Gladys said. "I have to take the title tonight."

"Well, Aunt Glad," Hoover stood up straight with his fists clenched as he spoke. "You tell that sawed-off bastard that he will never see that title if I have my way. Aunt Millie, do you know where it is?"

"Yes, Hoover, I do, and I'll get it for you."

"I promised I would take it to the funeral home tonight," Gladys whined.

"Well that just sucks Aunt Glad," said Hoover. "If I remember correctly, Aunt Millie promised Aunt Erm that she would be cremated and not buried, so I guess this family is known for breaking promises."

"Since you didn't have her cremated," Joan said, "where do you plan to bury her?"

"There has always been a spot for her in the lot near Mama and Poppa up in Dallas."

"Aunt Glad, whether you admit it or not, the only spot Aunt Erm ever wanted, after her death, was in the well at the old home place, and even you know that is the truth."

The kitchen conversation was interrupted by several phone calls and the arrival of neighbors bringing more food. I no longer went near the phone when it rang, as I knew Gladys would grab the receiver from my hand and talk in her slow, pathetic voice.

"That's right," Gladys said. "My nephew Flynn Shockley is going to preach along with Brother Jordan, and my son Leonard and his wife Estelle will sing several numbers, and if the Sweet Jesus Trio comes, they'll sing a few too."

"Mother of Moses," Joan said, "Mama, didn't you have any say in planning this funeral?"

"Not much," I said as I warmed food on the stove and refilled bowls and platters as they were emptied. "I was too tired to fight with Gladys."

"I'm sure you were, Mama," Joan said as she gently hugged me.

"I'd been up every night for the past few weeks and sort of dozed off at the funeral home. When Gladys woke me up, Mr. Moody practically held the pen while I signed whatever it was I signed." I poured a pot of turnip greens into a bowl and listened as Gladys continued speaking with Mr. Moody on the phone.

"I'm sure she'll look sweet in that color," she said. "That's real thoughtful of you, Mr. Moody, I know he'll do a good job. We'll be waiting to hear from you, bye, bye, now. Erma's not ready yet," she said, "but to speed things up and make her look real good, Mr. Moody asked Amos Gleason's boy Chunky to come and help him and Mr. Stump get Erma ready. They hope we'll be able to see her tonight. I told him that was just wonderful and really thoughtful of him to do that for us. You see, I told you Mr. Moody is a fine, thoughtful fellow."

"Yeah, I'm overwhelmed with his thoughtfulness."

"Let's all go barf off the porch in his honor."

"Is that Chunky fellow the ass-hopper that goes to school in Atlanta where he's learning to paint the dead?"

"Gross."

"You ever seen him walk?"

"Like his panties are in a wad?"

"It's probably from the lace in his crotch."

Hoover, leaning against the refrigerator and blowing smoke rings in the air above his head said, "You boys mind your language in Aunt Millie's house. She don't go for that kind of talk. Now, I've got a question for Aunt Millie. Is that brainless fool Shockley really going to preach?"

"I'm afraid so," I said.

"Flynn is not so bad since he got saved," Russell added.

"Saved from what?" Hoover asked. "Why does Aunt Glad insist on having him preach? That poor featherless loon with a double digit I.Q. ain't got a brain big as a chigger's thingamajig."

"Beats me," Russell said. "I don't know why she does half she does."

"She likes for folks to think she's got important kin."

"You call a chicken plucking, bootlegging thief important kin?"

"He's them things all right," Russell agreed, "but he is her kin, and she's proud of him. Besides that he gives me a job, so I ain't got no sweat about him. If he wants to preach, I say let him."

"Why isn't our illustrious cousin, Clyde Fenimore Bullard preaching?" Hoover asked.

"Is he the one that got kicked out of the church in Power Brook for doing something with a woman in a baptizing pool?"

"He's the one," Hoover answered.

"What did he do?" Russell asked.

"I heard he was trying to—"

"That's enough," interrupted Tillman as he pointed his finger at the young people around the kitchen table. "Hoover, a few minutes ago you scolded the boys for their language. Now, listen to you."

"Oh, come on, Tillman," Hoover said. "Let them know what kind of relatives they've got. It's not going to hurt them."

"Come on, Uncle Tillman, let Hoov tell us. He can clean it up. Come on, Hoov, clean it up, but tell us."

"Well now," Hover began, looking at me as if asking for approval. When I smiled, he began his tale. "It seems one Sunday morning old Fenimore had a bad accident. Way I heard it, he was running round the church during Sunday school naked." His audience laughed. "He just happened to stumble and fall into the baptizing pool that didn't have any water in it."

"Yeah, yeah, sure thing," they taunted. "Now, why was he naked at Sunday school?"

"Good point," Hoover said, "y'all are real observant. Seems old Fenimore had a very sensitive body and clothes irritated his skin."

"Go on."

"Seems that when he landed on the bottom of the pool, Kathleen Trickum was laying down there on a nice soft quilt all spread out on her back enjoying the spiritual air the place provided, and poor old Fenimore just happened to land right smack on top her." Hoover paused to light a cigarette while holding his audience in suspense. "Just by coincidence she was also buck naked. She, too, had a rash that didn't allow her to wear clothes. Now when this here deacon just happened to come along and look in the pool, there was old Fenimore struggling desperately to get up off Miss Trickum. That deacon, being a shallow brain fellow, like Baptist deacons have a tendency to be, got the wrong idea about what was going on down there, and you know how them Baptists are—they called a meeting, and by suppertime old Fenimore was out of town and ain't been heard from since."

"That's not a very nice story to be telling young folks," Gladys snarled.

"Nice is in the mind of the beholder, Aunt Glad."

"Aunt Glad, have you never told a bad story or listened to one?"

"I certainly have not, and with the help of the Lord I keep my thoughts and my words clean as a newborn lamb."

"Well, bully for you, Aunt Glad," Hoover said and looked at me. I shook my head and smiled.

"Mama," Joan said, "I wish you had called me to go to the funeral home with you this morning. We would have been a lot better off tonight." As she talked, she walked around the kitchen swatting flies.

"Yeah, and there would be one less jackleg preacher getting ready to run off at the mouth and tanking-up to spit in the artificial flowers that I'm sure Aunt Glad will have sitting around the pulpit and hanging from the church rafters."

"Hoov, did it have water in it?"

"What?"

"The baptizing pool."

"No, stupid, he told you they had a quilt spread on the bottom."

"Hoov, how did you know cousin Fenimore and that woman had a quilt spread on the bottom of the pool?"

"One night, years later, Kathleen got smashed and told me about it."

His audience laughed.

"Mama, is everybody coming tonight?" Joan asked. "Or will our more distinguished kin wait until tomorrow and come just in time for food and funeral?" As she talked, she hit a fly on the side of the refrigerator and kicked it under the cabinet.

"The funeral is not going to be tomorrow. It's going to be on Friday."

"Was that your idea, Mama, or did that also come from the wicked witch of South Georgia?"

"Gladys wanted more time to play with Erma."

"I figured as much," Joan said. "I personally am not going to sit around on my duff for two days waiting to bury somebody that didn't want to be buried in the first place. This is absurd, and I don't like it worth a tinker's damn."

"Me and Mr. Moody agreed that having the funeral tomorrow wouldn't give us enough time to get Erma ready," Gladys said. "Sides that, it's disrespectful to bury somebody the day after they pass. That don't give enough grieving time."

"Aunt Glad," Joan responded, getting louder with each word. I kept hoping she would explode, then things would change and for the better. "I don't give a cat's ass what you and Moody decided, and just in case you don't know it, there are other people in this family entitled to make decisions besides you. I say we are going to have the funeral tomorrow and no later. And I personally want to know how much of Aunt Erm's money that sawed-off little schmuck swindled out of this family because I intend to make every effort to get it back. Come on, Hoov, gargle and put on some socks. You and me are going to pay Moody a not so friendly visit, but first I've got to go to the john. Be ready when I get back. Take that worried look off your face, Mama," Joan said to me. "I promise to be the nice little girl you raised me to be, and I also promise to stand up for Aunt Erm the way she taught me to and the way she always stood up for me." She handed the fly swatter to E. J. as she said, "Here, for once, do something useful."

"Come on, Aunt Millie," Hoover said as he placed his beer bottle in the cooler and slipped a piece of Juicy Fruit in his mouth. "Walk on the porch with me and get a little fresh air while I wait for Joanie. Don't you fret about what has happened. Everything is going to be alright, I promise. I'm going to call J. R. and see if we can cancel those papers you signed and get Aunt Erm's money returned to you."

We walked out back, and after he and Joan left for the funeral home I stayed on the porch and petted poor little grieving Crowie. Only a few minutes passed before one of the grandchildren called from the kitchen door that Mr. Moody was on the phone and said Aunt Erma was ready to receive guests.

I did not want to go back to the funeral home, for I knew it would be an unpleasant occasion. I reached down and patted Crowie on the head as he looked up with sad, old eyes. I kept my arms around his neck and buried my face in his soft, clean wool as I made a feeble attempt to pray. Oh, Lord, have mercy on us sad, lonely creatures, for at this time I don't even know what to pray for except strength to get through this night and courage to face whatever tomorrow brings.

CHAPTER SEVENTEEN

Ewell Moody

South of the town square and separated from the Rock Church by the Bochimville cemetery stands the Maslow Moody Memorial Mortuary. While under the ownership of Grandpa Maslow, it was a handsome two-storied building with sash windows and an elaborate flight of twelve rounded steps rising to a porch with eight stately columns. Since Grandpa's untimely death, the grand old mansion has slipped off the list of the town's most elegant real estate, and in Bochimville lingo, is now a Dung Pile. During my growing-up years, the porch had at least a dozen white rocking chairs where day and night someone seemed to be rocking, spitting, and talking. It was on this porch that town folk gathered to cry, curse, or praise their dearly departed loved ones. Gigantic baskets of ferns, which I watered daily during the hot summer months, hung over the banisters, from which I cleaned tobacco juice weekly. Across the river and downwind from the county slaughterhouse, the mourners were provided with a unique odor while reminiscing or engaging in town gossip. It grieves me to admit that I recently heard it referred to as a *Gone with the Wind* reject, a somewhat true description of the place.

The chipped paint, rusty wrought iron railings, and scraggly magnolias and crepe Myrtles reflect the financial status and attitude of its present owner, me, Ewell Delray Moody. With the assurance that this scene was about to change for the better, I licked my lips in delight as I observed the first in a long line of pickup trucks bringing members of the Logan family up my long circular drive.

For one brief shining moment, on the eve of Miss Erma Mae

Logan's death, I experienced an overwhelming bliss. Dressed in my best funeral attire—teeth polished to baking soda perfection and hair parted on the side and held in place with a dab of Crisco—I welcomed the challenge ahead. With the assurance that my ship loaded with gold teeth had finally docked, I felt every pore of my body fill with ecstasy, and I am not referring to the mildly psychedelic derivative of amphetamine. I mean that heavenly, natural feeling furnished by Mother Nature's own pure breast milk when the planets are aligned in one's favor.

In this infrequently encountered state of bliss, I shifted from one foot to the other as I graciously greeted the members of the Logan family and welcomed them to my humble establishment. One by one they ambled up my steps, crossed the porch, and entered the viewing room where they looked upon the remains of their cherished departed, whose hair had been curled, face made up, nails polished, and body lavishly dressed.

As the family entered the Viewing Room, my capable assistant, Stump Dupree, stood with his hands over his crotch at the head of Miss Erma's casket, smiling and slightly bowing. With the family patiently waiting for further instructions, I took my designated place beside Stump. In my trained funeral voice, referred by some as my stained glass voice, I spoke in gentle, consoling tones to the family members.

"If there is anything either I or my aide-de-camp, Mr. Dupree, can do to make this occasion less painful, please let us know." I drug out the please. "We are here to serve your every need." I smiled, bowed, and, in-step with Stump, moved away from the coffin. Then, while looking over the room, we gazed upon the most ill-bred, tasteless dressed mortals we had ever observed under one roof.

The room remained almost silent until Gladys Gooch meandered up to the open casket and looked in. She wiped her nose with a small white handkerchief, a great improvement over the hem of her dress she had used during the morning, and began to lament.

"Watch her," Stump whispered to me. "The old gal is about to put on a performance the Bochimville Players or a group of professional mourners would envy."

"She would wail for a week if she thought anybody was listening. Before this night is over she'll probably tear her clothes and beat her boobs. Perhaps we should provide a few hot ashes to smear on her forehead."

"She can feign grief better than anybody I've ever encountered,"

Stump said. "I'm glad somebody else is holding her up and not me. I'd rather grope a hog."

"Don't Sister look sweet," Mrs. Gooch wailed, with spit foaming in the corners of her mouth. "I just want to reach down and squeeze her." Physically supported by her skinny little wimp of a son, Leonard somebody, she gazed into the coffin. Leonard arrived at the funeral home before the family, and it became my lot to entertain the mentally-delayed runt of a weasel from the North Georgia Mountains.

"Ohooo, Mr. Moody," Sister Gooch crooned, "you did such a fine job. She looks plumb real. I declare she looks so natural one would think she was not dead but in a komer."

"Thank you, Mrs. Gooch," I graciously responded with my best smile, somewhat like that of a wide mouth frog. "We wanted you to be proud of your dear departed sister, so we endeavored to create a beautiful memory picture." I smacked my lips and stepped back.

"Ohooo, you did just that," Sister Gooch assured me. "She's a living doll." She clutched Leonard's arm as she called to her sister. "Oh, Millie, you've got to see Sister. I wish I could put a mirror to her face and let her see herself."

Stump and I watched as Mildred Roper walked up to the open coffin and silently gazed at her dead sister. She shook her head in disbelief and then took a seat in the far corner of the room.

"For what you have done to that poor woman," Stump whispered, "if there is a God, He, She, It, or whatever is going to slap you right into a komer."

I ignored his frightful remark and said, "Poor soul, every now and then I have a tinge of guilt about ripping her off, for she is a good woman. Nothing like her sister. She looks so ragged out, I bet they'll have to prop her up to get her through the next twenty four hours."

"Grandpa Moody would rupture a hernia if he knew what we did to her, but life goes on. You've got to do what you have to do. If anything ominous happens in this place before this shindig is over, we can rest assured Grandpa Moody and the Logan gal are in the same place and retaliating like hell for what we have done today. It really scares the piss out of me."

"Don't go there," I said, a little whiny. "We've got enough problems dealing with the living, without conjuring up the dead. Talking about problems, here comes two of the worst ones we'll have to deal with until this little weenie roast is over."

"Who are they?"

"Hoover Murdock is the nephew of the Logan sisters, and Joan somebody is the daughter of the Roper woman. They came to see me shortly before the family arrived and demanded that the funeral be changed to tomorrow. I had to send Moss and Angus up to Paulding County to dig the grave in the dark. I was afraid not to do what they said, for the sooner we get the old gal in the ground, and I get my money, the better I'll feel. They demanded to know what the casket cost, the face value of the old gal's policy, and why the hell she wasn't cremated. They even went to see J.R., who thankfully told them that everything the sisters signed was legal and there was not a damn thing they could do to change it. That minute of legal advice will set us back the price of a damn pauper's box. The funeral will be tomorrow, which is fine with me, for the quicker we get the old gal out of the mahogany box, into a crate, and covered with dirt, the better off we'll be. Help me pass the word about the change, but I am not going to be the one to tell the Gooch gal. Somebody else can do that, but let's hope she is out of here before she finds it out. You need to call the radio station tonight about the change."

"Do you know why Murdock and Joan walked by the casket without looking in?" Stump asked.

"When they came earlier, they looked at the old gal and informed me that she didn't look like nobody they had ever known but more like a frizzy-headed, jaundiced monkey, and somebody was going to regret what had been done to their favorite aunt. Now, I'll admit, those two scare me fart-less."

"Me, too."

Stump and I watched as one by one the family gazed at the old gal, then walked away from the casket and found a place to nest.

"Have you ever seen so many exposed tits, tight-ass jeans, and cowboy garb in one place? Looks like the men would have enough respect to take off those damn western hats. This crowd must own stock in a chewing gum factory. They are like a damn herd of cows chewing their cud."

"Did you see the gal wearing the halter top with a string of Cheerios around her neck?" Stump asked. "Reckon she sucks on them when she gets hungry?"

"Look at the tattoos. Wish I could read them up closer."

"I'll bet there are not a dozen brain cells among the whole crowd."

Murdock and Joan moved to the far side of the room away from the crowd, causing me to tremble at the thought of what evil or retaliation schemes those two were attempting to conjure up. Like a hungry cat stalking its prey, I discreetly moved behind a couple of large plastic plants that shielded me from Murdock and Joan's view but hopefully enabled me to hear their conversation. I found it a lovely place to scratch as furtively as possible and hear the dialogue between the two family members that could turn my most beautiful dream into an unimaginable nightmare. When the time was right, I made eye contact with Stump and motioned for him to join me in my secluded spot.

"Those two are more irritating than a brier on the butt," I whispered. "If the Logan family has troublemakers, they're the leaders. I've heard that the Joiner gal, Joan, is meaner than a rattlesnake cornered in a rock pile. They don't like a thing we've done."

"Can't say as I blame them. I would be—"

"Be quiet," I said as I nudged Stump in the ribs, "listen to what they are saying."

"Can you believe that?" Hoover asked, shaking his head. "What a waste. If Moody gets his hands on Aunt Erm's money, I will fix his ass where only the buzzards will want it."

"If I were you," Stump suggested, "I'd keep the old hearse gassed up and ready to roll."

"Aunt Erm never wore nothing near that nice in her life," Joan said. "Did you see the orchid? It's big as a bush. She never wore a flower in her life. She believed flowers should stay on the stalk where they grew and not on somebody's shoulder."

"I'll bet that box she's spread out in cost more than her old Edsel did brand new. That sonofabitch wouldn't give us a hint of what it cost. At least we stopped him from getting the title to her old Edsel, since I have it right here in my pocket," Hoover said as he patted his coat.

"Damn, Virgil will be livid about not getting that old car, but hell I can't help it."

"I didn't know Moody could afford anything that nice," we heard Joan say. "I'd heard he was going broke. Look at this dump he calls a funeral home."

"Hell is not going to be hot enough for the jerks responsible for this royal rip off," Hoover said. "We've been took. Soon as the funeral is over, I'm making a beeline to Atlanta and hire me a real lawyer who will try like hell to get at least some of Aunt Erm's money back. That shyster J.R. is one sorry bastard, and there is no doubt he is in cahoots with Moody and Jordan. He said there was nothing we could do now that the papers have been signed. Did you notice how nervous he was? The entire time we talked, he sat behind his desk cutting out paper dolls. What kind of a lawyer is that? You know damn well Moody is paying him to get rid of us. Well, they ain't rid of us yet, and this little drama has just begun."

"Moody will probably have the money spent on booze or gambled away at the nudist camp before we have time to see the lawyer," I heard Joan say.

"They know you pretty well. Don't they?" Stump smirked.

"I'll promise you one thing," Hoover said, "I'm not going to let Aunt Erm down. Whatever it takes, this shit is going to be cleaned up."

Listening to Hoover and watching his tightly clinched fists caused my heart to flutter in my mouth.

"Let's get out of here," Hoover said to Joan. "I can't take this much longer."

"Wait a few more minutes," Joan said, "if we leave now somebody might notice."

"Does that mean you're going with me to the old home place?" he asked, "where we can do the fun things we used to do?"

I watched as he gently rubbed his hand up and down her back all the way from her butt to her shoulders. "Merciful hell," I mumbled to Stump. "This crowd has incestuous perverts among them."

"I need something to get my mind off this mess," Joan said.

They were talking loud enough for my sensitive ears to pick up every word, and I can also read lips, so I did not miss any of their frightful conversation.

"I can help you, there, Baby," Hoover promised, pulling down her zipper and running his hand in the back of her bra.

"In this town," Stump whispered, "we are the ones considered deviant, but those two are going out screwing. He's about to take off her dress right here in front of God and everybody. I thought they were first cousins."

"They are."

"Now I know why this family is so demented. It's the incest. How dysfunctional can one family be?"

"Look who just came in the door," we heard Joan say to Hoover. "Damn, he's coming over here. Hoov, zip me quick."

"Hello, Joan, Hoover," said a guy, definitely the offspring of two first cousins, I assumed to be Flynn Shockley. He shook hands with both of them as he spoke.

"May the Lord bless you real good, and may His Kingdom come

in your life and in your day."

"Why, thank you, Flynn, that's real kind of you," Hoover said, "but I have other plans for my life, especially for today, and it doesn't include nobody's kingdom. Tell me, Flynn, old buddy, is it true you done gone whole hog for Jesus?"

"Yes, Hoover, I have heard the call."

"You sure what you heard weren't a sick chicken?"

"No, Hoover, I'm sure it was the Lord."

"Well, now, that's mighty good, Flynn. Tell me, do them chickens of yours grow fatter now that you've found Him?"

Hoover was a real bastard to his cousin, and before Flynn had an opportunity to respond to Hoover's last ugly remark, Mrs. Gooch called Shockley to join her at the casket. The way she drooled as she spoke his name, one would assume he is right up there next to Jesus.

"Flynn, honey, come on over and see your dear old Aunt Erma. She looks like an angel in a box."

"I'm shore she does, Aunt Glad. I'm shore she does, and I've been anxiously waiting to see her. On the drive down from Covington, I found myself wallowing around in boyhood memories of the times I spent with her. I even wrote a song to her memory. I hope you'll be kind enough to let me sang it at her funeral."

"You know I will, Flynn, and I know Erma would be so proud."

"Is the whole family bonkers?" Stump asked.

"Listen and decide for yourself. Why is that damn Shockley staring up the old gal's nose? Did you leave your trimmers up there?"

"Family," Flynn Shockley said, standing at the foot of the casket with outstretched hands as if inviting the world to enter, "in this quiet time of sadness, let's all join hands and pray to our Lord Jeeeezus."

There once was a preacher name Flynn
Who didn't know where to begin.
He tried raising the dead
To get himself ahead
Claiming the Bible condoned him therein.

-Ewell Moody

CHAPTER EIGHTEEN

Ewell Moody

The Shockley fellow, with guidance from Sister Gooch, assumed the role of family spiritual leader by calling the family to join hands around the casket of their dearly departed for a word of prayer. The family reluctantly gathered and timidly reached for the hand of the nearest person. Joan and Hoover stepped from their chosen spot in response to Sister Roper, accompanied by her husband, walking up to the casket. With the circle complete, Flynn began praying.

Flynn had petitioned the throng for only a few favors when Delilah, my pit bull, came into the room and began sniffing the legs of the guests. She seemed especially fond of the aroma around Flynn's feet and lingered nearby even though I desperately attempted to gain her attention.

"You want me to get her?" Stump asked.

"Wait a few minutes. Maybe she'll see us or go away."

"Oh, Lord, we beg you, Lord, to come on down, Lord, and comfort the family of this dear, departed aunt, Lord, who lived a Christ filled life, Lord, from the day of her birth until the moment you took her home to be with you, Lord." Flynn prayed as he gently nudged the dog with his right foot. "We know at this very minute, Lord, she is sitting on your heavenly front porch, Lord, looking down at her dear family gathered here tonight, Lord, pleased they loved her so much, Lord. We know too, Lord, if you decided to do it, Lord, you can raise this beautiful body, Lord, from this box like you done Lazus from the rock, Lord, while his sisters watched, Lord. We know, too, Lord, that Lazus had been dead so long, Lord, he stunk, but you, Lord, brought him back after many days, Lord, and he smelled just fine, Lord. Now! Lord!" Flynn shouted, with his head lifted upward and his eyes tightly shut. "This dear lady, Lord, has only been dead a few short hours, Lord, and we beg you to let her jump off your porch of heaven, Lord, and sit upright among us tonight, Lord, to show the power in your hand, Lord. Now! Lord, Do it NOW! LORD! NOW! I COMMAND YOU, LORD!"

"If she do, that window is mine," I whispered.

"NOW!" Flynn shouted with such force he made the old windows with rotted frames shake like a thunderstorm had hit. It made me nervous. At the same time he commanded the Lord to raise Miss Erma, he gave Delilah a hard kick. When Flynn heard Delilah yelp, he jumped and hollered, "Aunt Erm, we hear you calling and we are waiting for you."

I knew I had better do something and do it quick, for nobody kicked Delilah without her retaliating. I grabbed her collar just as she made a dive for Flynn's leg. I gave her, slobbering, growling, and snapping, to Stump and returned to my place behind the thick plastic leaves of the banana plants.

Following a few encouraging Amens from Leonard and several cowboy hat-clad brethren around the casket, Flynn opened his eyes and glared at the casket. I sensed he was stunned that his dear aunt was not sitting up. He seemed extremely disappointed in the Lord.

The circle of prayer broke when Hoover and Joan dropped the hands of the person on each side of them, but not each other's, and returned to their spot in front of the plants that served as my hiding place.

"Hell, those two act like they're glued together," I whispered as Stump returned to his place near me in the viewing room. "What did you do with Delilah?"

"I put her in your apartment with a stern command not to devour the cats or parrot and to hold her pee until we return. Did I miss anything?"

"When that damn fool Flynn Shockley, or whatever his name, got through praying and demanding the Lord to do his wishes, I believe he really thought the old gal would sit up."

"All we need is a real, sure enough resurrection along with the other problems we've got at the moment. What else is going on?"

"Can't say those two over there are in the grief mode," I said and nodded towards Joan and Hoover. "They've got the hots so bad for each other it's a wonder they don't crawl behind the potted tree and get on with it. He has about rubbed the skin off her back. Mercy, what some men will do to get in a woman's drawers. Never understood it myself, but they're not the only loons in the crowd. Watch this bunch. We've dealt with some lulus in our time, but none compare with this gaggle of morons and jackasses."

Most of the women in the room, except Sister Roper and her daughter Joan, were crying. The men stood silently, looking down at the floor and shifting nervously from one foot to the other. Family members moved away from the casket and dispersed around the room. As small groups formed, whispering, sniffing, and the swishing of the funeral parlor cardboard fans could be heard. Mrs. Gooch refused to leave her dead sister. She stood over the casket crying and saying how much she had loved her. When her lamentations had faded considerably, other visitors entered the room.

"Watch the Gooch gal," I said. "Every new face that comes in the door cranks up more tears, and the front of the casket is wetter than the Wailing Wall. It's a damn shame professional mourners went out of style, for we could hire her out at funerals and make a killing. Remind me to tell you about her insistence that I take the old gal home for a sitting-up," I giggled.

Agnes Cullpepper, accompanied by her husband Melvin, walked up to the casket, and Mrs. Gooch threw herself in Miss Agnes' arms while Melvin nodded in silence to everybody looking his way. Behind the Cullpeppers came Flora and Bevel Mayhew and their disabled son, Grady Bruce. Flora and Mrs. Gooch locked arms while they hung over the casket, crying like a couple of ninnies. Grady Bruce, with an imbecile smile, walked with his feet turned in like a pigeon, stood before Mrs. Roper, and bowed. He walked over to Mrs. Gooch, repeated his performance, then looking in the casket, bowed, held up his hand, and said, "Go Dawgs."

Stump and I found it almost impossible to control our laughter.

"I didn't know the town simpleton was still living," I heard Joan say to Hoover.

"Sure he is. Old idiots never die, they just drown in their drool," Hoover said, still caressing her backside. He was so talented with his hand I began to wish I had him on my side of the tree to scratch my rash.

"Isn't he the old lunatic that killed Maslow Moody?" Joan asked Hoover.

"Yes."

"How come he's not in jail?"

"No judge or jury on God's green earth could convict a dunderhead like that."

"How did he kill him?" she asked.

"Damn," I said and nudged Stump. "Move closer to those two. They're talking about Grandpa."

"Grady Bruce, GeeBee as the town refers to him," Hoover began, "used to get his kicks by going to the funeral home about midnight with a big flashlight in his fat little fist and prowling around the rooms till he found an open coffin. If it had a stiff residing in it, he'd stand there eyeballing the sucker till he got whatever thrill it was he was looking for, then move on to the next one. One night, things were a mite slow around the funeral parlor, at least that's the way I heard it, and Grandpa Maslow decided to have a little fun. He parked an empty casket in the middle of the main room, turned out the lights, and him and the boys went about chewing the fat till they heard old GeeBee come in, then Grandpa ran and jumped in the casket."

"Oh, Lord," Joan said, "I remember the rest of the story. Don't tell me anymore. Mercy, I get a headache just thinking about it. It was a horrible way for a sweet old man to die. What time is it? I've had a long day."

"Merciful hell," I mumbled to Stump. "Will folks never stop talking about how Grandpa died? When you get right down to it, people are nothing but featherless buzzards. It never ceases to amaze me how folks flock to gawk at and talk about the dead. Yet you and me are considered the odd ones for being in this business, but I think a lot of folks would love to do what we do, especially the old Gooch gal. Mercy."

"You may be right," Stump said. "This place is already packed tight as sardines in a can, and look at the mob coming in the door. The word must have circulated around town that Miss Erma Mae Logan is bidding farewell to this town and doing it in high style. Why else would most of Bochimville be so anxious to see how an old maid, who in her youth kept this town in turmoil and then in her old age became a total recluse, is making her final departure? Look who just came in the door."

"Jeeeezus."

"Don't think so, but I wish it was him as long as he's not looking for me or you. I was referring to Lurlene Croker. I'm sure she's here to see if Miss Erma is being put away nicer than Elmo. Has she missed a funeral since the day we put him under?"

"She hasn't missed a funeral since the day she exited the womb.

She makes me nervous as hell. Watch her scrutinize that coffin."

"My word," Lurlene Croker said to Sister Gooch without formal greetings, "I do believe this mahogany box is just like Elmo's."

"It's a beauty, ain't it?" Sister Gooch asked. "And you'll never guess what it cost. Excuse me a minute, Lurlene, I need to do something. Oh, Mr. Moooody." I heard her bellow my name.

"Yes, Mrs. Gooch, how may I assist you?" I graciously responded as I stepped out from behind the large plant.

"Would you get me a brush, please? I'd like to change Sister's hair."

"Certainly, Mrs. Gooch," I said, then left the room and quickly returned with a brush and comb. "Mrs. Gooch, what would you like for me to do?"

"Oh, I'll do it myself," she said as she took the brush from my hand.

"Mrs. Gooch," I whispered, "please be careful. Your sister is very delicate."

In front of an audience of gawking women, Gladys Gooch brushed her dead sister's hair, tilted her head to a different angle, and when she pulled the brush from Miss Erma's head, most of the hair from the top came out in the brush.

"My word, Mr. Moody," she whined. "Erma's done gone bald. What in the world made her hair come out? What did you do to her?"

Stump hurried over to assist me as I whispered softly into Mrs. Gooch's ear. "When a person with a soul as celestial as that of your dear sister's leaves the body, it departs through the area known as the Anterior Fontanelle, and it has a tendency to loosen the hair. That is precisely what has occurred in your sister's case. Believe me, Mrs. Gooch, it is a sign of the most devout of souls with this type of leave taking. If you'll notice, my assistant has arranged your sister's hair again, and I beg that you leave it as he has placed it." I was sweating like a damn fox surviving a hunt.

"Oh, Mr. Moody, I will leave it alone. That is so sweet what you said about Sister's soul taking a leak through her Fontana. Thank you, Mr. Moody."

Stump placed the brush in his pocket, and we sheepishly returned to our hiding spot. I twisted like a rabid fox, as my rash was giving me fits.

"What the hell did you do to her hair?" I asked Stump through clinched teeth.

"I had her rolled on electric rollers when Festus Belmont came in to see if you had started on his buzzard. We got into a poker game, and I forgot about her until the smell kind of overtook us."

"You could have burned the old gal's head off. Merciful days, if lightning don't strike now, it never will."

"Calm down, Ewell. You did a magnificent job getting us out of that one. Where in the hell did you come up with that crock of excrement? Anterior Fontanella, my ass."

"Worked didn't it? Now what?"

"Mr. Mooody," Mrs. Gooch called again in her sweetest voice.

"Yes, Mrs. Gooch," I replied as I watched Lurlene Croker from the corner of my eyes.

"Bless my soul," I heard her say. "It has the same identical picture in the lid as Elmo's has."

"Mr. Moody, would you open the other end of the coffin so we can see Sister's feet?" Mrs. Gooch asked.

"Mrs. Gooch, full couch isn't usually done," I tried to explain.

"Oh, hogwash, I didn't say nothing about no couch. We just want to see Erma's feet. Open it, Mr. Moody, or I will."

"Yes, Mrs. Gooch."

"Ohoooo, ain't them sweet little oxfords, uh, oh! Mr. Moody," she whined. "Where is Sister's wood foot? I know she had it on this morning when you picked her up cause I helped put it on her before you got there. How come it ain't on her now?"

"I'm so sorry, Mrs. Gooch," I apologized. "My assistant obviously failed to place the foot on her lovely body. I'll check with him."

I rushed over to Stump with my teeth clinched so tight I felt my molars loosen. "Where in the bloody hell is the old gal's leg? Did you leave it in the kudzu? Go get it, and hope to God Delilah hasn't buried it or chewed it up." I stepped behind the tree to wait for Stump's return and took the opportunity to give my body a thorough scratching.

"That old half-wit," I heard Joan say, "shows how much she knew about Aunt Erm. She had not worn that leg in a coon's age."

"It hurt too much," Hoover said. "Now she's dead, that old dolt wants to put it back on her. Everywhere me and you took her, she went in her wheelchair."

"Or you picked her up and carried her like a china doll. She loved the attention you gave her, Hoov."

"Look what that old dunce is doing now," Hoover said with a crack in his voice.

I watched in amazement as Sister Gooch lifted Miss Erma's dress to show her burial attire to the audience of goggle-eyed women and stunned men. I gave thanks that Stump had put the old lady's drawers on, for most often he doesn't.

"I want y'all to look at these pretty undergarments Mr. Moody picked out for Sister," she said and smacked her lips with delight. "It looks kinda dingy, but it's brand new and soft to touch. It comes from a place called Endless Undies by Ruthie up in Atlanta."

Croker's widow looked in the casket as she remarked, "It sure is a long coffin for such a short woman. Elmo's feet come so close to the end in his that we mite near had to bend his knees to get him in there. Course he was over six feet tall. I thought they picked out caskets to fit the body."

"I'm not believing my eyes," Hoover said. "I swear Aunt Glad is going to undress Aunt Erm right here."

"Lord, help us all," Joan said. "She is holding Aunt Erm's leg straight up so everybody can see that damn shoe. Here comes Stump with her leg."

"Where's the other shoe?" Mrs. Gooch asked as Stump handed her the leg.

"Here it is," he said as he reached in his coat pocket. "Let me put it on for you."

"NO! I'll do it. Gayleen," Sister Gooch said to one of the women standing nearby, "would you hold Sister's leg while I put this shoe on it so Mr. Stump can fix it to her?"

"Would you believe they're attaching that leg to her?" Joan asked. "Merciful days, I've seen it all."

"I think the lovebirds have cooled off a little," I said to Stump as he returned to our place behind the trees. "Since the floor show is going so good they seem to have their mind on it. What took you so long? Had Delilah been chewing on it?"

"It was still in the kudzu, and she had nibbled on the toes. She and her friends must have peed on it a hundred times. It cleaned up, and the stocking hides the scratches and teeth marks."

"I didn't know they put shoes on the dead," I heard Hoover say, "especially on a fake foot."

"They usually don't, but Moody probably suggested them knowing Aunt Glad would buy anything, and it was another item to justify gouging us."

"They've got you down pat," Stump whispered, smiled, and smacked his lips.

"Yeah, I know, but at the moment, I am worried about Croker's widow. Can you hear what she's bitching about?"

We watched her rub her hand over the casket, and then heard her speak in a loud voice.

"There's a scratch on this one just like the one on Elmo's. Ewell put it on there when he ran the hearse off the road on the way to the cemetery. Ewell deducted twenty dollars for it. Gladys, has Ewell been driving Erma around town since he put her in the casket? You know he drives his corpses around town late at night. Gladys, do you know about this scratch? It's obviously had a lot of polish on it but still needs some more."

"Hoov," I heard Joan ask, "what is the problem with Lurlene Croker? What in hell is she doing? The fool is on her knees looking at the bottom of the casket. She licked her finger and is trying to rub something off the side. What did she just take out of her pocketbook?"

"Don't know, but I'll move in behind her and find out."

I watched Hoover as he glanced over widow Croker's shoulder, looked at the contents in her hand, and then returned to Joan.

"What did you see?" Joan asked.

"Looks like pictures of Elmo in his coffin. I think she's comparing Aunt Erma's casket with his, and she seems upset."

"Mercy, I knew things were going too good," I said to Stump. I pulled my collar out and rotated my head in an effort to scratch my neck. "We don't need those three getting suspicious about our business. Did you hear the conversation between them?"

"Think so, but listen."

"Maybe she's just a nut," Joan said. "There's one born every minute, but in this town they're born every second and live forever."

"Yeah, I know," Hoover said, "but she might have a reason for what she's doing. First chance I get I'll talk to her, but right now me and you have other things to think about." He placed his hand on her rear and fondled her gently.

We watched as they left the funeral parlor by a side door.

"Maybe the hots they have for each other will make them forget about Lurlene Croker," Stump whispered.

"Let's hope so. In the meantime, help me get these folks out of here. Tomorrow is going to be one hell of a day, and don't forget to remind them of the funeral change, but say it where the Gooch gal can't hear you. Lord, I can't take another one of her fits tonight."

"Is there anything else we can do for you people this evening?"

Stump asked each group of relatives, friends, and nosey thrill-seekers as he walked around the Viewing Room. "If not, I'm sure you would like to get some rest and meet us back here in the morning in preparation for the service which has been rescheduled for three o'clock tomorrow at the Rock Church." The relatives took the hint and most of them left without further coaxing, except Gladys Gooch. I figured she planned to crawl in the box with her dead sister and talk to her all night.

"Mrs. Gooch," I said, "the hour is late and my assistant and I need to apply the final touches to your dear sister in preparation for her final departure, and we're sure you, too, need rest." I placed my right hand on her elbow and gently led her to the door.

"Oh, Mr. Moody," she said before leaving the funeral parlor, "you be sure and leave a light burning all night for Erma. I don't want no disasters falling on this family because she got left in the dark."

"Of course, Mrs. Gooch, of course. I will personally see that the entire funeral parlor is well lighted throughout the night. I certainly do not want anything amiss to fall on your dear sister's family or my humble establishment."

With the family out of the mortuary, I locked the door and hurried around turning on lights.

"What the hell is wrong with you?" Stump asked. "Why are you turning up the lights? We can hardly pay Georgia Power now."

"I swear to God, I have never buried a body that gives me the frigging creeps like this old gal is doing. Something strange is going on. When I brought her in this morning I couldn't remember who she was, but now I do. I remember Grandpa saying that Erma Mae Logan had to be a witch because of the way she got things done. She never set her mind to a thing that she didn't accomplish. She kept a ruckus going on in this town all the time, and he used to laugh at her. Now I remember what she did when her mama died."

"Is she the one that wouldn't let Grandpa touch her mama, but hauled her off in a station wagon to God knows where and did God knows what with her?"

"That's the one. Erma Mae and Springer Yates hauled her up in the woods of Paulding County, and nobody knows to this day what happened to her. She said she promised her mama that nobody was going to give her a funeral like the one they gave her poppa, even though she held a damn shotgun in Grandpa's gut in order to get most of her wishes carried out for the old man. Mercy."

"We may rue the day we didn't cremate the old gal. When did

you start remembering this stuff?"

"When the Gooch gal told me to keep the lights on for her sister, it was like something hit me on the head. Another thing, when I saw her male relatives in cowboy hats, I remembered that she and the Yates guy were once tried for horse rustling and Grandpa served on the jury. Grandpa came home every day laughing about what went on in the courtroom. He seemed convinced the old gal had supernatural powers."

"Ewell, if it's all the same to you, I think I'll stay awake until this old gal is six feet under."

"I'll join you. Let's get Jim Beam and have him set up with us also. We're going to need his company real bad. Mercy. Insurance policies, gold teeth, and a fleet of old Edsels ain't worth this. Mercy."

I've buried virgins, villains, straight shooters, and whores,
But never had a witch at my morgue door
Grandpa's ghost this night will surely appear,
To remind me of my sins and increase my fear.

-Ewell Moody

CHAPTER NINETEEN

Mildred Roper

Leland insisted we leave the funeral parlor before the other relatives and ride around town so we could enjoy the calm before entering the heavy storm we knew awaited us at home. I did not look forward to relatives coming from everywhere, hungry, tired, and in need of a place to stay until this fiasco ended. I found myself wishing I could go to sleep tonight and in the morning wake to find it had all been a bad dream. We stopped at the 7-11 to buy coffee, eggs, and bread to keep from running out of provisions before the festivities were over.

At home we found our street lined with cars, pickup trucks, and motorcycles. A group of older teenagers played croquet and horseshoes on the front grass while the younger children chased lighting bugs under the pecan trees that lined the drive. They were putting the bugs in jars and probably had a prize in mind for the one who caught the most. It brought back memories of Joan's early years when she played with her cousins. If Erma was present when they caught bugs of any kind, they had to set them free for she believed it cruel to catch them in the first place. I made a mental note to see that they emptied the jars before coming in for the night. A young boy I didn't recognize, probably because of his funny looking Indian haircut, sat on a whitewashed stump strumming a guitar and singing. Nearby, a little girl held possession of the tire swing as she pushed herself backward then pulled her bare feet through the soft sand in the pit beneath the swing. I didn't know these kids, but I assumed they were related to me.

"Lord above, look at that," Leland said as he flashed his truck headlights on the door of a red pickup parked near the end of the drive. A painted picture of a guitar glowed in the light, and from the box of the instrument the head of a chicken could be seen. The bird had an open beak as if singing, and painted chicken feathers were around the end of the soundboard. Beneath the picture, in bold yellow letters, Leland read: "Plucking for Jesus."

"That must be Flynn's," I said, and we both laughed. "I sure do dread this funeral, for it's going to be everything Erma hated. I wish I could do something about what's going on, but I don't know what it would be. I certainly messed things up good. This afternoon my spirits were really high when I thought something was going to happen to change this mess, but now I guess it's not. Thank the Lord Joan and Hoover got the funeral changed to tomorrow. At least we'll get it over with quick."

"No, Millie, we won't get it over quick. When them long-winded, foot-stomping, spit-flipping preachers get in the pulpit it could go on for a week, and you know it."

"I reckon so, but at least it'll start tomorrow. That's better than waiting around till Friday."

Leland parked his truck on the street, and we walked the path leading to the front door without talking. The stillness of the warm summer night was broken with the sounds of high twangy voices singing *Asleep in Jeeeezus, blessed sleep, from which non-ev-ver wakes to weep. A calm and....*"

"Lord, what a racket," Leland said. "Sounds like a poor little animal being slaughtered. Bet it goes on all night, and we'll never get to bed. Here comes Joan and Hoover. Let's wait and walk in with them."

"I'm worried about Sophia," I said. "She ought to be here by now."

"Don't worry about that girl. She can take care of herself. Sides that, I'm pretty sure I saw her car out back when we drove up."

"Mama," Joan said as she hurried up the walkway to where we were standing. "Did you notice how strange Lurlene Croker acted tonight at the funeral home?"

"I didn't pay much attention to her, Joan, but me and your daddy left right soon after you and Hoover did. Why, what did she do?"

"That old gal was really upset," Hoover said, "and I think it has something to do with Aunt Erm's casket."

"I wouldn't pay much mind to what Lurlene does," Leland added. "She's a mite loony. When it comes to funerals, she's a lot like Gladys and loves a good one."

"Maybe you're right, Daddy, but I think there's something going on, and me and Hoov plan to check it out. We'll talk about it later."

Joan went in the front door with me and into the kitchen to make coffee and fix dessert to serve the guests. Leland and Hoover walked around the house to the back porch. In the kitchen I was so thankful to see Sophia, my granddaughter, Joan's only offspring from her marriage with Doyle Gibson, her first husband.

"Hello, Mother," Sophia said as she pressed her cheek to Joan's, and then walked over to me. "Hello, Grandmother, I'm sorry I didn't get here in time to go to the funeral home, but I drove by the place. I parked and went up to the door as the lights were bright as the town brothel, but it was locked. An animal snorted and growled through the crack in the front door, and it sounded like cats fighting in the back. What kind of a place is that? It appeared as ominous as the House of Usher." She hugged me long and gentle as she continued to talk. "Grandmother, I can't say I'm sorry to hear of Aunt Erm's death. I'm really glad, for she hung over the brink too long with that old hag Death gnawing at her. I'm happy she's now at peace and you can get some rest."

"I hope you're right, Sophia," I said. "If I knew Erma was at peace, I'd be mighty happy tonight."

"Is something wrong?" she asked.

Before I had a chance to answer, Gladys and her crowd of singers came out of the living room into the kitchen looking for drinks and food.

"Oh, my," Sophia said rather loud. "The creatures of the night are slithering from under their rocks to feed on unsuspecting prey. You had better step back, everyone."

Several older teenagers and Hoover came in the back door at about the same time the others came from the living room.

"Well, well, if it ain't the beautiful brain of the family," Hoover said as he reached for Sophia and held her in his arms. "How in the world is my favorite little second cousin?"

"I'm fine, Hoov, and you?"

"Now that you're here, I couldn't be better." I saw him look at Joan and wink. I watched them leave the funeral home early and wondered where they had gone. If what they did brought them pleasure, then so be it.

Joan filled glasses with tea, placed cups and saucers on the table, and then poured coffee. "While everybody is here in the kitchen," she said, "I have an announcement to make. In case Moody failed to mention it to you, the funeral has been changed to tomorrow at 3:00."

"Oh, my Lord, Joan," Gladys said, almost screaming. "I can't believe you did such an ugly, disrespectful thing to your dear old Aunt's memory. I think I'm going to f—"

"Aunt Glad, shut up until I'm finished. Then you can faint, fart, fornicate, fan, or whatever turns you on, and I really don't care which one you do. Now, as I was saying, if you know anybody that is waiting until Friday to come, you better call and tell them about the change, but don't put any long distance calls on Mama's phone, and I mean it. When the bill comes, I will call every number charged to her and embarrass the fool out of you, and I am not kidding."

"I'm so upset," Gladys whined and tried to cry. "It's mighty disrespectful to put one's own flesh and blood in the ground the day after they pass. I never heard tell of such in all my life. Why the time is so short I won't even have a chance to cut my toenails."

"Aunt Glad," Sophia said, "be glad you're not Jewish, for they are put in the ground before the sun sets on the dead body. So consider yourself lucky. At least you'll have enough hours to cry, squeal, scream, masticate, and beat your boobs before the party's over, and if you work at it, you might find time to trim your nails, shave your pits, plunk your chin hairs, and even bathe."

"You get more like your mama everyday you live," Gladys whined, "and I'm not going to stay in here and listen to this kind of talk. Come on y'all, Flynn, Leonard, Estelle, let's go back in the living room and sang a few more songs. Maybe it will help lift my poor, frazzled spirits."

I noticed Flynn lingering behind and not hanging on Gladys' coattail like he usually did. He walked over to Sophia and stopped in front of her as he spoke.

"Sophia, I understood some of what you said to Aunt Glad, but why did you tell her she would have time to masturbate. That's not a nice thing for a pretty, smart young girl like you to say to an older woman."

"Flynn, the word I used is masticate. It means to eat, chew, grind, whatever. It was my way of saying with the use of one word that she would have plenty of time to eat, stuff her face, and even haul home as much food as she can possibly carry. I doubt Aunt Glad has ever

152

heard the word masturbate, but I'm delighted you have. You've moved up one rung on the ladder of intelligence in my estimation. Jail was obviously good for you. At least it helped improve your vocabulary. There is a light in your little belfry after all. Now go on in the living room so Aunt Glad can cling to the cuffs of your pants and convince herself she is cured of all her maladies."

I smiled and shook my head at the expression on Flynn's face as he silently moved into the living room with the other guests.

"Joan," I said, "I know you're tired, but would you mind trimming your daddy's hair? He's beginning to look like the goat man."

"Don't mind at all, and while I'm at it, I'll cut a few locks from E. J. and Russell. They look like something that's been hibernating under a log and afraid to come out. Sophia, go look for your grandpa and bring him in here. He's probably on the back porch. Tell him to spit out that wad of tobacco before he comes in the kitchen."

I brought in a high stool and placed it in the far side of the kitchen away from the food and lay the clippers, scissors, comb, and bed sheet on a nearby chair. Through the back screen door, I saw Leland with Sophia on the porch. She held her grandfather's arm and whispered to him while Leland laughed like a small boy playing with a favorite friend.

"Child," I heard him say, "you get more like your great Aunt Erma Mae everyday you live. You even look like her with that pretty, shiny brown hair, sparkling brown eyes, and your skinny little body. Course that Indian skin you got from your Daddy makes you even prettier. You should have been born to Erma Mae cause you're as smart and full of as much mischief as she ever dared to be."

Leland sat on the high stool, and Joan wrapped a sheet around him and pinned it in the back. "Daddy, I can give you a better haircut if you take off your hat," she said. "Sophia, go look for Russell and E. J., and tell them they're next. You'll probably find them out front in a pickup listening to that god-awful music they play all the time. Tell them to be in here by the time I finish with Daddy. If they're chewing or dipping, make them spit it out and gargle with something they will find in the bathroom."

"That noise coming out of the living room is enough to clabber milk," Leland said, "and Gladys is sure in hog heaven tonight. Joan, me and your mama really appreciate you and Hoover getting the funeral changed to tomorrow. If Gladys had her way, she'd drag it out till doomsday. Now, Joan, what was it you and Hoover were upset about at the funeral home? Something about Lurlene Croker and

Erma's coffin?"

"Hoov, you tell them."

"I ain't never seen nobody check out a casket like Lurlene Croker checked out Aunt Erma's," Hoover explained. "She looked it over from top to bottom and inside out and was upset because according to her, it looks exactly like Elmo's. The more I think about it, I believe she is convinced it's the very same box Elmo was put in."

"If she's right," Leland said, "there is something mighty fishy going on in Ewell's business. What you reckon we ought to do about it?"

"I plan to talk to Lurlene Croker the first chance I get. Then we'll decide what to do. It's worth looking into."

"I don't know much about Ewell," Leland said, "but Maslow Moody was as reliable as the days of the week and wouldn't cheat nobody. The old man would have given the socks off his feet to anybody he thought needed them, and I know he buried a mighty lot of folks for nothing. He spent a small fortune on Ewell. He sent him to the best schools and tried to give him a good education, but all Ewell ever wanted to do was sit on a creek bank, read, write poetry, and stuff every critter he could get his hands on. Maslow also helped raise Stump Dupree—paid for his education and supported the boy's widow Mama. Just don't have a feel for how Ewell has turned out. Hoover, if you think there's some monkey business going on with Ewell, I say check it out, but be mighty careful about putting too much stock in what Lurlene Croker has to say. I never had much faith in nothing her or Elmo did or said. They was always too busy bragging about their money."

"Now, Daddy, you look like a human being again," Joan said as she dusted her father's neck with talcum powder. She carefully folded the sheet and carried it outside to empty the hairs and returned to the kitchen where E. J. and Russell reluctantly waited for her.

"Now, Mama," E. J. whined, "I don't want but a little bit off the sides. Don't want my ears to show, and keep the hair below my collar in the back. Please don't cut my bangs like you did when I was in grammar school. I know how wild you get with a pair of scissors when there's a head of hair in front of you."

"You're head is filthy," Joan said. "It looks like you've been shampooing with tobacco juice. When I get through cutting your hair, you're getting in Mama's shower and cleaning yourself up. You look like an orphan that has not had a bath since birth."

"Do we have to listen to that racket going on in yonder, Aunt

Joanie?" Russell asked. "They sound worse than a row of chickens hanging by their feet in a processing plant."

"Unfortunately, it is part of the price we have to pay when somebody dies, but just give me a minute to finish up a few things, and then I'll kick them all out. And the sooner I do it, the better."

"If you ask me, which nobody did," Hoover said, "this family is paying a mighty damn big price for Aunt Erm's death."

"How much is it going to cost to cremate her?" Sophia asked, sitting in the corner of the kitchen with her arms around Crowie. "It can't be much, and I know that's what she wanted."

"To make a long story short," Joan said, "the family fiend got to Moody before the rest of us did and made all the arrangements and signed over Aunt Erm's policy money to Moody. Nothing is going to be done our way."

"It's my fault," I said. "I let Erma down by signing those papers."

"No, Mama, you didn't let her down," Joan said.

"Grandmother, whatever happened I know it is not your fault, so don't take the blame," Sophia said as she moved to the back of my chair and placed her arms around my neck. "I know how close you were to Aunt Erm, and I have a pretty good idea what happened at the funeral home. Aunt Glad saw the opportunity to plan a barbaric funeral with Aunt Erm's gussied-up body lying in an expensive casket with the entire county parading by and extolling their praise upon Aunt Glad for the beautiful memory picture she painted, and she couldn't pass it by. Also, Grandmother, you must remember, Aunt Glad has a distinct tendency towards necrophilia. You also realize that Moody certainly had no intentions of discouraging Aunt Glad from donating a few coins to his coffer when he realized how anxious she was to win an Oscar for the most ostentatious funeral of the year. And Moody was certainly not going to let Aunt Erm escape his mortician's artwork. Grandmother, you were doomed the moment you walked up Moody's steps with Aunt Glad beside you."

"What in the world made Aunt Erm want to be burned up anyhow?" Russell asked. "I ain't never knowed nobody else in this family to want such as that done to them. Course I know she had some strange ideas but never did know what brought this one on."

"Well, boy, since you asked, I'll tell you," Hoover said.

"I figured you would."

"Just let me freshen up my Bud, and then we'll reminisce."

While Hoover reached for another beer, Sophia placed her hands on my shoulders and whispered in my ear. "Relax, Grandmother. Forget about this day, and don't think about tomorrow. Try to enjoy the moment as we reminisce about Aunt Erm, *for memories are the essence of life.*"

CHAPTER TWENTY

Mildred Roper

About thirty or so year ago," Hoover began after opening a fresh can of Bud, "Aunt Erm was told by Doc Frank to get her marbles in a circle cause the grim reaper was about to start cutting in her wheat field. Aunt Erm, not wanting to cause nobody any problems, whether she be dead or alive, decided to plan her own funeral."

"I've heard that tale so many times already, and I sure don't want to hear it tonight," Gladys said as she and her followers entered the kitchen for another singing break.

"Well, Big Mama, we want to hear it," Russell said, "so please let Hoover tell it."

Hoover blew a few smoke rings in the air, and then continued to spin his yarn. "One day, Aunt Erm got herself all dressed up in her Sunday go to meeting best, made up her face, and put on a hat. Then she called me and Joanie and asked us to go with her to the funeral home to visit Grandpa Maslow."

"She always wanted you and Joan to go with her everywhere she went," Gladys snarled. "She taught y'all to get into as much mischief as she got into."

"Go on with your tale, Hoover," I said, trying to cut Gladys off.

"Russell, what in the name of God is in your head?" Joan asked, as she held up the comb. "It looks like chicken mess on your scalp. I can't cut hair this dirty. It's enough to make me sick to my stomach. Come with me, I'm going to wash your head."

"You should find everything you need in my bathroom closet, Joan, go on with your tale, Hoover. We're listening."

"But I wanted to hear it," Russell whined. "I'm the one that asked him to tell it in the first place."

"It won't take but a few minutes to wash your head, and Hoov will talk slow until you get back. Stop whining," Joan said as she pulled Russell by the ear towards my bathroom.

"Let me open a fresh one, Aunt Millie," Hoover said as he reached into his cooler and pulled out a Bud. "Like I said, me and Joanie and Aunt Erm went to see Grandpa Maslow. Aunt Erm walked in and told him she wanted to plan her funeral. She reckoned her body would have to be put somewhere soon, and when the time came she wanted to be the one to say where even if she didn't have control over the when."

"Didn't do her much good to make that decision," Leland said, "seeing as how nothing she requested is being carried out."

"Well, I'm telling you that what's being done with her is a heck of a lot better than what she wanted done," Gladys said. "Just goes to show that nobody should have a say in what happens to them after they pass because their next of kin is alive and the dead ain't."

"Y'all let Hoover go on with his tale," I said. I didn't want to get Gladys started again. I was too tired to listen to her any more than I had to, and I did enjoy hearing good stories about Erma.

"As I was saying, before I was so rudely interrupted," Hoover continued. "Aunt Erm told Maslow she was there to plan her funeral, and she'd start by picking out a casket. Maslow had a funeral about to start, so he led us to the casket room and told us to help ourselves. Aunt Erma found one she liked and asked us to lift her in. She lay down, stretched out, and got real comfortable. I'll always remember what she said after she lay there a few minutes. She said it felt about as good as a motel bed her and Springer had been in a few months before he died. They put quarters in it to massage their backs. She told me and Joanie to look around and see if it had a slot we could drop a few coins in while she lay there dreaming. About the time she got relaxed, we heard women talking and coming towards the room where we were. Aunt Erm folded her arms across her chest, closed her eyes, and told me and Joanie to hide and stay quiet as field mice."

"I've never in my life heard such foolishness, and these young folk don't need to hear this," Gladys snarled between bites of whatever she was eating at the time. She really annoyed me, opening cabinets and removing foil from containers.

"Gladys," I asked, "what are you looking for? Have you lost something in my kitchen?"

"Where is the pound cake Janet Stansell brought this afternoon? Is there any more, or did the kids eat it up?"

"It's in the pie saver, Gladys. Get it and please get out of here or keep your mouth shut while Hoover finishes his tale. If you don't want to hear it, go on back in the living room and sing to yourself, and for once try having a little consideration for the rest of the family."

"Well, I've never," she said opening the pie saver.

"Aunt Glad, Hoover is going to finish this tale whether you approve or not," Sophia said, "and then I'm anxious to hear the story of how Aunt Erm got the land zoned for the nudist camp. I also want to hear how she saved the tree in the middle of the square and how she managed to keep Bochim Creek from being stopped-up. All my life I've heard everyone whisper and giggle about some of the things she did, but no one has ever told me the true stories. Tonight I intend to hear all of them even if I have to sit here snuggled up to Crowie until breakfast, so please do as Grandmother asked you to and get in the living room and please don't return until we've all gone to bed."

"Sophia, those tales don't need to be told to nobody, nowhere, no time, and y'all don't have to be so rude," Gladys mumbled with her mouth full of cake.

"I see nothing wrong with the stories, Gladys," I said. "If the young people want to know more about their great Aunt Erma Mae, I say let them. It's nothing to be ashamed of. I happen to be proud of the things my sister did for this town, and you ought to be."

"Hogwash."

"Uncle Leland will have to tell about the nudist episode," Hoover said. "I was probably too young to be there, but she had Springer with her on that occasion. I do remember the tree and the creek episodes," Hoover said, giggling. "Go ahead, Uncle Leland and tell it. I'll finish my story later."

"Your age never stopped her from taking you places before," Gladys reminded Hoover. "Lord, she had you driving her everywhere in that old car by the time you was twelve years old. You couldn't see out the windshield and had to sit on pillows or phone books. If Erma had not been friends with the sheriff both of you would have been put in jail."

"Tonight at the funeral home, some guys on the front porch were laughing and telling a story about Aunt Erm and Springer Yates being arrested and put on trial for horse rustling. Is there any truth to what they were saying?" E. J. asked.

Leland laughed. "Yep, there shore is, and before y'all leave to go back home I'll get around to that one, but let me tell about the nudists first. Like Hoover just said, Erma didn't need him on this occasion, she had Springer. I wasn't there either, but I had friends on the County Commission that stopped by the next morning and told me what her and Springer did. According to my recollection, Erma had a campaign going to get land zoned so a bunch of folks could build a place to run around naked. She tried everything in the world to get the commissioners to approve it, and course they wouldn't do it. One night when the commissioners were meeting, Erma and Springer showed up unannounced or uninvited whichever way you look at it."

"Her and Springer was always showing up in places they didn't have no business being," Gladys said. "Flynn, you want a piece of this cake? It's mighty good. Course a carrot cake would have been better."

"Go on, Leland," I said. "I'll fix a fresh pot of coffee."

"Anybody else need a trim before I clean up my mess and put up my tools?" Joan asked.

"Yeah, Joanie, I'll let you trim mine a little," Hoover said. "Just on the sides."

"That's the only place you've got any," Russell said.

"At least I don't have a head full of chicken shit."

"Now boys stop your bickering so I can go on with my tale," Leland said. "As I was saying, that night the commissioners was meeting in the basement of the Baptist Church, and all of a sudden the doors flung wide open and in walked Erma Mae and Springer Yates," Leland giggled. "'Good evening, gentlemen,' Erma Mae said. 'If I'm correct, the law is clear that any citizen of this county has a right to come to one of these meetings if he or she has something to say, and me and Springer intend to speak our minds. For months now, us and a lot of folks in this town have been trying to get you men to approve a piece of land so a few law abiding citizens of this State can exercise their freedom by discarding their clothes while participating in a few games and activities.

"'Somehow you gentlemen seem to feel that when people get naked they become murders, robbers, rapist, child beaters, and lose their faith in Jesus. Springer and I intend to show you that ain't so. We are here tonight to prove that a naked person is just as good a law abiding citizen and Christian as a person sitting in church wearing long Johns, brogan shoes, or a fur coat.' While Erma was talking, none of the men paid much attention to Springer, but all of a sudden he stepped out from behind the Coke machine buck naked." Leland began laughing so hard he had trouble talking.

"I have to interrupt you, Uncle Leland," Flynn said, "and ask if Aunt Erm and Springer was saved?"

"Don't know about that, Flynn," Leland said. "I never had the occasion to discuss their religion with them." He took his handkerchief out of his pocket and wiped his face.

"They never was saved," Gladys said as she ate a drumstick and licked her fingers. "Mama made Erma get baptized when she was twelve and when she come up out of the water she goosed the preacher in a place no decent woman would ever put her hand on a man. He got so upset he might near drown the next one he put under, and that's the Lord's truth. I ought to know cause the next one was me."

I looked around the room at the faces, and everyone with the exception of Flynn and Gladys were bent over laughing. The laughter seemed to lift my spirits and renew my physical strength a little.

"Go on, Leland," I said.

"When the commissioners saw Springer naked they was somewhat taken back. Mac Mars ran over and took a picture off the wall, turned it around, and sit it on the floor. Said he didn't want the woman who sewed the first flag for this country to see the goings on in that room. Millie, I'll have a cup of coffee if it's ready. Jimmy Rakestraw jumped up and locked the door. He then pulled down the blinds and turned out the lights, but the others made him turn them back on." Leland couldn't talk for laughing.

"Grandfather, what happened next?"

"All I can tell you, Sophia, is what the men told me. Springer picked up the Bible and started reading out loud, and when the men looked at Erma she was taking off her clothes. She looked at them and smiled.

"'You see, gentlemen,' she said, 'when a man is naked he can still serve the Lord. Does Springer read the thirteenth chapter of first Corinthians any different than if he had on his clothes? Don't you just feel the love in his heart he's reading about?'"

"That was plumb blasphemous," Flynn said. "I can't believe Aunt Erma did such a thing."

"Well, Flynn, old boy, nobody gives a freaking cat's ass whether you believe it or not, but she did it. Now sit down and shut up so Uncle Leland can finish."

"Hoover, you don't have to be so ugly to Flynn," Gladys said, with a whine and a mouth filled with the Lord knows what.

"I wouldn't if he wasn't such a dumb, greasy-headed, pompous, snaggletooth ass. Go on Uncle Leland."

"Erma Mae took off her clothes one piece at a time, folded them real neatly, and lay them on a table while she talked. 'You see gentlemen,' she said, 'now that Springer is naked, he hasn't developed an uncontrollable desire to run right out and rape young girls, stab old men, or molest children, and if you'll notice, no part of his body has increased in size since he became naked. Now, I ask you, do you see any reason why good, law abiding, God fearing citizens can't have the right to be as free as they want to be without any danger of harming others or themselves?' When Erma Mae got down to nothing but her brassier and step-ins, and they was red, Earl Larson, chairman of the commissioners, might near had a heart attack. He jumped up and said, 'Now, Miss Erma Mae you don't have to take off anything else. You and Springer have made your point. Y'all put back on your clothes, and I'll call for the question right now.'"

"That is the worst tale I ever heard in my life," Gladys said. "They ought to have locked her and Springer in the jail and left them there until they learned some sense, if that was possible? The next day her and Springer's pictures was in the Atlanta paper. If that wasn't bad enough, folks started calling from everywhere plumb aghast at what was going to happen in this county when a bunch of naked, white trash people moved in and all because of Erma and that trashy man she shacked up with all them years."

"Aunt Erm was way ahead of her time," Sophia said as she snuggled up to Crowie. "It takes a strong and rare woman to accomplish the good Aunt Erma did. Aunt Glad, the man you describe as trashy, I see as a role model for the way a man should be to the woman he truly loves. He supported Aunt Erm in all her endeavors, and they loved each other unconditionally. One day I hope to find a man that loves and cherishes me as much as Springer did Aunt Erm."

"Hogwash."

"The camp was established a long time ago," I said, "and it's still here. Folks drive from Atlanta and the North Georgia Mountains during good weather to spend the weekends here. They've never caused any problems and have done a lot of good for the town by buying from the storeowners. Way I see it, Erma did a good deed."

"Good deed, my foot," Gladys snarled. "What she did that night was might near as bad as her trying to organize a KKK."

"Aunt Erm was never a racist. She never disliked blacks, Jews, or gays, so why would she have wanted to organize a KKK?" Sophia asked. "I don't understand."

"Aunt Erma wanted a different kind of organization from the KKK as we know it," Joan explained. "She believed that if a bunch of white men could run around town in white sheets with their faces covered up doing all kind of mischief and meanness to anybody they chose to do it to, then she was entitled to form an organization to help the people they were persecuting. She wanted her organization limited to women, black men, and homosexuals, with their activities directed against preachers, hunters, and hypocritical churchgoers,"

"Sounds good to me," Sophia said, "that last group would have included just about everybody in this county."

"And they were going to wear pink sheets," Gladys added. "Erma had already started dying some. Lord, I was mortified at the thought of her walking up and down the streets of this town with a bunch of black men, queers, and women all dressed in pink sheets and pointed hoods. They would have looked like a flock of washed-out male Cardinals trying to breed. My word."

"If she had things organized well enough to be dying sheets, how come it didn't go through?" Russell asked.

"Because your dear aunt was in a corn crib fire the night before the big march and got her leg done in," Gladys said.

"The hand of the Lord certainly took over that time," Flynn added.

"Bullshit!" Hoover yelled as he stood up, kicked over his chair, and pointed his finger at Flynn. "If you say another word about the Lord being responsible for Aunt Erm losing her leg, I won't be responsible for what I'll do to you."

"Man, I tell you, I would have been scared to death if I'd been a preacher or a hunter in this town if she had gotten that organization going," Russell said. "Wouldn't you, Hoov?"

"Boy, you better believe it. She would have cut off their balls in the public square with a dull knife and enjoyed every whack."

"I never understood why she hated hunters so much," Gladys said as she spooned banana pudding into small dishes and passed them among the guests. "She ate meat."

"She did not," I said. "She didn't eat meat when we were children. When times were hard and about all we had was pork and Mama put grease into nearly everything we ate, Erma might near starved to death."

"Well, I know for a fact she ate worms, and if that ain't meat, I don't know what is."

"Aunt Glad, what the hell are you talking about?" Joan asked.

"Gurdy said the night the corn crib caught fire and everybody was standing around waiting for the ambulance that would haul Erma to Atlanta, Springer told the men in the crowd that him and Erma was licking salt out of each other's belly buttons and drinking liquor that had little worms in the bottle when he laid his cigar on a two by four and it fell in a pile of shucks."

The room filled with laughter, but Gladys and Flynn had no idea why we were laughing.

"What a woman. Aunt Erm is without a doubt my best role model. She certainly *burned her candle at both ends.*"

"Sophia, for the life of me, I can't understand why you would want to be like her. The woman had to be a little touched in the head. Come on Flynn and the rest of y'all. Let's go sing some more. I've heard all I want to hear about Erma for one night."

"Aunt Glad, there will be no more singing tonight," Joan said. "Mama is tired, and it's late. We have a big day waiting for us tomorrow, and it will start early and probably never end. Besides that, the racket y'all call singing could stop a lynch mob, and if there are any running around here tonight, I don't want them stopped. We might need them to—"

Before Joan completed her sentence, I heard Estelle banging out "Whispering Hope" on the piano.

"Joan," Gladys said, "We are just going to sang a few verses of "Amazing Grace" and then have Flynn lead us in a word of prayer. It won't hurt this family to pray together just once more. After all, we won't be together but one night since you changed the day of the funeral."

"NO!" Joan yelled. "Mama has been up every night for weeks, and she is worn to a frazzle. Nobody is going to sing another song around here tonight or pray a prayer unless they do it silently, and I mean it. You have already sung that damn, creepy song a dozen times tonight, and I don't want to hear about a worm such as you again, so hang it up."

I stood in the door of the living room and watched Gladys sit down and place her arms over her stomach. She stuck out her lower lip as if trying to cry. Flynn walked over to Joan and gently touched her on the right elbow.

"Joanie," he said, "I know your mama is under great strain, but that don't give you no cause to be rude to Aunt Glad."

"Look, Flynn," Joan replied as she jerked her elbow from his touch. "Get off your pious high horse, and get the bloody hell out of here so we can clean up this mess and get ready for tomorrow."

"Joan," Flynn said, trying one more time to deal with her. "There is no need for the use of bad language around our young people, and I don't see how singing one more song and having a short prayer is going to bring harm to nobody."

"Look, jailbird," Joan said, "to start with, you don't know how to pray, and if you did you sure as hell don't know when to stop. I for one am too tired to stand on my aching feet while you run your mouth off to the Lord about the poor condition of this family. If you want to talk to Him, find somewhere else to do it, but stop farting around and get out of here. You flatter yourself to think He would even listen, and if He does He's probably as sick and tired of hearing you bump your gums and say nothing as I am." Applause came from the young people.

"I honestly think Aunt Glad believes that if someone sick touched the hem of Flynn's coattail they would be healed," Sophia said.

"He probably believes it too," Hoover added. "Or if he spit in the eyes of the blind they would regain their sight."

"Wouldn't he be cute trying to spit with a front tooth missing?" Sophia said.

"Not only that, I'll bet he can't pull worms out of the ground like he used to do as a kid with his front tooth missing."

During the playing of "Amazing Grace," I watched Joan lower the fall board on the piano, barely missing Estelle's fingers but finally getting through to Gladys and the rest of the guests that she meant what she had said and it was time for all of them to leave.

Leland stood with me in the doorway as we said goodnight to everyone, then Flynn stopped in front of us as he spoke.

"Aunt Millie, I know you're a fine Christian woman, but Uncle Leland, I just want to ask if you have made your peace with Jeeeezus?"

"Well, Flynn, it never crossed my mind that me and Him had ever squabbled. I shore don't find no fault with Him, and if He ever found any with me, He ain't got around to telling me about it."

Flynn grunted and looked like he had been slapped in the face again for about the fifth time tonight.

Joan walked around the living room picking up handbags and holding them up as if auctioning them off. As they were claimed she pointed the owner to the nearest door. Reluctantly, the relatives parted and went their separate ways.

"That Joan gets to be more like your poppa every day she lives," Leland said as we watched her escort the last guest from the house.

"She gets more like Erma, and I'm proud of her. At least she knows how to handle Gladys."

"Grandmother," Sophia said, "Aunt Glad is a Leo and must stand out from the herd. Through her selfish, deranged greed she will attempt to have her own way regardless of the pain it causes others. Before this momentous occasion ends, Aunt Glad will be no more than one unnoticed fat cow in the herd where she belongs. Trust me, Grandmother, it will happen."

"Good night, Sophia," I said as me and Leland walked towards the bedroom. "It has been mighty good having you with us tonight. I appreciate you asking Leland and Hoover to tell tales about Erma. I needed to hear them."

"Don't fret, Grandmother," Sophia said as she hugged and kissed us both good night. "I have a strong feeling things will turn out differently than what you expect, and Aunt Erm shall triumph after all. Keep the faith. Our friends in the spirit world will not forsake us. I feel sure they have a plan in process even now, and it will be carried out. Have a good night, and I'll see you in the morning."

Yes, Sophia, I thought, I will keep the faith for it *is the substance of things hoped for, the evidence of things not seen.*

CHAPTER TWENTY-ONE

Mildred Roper

The night for most of the relatives gathered for Erma's funeral was much too long, and those sharing sleeping quarters with kin they had not seen since the last funeral was hardly a time to cherish. Most of the young kids and teenagers spread their sleeping bags on the floor of my front porch where chatter could be heard long into the night. To add a little excitement during the long, dark hours, the brave and daring among the clan ventured to the kitchen for food and drinks, but only after being assured Joan had gone to bed in the back bedroom and would not pose a threat to their lives.

I had not gone to sleep when I heard a young female cousin scream. She was using the bathroom in the side yard when Riverrunt, the neighbor's hound, touched his nose to her naked bottom. Unfortunately for the young folks, she woke up Joan who threatened to lock all of them in the corn crib if she heard another peep.

When all was finally quiet on the front porch, I drifted into a peaceful sleep, and during those hours when both my mind and body were at rest, I dreamed again of Erma.

I walked alone in the woods in late summer, and in the distance a fire burned brightly against the glow of dust. As I came near the blaze I heard the popping of dry pines and oak burning. The flaming wood gave off a pleasant odor. A circle of women seated on three-legged milking stools stretched their hands out to the fire in the middle of the circle as if warming their palms. They turned towards me and smiled.

There were no more dreams the rest of the night, but I slept soundly.

The night seemed short, but when I awoke at 7:30 and heard the early morning cooing of the doves and the cawing of Erma's favorite birds, the crows, I felt rested and somehow knew things would be alright. I knew beyond a shadow of a doubt Erma was trying to communicate with me, and in her own time and her own way her message would come through. I did not know what it would be or what would be expected of me, but I would wade that creek when I came to it. If I needed help, I felt sure I could count on Leland, Joan, Hoover, and Sophia, and if they thought me crazy they would never admit it like the other relatives would do. I wanted to talk with Sophia about my feelings, as I knew she would be the most understanding and could give me insight about the situation with Erma, but it seemed I was never alone with her.

At this early hour, board games were in full force on both porches. They were playing chess, checkers, pickup sticks, monopoly, and Chinese checkers. All the games belonged to Erma. When she was not reading, she looked for somebody to play games with her. Leland was always ready to play checkers, and they must have played hundreds of games during her lifetime. Any kid that came into the house never left before he or she had played a game with Erma. Even when she took to her bed with her final illness, she still read and played games until a few days before her death.

"You look more rested this morning, Mama," Joan said, turning pancakes off the griddle, as I entered the kitchen. "Did you sleep well?"

"Yes, I did sleep well. I can't believe you got breakfast started without me. I guess I was dead to the world."

"You needed the rest, Mama, and I'm glad you were able to sleep. I hope that bunch of wild hyenas on the porch didn't bother you too much. I should have made them sleep in the crib or the barn loft. Course if I had, the whole place would have gone up in flames the way they were smoking out there during the night. Fix your plate, Mama, and sit at the table. You are not going to do anything strenuous today, and I mean it."

I obeyed Joan's orders and filled my plate from the food on the counter top and sat at the kitchen table. Platters of sausage, bacon, fatback, and pancakes, prepared by Joan and several women from the church, filled the table. Eggs were fried, scrambled, poached, and boiled. Large pans of homemade biscuits and blueberry muffins were taken from the oven and doused with butter. Maple syrup, strawberry and blackberry jam, sorghum syrup, honey, and sawmill gravy were available to make the biscuits tastier. I found it enjoyable to eat food cooked by somebody else, especially in my house. When I finished my breakfast, I walked around the kitchen, dining room, and porches to see if anybody needed anything.

The teenagers and young kids filled their paper plates and returned to the front porch that now reeked of stale cigarettes, sweaty bodies, fried bacon, and where heavy betting was in progress over the games being played. The men carried their plates to the back porch, and the women sat around the kitchen and dining room tables.

Hoover, among the early risers, leaned against the refrigerator nibbling a slice of fatback. I heard him make remarks to those who crossed his path.

"You babes get wasted last night?"

The hefty young blond, dressed in a Bull Dawg sweatshirt with her hair in plastic curlers, smirked and walked on by. She carried a diet Pepsi and a plate of fried bacon.

"You're a pretty little slip of a thing," Hoover remarked to a younger cousin.

"And you're a dirty old man," she answered, stuck out her tongue, and walked on.

"Them pants you're wearing are tight enough to give you varicose veins in the rear," he said.

"At least I've got something to put in mine. Get my drift?"

"You're a brazen little tart, now ain't you?"

In the hustle of feeding the crowd, no one noticed Gladys missing until the phone rang around 8:30 and I answered.

"She has done what? Goodness gracious. How long has she been there? I'll send some help right down." I placed the receiver in the cradle and shook my head in disbelief, debating to myself as to what I should do. The temptation was not to send help. My day would be a lot better if she did not come, but I knew I could not do that.

"That was Gurdy," I said. "Gladys decided to take a bath this morning."

"But it ain't Saturday," someone remarked.

"But it's the right occasion."

"It's a good thing somebody dies every now and then or she'd never get a bath."

The kitchen quickly filled with curious minds to hear what Gladys had done to make her late for her favorite festivities.

"Bet she hasn't had a bath since the last funeral."

"Don't knock it, man. Every time she takes one, we have a water

169

shortage."

"The only time she changes her clothes is after a bath, or have you noticed?"

"Aunt Glad is like Mother Nature," Sophia added. "She only changes with the seasons. I'd like to do a life reading on her. Perhaps that would shed light on her eccentric behavior."

"Eccentric behavior my foot," E. J. snarled at his sister. "Where do you get them big words and dumb ass ideas?"

"Baby Brother, it would be impossible for someone with a head filled with hayseed to understand what I'm talking about so don't even try," Sophia responded.

"Whoever said educating a woman is like putting a knife in the hand of a gorilla sure knowed what they was talking about."

"Well, Beetle Bailey, I'm impressed. You can actually quote an entire line without stuttering, and I wasn't aware that you could read. That is truly an accomplishment from a member of the sex that often cut their wisdom teeth late in life, and for future reference, please use were with they and the correct conjugation of the verb know is knew. There is no such word as knowed."

"You can shove it up your—"

"E. J.," Joan interrupted her youngest child, "you and Sophia stop bickering so Mama can tell us what happened and what we need to do."

"Gurdy said Gladys can't lift herself out of the bathtub because it's so slick from the bath oil she poured in the water."

"Either the Lord or Avon is on our side today," Hoover said, still munching a slice of fatback. "Whichever, it don't matter, but we're mighty grateful. I vote we leave her there until after the funeral."

"I agree with you, Hoover," Leland said. "It sure would be a lot less ruckus going on around here today if we did. Shame we can't throw Flynn in there with her. Course ain't no way his feet would touch the bottom of the tub seeing as how he can walk on water."

"If you give her enough cough medicine and a can of snuff, she could stay there forever."

"Laying in that tub, I'll bet she looks the world like a washed-up whale laying in the gutter."

"Why did Gurdy call us?"

"He needs help to get her out."

"Don't hear no volunteers."

"Bet we could put a fur coat on an irate bull easier than we can get her out of the tub."

"How come Leonard and Gurdy can't do it by themselves?"

"They're not strong enough."

"Nor got enough sense."

"Aunt Glad and Uncle Gurdy remind me of Jack Sprat and his wife," Sophia said.

"Who the hell are they?"

"Probably somebody she met in Athens."

"How many men you think it will take to hoist her out of the tub?"

"About six and a crane."

"Y'all stop being ugly and go on down there and help her out," I said, even though I knew how most of them felt. "For Erma's sake, please be nice to one another for one day."

The remarks stopped immediately. Leland, Hoover, and two other adult male relatives left the breakfast party to assist Gurdy in lifting Gladys from her bath.

"Call us if you need more help," I said.

The men were able to get the job done, and Gladys arrived at my house around 9:30 dressed in a dark green sleeveless dress with a white square collar and two large pockets. With the aid of her cane, she made her way into the kitchen and placed her order for breakfast with one of the churchwomen. She then took a seat at the dining room table.

"I ain't real hungry this morning," Gladys said, "seeing as how I am a tad lightheaded from no sleep and too much soaking in the tub."

"Your lightheadedness might be from that blue stuff on your hair soaking into your brain," Hoover said.

"I'm telling you right now," she said, ignoring Hoover's remarks. "I have never been so embarrassed in my life just sliding around in that tub like a greased hog and not able to get off my rear. Estelle helped me get on some step-ins and a blouse before the men came in to help me out. I wanted to shave my underarms and my legs but by the time they got me out I was so stove-up I couldn't raise my arms up to my pits or bend over to put a razor to my legs."

"Did you trim your toenails, Aunt Glad?"

"Lord, no, Sophia. It'll be a long time before I can do that since I can't squeeze scissors with the hand that got caught in the casket lid yesterday, and it's the same hand that got a stapler in the thumb. I've had a lot of bad luck in the last day or so, and I got so bruised up bumping around in the tub that there ain't no way I can get my hands down to my toes even if I could squeeze my fingers. I'll just have to wear these old flip-flops to the funeral. I can't help it. Now if I had a lot of money like Lurlene Croker, I could get Doc Frank to trim my toenails for me. You know it's a disgrace that she pays him thirty-five dollars just to trim her toes. Course that's neither here nor there. As I was saying, while I was sitting in the tub I just knew all that water would make me pass a rock right out my bladder and cause me to miss Erma's funeral after I had worked so hard to get it just right. Y'all know I believe it's more than luck that got me here. I think it was meant for me not to miss the funeral."

"Aunt Glad," Sophia said, "I'm sure you are correct. *A lucky man is rarer than a white crow. Shallow men believe in luck, wise and strong men in cause and effect.*"

"Jesus Christ!"

"No, Emerson."

"I would have been here a lot sooner, if I had not had to clean last winter's coal out of my bathtub before I could take a bath."

"She keeps her winter coal in the bath tub?"

"Yeah.

"Does that tell you how long it has been since she had a bath?"

"Here's your breakfast, Gladys," Maureen Cox, a long time friend of the family, said as she placed a platter in front of Gladys. It held six slices of fried fatback, three sausage patties, four eggs sunny side up, a scoop of grits, three large buttermilk biscuits, and a bowl of gravy on the side. Gladys covered the entire platter with the gravy, then took a bottle of cough medicine from her dress pocket and added a few tablespoons of liquid to her mug of coffee.

"Aunt Glad," Hoover asked, "what is that you're putting in your coffee?"

"Medicine for my liver."

"Does it make it better or worse?"

I smiled at Hoover's remarks and then turned my head to speak to Leola and Luther Hightower, who were arriving from the old home place where they slept the night. Leola sat down at the dining room table with her cat Funky on her lap. Luther joined the men on the back porch.

"Would you like some breakfast, Leola?" I asked.

"Yes, me and Funky would like some eggs."

"Would you like to put your cat on the back porch until after you've had your breakfast? How would you like your eggs cooked?"

"Funky likes his cooked with butter and cheese, but cook them just a tad. I don't let him eat raw ones. It causes worms." Funky did a little dance in an effort to get out of her lap, but she kept rubbing him and wouldn't let him go. "Funky will have to stay in here with me. He gets nervous on the back porch and might throw-up his eggs. Sides that, you've got outside cats and he can't be near other animals. He might catch something."

"You mean something like a rat or a chicken?"

I liked Hoover's remark. Course nobody else seemed to pay any attention to it. I looked at him and smiled while listening to Leola continued to give her food order. "My eggs need to be boiled real soft, almost raw. Since my accident, I can't hardly swallow nothing."

"What accident was that?" Hoover asked.

"One night about a year ago, I got a rope hung around my neck, and it might near choked me to death. Now about all I can eat is real soft eggs and crackers soaked in sweet milk. I still wake up in the middle of the night and feel that rope around my neck. It makes my tongue swell up real big."

"What in the world is she talking about?" Hoover asked as we walked into the kitchen.

"She tried to hang herself. That's why she always wears a scarf around her neck. It left bad rope burns. The only thing that saved her was that the shower rod fell and hit her on the head and caused a concussion. I wish she would take that cat away from the table before it makes Joan have a fit." I gave her breakfast order to the women and then went back to the dining room with Hoover following behind me.

"Leola, is that the only cat you brought with you?" I heard Joan ask.

"Yes, it is," she said as she kept massaging the back of the cat's head. "Funk is the only one that don't puke when he rides a long ways."

"Leola," Gladys mumbled with her mouth full, "since you and Luther didn't go to the funeral home last night to see Erma Mae, I thought you might like to go with me this morning. Then we can get back here in time to have a bite of lunch before the funeral."

"I don't know, Aunt Glad," she answered real timid like. I watched her rub the cat's hair backward as if looking for fleas. Cat hairs were flying around the table. "I don't do real good around dead folk."

Gladys poured her coffee in a saucer as she spoke. "You must see Erma one more time. She looks so natural you'd think she was going to sit up and say something. It's a crying shame not to see her. She might even talk to you."

"Natural my ass," Hoover snarled. "There ain't no way on earth Aunt Erm would be caught sitting up talking to nobody looking like she does right now, especially with that damn bush pinned on her shoulder, and you better be glad she can't speak. You wouldn't like what she would say." He winked at me.

Gladys got up from the breakfast table and burped so loud I thought a stream of blue gas would surely cover the dining room.

"Lord, I don't know why I've been so bloated since Erma died." She belched again. "It must be from stress."

"Yes, Aunt Glad," Sophia said, "I'm sure you're right, for it is a known scientific fact that a person may experience extreme stress when eating twice his or her body weight in such a short time, as you apparently have done in the last two days."

"As I was saying, Leola," Gladys said, obviously not hearing a word Sophia spoke, "I really wish you would go with me."

"I don't know, Aunt Glad," Leola whined. "I've not been real good around the dead since Quida got sucked up in the chimney sweeps vacuum cleaner and when we got her out, she was all covered with soot."

"You won't have no trouble looking at my sister," Gladys assured her. "There has never been a more beautiful corpse."

"Aunt Glad, there is no such thing as a beautiful corpse," Sophia said, "and your public exhibition of Aunt Erm's embalmed and heavily made-up body is a revolting spectacle and a disgrace to her memory."

"Sweetheart, you're wasting your time and talent trying to get a message through her thick skull," Hoover said to Sophia. "She has two things on her mind today: food and funeral, and she don't hear nothing else. Ain't that right, Aunt Millie?"

"I'm afraid you're right, Hoover." I heard the ladies call from the kitchen that Leola's eggs were ready. I brought them to her and placed the plate on the table. "If you'll put the cat on the floor, Leola, I'll bring him his eggs."

"He'll be fine eating with me," she said as she broke the eggshell on the side of her plate and scooped out the insides with a knife. The cat stood on the table and ate from one side of the plate as Leola ate from the other. Funky's large fluffy tail swished back and forth and hit Joan in the face.

Joan coughed, pushed her chair back from the table, and stood up. "I'll be damned," she said.

I picked up the coffeepot and followed Joan to the back porch where some of the male guests were eating. Leland turned the handle of an ice cream freezer while two grandkids argued over who would lick the dasher.

"Joan," I said, "please let me bring you some breakfast out here. I know you haven't eaten much, and you did most of the cooking."

"I've had all I want. Thanks anyway, Mama."

"What's wrong, Joan?" Leland asked.

"Leola is feeding that damn cat on the dining room table out of her own plate."

"I know now why they keep her locked up most of the time," Leland said. "She must have drunk a little Nux Vomica like Erma did once a long time ago."

"Uncle Leland, did Aunt Erm really drink that poison?" asked one of the grandchildren.

"Yeah, I'm afraid she did, but she didn't do it on purpose."

Leland turned in his chair like he was ready to spin another yarn. He crossed his legs and spit his tobacco juice in the coffee can.

"It was her poppa's fault."

"Why?"

I walked around the porch refilling coffee cups as I listened to another of Leland's tales of Erma. I then put the pot on the table and sat down for a short break.

"Erma's Poppa fixed some Nux Vomica with sweet milk to give Halfmoon and left it in the icebox and didn't tell Erma about it. She thought it was sweet milk and drunk it."

"Why did he give it to Halfmoon?"

"The old dog got blood poison from hanging out at the sawmill, and before Erma's poppa got around to giving him the Nux Vomica he was might near dead."

"Maybe we ought to give Leola's cat a little dose," Gurdy said.

"Wouldn't be no bad idea," Leland agreed. "Never did have much use for cats unless they stay in the barn where they supposed to and live off mice and milk."

"What's she going to do with it during the funeral?"

"Probably take it with her."

"Joan," I said when Leland and Gurdy had finished talking about the cat. "Please come back in the kitchen and help me and the women clean up. We need to start fixing lunch. The Lottie Moon Bible Class will be here shortly with more food, and we need to clear some places to put it."

"Is nobody going with me to the funeral home early?" I heard Gladys whining.

"I'm sure The Bad Taste Boys, Lunacy and Insipid, will accompany you," Sophia said to Gladys.

"Who the hell is she talking about now?"

"Flynn and Leonard, who else."

"There ain't going to be no time at all to spend with Erma since the funeral's today," Gladys whined and looked at me. "It shows mighty little respect burying somebody the day after they pass. Never heard tell of nothing so bad in all my born days, and I'll never forgive them relatives that have been so disrespectful to my sister. I just hope and pray nobody is that unkind to my memory when I pass."

"Aunt Glad," Joan said, "If I'm around when your time comes, I'll do everything in my power to have you on public display for a month."

"Yeah," Hoover added, "we'll put you in the Town Square where the Buzzards of Bochimville can eyeball you day and night."

"Aunt Glad, I don't understand your behavior," Sophia said. "When Aunt Erm lived, you hated her and disapproved of everything she said and did and, according to you, she has always been an embarrassment to the family. Now that she is dead, the way you carry on one would think the stars in heaven were seen at noon the day she died."

"Y'all don't have no respect for nobody," Gladys whined. "I just want my sister to have a good, wholesome funeral like I hope to have when my time comes."

"Aunt Glad, if I'm still in my earthly body at the time of your departure, I promise to personally see that you are stretched out in Moody's Cuckooland until rigor mortis sets in and your body is turned into an ornamental keepsake. I will then have it permanently encased at city hall where we will make every effort to preserve your body forever just like Eva Peron."

"Yeah, and after you get all stiff and green, we'll stand you in a flower pot and enter you as a nut tree at the Bochimville Goose Fair."

I smiled at Sophia and Hoover's remarks, and then spoke to Gladys. "I'll go with you. There are a few things I want to look over at the funeral parlor, and as Sophia said, I'm sure Flynn and Leonard will go with us. It'll give them a chance to pray and maybe convert a few souls." I looked at Hoover in hopes he would volunteer to come with me.

"Come to think of it," he added. "There are a few things I'd like to check out too. Come on Joanie, we'll drive your mama. Who knows, we might be lucky enough to run into Croker's widow and have a little chat with her about a very important matter."

"Why are y'all so chummy with Lurlene Croker all of a sudden?" Gladys asked. "Hoover, are you thinking about courting her?"

"Can't ever tell, Aunt Glad. If she is willing to support me in a manner to which I would like to grow accustomed, I'm willing to give it a try, but I will tell you one thing. You better enjoy yourself today, because me and Croker's widow might be real close to opening a can of big, juicy worms, and if we do, you ain't going to like the flavor."

And Gladys, I added silently, enjoy yourself today for *we know not what tomorrow will bring.*

CHAPTER TWENTY-TWO

Ewell Moody

The Logan cortege arrived at the mortuary around 11:00 to visit one last time with their dearly departed loved one before me and my boys laid her lavishly clothed body in the red clay of Paulding County. When the family arrived, I was not available to greet them, as my services were needed in the rear of the funeral parlor to supervise the loading of a plywood casket onto the funeral parlor pickup truck.

"Now y'all make sure that box is covered real good," I said, "and tie it down tight. If it slips off on the interstate, I'll most likely be the next one to occupy Stump's slab."

Moss Scofield, the funeral parlor's head gravedigger, truck driver, and all around handyman stood near the cab of the truck. He cut a plug from his chewing tobacco and worked it from one side of his mouth to the other before he spoke.

"Ewell," he said slowly, "we've done this enough times already so don't see no need in your getting yourself all worked up over nothing. You best take it easy. You're sweating like a mule in a log pulling, and your hands are shaking like you need drying out from too much moonshine."

"Moss, I know, I know," I said, "but in this business a body can't be too careful."

"Ewell, why don't you put on your funeral face and go on in yonder and take care of that tacky dressed crowd I just seen come in the front door," Moss suggested as he spit tobacco juice in the dirt. "It looks like all the kinfolk that Logan woman ever had is up yonder waiting for you, but before you go I want to tell you something. The way my joints ached when I crawled out of bed this morning, and the cracking sound my spit makes in the sand, I got no doubt before this day's over it's gonna pour bullfrogs, and I do hate burying folks in the rain especially when I've got to swap them from one box to another."

"Moss, I'm sure it's going to be a hell of a day just from the way it's starting. Mercy, the damn funeral isn't until 3:00 and it's just now 11:00, so why in the hell are they here this early?"

"Must want something mighty important seeing as how they're all dressed up in their Sunday go-to meeting frocks. Maybe they just want to look at that expensive box you sold them."

"If I'd paid that kind of money for a box, I'd want to do more than just look at it," Angus Creek, Moss' son-in-law and assistant gravedigger, said as he helped me tie down the sides of the quilt to the pickup truck. "I'd sit on it or eat out of its lid. Better still, I'd get me a good woman and spend the night in it. Them springs look like they'd have a mighty good bounce to them. Never seen a family so anxious to get one of their kin in the ground. I been digging graves for a long time, but this is the first one I ever dug after dark."

"I'm sorry I had to send y'all up there last night," I apologized, "but the reason she is being buried so quick is because them two old sisters couldn't agree on nothing. The Roper woman didn't want no funeral at all, and when she knew she was going to lose the battle with her sister, her daughter and that Murdock guy insisted the funeral be today, which suits me fine. The quicker we get the old gal in the ground, the mahogany box back in the Selection Room, and these people out of my face, the happier I'll be. Did you get the tent up?"

"Course we did, and talking about digging in the dark, I don't have no hankering to do no more like last night neither. I tell you, Ewell, it was plumb spooky up there in Paulding County digging by lantern light. Angus, did you tell Ewell about the old man?"

"What old man?" I asked.

"Me and Angus was minding our own business, digging away, when all of a sudden here stands this old man beside the grave. Just sort of watching us. In one hand he held a big stick, and in the other hand he held the end of a rope tied around the neck of a scrawny little old white heifer. White as snow. Never seen nothing so white. Man didn't say nothing. Don't know where he come from. Don't know what he wanted. Don't know where he went. Just sort of like he appeared and then disappeared. Make matters worse, an old hoot owl sit on a limb and watched every move we made. I tell you, Ewell, something is off kilter about all this casket swapping. When folks find out what we're doing, you are one greased goose."

"Moss, you believe in too many old wives' tales. Get your mind on the business at hand and stop fretting over white heifers, old men, and hoot owls. Mercy. When you get the truck up there this afternoon, you better hide it way back in the woods and keep an eye on it."

"Lord, Ewell, we know what to do," Moss assured me. "By the way, it was a full moon last night when we dug the grave, so there ain't gonna be enough dirt to fill it up. Better throw some lumber scraps and junk in the truck, seeing as how I know you ain't about to bury the vault you sold them."

"Plenty of broken concrete blocks on the other side of the barn. Take what you need. I know you can take care of things, Moss, but I'm a little antsy about that Murdock man and his gal cousin. She's the daughter of the Roper woman, and they ain't a bit happy with how the old Logan gal's money is being spent, and I'm mighty afraid they're going to retaliate somehow. I know I should get enough money for this funeral without swapping the box this time, but if something happens and I don't get that lovely green stuff, without the mahogany box I'm done." I threw a rock at several male dogs in my parking lot, then picked up Delilah and put her on the loading dock. "Besides that, Croker's widow made me a mite edgy last night comparing pictures of her old man's casket to the old maid's, so I have a right to be fidgety as a bitch in heat."

"I know, I know, Ewell, but we got things under control now, so you take it easy. Before this day is over maybe we'll all be walking with the wind on our backsides."

"I sure as hell hope so, Moss."

With the truck loaded to my satisfaction, I sent Moss and Angus on their way with a few additional words of caution. "Keep that truck within the speed limit there and back, and stay out of the fast lane. The thought of that mahogany box being impounded makes my hemorrhoids act up so bad I can't think about ever sitting down again."

I watched until the truck was out of sight before I stepped into the cool funeral parlor, bowed my head, and prayed softly. "Lord, if there is a Lord, don't let nothing go wrong with this deal today because if it does I could lose my ass. You remember me just this once, Lord, and when that wad of loot is placed in my hands, I'll remember you. I promise, Lord, I promise."

I wiped the sweat from my brow and decided to sneak down the hall to my office and tidy up before coming face to face with the Logan vulture squad. I noticed Stump waiting for me near the surgery door.

"Ewell, you'll never believe who is waiting for you in your office."

"Who?"

"Freddy Featherbone."

"Mercy, do you know what he wants?"

"Don't have the slightest idea," Stump answered. In one hand he carried a rolled-up Batman comic book and in the other a kraut covered hot dog. "Probably wants to sell you something."

"He certainly didn't come to give me anything, that's for sure. Don't you have anything better to do than read comic books and eat cabbage covered dogs?"

"It's lunch time, Ewell. Man can't live by booze alone, at least not all of us can. Freddy's got a suitcase with him, so he might be planning to move in. What do you want me to do with the buzzard?"

"Stick it in the freezer. I'll stuff the damn thing tomorrow or the next day, or the next. Mercy!"

> *There was a mortician named Moody*
> *Whom some thought very fruity.*
> *At night he did prowl and by day he stuffed fowl.*
> *That fruity mortician named Moody.*
>
> - Ewell Moody

CHAPTER TWENTY-THREE

Ewell Moody

It had been a long time since I had seen Freddy Featherbone, and I wasn't exactly thrilled with seeing him today. He was always full of surprises, and hell, I had enough to do just dealing with the Logan family without my past catching up with me. I remembered Freddy as a short, stocky man, now in his late forties and probably bald as a mosque. I wondered if he still had the lizard on his left arm that he had tattooed there one night when we were half crocked. I won't say what I got tattooed at the same time, but at least mine doesn't show except when I'm at the nudist camp. Down there nobody gives a crap, except the time I won first place in the camp's Tattoo Contest for the Most Original Tattoo in the Most Unique Place.

As I entered my office, I saw him sitting at my desk dressed in a pink shirt and brown slacks with his brown, untied, scuffed wingtips on my desk. When I saw his swollen ankles I knew why he couldn't tie his shoes. From what I could tell he hadn't changed much in appearance. He still chewed on an unlighted cigar like he did when we were teenagers. When I entered the office he stood and offered his hand, but before I had time to shake it, he went into a coughing fit and jerked his hand back to cover his mouth. I didn't want to touch his damn hand or even be in the same room with him. Mercy.

"Well, well, well," Freddy said when he finally stopped whooping. He then moved to the front of the desk and sat in one of the side chairs. "If it ain't my old buddy, Ewell. How in the hell are you?" He placed a worn suitcase on the floor near his chair, opened it, and began taking out items and putting them all over my damn desk.

"Freddy, I'm fine, but you sound like hell. What's the matter with you, and what brings you to this neck of the swamps?"

"Well, now, I'm not near as bad off as I sound."

"Hell, I hope not."

"I just had a little bout with TB, but I'm better now. As to what brings me here, I'm trying to get settled in a new business venture and thought you might be willing to give an old buddy a little boost. My sources tell me that your business is on the brink of doom, but my sister informs me that you and her husband are making a killing off the old Logan gal's funeral. Thought maybe we might be able to scratch each other's backs, so to speak. I got some ideas that might help spruce up this joint, and I could use a little compensation for my efforts."

"Mercy, Freddy, the old gal only died yesterday. News travels fast within your family circle."

"Yeah, yeah, we're real close," he said and grinned. "I'm here to help you pull you starving ox out of the ditch, put your newly acquired green stuff in a place where it'll grow like kudzu, and put you on top in this dismal trade."

Before he could expound upon his great ideas, he went into another coughing fit and started spitting all over everything. I went to the bathroom and got a roll of toilet paper to catch his spit. Mercy, what a germ-spreading slob.

He finally stopped hacking and went on talking. "You got anything to drink? My throat is scratchy as a bundle of fodder."

I opened the bottom drawer of my desk and took out a bottle from beneath a pile of papers and folders. I poured a small amount into a used paper cup and handed it to Freddy. I then lifted the bottle to my mouth and drank the wonderful, soothing balm.

"As I was saying, Ewell, as your new business partner, I can make us both rich in no time, but we'll have to change a few things around here." He moved the cigar from one side of his mouth to the other as he spoke. His lips were covered with spit and little brown tobacco specks. He kept dabbing his mouth with a wad of toilet paper. "First off, you need to get somebody in here, like myself," he smiled, "to handle the customers. In this bleak business you've got to be a go-getter and get them when they're hot. If you didn't have that bastard Virgil Jordan helping out, you'd never sell a pauper's box. Ewell, you're not aggressive enough. To put it bluntly, you're a wishy-washy wimp, and you need a bloodsucker to deal with the kind of folks that come through your door. When families come in here all grieving, you can't pussyfoot around. You've got to play on their emotions."

"I did alright with the Logan sisters. Didn't I?"

"That funeral was sold by the time the Gooch gal waddled in the door, and you know it. Well, maybe it did take a little assistance from Jordan to change the mind of the sister, but that old Gooch gal was determined to have the biggest funeral this town has ever seen no matter what it took. Hell, she would have sold her soul to the devil or anybody else that would buy it to get what she wanted. Let's just say you got lucky on this one, but the next time around Lady Luck might not be on your side, and you can't always depend on Jordan to do your selling. Let's face it Ewell, it ain't good business having the preacher as your salesman. Sides that, I figured when you get the Logan money you'll pay him off, and that's why I'm offering to become your new partner."

"You better believe I'm paying off Jordan. That bastard gives me more pain than a risen on the rear, but what makes you think you know how to run a business for the dead?"

"I guess you forgot how I hung around this place when we were boys," Freddy said, taking the cigar out of his mouth to take a drink. "You and Stump ain't the only ones Grandpa attempted to teach the tricks of his trade. Fill me up again, will you? I know you've got the stuff hid all over the place just like you did when Grandpa was alive. Old habits are hard to break, and if you notice it stops my coughing. I never understood why you didn't learn how to run a successful business from Grandpa. The old man had to be the best teacher that ever breathed."

"Don't start on him."

"I've seen Grandpa Maslow do whatever it took to get what he wanted. Lord, he would cry with the family, drink with them, pray with them, eat with them, or roll over and play dead if need be. One time I walked in here and he was shooting craps with a guy to settle the price of his wife's casket. No family ever left this place unhappy if they dealt with Grandpa."

"Yeah, yeah," I said as I leaned back in my chair and started scratching.

"Grandpa could look a sucker in the eye and tell in a heartbeat how much he was going to gouge out of him, and make the fool appreciate him for doing it. He could put his arm around your shoulder while peeing down you leg and make you like it. He could smell moolah a mile away. Course he could also tell if the poor sucker didn't have a penny to his name, and in those situations Grandpa buried the dead for nothing. He was a good man."

"Okay, Freddy," I said as I lifted the bottle to my lips and drained the last drop. "You've made your point. Tell me what you have in mind for me to do to get this hearse ride to Goshen as you put it. I don't mean to be rude, but haven't you been spending time in Buttsville at the expense of the state?" I leaned back in my chair, placed my feet on the desk, and awaited his answer.

"Yep, I was there, but it was probably the luckiest break I'll ever get. I got TB and my hospital roommate was in the funeral business until he got caught doing things to corpses that some folks don't understand. He taught me how to run a successful funeral business, and I spent time in the hospital reading psychology books about how to play on people's emotions. Ewell, I'm here to tell you, it works."

"But your jail buddy got caught."

"Not for everything," Freddy said as he took the cigar out of his mouth and smiled like a damn Cheshire cat. "Now, Ewell, don't sit over there so pious and smug like you never did anything that could send your ass to the slammer."

"I keep my nose clean."

"Like hell you do. For instance, how can you have so many nice funerals without buying any more caskets? You haven't got any floor planning."

"What are you talking about?" I asked as I took my feet off the desk. I opened the bottom drawer and took out a bottle with just a little booze in it. Freddy was making me nervous.

"Pour me some of that before you guzzle it all down," he said. "If I asked you right now to show me a mahogany box you couldn't. I mean an empty one." He smiled that old idiotic smile I hated. "Course, now, if I should came back tonight or in the morning, you might have one. It would be a little dusty and have a few scratches before Moss and Angus took the dust rags and polish to it. That's not important, Ewell, but mark my word, your luck is running out, and you better get ready for a new game." Freddy raised his cup and drank the last of the Jim Beam, and it did seem to help his cough. "Let's face it, Ewell; I hate that damn Virgil Jordan as much as you do even if he is my brother-in-law. So pay him off and let's get this business rolling. First off, you ought to advertise."

"Why the hell should I do that? Every fool in Bochimville knows I'm the only undertaker in town unless somebody moved in last night?"

"Okay, okay, so you're the only game in town, but you ought to be getting business from the neighboring counties, and you sure as hell need to stop folks down here sending their dead to old man Feinstein in Atlanta. He gets a mighty big slice of your business every year, and you sit with your thumb up your rear doing nothing about it."

"Okay, so how do you suggest I advertise?'

"Do you remember how Grandpa Maslow used to do it?"

"Hell, Grandpa had money to do a lot of things. I don't."

"That's right, but you can have as much as he had. You just need to be creative. One way to advertise is giving stuff away." He turned his head to the side and spit cigar particles from his tongue. Mercy, what a slob. "Do you remember how Grandpa used to have a big barbecue once a year in the middle of town?"

"Yeah, reckon I do, but I don't have any money for that kind of stuff."

"You will if you get rid of Virgil Jordan and follow my advice," Freddy assured me. "Ewell, you can have coffins full of money in every corner and neon signs out front bigger than the revolving blue one on the Rock Church. You can afford a Cadillac hearse filled with sexy women, men, or animals—whichever suits your fancy—a little hide-a-way on Lake Jackson, and the best news is that your clients will not have to share the same coffin. How is that for starters?"

"Sounds great, Freddy, so what do you suggest we do first, and how much moolah are you going to take me for?"

"We'll discuss money later. First we need to have a big barbecue like Grandpa used to have. This gets their attention. Then, we give away little stuff to keep your name in front of them all the time. You remember how folks used to come from all over the county to get pig cooked by Grandpa's boys."

"Times have changed. I have neither pigs nor boys."

"Stick with me, and you'll have both. You'll also have a big house, the largest taxidermy shop in Georgia, and someone else to gut your animals and embalm your bodies. All you'd need to do is count the money. The rest of the time you can be out in the ocean chasing *Moby Dick* or sitting in your cabin on the lake reading and writing poetry."

"What do you have in mind to give away?"

Freddy reached down into his old, worn-out suitcase, took out a stack of cardboard fans, and put them on my desk. "Everybody gives away fans, but be patient. I got some real jewels in this case."

"Nobody wants a piece of cardboard stapled to a stick," I reminded him. "We've all got air conditioned buildings. Besides that, I'm sick to death looking at that picture of Jesus riding a mule with a bunch of sick little urchins running after him waving banana trees. Those things have been around forever. I used one of the handles for a teething stick. Talk about creative, mercy, Freddy, you've got to do better than that."

"I will, I will, give me time. Fly swatters with the funeral logo on them are good takers. Everybody's got flies. You want the whole family involved, so for starters we got baby bottles with the imprint, *Suck with Moody*. For the older kids we got pencils and crayons with *Color rite with Moody*. For the old folks in the house, here's a glass to hold their choppers with the logo, *Keep them clean for Moody*. Soap for the whole family in all shades and smells with your logo. Dog and cat dishes *Let Moody make your pet immortal*. You might even get a little taxidermy work out of that one. Beer glasses and coffee cups, *Drink with Moody*. Candles and candleholders, *Let Moody light up your life*. Doormats, *Wipe with Moody*. Towels, *Dry with Moody*. Screwdrivers, well you get the picture."

"Freddy, you leave me too stunned for words," I said as I fondled each item he placed on my desk.

"That's just the simple stuff, Ewell. Here are the real go-getters. Bet you've never seen a paperweight made of real Georgia marble in the shape of a tombstone with *Maslow Moody Memorial Mortuary* engraved on it. We got little casket earrings that any woman would wear long as they're free. Horse drawn hearse tie tacks for the men and real candy shovels for the little ones to lick and candles for power outages shaped like—" Before he completed his sentence, there was a knock on the door.

"Come in," I said.

Lucinda Faye opened the door and stepped into the office. "The Logan family wants to see you, NOW!" She said with her hands on her hips, like I gave a shit. She then turned and walked out without waiting for an answer.

"That gal moves like she's got briers in her crotch. You need to replace her with a good coon hound."

"Yeah, you're right, Freddy," I agreed. "There are a lot of things I need to replace around here. You better hurry if you've got something else to show me."

"The best is yet to come," he said. "Here's a winner." He placed a small silver casket on my desk and opened the lid to the sound of an organ softly playing "Asleep in Jesus."

"I don't believe you, Freddy."

"This little sucker will feed big bucks into your coffers. It not only comes equipped playing old funeral favorites, but you can special order them playing country, western, popular, rock, rap, and for the more highfalutin folks they'll make them playing that classical stuff. Folks can have their dead mama's name engraved on the top and her picture inside the lid."

"That's not bad, Freddy. The old Gooch gal would have bought a dozen of them mothers to give to her friends and family just to show off."

"The good thing about this little doohickey," Freddy explained, "you can make the whole casket a music box. I went to a funeral where a man's wife had passed, and one of these little thingamajigs installed in the lid of her coffin played "You Picked a Fine Time to Leave me Lucille" the whole time the old gal lay a corpse. I tell you, Ewell, it was real moving. Course her name weren't Lucille, but it didn't make no matter."

"That's not bad," I agreed. "How much do they sell for?"

"We'll talk about money in a minute, but first look at a few more goodies. Playing cards, ash trays, matchbooks, Christmas tree decorations, and this little item will make you a vast bundle."

Excited as a bitch in heat, Freddy spread a pair of black lace panties with the *Maslow Moody Memorial Mortuary, Bochimville, Georgia* printed in red across the crotch. "I knew Virgil would be eager to have a few of these, so I took the liberty of having a couple of dozen done with your logo."

Looking at Freddy's stuff put me in a mild stupor. I sat at my desk holding a pair of the panties in my hand turning them from side to side. I got the nicest feeling.

"Ewell, have you ever wondered where folks look first when they find a dead whore?"

"Nope, can't say I've given it much thought," I said as I held the panties up to the light.

"The crotch of course. We'll have Virgil give these out at the cat houses in Atlanta, and you'll be swamped with every dead whore this side of Kennesaw Mountain. Along with the barbecue you could have a real tear jerking hillbilly singer come in and get the people all emotional then have a drawing."

"For what?"

"Oh, for instance, you could have a nice plush coffin on the square, maybe the one the old maid is in now." Freddy paused from speaking, took out his cigar, and smiled as if waiting for me to respond some special way. "You could have folks put their name on a ticket and drop it in the coffin. A cute chick dressed in two black titty tassels and a G-string draws a name from the casket, and the winner gets a whole funeral paid for. Course we'll have a few stipulations in the contract, like it's non-transferable and must be used within thirty days."

"With my luck, the only terminal person in town would win. Freddy, I've got to go. We can finish this chat later."

"What time you think you'll be back from Paulding County?"

"Probably late."

"I'm spending the night with Rosalee, so I'll hang around and see you when you get back." He picked up his trinkets and placed them in his suitcase. "One last word, Ewell, if you're serious about making money in this business, you ought to fill this county with your name on as much stuff as the Braves have theirs on."

"I'll give it some thought, Freddy," I promised. "I'll give it some serious thought, but I've got to go now."

On the way to meet the Logan family, I gave it some thought. Freddy might have some good ideas. If I decide to stay in this business, after I clean up from the Logans, I might add a trinket here and there. This time tomorrow I ought to be a pretty rich man. After all, this is one elaborate funeral that's costing me almost nothing. I swung my arms and attempted a little fancy footwork then pranced down the hall. I'll go up to Atlanta mañana—pick-up the check from the insurance company—pay off that damn preacher—then I'll have my ass in high grass. Jeeeezus, it feels good.

> *With money I'm somebody,*
> *Without it I'm a bum.*
> *If you want to know its value*
> *Just try to borrow some.*
>   - Ewell Moody

CHAPTER TWENTY-FOUR

Mildred Roper

The Doleful Doofus Donkeys, as Sophia referred to Gladys and her followers, left the funeral home and went back to my house hungry and ready for a gigantic lunch. The enormous breakfast they consumed a few hours earlier had hardly been adequate to carry them through the morning. I was grateful that, while we were at the funeral home, more food arrived from the town saints and sinners, and the Lilly Moon Sunday School Class, under the leadership of Dafney Honeysuckle, graciously accepted the responsibility of feeding the noon meal to the gluttonous multitude.

Dafney, fifty-five, tall, and with a touch of gray to her tightly curled brown hair, wore large round glasses and usually dressed in skirts and blouses with a bow tied under her chin. She had worked as the church secretary since the day the Rock Church that Loves Jesus opened its door. The bossy type, and an authority on every subject, she usually took charge of all occasions, and funerals were her specialty.

When I walked into the dining room, she was busy removing the foil covers and checking to see if the dishes were hot by pressing her little finger into each dish. If the temperature was not up to her expectations, she sent the dish back to the kitchen.

Thelma Fife, Dafney's assistant, filled plastic cups with crushed ice and placed them on the table. She then poured tea from the gallon milk jugs lined along the countertop and added a slice of lemon and a sprig of fresh mint picked by Leland in our backyard.

"Y'all have been mighty kind to us," I said as I walked around looking at the food.

Dishes of cranberry relish and large platters of baked turkey and cornbread dressing were placed in the center of the dining room table. Dutch oven meatloaf basted with tomato sauce, roast beef, and venison were a small portion of a feast fit for royalty. One table held barbecued chicken—chicken-rice casserole—chicken salad—fried chicken—chicken with dumplings—chicken pot pies, and baked chicken.

Hoover entered the dining room with Joan and gasped when he saw the amount of food spread before us.

"My Lord, what a fowl banquet," he said. "One thing for sure, come funeral time in this town the mortality rate among chickens goes sky high. All this good food reminds me of being in Savannah and eating with Paula and her boys. He reached in a pan of barbecued chicken, took a drumstick, and began munching it.

"I'd like to pop him on the hand," I heard Dafney say to Thelma. "He needs to wait until the Christians have eaten before he starts. He especially ought to wait until the blessing is said. He never had no manners as a kid, and the way I see it, growing up ain't improved him one smidgen."

"Well, well, well, I do declare," Hoover jeered, "if it ain't Miss Rock Church in the flesh buzzing around like a queen bee seeing that everything is done to her liking." Hoover winked at me and Joan as he sucked on the chicken bone. "How are you, Miss Dafney?"

"I'm fine, thank you, Hoover," Dafney replied without looking in his direction. She kept picking up serving spoons and placing them among the dishes.

"Is everything okay?" he asked. "Or should we just feed it to the hogs?"

"Everything is fine, Hoover, just fine," she responded without opening her teeth. Joan giggled and poked me with her elbow.

"You do know how to enjoy a good funeral, now don't you, Miss Dafney? Seeing as how it gives you and the girls in the Missionary Society and Miss Moon's Sunday School Class an opportunity to show off your culinary talents," Hoover taunted as he laid the leg bone on the side of the table and reached for a fried chicken breast.

"Hoover, I enjoy cooking, but I don't enjoy seeing people grieve."

"Well, now, Miss Dafney, you and Miss Moon don't need to worry none about that around here," Hoover said. "I'm here to tell you, that except for Aunt Millie, none of these people understand the meaning of the word."

I picked up the leg bone from the side of the table, wrapped it in a paper napkin, and put it in my apron pocket. I then turned to Hoover and said, "Hoover, would you please gather everybody together so we can eat?"

"Aunt Millie, it would give me great pleasure to call this herd to the feeding trough. I'll be right back." He walked through the kitchen and out on both porches calling to everyone. "If you want anything to eat, you better make tracks to the table now! This is the last call."

The kitchen and dining room filled up quickly. Gurdy walked through and seeing the table said, "I do believe there's enough food in this house to feed half them starving countries over yonder that the President's always wanting to shoot up."

I agreed with him. Somehow it seemed a sin for us to be eating so much food in such a short time just because somebody had died.

Gladys and her chosen mourners made their way through the crowd and stood near the dining room table. Hoover and Joan stood with me in the dining room door waiting for somebody to ask the blessing.

"You watch," Hoover mumbled, "Aunt Glad is going to ask that fruit fly Shockley to pray over the grub, and if she does it will be cold and moldy before he shuts up, not to mention the spit he'll throw all over the table."

"He ain't about to spit all over this food," Joan said as she handed me her plate. "Don't worry Mama, I'll handle this like a real Christian lady."

She stepped into the center of the dining room, tapped a few times with a knife on the side of a glass, and waited for silence.

"Okay, everybody," she said. "Let me have your attention. It's getting late, and we need to eat and get back to the funeral home. Bow your heads while Hoover leads us in a word of prayer."

Gladys choked—Dafney gasped—Flynn coughed—Leola passed gas—I smiled, and Leland giggled.

Hoover strangled on his tea but managed to step to the center of the circle and cleared his throat before saying, "Let's pray y'all." Following a few seconds of silence, he began. "Lord, we ask that you bless all this food we don't need and forgive us for making hogs of ourselves. Most of all, Lord, help us remember the good things about Aunt Erm, and, Lord, please give her real leg back to her so she don't have to hobble around heaven. Amen."

Gladys hobbled across the room and stood in front of me, Hoover, and Joan. She banged her cane on the floor before speaking.

"You have no shame. That was the worst praying I ever heard anybody do. You know Leonard or Flynn should have said the blessing. Hoover, you ain't no preacher, and you don't even know how to pray."

"You're right on one count, Aunt Glad. I ain't no preacher, but I do know how to pray, and whether you believe it or not, the Lord has answered my prayers many times. And another thing nowhere is it written that some jack-leg needs to spit all over the food every time it's blessed like them two do every chance they get. I know the Lord heard me today just as good as he would have heard one of them old boys. And if I know the Lord like I think I do, He's probably as grateful as we are that He didn't have to listen to one of them pious farts run off at the mouth for half an hour and say nothing. You agree with me, Aunt Millie?"

"One hundred percent, Hoover, and I know Erma would also."

"Hogwash," Gladys mumbled as she waddled to the other side of the room.

Relatives stepped up to the table, filled their plates, and then moved to one of the rooms in the house, the porches, or the yard. I excused myself from Joan and Hoover and went to the kitchen, filled a pitcher with tea and a bucket with ice, then walked among the guests intrigued with shreds of conversations as I refilled their plastic cups.

"I was up there in that balloon playing my harmonica when I had this sudden urge to piss. Sorry, Aunt Millie, I didn't know you was standing behind me. I'll have more of that good tea of yours. You always did make the best. Sure beats that instant stuff Jean Ann is always pouring down me."

"Glad you like it, George. There's plenty more."

"As I was saying, a woman in the basket with me and my buddy, Ben, said, 'if you take a leak, I am too.' Weren't no trouble for me. Just stuck my weenie through a hole in the basket and relieved myself. Ain't no feeling on earth like peeing on a cloud. Next thing I knowed, she had dropped her drawers, and I heard her say, 'now boys y'all hold me real tight while I hang over this basket and relieve myself.' I got so damn tickled I might near dropped her over the side."

"How did Flynn get his front tooth knocked out?" I heard E. J. ask.

"In a jail fight, I think."

"I thought he was talking to God in a whirlwind and ran face first into a tree." The table filled with laughter. "Sorry, Grandmother, I didn't mean to be disrespectful."

I smiled at Sophia and then listened as Hoover spoke to a distant cousin.

"Are you still babbling out of your head with them Holy Roller snake handlers?" He asked. "I love them fang marks on the side of your face. The color goes well with your lipstick. You must have made that little old adder mad from the way it gnawed on your face. By the way, what do you feed them vile vipers? Sinners? Which do they like best, Baptist or Methodist? Mighty good tea, Aunt Millie."

"Glad you like it, Hoover," I said as I filled his cup. I then turned to listen to the cousin at the end of the table.

"Sure hope I have better luck next hunting season than I did last fall," I heard him say. "Man, I shot the biggest damn buck in Butts County—lashed that joker to the roof of my old Ford station wagon—circled the square in Jackson blowing my horn so everybody would come out and envy my kill. I could see me wearing a vest made from its hide and them big old antlers hanging in the hallway loaded with hats and caps, and I could might near taste the venison on the grill. Thanks, Aunt Millie, mighty good grub you serving up here today."

"Glad you're enjoying it, Horace."

"As I was saying, I hit I-75 doing about sixty, and the damn ropes broke. That old buck hit the concrete and bounced like a tennis ball. Before I could get my foot on the brake one of them Peterbilt's come along wide open, and the last time I looked in my rear view mirror, there weren't a piece of that deer big enough to hold in my hand."

As I filled E. J.'s tea glass, I heard him talking to the person sitting nearby. "I hope they don't use that awful scripture that goes something like O grave where is thy sting? When I hear it, I see this big old bumblebee swooping down on the grave and stinging the shit out of everybody present."

I kept filling glasses with tea and ice even though the pitcher seemed to grow heavier in my hand, but the assorted conversations helped keep me going, as I enjoyed being with the family so much.

"Grandmother," Sophia said as she stood and took the pitcher from my hand. "Sit, eat, drink, and be not discouraged. I'll fix you a plate, and then I'll pour tea for everyone. You seem so exhausted, and the day has hardly begun."

"Thanks, Sophia, I think I will, but please don't fix me much. I'm not very hungry." I did not realize how tired I was until I sat down. I had hoped the fresh surge of energy I had when I woke up would see me through the day, but I seemed to be wilting at a rapid pace. When Sophia put a plate of food in front of me, I ate slowly and thought of my dead sister. Erma would have hated the thought of a funeral but would have loved being with these people. She enjoyed a crowd, especially the conversations.

"I'm sorry to hear your daddy died," I said to the wife of one of my nephews sitting across from me. "What killed him?"

"Just died. He told Mama a week or so before that he was going to die. He didn't get along with my sister Asilee because she was always bossing him. Seeing as how they lived in her doublewide, and her and Mama was thick as the hairs on a dog, they made life miserable for Daddy. One night about a month ago, Daddy said he couldn't breathe through his nose, so Asilee tried to make him eat a spoonful of Vicks VaporRub. When he spit it on her, she rolled him over and slapped him right hard on the butt. Next morning he told Mama he was ready to die and get out of that shit. He never said another word to nobody including me.

"A couple of mornings later, Mama woke up and looked over in his bed, and there he was stiff as a hoe handle. They had stopped sleeping together about two years ago when Mama said she had stood him long as she could waking up in the middle of the night hollering, 'Old Lady, I hear something. Get up and check it out.' If she didn't jump right up, he would hit her on the head with his shoe. She made Asilee move in two twin beds and put them as far apart as she could get them. It didn't change things much. He just started throwing his shoe across the room. Anyways, there he lay with his mouth wide open like he was catching flies and his eyes blaring like headlights on a new tractor. He was dead as a stump."

"How is your little boy?" I asked to change the subject, since she had already told me far more than I wanted to know.

"Mean as hell. I left him home with Mama. That kid is a humdinger."

"Why didn't you bring him with you?"

"Lord, Aunt Millie, you better be thankful I didn't. I put him down for his nap the other afternoon, and he didn't want to take one, so he pulled the helmet off his little soldier and stuck it up his right nostril. I had to take him to Atlanta to the Baptist Hospital to a nose doctor that charged me a small fortune to dig the helmet out. My nerves are shot, and I needed a break from him. I left him with Mama and Asilee. Hoover, why do you have your hands in my hair?"

"I'm just trying to figure out your natural color."

"Well, don't bother because I don't know and don't plan to find out. As long as I can buy them little bottles of color at the drug store and pour it on my scalp, nobody but the Lord Himself is ever going to know for sure, and I doubt that He's interested. Get your hands out of my head and leave my roots alone."

"Aunt Millie," one of the nephews across the table called to me, "is that Dafney Honeysuckle passing around watermelon?"

"Yes, Henry, it is."

"I haven't seen her in a long time. I thought about her a couple of weeks ago after that big storm, and Georgia Power sent me over to the nudist camp where they had a power outage. Oh, man, that is some place. You don't know who you'll see there. I couldn't go in unless I was naked, and I couldn't bring myself to strip, as I had a fear of climbing a pole in nothing but my birthday suit. I was afraid I might hang something on an insulator and it stay there when I slid down. Anyway, I got to the top and looked down over the fence, and I swear there was Benny Honeysuckle, Dafney's boy, naked as a jaybird playing croquet, laughing, and having the best time. If I went over there right now and told her about seeing him she would call me a liar."

Henry's tale was interrupted by a woman's scream, and when I turned around, I saw Leola with her face down in her plate. I watched as her husband, Luther Hightower, picked her up and carried her out of the dining room followed by Funky shedding hairs all over the place. I figured he knew what to do when she had a fit, so I didn't get up to see what was wrong. I learned later that when Leola saw the platter of watermelon slices that Dafney was passing around, she thought it was a platter of heads, so she fainted.

"Hoover, how about finishing the story you started last night about why Aunt Erm insisted on cremation instead of being put in the ground," E. J. said. "I want to hear it."

"Where was I?"

"Hoover," I reminded him, "you were at the place where Erma had crawled in the coffin, and then y'all heard women coming in the room. You and Joan ran and hid."

I was so glad when E. J. asked for more tales of Erma, for then I could just sit, drink my tea, and not have to carry on a conversation with anybody. I was about at my physical limit, and I needed time to recuperate before the big event began. I hoped Gladys would not come in and start a ruckus before he finished, but I knew that was probably just wishful thinking.

O Lord, I silently prayed. Help us remember that until there is peace within families, there can be no peace upon this earth.

CHAPTER TWENTY-FIVE

Mildred Roper

"Oh, yeah, I remember," Hoover said as I reminded him where he had stopped on the story the previous night. "Little cousin, how about pouring me another round of that good old tea," he said to Sophia as he held his plastic cup for her to fill.

"Aunt Erm was laying there in that casket with her face all painted up, still as a wet hunting dog by a warm fire, when these two old gals walked up to the casket. They was carrying on about how sweet their mama was going to look laid out in one of them fancy boxes when they suddenly stopped talking. I peeked out from my hiding place, and they were standing over Aunt Erm not saying a word. Then they started discussing her.

"'There's a corpse in this one. Do you know who it is?' I heard one of them say. 'No, I don't, but why you reckon Maslow has her back here instead of in a slumber room?' Then the other one said, 'If you was that ugly wouldn't you expect to be put back here? Take a look at her face. You reckon it is a her? Look at them lips. They look like plastic ones kids wear at Halloween. Lord, look at the color of her skin.'"

"Aunt Erm should have crawled out of that box and beat the crap out of them two old gals. I'll bet one of them was Dafney Honeysuckle."

"Wait until you hear the whole story, E. J.," I said. "Hoover go on."

"Save me a slice of that pecan pie, Joanie," Hoover said, "I'll be finished in a few minutes. Where was I? Oh, yeah, these two old gals was hanging over the casket looking at Aunt Erm and expressing their opinions. 'Her skin looks bilious,' one of them said. 'You reckon she died of a liver disease?' The other one asked. 'Maybe she's an Indian. When I was a girl I went to the funeral of an Indian woman, and her skin looked like summer squash—rotten summer squash I should say, because it was not only yellow but wrinkled. You know how summer squash looks when it gets too big to use except to fry, and then it turns like rubber with little ridges on it and the most awful yellow color in the world. I wonder why she's wearing that silly hat with a little veil on her face. I've never seen a corpse wear a hat.'

"By this time, me and Joanie was wondering how in the world Aunt Erm was managing to stay there with them old gals talking about her so ugly. They just kept on. 'Maybe she's wearing that hat to hide her skin,' one of them said. 'Look at them hands. Why do you reckon she's just got on one glove? She sure needs to have on two. The hand that's showing looks like a buzzard's claw.'"

"If they said that about her thirty years ago, what do you suppose they're saying today after she has been sick all these years? It makes me angry, and I must cry."

"I know how you feel, Sophia," I said, "but let Hoover finish."

"'Round her fingernails are stains like she's been shelling black walnuts or canning beets,' one of them continued. 'Have you ever seen nose holes that big? It's like looking down Grand Canyon. I'll bet that dress is a hundred years old, and the collar has never seen a bar of soap.' By this time me and Joanie was getting a little pissed, but we knew Aunt Erm would handle things her own way, so we stayed out of sight and listened. 'She's mighty flabby in the middle,' one of them remarked.

"Then there was a little pause before the other one yelled, 'Oh, Lord, I do believe she has busted wide open. You shouldn't have pressed on her stomach. Smell that?' 'Course I smell that,' the other woman said. 'My nose is perfectly clear. Did you get anything on you?'

"'No, but let's get out of here before Maslow gets back.' I could tell she was holding her nose."

Hoover's audience sat silently waiting for the next line when Gladys waddled through the room.

"My Lord, Hoover, I hoped you had forgotten about that tale and we wouldn't have to hear the rest of it, especially while we're eating.

It's so nasty."

"Aunt Glad, you don't have to listen to a word of it," Sophia said, "and if you plan to throw one of your don't-get-your-way-fits, don't bother. We plan to remain here until Hoover finishes even if the funeral has to be delayed, and in case you have forgotten, you are in my grandmother's house and you have no say. Also, just in case no one has told you so, you are not by divine right this family's spokesperson. Please go on Hoov, what happened next?"

"Soon as the women were out of the room, me and Joanie walked up to the casket and looked in. I was beginning to worry that Aunt Erm had died, but she was laughing so hard, tears ran down her face. It seems Aunt Erm had eaten a few beans for supper the night before and a couple of prunes for breakfast, so when the old lady pressed down on Aunt Erm's stomach, she expelled a little gas."

Hoover's audience roared with laughter. The cheerful atmosphere seemed to lift my failing spirits, but only for a moment.

"But that don't tell us why she decided to have Moody cremate her," E.J. added, a little disappointed.

"Well, boy, I'm getting to that part. When Aunt Erm got back home she was so upset over the things the old ladies had said about her while she was laying there in the casket that she swore she would never have anybody hovering over her coffin, crying, hiccupping, and carrying on like a bunch of fools."

Just like last night, I thought but didn't say anything, as I was sure they would do it again today.

"A few days later when we went back to see Grandpa Maslow is when she told him she wanted to be cremated when she died, and she wanted her request placed on file in his office, and she wanted it done that day.

"'Erma Mae,' he said. 'I'll put your request in my Not Dead Yet file, and if I'm alive when your time comes, I'll see that your wishes are honored, but I can't vouch for what my grandson will do if he happens to be in charge.' Unfortunately, today we all know what his grandson, the yellow belly sonofabitch, is doing."

Hoover finished his tale, and no one spoke for a few minutes. I was thankful Joan was not in the room but on the back porch with the men. I knew she would have a lot to say to Gladys, and I did not want another scene before the funeral.

"Just goes to show that Ewell has more sense than his grandpa ever did, at least I think he does."

Hoover turned towards Gladys ready to retaliate. I reached out my hand and gripped his arm. "Don't, Hoover, for my sake, please. Let's just get this day behind us so we can all rest in peace."

"For you, Aunt Millie, I'll bite my tongue." He then got up and left the room.

"Erma had Maslow wrapped around her little finger, and he would do anything she wanted. I never did understand why the men in this town all seemed to cow-tail to her every whim. I'm mighty glad Ewell didn't know her and he's in charge today and not his grandpa. Like I already said, he has more sense than his grandpa ever thought about having. If Erma had her way, she would have embarrassed this family with her passing just like she embarrassed us with her living, but like Mr. Moody said yesterday, funerals ain't no time nor place to be cheap. We need to make up for all the things the deceased didn't have when they was alive, and that's what I'm doing for Erma. In her last years my sister didn't have nothing but an old slip she wore most of the time and that old coat that a dog wouldn't have slept on. But I'll tell you one thing, today I have her dressed fit to kill and that is how the people in this county are going to remember her. Just wish Mr. Moody could get the tires fixed on his limousine so we could all ride to the church in it, and he could take some of us up to Paulding in style."

"Aunt Glad, it is only one block from the funeral home to the church. Do you mean you would ride in a limo that short distance?"

"Sophia, you bet I would. Nothing shows how rich a corpse is more than having the family ride in one of them limos. I remember going to a funeral years ago over in Covington, and that funeral home furnished limos for everybody to ride in from the house to the funeral home, and it was only one mile. It made the man look real rich, and I know for a fact he never owned more than one pair of overalls at a time in his whole life. People took time off from work and watched as we rode through town, and you can bet today that nobody in Covington ever thinks about how poor he was when he lived, but they sure remember how rich he was when he passed because of the funeral he had."

While I drank a cup of coffee and ate a slice of pound cake, I remembered the funeral Gladys was talking about. Erma had made fun of the family for spending almost every penny they had to bury the man and left his wife with practically nothing. I wished I could drown-out Gladys' chatter, but it seemed impossible. At least this time tomorrow it would be over, and Gladys would not speak to the family again until the next funeral and only then if she were in charge. I now knew what Erma meant when she said being around Gladys allowed her to answer the biblical question, *Why the heathen rage*?

"I think it's a shame to bury my sister the day after she passed and not even have time to get her name in the paper," Gladys whined. "All we have done is hurry, hurry, hurry since the minute she passed, and I'm plumb worn out."

"Aunt Glad, if you want more time to solemnize Aunt Erma's death why don't you ask Flynn to stop the earth's rotation. I'm sure with his closeness to the Almighty he can hold back the night until you've had time to do your thing, whatever it is."

"Sophia, I'm just saying we didn't even have time to put her name in the paper, and that's a disgrace. I can't imagine dying and nobody seeing my name in print. The only time most folks get their name in the paper is when they are born, get married, and die."

"Aunt Glad," Sophia said as she placed the tea pitcher on the table and used her hands in a dramatic way as she talked. "When the time of your sanctimonious death comes, I will send notices to every publication known to mankind, including *the Watchtower*, *The Farmer's Journal*, and *Grier's Almanac*. I will also have *The Market Bulletin* print your funeral plans in the column beside the market price of hogs and butter beans. I will also enclose a picture of your well-fed carcass laid out in a pink satin-lined casket for the whole world to gaze upon if anyone desires to do so. Also, may I remind you that Aunt Erm's name has been in the paper more than all the members of this family put together because of the good she accomplished in her lifetime. She doesn't need an obituary to remind the world of her lifetime achievements. And since I have seen no positive contributions you have made for the good of humanity, the notice in the paper regarding your death will no doubt read as follows: Gladys Odiva Logan McTyre Gooch is dead—forgotten—the day of her death."

"Sophia, I—"

"Silence please, I am not finished. May I remind you that Aunt Erm's name is on a bronze plaque attached to a large oak tree and also engraved in concrete on a beautiful bridge? Both epitaphs are located in the county in which she was born, lived, and died, and they will still be there when your obese, hypocritical carcass has long been decayed and forgotten by everyone who ever knew you existed. So dear Aunt, enjoy yourself today as you make others miserable, but remember that Aunt Erm's name will live forever in this county, whereas yours is no more that a dew drop on a leaf of bitter weed."

Hoover and Joan, standing in the door of the dining room, began applauding when Sophia finished speaking. E.J. and Russell stood and applauded along with most of the other relatives except Gladys, Flynn, and Leonard. Then, silence fell over the room and no one spoke for a few minutes. Gladys seemed oblivious to Sophia's words and continued to stuff her mouth with God only knows what.

"It's about time to go back to the funeral home," I said in the hopes that Gladys would not attempt to rebut Sophia's speech. "We need to help the ladies clean up before we go."

"Don't we have time to hear about Aunt Erm's tree?" E.J. begged.

"Sure," Leland said, jumping in like he was willing do anything to keep Gladys' mouth shut.

"Wish I could stay and heard the story," Russell added, "but I got a load of chickens waiting to be hauled, so guess I'll see y'all at the church."

"Many years ago when Erma Mae was young," Leland began, "the developers were hitting this county pretty hard, and Erma was upset about the way they were destroying the trees. When the commissioners voted to re-do the town square and cut down a five hundred year old oak tree, Erma Mae went temporarily nuts."

"Erma was always going nuts ab—" Gladys attempted to say with her mouth filled with something.

"Keep quiet, Aunt Glad. Enough is enough," Sophia interrupted. "Continue, Grandfather," she said to Leland.

"Erma got her a blanket and a pillow, and Springer helped her climb a ladder to the biggest branch of the old oak. She said she would stay there until the commissioners voted not to cut the tree. If they were cruel enough to cut that tree they would take her down with it, for she was there to stay until they voted to save the tree."

"Anybody that loved an old tree like that couldn't possibly be right in the head," Gladys snarled.

"Dear Dumb Aunt Glad, William Blake, the great English poet, artist, and mystic said, *The Tree which moves some to tears of joy is in the eyes of others only a green thing that stands in the way.* Aunt Erm's courage and action regarding the tree just goes to show once more what a wonderful, marvelous individual she was. I am honored that my middle name is Mae, as I was named for her, and I strive daily to live up to her name. Just in case you don't know, Dear, Dumb Aunt, Mae is a derivation of Mary, the mother of God and the name of many queens. While we are still on my name, I am proud that my father chose Sophia, whose meaning is holy wisdom, for he has great hopes that I will develop in courage and knowledge like my namesakes. At the time of my death, it is my hope that I, like Aunt Erm, will be remembered for the good I accomplished during my lifetime and not for the price of my funeral."

"Hogwash."

"When my sister stops spouting off at the mouth like she always does," E.J. said, "I have a question, Grandpa."

"What is it?"

"How did Aunt Erm go to the bathroom or eat?"

"Springer used a bucket tied to a rope, attached to a limb, to send up food and books. When she was forced to do so, she peed in a coffee can and sent it down in the bucket. Course late at night she would sneak down, take a quick bath, change her clothes, use the bathroom and head back up the tree before dawn."

"Springer must not have fed her much, cause one day Mable Davis went by the tree and saw Erma gnawing on a piece of bark like folks eat French fries."

"How long did she stay up there?" E.J. asked, ignoring Gladys' remark.

"A week."

"Springer made sure the radio and television stations and newspapers all over the state got hold of what she was doing and publicized her actions, so folks came from all over to see her and applaud what she was doing. It caused great embarrassment to the commissioners, so they had no choice but to recant. Erma still wouldn't come down until she had a written document, witnessed and notarized, from the town officials that the tree could never be cut unless it became diseased through natural causes."

"Man, she had guts," E.J. said.

"Yeah, she did," Leland continued. "Not only did the commissioners recant, they voted to place the plaque that is still on the tree today. The day they put the plaque on the tree, they had a barbecue and honored Erma Mae."

"Before we go to the funeral home," E.J. said, please explain why the bridge over Bochim Creek is also named for her? How did that happen?"

"We don't need to hear no more about Erma's shenanigans," Gladys whined. "I'm sick of them."

"Well go sit on the porch and suck your toe, or better still braid the hairs in your arm pits. For the sake of what dignity this family has left, please put on a jacket or blouse before you go to the funeral. Your pit hairs are repulsive to anyone with a civilized tendency, and please put on socks."

I smiled at Sophia's remarks, as Gladys, with food oozing out of her mouth, glared at Sophia.

"E.J., I want you kids to hear the story of the bridge," I said, "but I'm afraid it will have to wait until after the funeral, and then I promise that your grandpa will tell it to you. We do need to go to the funeral home now." I dreaded the hours ahead so much I felt a headache coming on, but I knew I had to go.

"Ever time I drive over that bridge I think it just plumb disgraceful to have her name in great big letters for the world to see."

"Aunt Glad, until you accomplish something worth having you name on a plaque for the world to see, I suggest you refrain from condemning Aunt Erm for her accomplishments."

Gladys didn't answer Sophia but turned her head away as she stuffed a boiled egg in her mouth. I wondered how many unborn chickens she had consumed since Erma died.

"I would like to thank Grandfather and Hoov for sharing stories of Aunt Erm with us these two days," Sophia said. "I also vow that I will not return to Athens until I have heard the story of the bridge plaque and the trial for horse rustling, but Grandmother is right, we need to leave for the funeral home."

"Yeah, thanks Uncle Leland and Hoov." E.J. added. "When we get around to hearing the bridge story, I want to hear how and where Aunt Erm got Crowie and why she loved him so much. Course I think he's a pretty cool sheep, but never knowed nobody that had one trained as a pet. That sheep has even been crying since Aunt Erm died. Look at him lying over there in the corner. I think we ought to take him to the funeral."

"He'd fit in fine," Hoover said. "Put him right up front with that load of chickens and Funky, the egg sucking cat."

"I think we ought to barbecue that old sheep and get it out of the way once and for all."

"Aunt Glad, it is not my nature to threaten others, but there are exceptions to every rule, so hear me out with this family as witnesses. If Crowie dies from something other than natural causes, I will personally see that he or she who caused his death will meet the same fate, and believe me I have no problem with placing your carcass on a barbecue grill. Also, Dear Aunt, when I do make threats, they are not idle ones."

Gladys continued to chew whatever was in her mouth and seemed oblivious to Sophia's threat.

Silence hung over the room for a few seconds, and then several other relatives expressed their appreciation for the stories told about Erma. I waited for comments from Flynn, Leonard, or the other more pious ones, but they did not respond.

Joan, with tears in her eyes, hugged her daughter, and then the two of them cleared the tables. Sophia insisted on staying at the house to help the women clean the kitchen and promised to meet us at the church for the funeral. Gladys packed boxes and bags with food for Leonard, Flynn, Tillman, and her grandchildren to have a little something to eat on their way home. She then packed a large box for Gurdy to take home for their supper, so she would not have to cook when they returned home worn out from the trip to Paulding County.

"Storing up till the next funeral, Aunt Glad?" Hoover asked.

"Just taking a few things for supper."

"You must be expecting a crowd tonight the way you filled that box," he said, then turned to Flynn. "Well, cousin, old buddy, it looks like you've got enough stuff in that bag to feed them chickens until you get through serving your next sentence in the slammer. You've enjoyed this funeral so far, now ain't you cousin? Mighty glad we could oblige you. Aunt Millie, the way relatives are carting off food from your table, looks like you are going to have to cook for you and Uncle Leland tonight."

"It makes no difference, Hoover, when Erma lived she shared everything she had with somebody else, and if she was here today she would do no different."

"I am so tired of all that hogwash about how good, thoughtful, and sweet Erma was. I'll be glad when I never have to hear another story about her. I know how she was."

"Aunt Glad," Sophia said, "would you please tell me what Aunt Erma did during her lifetime that was so disgraceful? I have listened to the stories about her accomplishments, and I have wonderful memories of her playing and reading to me during my growing up years. I've heard her praised by others, but only criticized by you. Perhaps you know something about her that the rest of the family is not aware of."

"My Lord, child, ain't you been listening to all them tales Hoover and your grandpa have been telling about her? If they ain't disgraceful I don't know the meaning of the word."

"Aunt Glad, those tales say to me that Aunt Erm simply heard a different drummer. Like Edna St. Vincent Millay, Aunt Erm burned her candle at both ends, and I personally thank God for women like her. The world needs more of her breed."

"Lord, I don't know where you get your ideas about her being a saint or hearing a drummer and all that other foolishness. Let's get on down to the funeral parlor and have ourselves a good time and stop talking about Erma. Like I said, she don't count no more, and thank God she ain't here to be giving nobody a hard time."

"I got one more thing to say," Hoover said, speaking very loud. "Now y'all listen up. Before you fool preachers get in the pulpit and start running off at the mouth and spitting out nothing but spit, just remember the fine sermon you heard here today by little cousin. None of you, including Jordan, can hold a candle to her." Hoover clicked his teeth and smiled.

"Thank you Hoov," Sophia said. She then turned to me and placed her arm around my shoulder. "Grandmother, a great tragedy has occurred in this family, and I am not speaking of Aunt Erm's death. The tragedy of which I speak is that of Aunt Glad getting what she wanted regarding Aunt Erm's funeral, as it is in complete opposition to the wishes of Aunt Erm and other family members. But I firmly believe that time will soon tarnish what Aunt Glad thinks is now shinning in splendor, for *what this moment brings, the next moment may take away.*"

CHAPTER TWENTY-SIX

Mildred Roper

By 1:30 the family had finished lunch and returned to the funeral home to supposedly say goodbye to Erma, as Gladys insisted Mr. Moody move her to the church to lie in state before the funeral.

I did not say goodbye to my sister's body, as I knew her real self was not in that expensive box, but her spirit was still with me. These things I kept to myself, for I learned long ago that few people willingly talk about death, but sweep it under a rug in the hopes it will stay there. Erma was not like that. As her time drew to a close, she often told me that old lady Death, in the form of a crow, visited her everyday and sat on the foot of her bed. They carried on meaningful conversations.

"Why in the hell is she being carted-off to the church?" Hoover asked. "Ain't folks gawked at her enough already?"

"You'll have to ask Gladys," I said. By now, I didn't try to figure out what Gladys would do next, and I was really too tired to care.

"I want to make sure everybody gets to see her," Gladys whined.

"Why don't you hang her on the flag pole in the middle of the square? Then you can lead the town vultures in a parade around her and view her from every angle."

"Hoover, you're shallow as they come," Gladys said, "and you ought to be ashamed of yourself, but I know you're not." She turned towards the family and motioned for them to gather around the casket again, but only a few paid any attention to her demand.

"There they go again," Hoover sneered, "hunkering around that coffin like a pack of Georgia Dawgs around the pigskin."

Flynn stood beside the casket spitting and sputtering in an effort to pray another of his usual senseless prayers while Gladys hung over the casket blubbering and rubbing Erma's head.

"She looks so peaceful and calm," she said as she gently patted Erma's cheek, smoothed her dress, and rearranged her arms. "She must already be on streets of gold playing with fat little angels."

"God have mercy on us," Hoover snarled. He stood with me and Joan in the far corner of the room. "Any minute she's going to take her out of that damn box and stand her on the floor."

"It's bad enough they talk about her like she's a household fixture," Joan added, "but Aunt Glad has kissed her on the forehead, rubbed her stomach, and combed her head until her hair is about to fall out."

"Can you imagine what Erma would say if she could speak?"

"I'll be really disappointed, Aunt Millie," Hoover said, "If she don't speak, and as this show gets worse, I am convinced we will hear from her."

"Mama," Joan said, "If Aunt Erm spoke at this moment she would tell them all to simply but quickly piss off."

As she talked I noticed her twisting the strap on her handbag as if trying to break it.

"You know, I've thought a lot about Aunt Erm in the past few days," Hoover said with a note of sadness in his voice. "I'm going to miss her."

"Me and you were always her favorites," Joan said.

"That's because y'all are so much like her."

"She was a little odd, but a good old thing."

"Anybody that didn't wear anything but a slip in the summer and a fuzzy coat in the winter was more than a little odd."

"You remember that old pocketbook she carried around with her?"

"Sure, and I'll bet Aunt Glad has it now."

"You know, I was thinking last night if it had not been for Aunt Erm, I would never have gotten much for Christmas or my birthdays when I was growing up," Joan said. "You and Daddy didn't have much to give me. Did you Mama?"

"No, we didn't. Times were hard when you were little, and I never understood how Erma could buy for all her nieces, nephews, and sisters at Christmas and on their birthdays and graduations from high school, but she did." As we talked, I watched Joan's eyes fill with tears.

"I remember how we would each pick something from the Sears Catalog, and it would be under the tree on Christmas morning."

"She bought my first set of watercolors," Hoover said, his voice trembling as he spoke. "Then when I was about thirteen she gave me an expensive set of oils and the easel that I'm still using today."

"I'll never forget my first prom dress. I picked it out of the catalog, and she ordered it and paid for it."

"When Poppa was sick, Erma paid all the doctor bills. Did you kids know that?"

"Yes, Mama, I think you mentioned it before."

"She gave away everything she ever had," Hoover added. "It's no wonder she didn't have anything but an old slip and a moth eaten coat. And look what they're doing to her today."

"They have made a mockery out of her death."

"And her life."

"You remember the family with six kids that lived in Grandpa's tenant house when me and you were about twelve?" Joan asked Hoover. "Their mama was sick a long time and finally died. Aunt Erm took money out of her retirement fund at Sears and paid for the funeral, and as long as the family lived there she bought groceries for them every week."

"That's not all she did for them," I said. "She bought Christmas presents every year for the kids because I helped her pick them out of the catalog. Not many people knew these things about her. Most people thought she was just a crazy old woman. She struggled so hard to pay the premiums on that insurance policy because she wanted it to help somebody else, and I foolishly signed the papers and gave Gladys the right to do this to her. I promised Erma that a day like today would never come to pass if I was alive when she passed on. I have failed her so badly." I began to cry like I had not cried since I was a child.

"Mama, please don't blame yourself," Joan said. "You didn't know what you were doing in your state of mind and worn out body. Aunt Glad was well rested when y'all were at the funeral home, and you were not, so she purposely took advantage of the situation. Mama, please don't cry so hard. It will make you sick."

"Aunt Millie, don't let it get you down," Hoover said. "You did the best you could with that sister of yours, and Aunt Erm forgives you. She knows you tried. There is one thing I would like to do that would give me great pleasure, and that is take that infernal orchid off Aunt Erm's shoulder and cram it up Aunt Glad's nose, and before this day is over I might do it. Sorry, I didn't mean to get off the subject, Aunt Millie. Now, don't you fret none about signing them papers. All is not lost. I can't do a thing today, but I have an appointment with a lawyer in Atlanta Friday, so maybe we can get some of Aunt Erm's money back to give to the people she wanted it to go to. The lawyer is going to see me on short notice because I told her it was an emergency. We don't want Moody drinking, gambling, or high-tailing it out of town with Aunt Erm's money."

"I appreciate what you're doing, Hoover, and I wish you luck, but the only person who could handle Gladys was Erma, and because she's not here today, Gladys is having a field day. It seems she is doing all this just to get even with Erma for not letting her have her way all them years, especially when Mama and Poppa died."

"You might be right, Mama," Joan said. "We are going ahead with the funeral to keep peace in the family, but you wait until it's over. We're going to find a way to get even with Gladys, Moody, Jordan, and anybody else with a part in this fiasco, and I mean what I'm saying. After the funeral, Hoov will talk with Croker's widow and the lawyer, and in a few days I'll climb on the rooftop and scream, vengeance is ours! Mark my word."

"Come on, Aunt Millie; let's go on to the church. No need staying around this joint. It gets sicker by the minute," Hoover said as he took my arm and helped me from the chair. "It's not over yet. The fat lady has a few more acts to perform and more food to consume, and you know which fat lady I'm talking about. We've got a lot more miles and hours to go, but I'm going to make you a promise. If there is a God in heaven, and I know there is, He is my witness, and like Joanie said, vengeance will be ours. I don't know how or when, but somebody is going to pay for this and pay well, and I am not talking about paying with just money."

As Hoover and Joan were leading me across the room to the door, we noticed Gladys pulling up Erma's dress and showing her underclothes to a group of women who were not at the funeral home last night. Mr. Moody, standing in the doorway, smiled broadly as we came near.

"This little old side show you got here today is making you frisky as a camel with mange, now ain't it, Brother Moody?" Hoover said. "Wait until the funeral when you get to entertain a truckload of chickens, a human loon, and a cat." Hoover squeezed my arm, chuckled, and clicked his teeth.

CHAPTER TWENTY-SEVEN

Ewell Moody

Founded as a break-off from the Church of the Exiled Baptist over the dispute of calling a member from the local nudist camp to fill the pulpit, the Rock Church that Loves Jesus claimed status as the largest of the six churches in the town of Bochimville. The church perpetually reminded the town residents of its presence with the playing of hymns for one hour each day from the church tower and at night with a bright blue message, *Repent the time is near* circling the neon cross on the church spire.

At the time of its organization, the Rock Church issued a call to the Reverend Virgil Jordan, a polished, self-ordained, fast-talking man of the cloth, and for twenty years Jordan effectively led the flock of the Rock Church, annually increasing the membership and his income. He planned to continue in this capacity until his death or the demise of the church. However, Fortuna, the cruel goddess of fortune, simultaneously turned on both Jordan and me by taking us to the highest point and dropping us on our heads.

Under the heavenly glow emitted from its staunch members gathered for the funeral of one that never belonged to its membership, or even entered its door, I stood between Jordan and Stump on the steps of the Rock Church. The heavy rains which began the moment we placed the old gal's remains in the sanctuary had ceased for the present, but black clouds hung low in the sky as thunder sounded in the distance, threatening the return of another violent storm. We waited patiently as Mrs. Gooch, with the aplomb of an army sergeant, instructed everyone present of their duties and her desires.

"Mr. Moody, I hope you moved Sister into the church feet first," she said. "I don't want her having no problems walking into glory land. If she was heading in the wrong direction, she might have a hard time turning around on just one leg, and if she got lost they might never find her."

"Mrs. Gooch, I assure you we transported your sister in the proper manner."

"That's good to know," she said. "I thought you would do the right thing, Mr. Moody, seeing as how you are a good man. Why just last night at the supper table I was telling some of the relatives what good men you and Brother Jordan are. Course some of them didn't believe me, but it don't make no matter. When this day is over they'll know for themselves what kind of men y'all are." With that prediction, I felt the need to drink hemlock. She turned towards the family as if preparing to make an announcement.

"When the time comes to go in the church," she said, "I'm going in right behind Brother Jordan, and I want my grandkids to follow me. After that, y'all can come in any way you want to. Don't make no matter after me and the preachers get in. Seeing as how I'm the oldest, I get the place with the most respect." She pointed her cane over their heads as if counting. "Everybody is here except Russell, and we're going to stand right here until he comes."

"Aunt Glad," Hoover Murdock said, "you can stand in this murky humidity until snowballs stay firm in the desert, but I'm not waiting another minute for that pimpled headed, chicken plucker."

"But they need him to help tote the casket."

"No sweat, Leland over there can fill in for him."

"NO!" she yelled as she lifted her cane over her head and brought it down on the railing of the steps.

"Mercy," I mumbled. I looked at Jordan and shook my head. "That demented old gal could cause someone to become momentarily deranged."

"Here he comes, Big Mama," one of the children called from the rear of the line. "He's driving a chicken truck, and feathers are flying all over the place. I can smell him this far away."

Mrs. Gooch grabbed one of the pallbearers by the arm and handed him a paper bag. "Give these clothes to Russell and tell him to change in the Sunday school room closest to the back door. Now, E.J., don't y'all dilly dally around none. It's about time to start."

"Way I see it. It's done past time. Don't you agree, Mr. Moody?"

"Yes, yes, Mr. Roper, I do agree. As a matter of fact, the congregation has been waiting for some time."

I watched as Mr. Roper turned his head and spit a flow of tobacco juice into the bushes. I then heard him speak to Mr. Gooch.

"Gurdy, don't you think we might better take out our chaws? Once we get in there we probably won't get out until the crickets start chirping, especially if Gladys has another one of her conniption fits and starts whacking around with that cane."

"Nope, don't think I want to take mine out. If Gladys has another hissy fit I've got to have something to keep my nerves together."

"You've got a point there," Leland Roper agreed. "Course if them preachers get all fired up, we liable to be in there until the horns blow on judgment morning, so I better cut me another chaw too. Look at it this way; I ain't never in my whole life heard of nobody dying from swallowing a little tobacco juice."

"Before this thing is over, me and you both will probably hope to be the first victims of such a death. I think I'd ruther die from swallowing my juice than sitting through the next few hours with dry gums." The men looked at me as if expecting sympathy. I gave them the old Cheshire cat grin.

Russell and E. J. came to the front of the church after Russell's quick change into a brown sport coat, navy pants, a yellow-striped shirt, and a red tie. I had seen better dressed tramps and paupers in my time. Mrs. Gooch took a comb from her big old bag, ran it through Russell's hair, licked her fingers, and pushed his hair away from his face.

"Now, you'll look plumb good toting your great aunt's casket," she said. "Get over there in line where Mr. Moody tells you to, stand up straight, and act proud. It ain't everyday you get to do something this exciting."

If this is exciting, the poor boy has never had a life, I thought. I waited until I was sure Mrs. Gooch had finished grooming her grandson before I spoke.

"The pallbearers need to line up behind Brother Jordan," I said. "You'll march in two by two and be seated on the right front pew." I turned to Stump and whispered, "They look like a troop of defeated rebels. Look at Russell's shoes. They're covered with chicken shit and feathers. Why are so many of the men dressed in camouflage hunting clothes? No hunting of any kind is allowed in Chemosh County during August. For the sake of this county's future, why don't I return some of the old maid's money for the whole lot to be neutered? Be ready to go in as soon as I get the herd moving."

"I want to be behind Brother Jordan and Flynn," Mrs. Gooch whined.

"Mrs. Gooch," Jordan said, "the pallbearers must come in directly behind me, as they'll need to be up front. Now you just hold tight to your husband's arm, and you can be the first family member the congregation sees. This will give you a special spot." He looked at me and rolled his eyes.

"Well, okay, but I wanted to walk in with Flynn and Leonard."

"You would think Flynn Shockley has the unlisted number of Jesus Christ the way the Gooch gal carries on about him," Stump whispered. "I'll bet she even prays to him. At least we know he can't perform miracles since the Logan gal didn't sit up in her coffin last night after he yelled and spit all over her. Talk about spiting, he doesn't do that too well. Remind me to look in your tooth jar and see if we can find something to replace his missing incisor."

"Listen to this crowd," I said. "They squabble among themselves more than any family we have ever served."

"Man, you stink," E.J. said as he took his place beside Russell. "Stay as far from me as you can. You smell like a giant chicken turd."

"Looks like one, too," Stump whispered.

Satisfied the family was properly in line, Stump and I pranced down the aisle and took our designated places at the foot of the casket. The family's arrival at the door provided a signal for Mary Gay Hunter to increase the volume of the organ and the choir, dressed in bright red robes and yellow collars, to stand and sing, *When the trumpet of the Lord shall sound, and time shall be no more, and the morning breaks eternal bright and fair....* It was also a signal for us to close Miss Erma's casket. As the lid went down, I knew I would have to look on the old gal's face one more time when we swapped the box at the cemetery. That I could deal with, but for the sake of Mrs. Roper and her family, I hoped this would be the last time we placed Miss Erma on public display. I turned towards the congregation, raised my arms, and signaled them to rise. I then moved with Stump behind the floral arrangements, out of sight of the congregation but in a position where we could observe and hear the happenings around us. I did not look forward to this barbaric ritual planned by Mrs. Gooch and me. Me for money, she for glory.

"There are more fresh flowers in here than in the Garden of Eden before the fall," Stump whispered, "and enough plastic ones to plug a landfill."

"No doubt Sara Nell made a killing this time," I said. "The old Gooch gal must have told everybody what to bring, for I have never seen so many potted plants. What a waste. Think of all the booze that could have been bought with the money spent on this stuff. It's useless as a truckload of hen's teeth. Mercy, just look around you. I thought this town would never see another occasion that compared to Elmo Croker's, but I believe the Gooch gal has succeeded in throwing a bigger and more vulgar bash. Croker's widow will piss a rock." I clicked my teeth and smiled.

Every window in the church served as a shelf for at least one pot in full bloom or an artificial arrangement suitable to bring perpetual beauty to the grave of Miss Erma Mae for months to come. It could also serve as suitable roughage for the rats in the corncrib if Sister Gooch did with them as she promised.

A large round wreath with *Sister* spelled out in press-on gold letters on a bright red satin ribbon occupied the prominent spot immediately behind the casket. On top of the casket, a row of white orchids tied together with pink satin ribbon sparkled in the bright light from the church ceiling.

"Everybody is a star today," I said to Stump. "Look at Bochimville's self appointed spiritual leader and protector of the Word leading the procession of mourners down the aisle. He is not happy with Shockley and his Holiday Inn Gideon Bible tucked neatly under his arm walking beside him. But we all have our crosses to bear, now, don't we? Looks like Shockley, the poor, pathetic doofus would take off that damn cowboy hat. Mercy."

Following a signal from Jordan, the choir stopped singing and began mournfully humming to provide background music for Jordan's recitation of scripture as he paraded down the aisle. His large open Bible in the palms of his outstretched hands reminded me of an ancient priest laying a sacrificial lamb on the altar. His loud oration, clearly heard over the congregation, sprung forth like a bubbling fountain.

> *"There shall be no more sorrow, nor crying*
> *Nor will there be any more pain for all*
> *These things are passed away.*
>
> *O death where is thy sting?*
> *O grave where is thy victory?*
> *I am the resurr—"*

Before Jordan completed the verse, Flynn's loud voice overpowered the preacher's words.

"O praise the Lord, ye dead where have you been stung? Where in the name of Jeeeezus is your victory?"

"Jordan is pissed," I whispered. "Look at his face."

As Jordan and Flynn walked up the steps on the way to the pulpit and were facing us, I heard Jordan say, "Shut up you damn fool."

Flynn didn't hear or paid no attention to Jordan. The next voice the congregation heard was Flynn's. "I am the erection of the dead and the living. All that come into me will be made lily white and purple-plumb pure. Brother, you'll be made pure as a breeze."

"That fool hasn't got an educated bone in his body."

"If he did, he would still be a fool."

"They act like a herd of swine being led to the slaughter," Stump whispered as two by two the family of Erma Mae Logan ambled down the long aisle to the seats reserved for them at the front of the church. Mrs. Gooch, supported by her husband and one of her granddaughters, followed the pallbearers down the aisle.

"I'm glad I'm not the one holding that old gal up," Stump said. "I would rather drag a beached Moby Dick back to the water."

We watched in amusement as the family took their designated seats. Mrs. Gooch's children and grandchildren walked immediately behind her, then the Roper family. Mrs. Roper walked between her daughter and Mr. Roper. Sophia, the granddaughter with the mouth, followed close behind. The teenage cousins walked with their dates or a sibling. Most chewed gum, others giggled, and one little guy picked his nose.

Stump and I watched as Mrs. Gooch took her seat in her chosen place and looked over the floral crop. In a loud voice we heard her say, "We sure got oodles of flowers, didn't we? Lord, Erma would be so proud of this sweet-smelling sacrifice we did just for her."

I then turned towards the pulpit and listened as Jordan greeted the congregation.

"It is with a sense of joy that I stand before you today," he said. "Before this gathering ends, you can count on a miracle."

It was the largest crowd I had ever seen in the Rock Church.

"I bet this is the first time Jordan has ever seen all the pews filled," Stump whispered. "I don't understand why the whole damn county turned out for this funeral. The old gal might have been well-known in her younger years, but she has hardly been out of the house in a decade."

"Word got out that the old lady who is responsible for getting a nudist camp in this county—has a tree and a bridge named for her—a black sheep for a pet—and tried for horse rustling is being put away in style, and everybody wants to see for themselves. It was on the radio last night and this morning. Radio Ralph made it sound like a celebrity had died. I'll bet Virgil will use this opportunity to take up a collection, as there is no way in hell he's going to pass up an opportunity like this to fill his coffers."

Jordan smacked his lips, smiled, and then raised his arms out over the congregation as he read from his big, floppy Bible. *I am the resurrection and the life. He that believes in me shall never perish but—*

"Amen, Amen, brother," Flynn Shockley shouted. "Yes, yes, he that believes shall never flourish."

"This may be the beginning of a modern day holy war," Stump said. "Look at Virgil's face. If he died at this moment we'd have one hell of a time bringing back his natural color, but then he would have rosy cheeks. Why is Flynn Shockley looking heavenward? Is he expecting a vision?"

"He thinks his name is Paul."

Virgil Jordan lifted his Bible from the pulpit and continued speaking. "Let us hear the words of the Lord from His own book. *God is our refuge and strength, a very present help in trouble—.*"

"Amen, hallelujah, yes, He is present in trouble," Flynn agreed. "I know, I know. I've been in lots of trouble, and He has always been there for me."

"The Lord is my shepherd. I shall not want."

"No, we shall not want, Amen brother," Flynn Shockley shouted, patted his foot, and shook his head.

"In my father's house are many mansions. If it were not so I would have told you." Jordan spoke hurriedly. *"I go to prepare a place for you... Our help is in the name of the Lord who made heaven and earth."*

After ten minutes of scripture reading, with frequent interruptions from Flynn Shockley, Jordan took a break for Mrs. Gooch's son, Leonard, the wimp of the mountains, and his gum smacking wife with sagging eyelids, to sing.

"What a show," I said to Stump. "That old Wurlitzer upright with its yellow ivory keys resembles a smiling skeleton intrigued with its surroundings. If she continues twirling the top of the stool it's going to come off in her hand. She looks like something that would show up to unclog your drains." She finally sat down, still chewing her gum, and started playing softly as Leonard spoke.

"At this time, me and my wife Estelle would like to sang a few songs in memory of my dear departed dead aunt who succumbed early yesterday morning," he spoke in a soft voice, characteristic of his usual timid personality. If somebody had booed at him, he probably would have wet his pants. He took out a handkerchief and wiped the perspiration from his forehead.

"Gooch's son, Leonard what's his name, is deader than the old gal in the box," Stump whispered. "I wonder if he always sleeps standing up with his lips moving. What did he just say about suck comb?"

"He is so pale. You reckon he has worms?"

Estelle played a few measures of "There is Power in the Blood" and came in on the first word with Leonard a few words behind. By the middle of the fourth measure they were together.

"Mercy, how I hate those damn vampire hymns," I mumbled. "The things these so-called Christians love to sing about is beyond my comprehension."

They sang one stanza, and then Estelle began the second while Leonard came in on the third. Estelle changed and joined him. At the end of the hymn Estelle changed keys and began the introduction to "Precious Memories." I was so thrilled I needed to pee.

"Watch the Gooch gal," I said. "She is getting ready to put on a show that I bet we'll regret not selling tickets for."

At the beginning of the second stanza, as the duet sang *precious father, loving mother, fly across the lonely years,* Mrs. Gooch used the back of the pew in front of her for a wailing wall. She began moaning with every beat of the old upright. During the last stanza, *as I ponder, hope grows fonder, precious memories flood my soul,* she threw her head back on the pew, and a teenage granddaughter fanned her with the back of an open hymnal.

"The old gal looks like a damn heifer lowing at the skies," I said. "She is enjoying the hell out of this occasion."

Jordan stood to go to the pulpit as Leonard and Estelle finished their songs, but before he had taken a step from his seat, Flynn Shockley was there ahead of him.

"Now the fun begins," Stump said with a smile.

> *There once was a man name Flynn*
> *Who got saved in a chicken pen,*
> *He was then called to preach,*
> *but had trouble with his speech*
> *That poor, ignorant preacher named Flynn.*
>   -Ewell Moody

CHAPTER TWENTY-EIGHT

Ewell Moody

Dressed in a green leisure suit, plaid shirt, string tie, snake skin boots, and still wearing that damn cowboy hat, Flynn Shockley jumped to his feet the moment the Looney twins, Estelle and Leonard sang the last word.

"My dear friends in Jeeeezus," he began, "I stand before you today as a new convict, ugh...ugh... convert for my Jeeeezus. It's a real thrill to be here to say a few words in memory of my dear departed aunt who meant so much to me all my boyhood days. My dead aunt Emmer...Eunice was a good upright soul while she walked this earth, and today there is no doubt she is sitting on the rock of ages with the little Lamb of God right there on her lap. We all know she did love lambs and goats."

A weary amen came from Leonard on the front pew while Gladys, with her composure regained, looked up in the face of Flynn with a beam on her own.

"Look at the old Gooch gal," Stump said. "She thinks she's sitting right smack under the droppings of the Word. If she don't shut her mouth she might get a little taste. I wonder why she's wearing that big old faded flannel shirt. You think she's cold?"

"Have you noticed how she's burping? She must have been eating non-stop with free food flowing in. I'm thankful belching doesn't come out colored or this whole place would be a putrid green."

"She is definitely hyped on deviled eggs and excitement."

Flynn opened his Gideon Bible and began fanning the pages as he spoke. "I'd like to read you a few words of comfort at this time," he said. "You may follow me along in the Bibles there on the backs of the benches if the spirit moves you to do such." With the Bible opened from the back, and upside down, he glared at the printed page. "It says," he quickly turned the book to an upright position. "Now these are the words of Jeeeezus as found in reva....reva....reva....lations." He cleared his throat before reading. *"Then come one of the angels who had the seven bow...seven bowels on his head and he said to me come, and I'll show you the great whore's judge....judgment who sits on the waters fornicating with Kings. He took me way into the, into the wilder, wildness, wilderness and there he showed her, me a beast with seven names on his head and ten horns of scar...scarlet. It was full of blas...blasted...balas...mous names and holding in her hand a golden cup full of impure forni....fornications and on her head was wrote a, a mystery, which read the Mother of Harlots and abo... aberni...abor.... nations of the earth. Then I saw the woman drunk, drunk with the blood of the saints and the blood of the mar-turds, the mar-turds of Jeeeezus. Then I saw the woman's bottomless pit that had seven horns and ten heads."* With great difficulty and perspiring profusely, he read the entire seventeenth chapter of Revelations. "Now, let that lean on you for a bit," he added.

I rolled my eyes and exchanged glances with Stump. "He should have kept the Bible turned wrong side up," I said. "He probably would have sounded better."

"Now," Flynn continued after thumbing through his Bible for some time, "I'd like to read a portion of my aunt's favorite scripture. Anytime you went to see her she was sitting in the swing under the big old shade tree or in her rocking chair in the living room reading her Bible to her pet sheep, Chopper. Most of the time she would be reading this part I'm going to read to you now. It's the 23rd chapter of palms, and it says, *The Lord is my shepherd, I shall not want for nothing. He makes me lay down in, in green pastures. He leads me beside, beside waters, still waters. He stores my soul in paths of rightness, for his own sake sets a table before me. In the presence of all my enemies my cup runs over.* I know you will agree that them are mighty comforting words in days like these." He closed his Bible but continued speaking. "Now I've been told that a funeral is no place for a personal testimony. But when somebody has been as sinful as I've been most of my life, and the Lord thought enough of me to reach right down and lift me up out of that chicken sh.... that, ugh mire that was drowning me then I know you will agree I ought to talk about it every chance I get. At funerals, weddings, on the street, in chicken houses, or anywhere I might be. A man that is as full of joy as I am can't wait around until the next revival to shout his salvation. The hour is now! Brothers and sisters it is now!"

He looked in the flowers around the casket as if searching for something then reached down and brought up a guitar. He began strumming as he spoke.

"Before this day is over, we just might have a new client," Stump said, smacked his lips, and smiled. "Old Virgil is about to blow a carotid. Look at his neck all puffed up like a goose's."

"Now it come about this way," Flynn said, then hummed a few measures. "I was down in the chicken house one night in a hail storm, hmmmmmmmm, and I thought I heard somebody call my name, hmmmmmmmm, when suddenly the tin roof of that old chicken house was lambasted with a noise like none you ever heard in your life, hmmmmmmmm. It was like the Lord put his foot right down on top it." Flynn stomped his foot and strummed a few loud chords on the guitar. "Then I heard my name," he whispered into the microphone. "I thought at first it was a sick chicken calling to me for help, but then," he shouted, "I knowed it was the Lord. Hallelujah, praise Jeeeezus! It was the Lord!" In his excitement, Flynn spit in the flowers and with his fist hit the pulpit so hard it shook under his blow.

Fearful the pulpit had come loose and would topple over, I quickly moved from behind the flowers and laced my hands around it and held it in place until it felt secure.

Flynn continued with his testimony. "Now, my dear brothers and sisters in the Lord, I feel it my duty to tell about another experience I had just last night." He paused a few seconds to tighten the strings on his guitar. "I went to bed on the back porch of the old Logan home place, hmmmmmmmm. By the time my head hit the pillow I was fast asleep. I was plumb worn out from everything that went on yesterday, hmmmmmmmm. During the night I woke up when I heard a man's voice, hmmmmmmmm calling somebody by the name of Oral." He leaned over the pulpit as if trying to get closer to his audience. "Oral, Oral, the voice kept calling. Then all of a sudden I felt a hand on my shoulder, and I knowed that voice was calling me. Hmmmmmmmm, but my name ain't Oral. Not even my middle name is Oral, and nobody I know is named Oral."

I had never seen anyone sweat like he was sweating. His old hat must have been hot as hell. He continued to wipe the perspiration from his forehead with the back of his hand.

"I tell you brothers and sisters in the Lord," he screamed, "I was scared!" Then he began to speak softly. "I knowed it was the voice of Jeeeezus. For a few minutes I thought maybe Jeeeezus was confused and might be talking to the wrong fellow. Then all of a sudden I knowed he was talking to me even though He was calling me something different than my name."

I watched as Virgil Jordan clinched his fists and bit his lower lip. "Virgil is about to piss a rock," I said. "Look at him. I love seeing him suffer. Mercy, what a show. If I could pee and have a drink I could enjoy the performance much better."

"Yeah," Stump agreed, "but watching Virgil suffer is better than a drink. He's as agitated as a house trailer in an Alabama tornado."

"The voice said to me," Flynn continued. "My son, you're doing a fine job for me, and this night your name has been changed."

"To Swine's Ass, I'll bet," Stump whispered.

From the congregation came several Amens, a few yawns, and a lot of throat clearing. The Gooch gal screamed, "Hallelujah," then fainted, or at least pretended to.

In a soft voice, Flynn continued to speak. "The voice said, from this day on you will be called Oral, Oral!" he screamed then kicked a pot of flowers that toppled over onto the carpet. "I'm changing your name to Oral because you have a call from me. You will tell my people at the Rock Church that I want them to support you in your mission for me, hallelujah. Yes, sir, brothers and sisters that are what the Lord said to me just last night. So from this day on, my name is no longer Flynn Shockley but Oral Shockley. He didn't say nothing about changing my last name. Guess it pleases Him. He just said Oral! Oral! Hallelujah! It's Oral. With your help dear brothers and sisters in the Lord, I'll build hospitals, schools, dope houses, orphan homes, and together we'll find a way to get rid of jails and all them other places of affliction heaped on good men."

"Mercy," I mumbled, "had I known he was going to carry on like this, I would have backed over him with the hearse."

"Wait! There is more dear brothers and sisters in the Lord," Flynn cried. The congregation seemed to be silently waiting in anticipation to hear his next commission. "The Lord said Oral, my boy, you and The Rock Church That Loves Me has a mission. You," he screamed, "are going to stomp out, crush, tromp on, and trample under foot every queer known to mankind."

"Sonofabitch has stopped ranting and gone to meddling," Stump said. "Maybe it isn't too late to run over him with the hearse. All we need is an opportunity, and we just might find one."

"Amen, Brother Shockley, Amen," came a voice from the congregation. With encouragement from the audience he continued his sermon or fit, whichever it might be called.

"Yes, dear brothers and sisters, that's what I just told you. The Lord said, Fly...Oral, my boy you will stomp on, spit at, and kick out every queer from the face of my earth."

"Hallelujah, you tell them, Brother Oral."

"You, my boy, He said are called by Me to get rid of the thorn in the flesh of Humanity that is heaping nasty life sucking diseases upon good, God fearing people." He strummed a few more chords and then continued his idiotic performance. "And the Lord said, Oral, you'll have a tee vee show right from the Rock Church every Sunday morning. Them good folks of Bochimville will build you a glass prayer tower that'll reach right up to my front porch, and the money will flow in to do my work."

"Over Virgil Jordan's dead body," Stump giggled.

"I wouldn't mind that at all," I smiled. "It would save us a lot of money."

"I want y'all to bow your heads while I sang a few verses of a song that I wrote on the way down here yesterday. It is for my dear old dead aunt."

"Look at the fools," Stump said. "They will not bow their heads or shut their eyes in fear of missing the next act."

> *On the Banks of that beautiful river,*
> *In glory and in bliss,*
> *I know we'll meet Aunt Erma,*
> *And live in righteousness.*
>
> *On the Banks of that beautiful river,*
> *Where queers can never come,*
> *We'll hear dear Aunt Erma*
> *Playing her heavenly drum.*
>
> *On the Banks of that beautiful river*
> *Where kin will live in peace,*
> *There with dear Aunt Erma*
> *Our sorrows all will cease.*
>
> *On the Banks of that beautiful river*
> *With our sins washed lily white,*

We'll sing with dear Aunt Erma
Wearing a new leg fitted tight.

"Eat your heart out, Ewell," Stump teased, "looks like we're in the presence of a modern day Frost."

I ignored Stump's remarks as I listened to the loud Amens from the congregation at the end of the song. Flynn picked up his Bible, placed it under his arm, and walked towards his seat. Before Jordan could claim the pulpit, Flynn stopped and again faced the audience.

"Oh, I forgot something," he said. "My dear Aunt Glad asked me to read a poem that has a special place in her heart. This same poem was read at the funeral of another of her dear departed sisters who is this day with my dear Aunt Erma Maude."

Flynn turned towards the piano as he spoke. "Sister Estelle, it would please me mighty much if you would be so kind to play "Amazing Grace" on the piano, kind of soft like while I read this poem." He fumbled in his pocket for some time before locating what looked like a wrinkled old piece of tablet paper. He then attempted to read.

Sunset and evening star,
And one clear call.
May there be no morning, morning in the bar
When I pull out the sea.

But such a tide, as moving seems to sleep,
Too full of sound and form
When that which drew, from out the deep
Turns again home.

Twilight and evening bell
And after that dark
May there be no sad farewell
When I – When I bark.

For from out our born of time and place,
The flood that bears me far
I hope to see my Pil-pil-lot's face
When I go in the bar.

"Mercy, that was a disgrace to the memory and talent of Tennyson," I said.

He folded the paper and placed it in his pocket as he spoke. "Them is mighty pretty words writ by a fine Christian Brother by the name of Tennis-son who lived right here in Bochimville till he passed on a few years back. May the Lord bless his soul real good. Now brothers and sisters in the Lord, I have just one more announcement for right now before I turn the pulpit over to Brother Jordan. I must say one more thing about the mission we have before us. The Lord told me last night that He was calling the Rock Church that Loves Him to furnish the money, and He was calling me to do the footwork."

"Look at Virgil," I said as I smiled. "The way he looks, he's a damn good candidate for Elmo's box. The crowd likes that fool Flynn...Oral, whatever his name, and it's scaring the pee out of Virgil. Lord, I'd love to get him on our slab. With that snarl on his face, he makes Scrooge look like the angel of mercy."

"Seeing as how I didn't think it fitting and proper to take up a collection during my aunt's funeral," Flynn continued, "I asked that dear little lady from Mr. Moody's funeral home if she'd be nice enough to stand in the back of the church after the service and hold my hat for y'all to make a little free-will offering to a big cause."

"Mercy, what a damn schmuck," I said. "Listening to him makes me feel like the cloven hooves of stupidity have run roughshod over my entire body."

"When you leave this holy place today," Flynn said in a humble manner, "if the Lord lays it on your heart to give to a cause we're in together, just see Miss Lucinda Faye. She will be glad to oblige you. I think you for your kindness."

"Damn, what a nervy bastard," Stump said as Shockley came out of the pulpit. "Grandpa used to say a *man's soul belongs to God, but his ass belongs to whoever can whip it.* I hope somebody in the Logan family whips his ass and does it soon."

CHAPTER TWENTY-NINE

Ewell Moody

By the time Flynn Shockley left the pulpit, the weather had taken a change for the worse, and I was beginning to think God in His infinite wisdom was looking down on us fools in anger and letting us know how He felt about the whole spectacle, especially my part. I was extremely agitated, and Stump was in no better condition.

The first act had been worth watching mostly because it brought emotional pain to Virgil Jordan through the realization that he just might be kicked off his throne and soon. I was now ready for a finale and to get the show on the road, but I had the strong feeling the fat lady had just gotten started and might bring down the whole house before this fiasco ended.

"We can't get to Paulding County and back before dark even if we start now," Stump whispered as he looked at his watch. "Hell, we can't leave this place until the thin one, the fat one, and the fool have finished the show. Shockley was up there over an hour, and the old Gooch gal is giving signals to her son and his cud-chewing wife to keep on singing. Virgil is dumbfounded as hell since he can't get a word in over the old Gooch gal's daughter-in-law pounding the life out of that old worn out piano. Virgil must have pissed-off the old Gooch gal, and she is retaliating."

Before Virgil Jordan could gain the pulpit, Mrs. Gooch screamed, "Oh hallelujah, I know my sister is in heaven this very minute, and I rejoice in the thought." In the next breath she signaled for Leonard to start singing.

He touched his wife on the shoulder, and she began beating out

"On Jordan's Stormy Banks I Stand." I found the hymn very appropriate in view of the weather.

> *On Jordan's stormy Banks I stand, and*
> *Cast a wishful eye,*
> *To Canaan's fair and happy land,*
> *Where my possessions lie.*

The couple sang the first and second stanzas together and when they finished, Leonard began talking while his wife smacked her gum and played softly in the background.

"Since this song means so much to my mama, and meant a lot to my dear departed aunt, I want y'all to stand and sang the last verse with me and Estelle." He raised his hand as an indication for the congregation to rise. "Now let's all sang together. It's on page 194."

> *When shall I reach that happy place,*
> *And be forever blest?*
> *When shall I see my Father's face,*
> *And in his bosom rest?*

Before the last words died from the tongues of the congregation and Estelle could introduce another hymn, Jordan jumped into the pulpit.

"Thank you Brother Leonard," he said. "That was mighty fine singing."

"Look at his knuckles. They're white from clutching the pulpit, and listen to how fast he's talking," Stump said. "I think he's afraid the old fool will try to take the pulpit away from him. They act worse than a couple of pit bulls fighting over a dead cat."

"We're gathered here today to pay our last respects to a dear soul who passed from our midst just yesterday morning, bright and early. As you know, she lived a long, fruitful, and unselfish life, and we're all going to miss her mighty bad," Jordan said. "This dear departed soul came into the world many moons ago as our red brother would say. She was the oldest of six girls and never had a man to care for, but instead she spent her life taking care of her parents, her sisters, her nieces, nephews, and her neighbors. We are here today for the purpose of paying our respects to one so great in the faith and so generous with her worldly goods."

"Since big money is involved, he has forgotten about her escapades and the man she screwed for years," Stump said. "Her sins are forgiven, and he's preaching her right into heaven. That loudmouth, hypocritical, immoral clod slips in and out of his preacher role as easy as he slips in and out of Atlanta's whorehouses."

"Well, let him go ahead and preach her into heaven, but it's like Grandpa often said, *if you are not through the pearly gates by the time your body is placed in a fancy box, you ain't going to get there. Funerals are a waste of time, for every man and woman preaches his or her own.*"

"Me and members of this dear one's family worked hard planning this service in order to show our appreciation of her," Jordan continued. "We knowed it would please her mightily."

"Amen," shouted Shockley, Flynn, Owen, Oral, or whatever the hell his name happened to be at the moment. He clapped his hands together like the town idiot and created a loud pop.

"Yes, yes, that's right," came from the congregation, along with several Amens and a lot of sniffing.

"With the emotional storm he's brewing," Stump said, "we'll be lucky to get home from Paulding in time for breakfast."

"One day," Jordan continued, "we'll all meet beside that beautiful river that Brother Leonard and his dear wife sang about. That is, them of us that are saved will, but sinner among us," he screamed and pounded the pulpit, "you won't be there unless you change your ways and do it today." Lowering his voice, he leaned over the pulpit as he spoke into the microphone. "Even though we know this dear sister will be in heaven when the roll is called up yonder, I have a few words for the grieving family this day." He looked down at the family as he spoke. "It's going to be hard not having her in your midst."

"Yes, yes, oh, Lordy, yes," Mrs. Gooch screamed then fell over on her husband Gurdy. He took his hand and pushed her back up, never losing the rhythm of his chewing.

"When you return home this afternoon, you'll look at that old swing where she used to sit, and she'll not be there. You'll go to the bathroom where she passed, I ugh, you'll go to the bedroom where she passed over from this world, and there'll be no sign of her. When the nieces and nephews come to visit in a few weeks there won't be no Aunt Er...to greet you with gifts like she used to."

"Mercy, he doesn't even know the old gal's name," I whispered. "The way he carries on it's a wonder the Lord hasn't zapped him like a horsefly on a mule's ass."

"The way things are going on outside," Stump said, concerned about the weather, "the Lord might be planning to do a lot of zapping before this day ends. I wish the rain would let up. I've never been afraid of the weather, but at this moment I am scared shitless. Don't know why, but I feel evil in the air."

"When you go down to the old home place," Jordan continued, "you'll see things that'll remind you of her. It'll bring tears to your eyes, but don't be sad for her, be glad, for yesterday morning she mounted a pale horse and rode off to her earned and just reward."

Stump and I watched in amazement as Mrs. Gooch and her followers continued to wail in rhythm to the whish, whish of the cardboard fans in the hot stuffy church. They never removed their eyes from Jordan, as if gazing into the face of the anointed one.

"When tears come to your eyes," Jordan spoke in his soft, consoling voice, "just remember that somewhere in glory your dear loved one is having a real happy time rocking in the bosom of Abraham."

"Poor old Abe, I'll bet he's sick and tired of all that rocking on his tits. I wonder what he did in life to deserve that kind of punishment throughout eternity. But from what we know about the old gal, he has a viper in his bosom this time."

"It must have been something really bad to get that inflicted upon him." Stump said as we continued to listen to the fool in the pulpit. "Jordan's got them now. Shockley didn't hold a candle to Jordan's performance. Look at the Gooch gal. Is she dead?"

"Naw, she's just getting ready to yodel or catch flies. Why else would she have her mouth open like that?"

"Brothers and Sisters," Jordan continued, "I've been a preacher for might near twenty years, and I have never preached a funeral without giving an invitation for sinners to come and kneel at the casket and make themselves right with the Lord." He turned towards the piano as he spoke. "Brother Leonard, would you come up here and lead us in a few verses of "Just As I am without One Plea" while I stand at the head of Miss Era's—at the head of the coffin ready to receive any lost souls that want to come."

We watched as Jordan took his place at the head of Miss Erma's casket, and Flynn quickly stationed himself at her feet and stood with the exact posture as Jordan, his obvious role model.

No one came during the singing of the first stanza, so he asked for another and then another and finally sang all five stanzas without saving a single soul, a deflating blow to his ego.

"Hell," Stump said, "there's nobody around here today interesting in being saved. There's too much other stuff going on. Why don't he hang it up?"

Desperate to write another name in red on the last page of his Bible indicating a soul he had personally saved from the burning pits of hell, Jordan charged the congregation with frightening words.

"Dear brothers and sisters that are lost here today, you may be the next one to lay in this box where Miss...this fine lady is laying right now. We rejoice that she made the right decision in time, but you dear brothers and sisters may not have another chance. Time is running out." While Estelle played "Just as I am" softly on the piano, Jordan made one last plea. "Today, dear brothers and sisters, may be your last chance to walk down this aisle and place your hand in the up-turned palm of Jeeeezus. Tomorrow you might be a guest in Brother Moody's house like this dear lady was yesterday."

"There is nothing that pisses Virgil off more than not being able to save a soul," Stump said. "He takes it personally."

"I'll bet he was hoping to get them squalling again so he could out-do Shockley and take up a collection."

"Brothers and sisters," Jordan continued in a voice seasoned especially for funerals. "I have a request to make of you today." He shifted his weight from one foot to the other and continued to roll his Bible into a tube as he spoke. He began walking back and forth behind the pulpit. "As you all know, this dear departed lady was a lover of everything that breathed upon this earth, both human and animal, and gave away most everything she ever earned. Today I want this community to return a portion to her."

"Here comes the collection."

"Yep, believe you're right."

Faces seemed lifted in anticipation of Jordan's next words. "I want us to take up a collection that will be used for the sole purpose of helping feed the hungry and needy of this town. We'll set up a memorial fund in her name, and every time a hungry mouth is fed they'll know who is responsible for the feeding. Dear brothers and sisters I'm going to ask Brother Moody and Brother Stump to come up and open the coffin of this dear lady even though she lay open before the funeral started."

"Mercy, what a prick," I grumbled. "Will they never let that poor old soul rest in peace? They're going to drag her out of that box until the buzzards get a whiff and start flocking through the front door."

"I would like some of my deacons to come up front and stand on each end of the coffin and hold the collection plates," Jordan said. "When you good folk pass by and look on the face of this dear lady,

I hope your hearts will be inspired to impart real good to a heavenly cause. Remember Jeeeezus said *in as much as you have done it unto the least of these my brethren, you have done it unto me.*"

While we opened the casket and made a few adjustments to Miss Erma's appearance that was beginning to concern me, especially her jaundiced skin, Jordan handpicked the self-appointed saints he wanted to assist him.

"Brother Harley Fields, Brother Cecil Porter, Brother China Peppers, and Brother Floyd Cotton, y'all come on up and get the plates. Sister Estelle, I would be grateful if you would play that old favorite 'There is Sunshine in my Soul Today" while we give everybody here a chance to recipi...repro..cate, give back to somebody else a portion of what this good soul give to others in her lifetime."

I carefully placed Miss Erma on public display and turned to direct the masses to the front of the church to gaze once more on her well made-up face. I was pleased with Stump's superb artwork as I admired Miss Erma's tightly bonded eyelids, firmly stitched lips, and spotless, hair-free nostrils, but was concerned that her skin had a yellow tint, probably from lying in the kudzu too long. I hoped Jordan would bring this performance to an end soon so we could get the old gal in the ground. I was also concerned that it was still raining extremely hard, making our job at the cemetery more difficult. I perspired profusely and badly needed to scratch as I joined Stump behind the floral arrangements. Suddenly I heard an unfamiliar, irritating noise near the casket. When I turned, I saw Flynn Oral Shockley blowing a damn harmonica.

"Mercy," I said, "we should have charged admission for this one. These fools are having a better time than when the circus came to town."

One by one the congregation meandered down the aisle to gaze once more on the face of Miss Erma Mae Logan. A face, before yesterday and today, few had seen in over a decade. And if most of them had seen her they wouldn't have had the foggiest idea who she was and really wouldn't have given a tinker's damn. But today, they reluctantly, but with a sense of obligation, dropped a few bills or loose change from their pockets into the offering plates held before them.

"That damn Virgil ought to be castrated. Look how he stands there scrutinizing every tinkle in the collection plates," I said to Stump. "What will he do next? Go see how the weather is. We might better talk to Virgil and keep the old gal another night and take her to Paulding County in the morning. God forbid we have to put up with the Gooch gal another night, but we can't swap a casket in this mess."

The last to view the remains was Mrs. Gooch. Supported by Mr. Gooch and one of her granddaughters, she stumbled up to the casket, looked in, threw her arms above her head, screamed, and then fell prostrate to the floor. She bumped her nose on the side of the coffin and began to bleed.

"Shit," I mumbled. I knew it was a mistake to open that damn box again. The old gal appeared to have encountered an aberration, and I vowed I would not move a muscle to lift her off the floor. Virgil looked straight ahead and acted as if he did not see her even though the blood from her nose splattered his shoes.

"Oh, Lord, I do believe she is dead," screamed a woman from the congregation.

I thought if I had a casket to put her in, I'd be for that, but right now I'm all filled up. And the bad part about her being dead, in a couple of days we would be back where we are now, and I sure as hell don't want that. Insurance policy, gold teeth, old Edsel, or whatever, it ain't worth it. Mercy.

People stepped into the aisle of the church or leaned over the pews to see the cause for the bedlam down front. Jordan continued to talk and quote scripture. Flynn played his harmonica.

Stump returned to his former spot, and together we observed the crowd. "Is anybody going to help the old gal up? She looks like a run-over cow in the street," he observed. "Did you notice that she's wearing socks and no shoes?"

"Didn't notice, and I sure as hell ain't helping to get her up. She probably passed out from consuming so much chicken and pig, and my first aid training went out the window the instant she hit the floor. She's probably faking it anyhow. Oh, boy," I said, "help is on the way. Here comes Dafney Honeysuckle like a martyr bearing her own fagots to the fire. All is well."

Dafney knelt beside the prostrate Mrs. Gooch, lifted her head in her left hand, and wiped the blood from her face with a wad of tissues. She then instructed the few women who had stepped forward to help.

"Margaret, lean down here and fan her in the face. Sarah, get more tissues, and Sally, you get a wet rag."

While the women ran around in a dither helping Dafney, Leonard led the congregation in singing "Blessed Assurance, Jesus Is Mine." By the time they had sung the same hymn through several times, Mrs.

Gooch began to revive. When she stood up, she burped and passed gas so loud it could be heard throughout the church. The Caring Souls Committee hovered around their victim until her face was clean, her spirits perky, and she was safely back in her pew.

"Look at Jordan," Stump said. "He hasn't taken his eyes off the collection plates since the first copper hit the bottom. He's like an old bitch wallowing in rapture while watching her first litter. I wish Shockley would swallow that damn harmonica. I don't know much about music, but I don't think he's playing in the same key as the piano."

I didn't listen too attentively to Stump, as I was more concerned with what was happening outside. "Did you check the weather?" I asked.

"It's raining like hell. The streets are knee deep, and the wind is getting stronger. I can't see risking our necks going to Paulding County tonight, and we can't afford to take a chance on swapping Elmo's box. We could ruin it if we have to drag it through the mud. You need to talk to Virgil. In the meantime, I better see what Russ Raiford wants. He's standing in the back waving his arms like the wings of a dying sea gull. He must have something important to tell us. I'll be right back. This is just not appropriate weather for this time of year."

With outstretched hands, Jordan began to pray. "Lord, we give you thanks for the generous folks who have reached deep into their pockets this day to give to a good cause. I give you thanks for giving me divine wisdom to know what to do with these funds to further your kingdom."

"Yes, thank you, Jeeeezus," Flynn echoed, with head lifted upward and hands locked in the prayer position. The harmonica protruded above his thumbs.

"Help us spend every dime of this money in a way pleasing to you," Jordan beseeched the Lord. He lifted his arms again and motioned for the congregation to stand as I walked up the chancel steps after Stump relayed Russ Raiford's message to me.

"Virgil," I whispered, "I have to tell you something before you dismiss the congregation. Russ Raiford got a call from Moss. There has been a bad storm in Paulding County, and a huge oak fell on the old lady's grave. There's no way in hell they can get it moved before morning. You need to tell the congregation we will have the burial about noon tomorrow."

As the pallbearers came to the front to bear the casket away,

Jordan raised his hands to speak again.

"Brothers and sisters, Brother Moody tells me that the folks in Paulding County are in the midst of a terrible storm. A tree has fallen across this dear sister's grave, and unfortunately there is no way it can be moved before morning. Brother Moody and Brother Stump will move the body of this dear soul back to the funeral parlor where she will remain this evening. If any of you want to visit with her again, please feel free to do so. We will meet in the morning in Paulding County at the family burial site for the internment at 11:30."

"Oh, hallelujah," Sister Gooch cried. "I'll get to spend another night with Sister before they put her in the ground. I knew the Lord was on my side."

Followed by the pallbearers, Stump and I pushed the casket down the aisle while Jordan and Flynn walked side by side and Jordan extolled the benediction on the members of the family and congregation.

"As you go out these doors today," he said in his loud gravelly voice, "remember the Rock Church that Loves Jesus is here to serve your every need. Remember that I am the only pastor this church has ever had. Remember that I plan to serve here until the day I answer my phone and the caller is Jeeeezus. Remember we will meet in Paulding County at 11:30 tomorrow."

As the two men reached the door, Flynn stopped and in a loud voice reminded the congregation to "remember it's the Lord that blesses you real good every day, so please remember to give to the new mission He has called us to start."

As I guided the head of the casket through the door to the vestibule, I felt my blood pressure shoot to the top of my head when I saw Lucinda Faye, in her assigned place, holding a hat. On a cardboard sign attached to the wall behind her, painted in large letters, was the message: ORAL SHOCKLEY CAMPAIGN FOR THE LORD AND THE STOMPING OUT OF ALL ABOMINATIONS FROM THE FACE OF THE EARTH.

After observing Flynn Shockley and Virgil Jordan during this entire ordeal, I thought about Grandpa and felt he surely had those two in mind when he said: It *is the coward and scoundrel who use the church to justify their evil deeds.*

CHAPTER THIRTY

Mildred Roper

During the funeral, a summer storm hit the small town of Bochimville, and the wind blew chicken feathers from Russell's truck over the churchyard. The hearse and cars in the parking lot looked as if a snowstorm had drifted through, and the rain wet the chickens, casting a stifling odor over the area.

Leola and Funky came to the church, but most of the time she sat on the fender of Russell's truck while Funky climbed around and harassed the chickens. During the heavy rain, they sought shelter under a small pavilion near the end of the parking lot. When her husband told me that Leola often went nuts when she was around the dead, and because of the screaming fit she had at lunch over the watermelon slices, I decided it best that she not go to the church or the funeral home even though Gladys insisted she do so. He said the last funeral she went to, she got so upset she ran from the church, and he later found her in a pasture down on all fours eating grass like a cow. I felt we already had enough crazy, weird people attending the funeral without adding a human cow.

People left the church in a hurry as the rains fell hard. Umbrellas opened quickly and were shared as folks dashed to their cars. Leland seemed to think they hurried as if glad to be out of the place. The family and pallbearers waited under the church canopy for the hearse to be loaded.

"I feel well cooked in the cauldron of Aunt Glad's selfish desires and insane ambitions," Sophia said, standing near me and Leland. "I also feel I have just left the City of Pandemonium. If Flynn Shockley has been called to be a leader of God's people, it certainly doesn't say much for the Almighty's judge of character. A kangaroo imitating a crow would be more effective than Flynn Shockley imitating a person called by God. And Grandmother, if he is called, I do not wish to be considered among the chosen. It looks like Aunt Erm might be tilting the water jars of heaven in an attempt to let us know her spirit lingers on, and she is still in charge. God help some folks I know if she is."

"I don't see it that way, little cousin," Hoover said as he stood with the other pallbearers. "I like to think old Gabriel is trying to piss on Aunt Glad's head and so far is doing a pretty good job."

"I'm here to tell you that there ain't never been so damn much non-stop babble under one roof since the beginning of creation," Leland said. "I never realized Flynn was such a loony halfwit. It scares me to know he has six kids loose in this world."

I agreed with their remarks and tried to hold back my tears as I had done during the service for Erma. The performance by Brother Jordan, Flynn, and Gladys left me in a daze, and now I watched in amazement the commotion going on in the yard of the church.

The hearse parked under the canopy and near the front steps was surrounded by most of the male dogs of Bochimville, and I assumed that Moody's pit bull was in heat. She sat in the front seat of the hearse under the steering wheel as if preparing to drive off and leave her pursuers. Moody opened the back of the hearse, and two large dogs jumped in and tried to join Delilah up front. Moody shoved the dogs out with a broom as Stump grabbed Delilah and put her in the flower wagon.

The men carrying the casket stood at attention while Moody once again chased the dogs out of the hearse. Russell, the smallest, could not hold his part of the load.

"I'm going to have to sit this sucker down," he whined. "It weights a ton, and my hands are slick as chicken grease."

Before the other five could tell him what to do, Russell let go of the front right handle. Dale, immediately behind, quickly dropped his also, and E.J. at the back right did the same.

"Holy shit," E.J. yelled, "get this damn thing off my foot. It weighs a ton."

By the time the dogs were cleared out, E.J., in severe pain, gave his place to Moody who helped lift the coffin into the open door of the hearse.

"I think E.J. is hurt," I said to Leland. "Please go see about him. He wouldn't complain if he wasn't in pain."

The rain began to slow as the family waited around the front of the church for the body to be loaded into the hearse. Gladys and members of her mourners club mingled among friends and kin at the bottom of the church steps.

"I feel so good since Flynn's sermon give a big plunk to my heartstrings," I heard Gladys say. "And to make things even better, we can spend another night with Sister." I could feel her looking over her shoulder at me and Joan as she spoke. "Just goes to show that folks don't get their way when what they want is against the will of the Lord. I'm going to make a beeline over to the funeral home and stay there all night if I've a mind to. Just wish folks would bring some food."

Joan quickly turned to Gladys, but did not speak when I laid my hand on her wrist.

"Please, Joan, leave it alone," I begged. "Let it be."

"Mr. Moody," Gladys called, when Erma was finally loaded in the hearse and ready to return to the funeral home. "Since we're not going to Paulding County until morning, I want you to drive Erma through town and let all the folks that didn't come to the funeral see that she's having a proper send off."

"Fine, Mrs. Gooch, I will do just that. Is there any place you wish for me to stop or should I simply blow my horn as we go down Main Street?"

"Oh, Mr. Moody," Gladys said and then giggled. "That would be real nice. Me, Estelle, Leonard, and Flynn will be in the car right behind you, and if we see anybody you ought to stop for, we'll blow the horn. Come to think of it, how about me riding with you? That way I can tell you where to go and when to stop."

"Damn, I am not believing this," Joan said. I did not reply, but simply shook my head.

"Let her cluck," Leland said, having returned to the steps after checking on E.J., "maybe she'll fall off her nest and break her damn neck."

"Grandmother," Sophia said, "nothing can be done with Aunt Glad. She has Leo ascending, and Leo loves center stage. I was thinking during the funeral that if Aunt Glad had been alive during the Grand Inquisition, she would have been front and center at every stake burning. She would have loved the sound of flames crackling around the heretics. Or if she had been present at the witch hunts and trials, she would have participated in every execution. Have patience, Grandmother, *even this shall pass away.*"

"Well, I sure as hell hope you're right and it passes soon. I've about had enough," Leland said. "Since Erma died she has been hauled from one place to another like a country politician jumping from stump to stump. It's high time it stopped. Joan would you and Hoover give your mama a ride home? Me and Sophia need to stop off at the feed store for a few supplies. She tells me her little horse down there in Athens is gonna be mighty hungry if she don't take back a little grub for him."

"Sure, Daddy, but there is no need to hurry home seeing as how we'll probably have a house full of company when we get there, and I agree with you, it's about time this mess ended." Joan held my arm as we walked down the steps and got in Hoover's car.

As we pulled out of the church parking lot, Mr. Moody passed in the hearse with Gladys' arm hanging out the window waving.

"Look at them fools tooling down the street in that damn meat wagon," Hoover said. He drove the few blocks to Moody's Mortuary, pulled in, and parked under the funeral home sign which read:

> *Maslow Moody Memorial Mortuary*
> *Offstreet parking*
> *Remains Shipped Anywhere*
> *Taxidermy of any animal*

Attached to the post under the sign hung a piece of cardboard with the words, *Vidalia Onions. See head embalmer.*

"Hoover, when you go inside would you get me a few Vidalias? I'm about out."

"Sure, Aunt Millie, be glad to, but I'm not going to drive around town like a damn fool. I don't give a toot what Aunt Glad wants. I'll have to stay here to help tote the coffin back inside, and if you don't mind, Aunt Millie, I'll drink a beer while we wait for the party of fools to return."

"You know I don't mind, Hoover. Help yourself. I wish I liked the stuff because right now I need something."

Joan, seated in the back seat, opened a small cooler and took out two bottles of beer. "Hoover," she said, "for goodness sakes turn off them windshield wipers. That slisk, slisk, slisk is driving me ape shit. Sorry, Mama, I didn't mean to use bad language, but I'm nervous as an unemployed whore."

She uncapped two long neck bottles of beer and handed one to Hoover. After her first swallow, she sighed and said, "Oh, I needed that. Mama, I wish you liked this stuff, as you call it, because I know you need something to smooth your frazzled nerves." We sat in silence for a few minutes before she spoke again.

"Have you ever been through anything like that funeral in your whole life? The entire time I sat there thinking about the two things Aunt Erm hated the most. Preachers and funerals, and look what they did to her and what they put this family through."

"Did you notice that Brother Jordan never one time called Sister by her name?"

"Yes, Mama, I noticed. It was obvious he didn't know it, and really didn't give a tinker's damn."

"You know something, ladies," Hoover said. "All night I lay awake thinking how we could find a way to get even with Moody and Jordan. Now may the Lord forgive me for sounding like that brainless bastard Shockley, but a little voice within kept telling me that my answer is with Croker's widow. That old gal is really upset about something, and I'm convinced it has to do with Aunt Erm's casket."

"I guess I don't know what you mean, Hoover. I know you explained it to me last night, but I'm getting a little muddled and don't remember like I ought to. Tell me again what you're thinking."

"Aunt Millie, you are not muddled, you're just tired and you have every right to be. I believe Croker's widow is convinced that Aunt Erm is right now in the same identical casket Elmo was in a couple of years ago, or however long it has been since he died."

"But how can that be. I don't understand."

"It means that before Elmo was put in the ground permanently, Moody took him out of the expensive casket and kept it and has been reselling it. God only knows how many times the same casket has been used. If it's true and we can prove it, we can have Jordan and Moody locked away for a long time since Jordan is part owner of the funeral home. Then we can even the score a little for Aunt Erm."

"If that is true, and you can prove it and make everything right, then I will believe with all my heart we were meant to go through what we have been through since Erma died, even if it was against everything she believed in. Sometimes in life we have to endure the worst to reap what is best in the end. Hoover, you give me so much hope."

"Before this is over, Aunt Millie, if I have my way, you will get a lot more than hope. Vengeance is what I am shooting for, and that is much sweeter than hope. Do you know how many so-called big funerals Moody has conducted since Elmo died?"

"Elmo died about two and a half years ago, and I'd be willing to say Moody has had at least four or five good size funerals since then, but if what you are saying is true, why hasn't Lurlene noticed the use of the casket before? You know she goes to all funerals."

"Maybe she has noticed it, Aunt Millie, but has been unable to get anybody to listen to her. Let's face it, most people think the old gal is crazy and ignore what she says and does, but if we can get her on our side we might have it made. What's her first name? I forgot. I hope I'm not getting like Moody and Jordan and can't remember one simple little lady's name."

"Her name is Lurlene, but she likes to be called Mrs. Croker. She's a very proud woman, and if you talk to her, be sure you don't call her by her first name, and when referring to Elmo, call him Mr. Croker. Are you thinking about digging up Elmo?"

"Would you be against that, Aunt Millie?"

"Oh, heavens, no, I'm for doing anything that will make up for what has happened to Erma and her money. I will even help with the digging if you need me."

"That won't be necessary, Aunt Millie, but you might like to watch. Once we get a court order to have it done, the sheriff will be in charge of the digging."

Hoover seemed in deep thought as he sipped his beer, and I remained silent until he spoke again.

"You know, Aunt Millie, I have always loved the book of Ecclesiastes, especially the part where there is a time for everything under heaven. I've been thinking about the preacher's words, and I don't mean that fruit fly Jordan. *For everything there is a season, a time to kill, a time to plant, and a time to dig up.* It just might be the time this little old town did some digging-up."

"Here comes the hearse," Joan said, "and I wish you would listen to those damn horns. They sound like a flock of buzzards with cowbells around their necks. Look how it's raining. Hoover, you will never be able to get the casket inside in this weather, and the lightning is terrible. It could strike Aunt Erm's box."

"At this stage of the game, Joan, a little rain ain't going to hurt nobody, especially me and Aunt Erm, and the lightning might help sterilize the muck hanging in the air. You ladies sit tight. I'll be right back. It's a shame Aunt Erm had to die to get this much attention from her relatives. This time last week most of them didn't know she existed, and this time next week she will again be forgotten. Oh, well, what the hell, life goes on, now don't it? I won't forget your onions, Aunt Millie. I'll even have them charged to Aunt Glad's account. At least that way we can get something back for all the money she has wasted on this little fiasco."

I watched Hoover as he patiently took his place in the rain to help carry the body of his old Aunt back into a place she never wanted it to go in the first place. The rain had started again and was not like any I had ever seen in August. It was a frightening rain to those that believe in such things, so I kept my thoughts to myself.

My heart bled for this family, as there was so much needless disagreement and hurt. I bowed my head and silently prayed. O, Lord, I am confused. I am a fool. Help me not to look for answers in the wrong places, and when I find those answers for which I seek, give me the wisdom to know I have found them, and give me the strength to act accordingly.

CHAPTER THIRTY-ONE

Mildred Roper

Once again the coffin containing the body of my sister found a place on the worn velvet draped catafalque in the Maslow Moody Memorial Mortuary. Many of the folks who looked at her for two days returned to look some more. I began to wonder if she had been on display for a week, would the same people have continued to look at her. As soon as Hoover had completed his duties, the three of us left the funeral home and went back to my house where I hoped peace had returned to my humble dwelling.

Before leaving my house for the funeral, the Women's Missionary Society covered the food and refrigerated the perishables, but they left the place in a mess, as they had no idea the relatives would be in town another night. I guess they figured I was able to clean my own place.

"Mama, you are not going to stand on your tired feet tonight and feed this crowd another bite," Joan decreed. "They can eat at the Burger King or go hungry, and I frankly don't care which they choose."

While Joan prepared three glasses of iced tea and sliced a cake, Hoover took off his wet shirt and placed it in my dryer. I used my hair dryer to dry his jacket. He then looked in the phone directory for the number of Lurlene Croker. I sat at the kitchen table and rested. I was so overwhelmed with the strong feeling that someone other than the three of us was present in the house, I continued to look around the kitchen. Whoever or whatever it was, was a kind and good feeling. I did not mention it to Hoover and Joan. I wished that Sophia was there for I had a feeling that she, too, would feel what I felt.

"What's wrong Mama?" Joan asked. "You keep looking around like you expect to see somebody. Are you okay?"

"It's nothing," I said, but the feeling was so overpowering I could not ignore it.

"Do you think Mrs. Croker is home by now?" Hoover asked.

"I would think so. There was no reason for her to go back to the funeral home unless she wanted to take another look at the coffin. I see no reason for that, seeing as how she checked it from top to bottom last night, and today she looked it over as careful as possible short of making a scene at the funeral."

"Last night I thought she was going to dust it for fingerprints," Joan added. "And you're right Mama, I noticed at the funeral when she walked up to the casket, she never even glanced at Aunt Erm, but kept running her hand over the coffin. I'm convinced she knows something or at least suspects it."

"I'm going to call her," Hoover said as he reached for the phone.

Joan lit a cigarette and took a seat at the table near me. We drank our tea and listened as Hoover spoke into the phone. While he talked, he smoked. When they were nervous, they seemed to blow out more smoke, and within a few minutes a blue haze covered my kitchen. It made my headache worse, but I did not complain. When Erma was alive no one smoked in the house, and I wished I had been strong enough to keep the rule enforced.

"Mrs. Croker? Hoover Murdock here. I'm fine, fine. Thank you. I wonder if I might come over and talk to you about the subject we discussed briefly last night at the funeral parlor? That's right. Yes, it does concern Aunt Erm's casket. You mean you found out something else since I talked with you? That's good, mighty good. Thank you. I'll be right over."

"I would like to go with you, Hoover, but I am going to stay here and make Mama go to bed early and see that the relatives don't congregate in this house another night. They can go to Gladys' or find themselves a motel after they forage for their supper. Please wake us up if we're asleep when you get back. We want to hear everything. I can probably find you a bed or a couch tonight so you won't have to sleep on the porch floor like you did last night."

"Joan, I can stay by myself if you want to go with Hoover. Your daddy and Sophia will be home shortly. Hoover, I'm sure we can find you and Sophia a place to sleep inside, even though I know she loved having you sleep with her on the porch last night, as she was determined to sleep outside near Crowie."

"Mama, you haven't slept in weeks, and you said yourself that last night when you did sleep you dreamed about Aunt Erm all the time. I am not going to let you stay here tonight and have Aunt Glad and that bevy of buzzards run all over you."

"But I want so much to do something to help make up to Erma for letting her down. I can't get over this feeling that Erma has been trying to tell me something ever since she died, and I don't know what it is. Maybe it's about the casket, and I'm just too dumb to understand. All afternoon I've been thinking that maybe this storm happened to give me more time to figure out what Erma wants me to do."

"Aunt Millie," Hoover said as he put on his shirt he had taken from my dryer, "don't you worry none about Aunt Erm getting a message to you. If she has something to say, she will see that you hear it in her own good time. You get some rest. According to the radio we are in for a real storm tonight, and you don't need to be out in it."

Shortly after Hoover left the house to visit with Lurlene Croker, Gladys and her followers returned to my house. Leland and Joan were in the kitchen when I came out of the bathroom following the warm bath Joan insisted I take to help me relax.

"We're about starved," Gladys said as they entered the kitchen. "Running around showing off the dead can make a body mighty hungry, and rain always gives me a whale of an appetite."

She looked at the kitchen table and then stepped to the dining room door. "I thought supper would be ready with all that food left from lunch. I didn't even taste the corned beef and cabbage Dorothy Haywood brought, and I do hope there is some left. She asked me at the funeral if I enjoyed it, and I was plumb embarrassed to tell her I hadn't even tasted it. So how long before supper is ready, Joan?"

I stood at the kitchen door and smiled as I waited for Joan's reply.

"Aunt Glad, read my lips. Supper is not going to be served in this house tonight to a living creature except Mama, Daddy, me, and Hoover, and we have already eaten. When Sophia comes in from visiting friends, I'll feed her, but that is all that will be fed at this table tonight. I can't imagine how you passed up a single dish, but that is your cross to bear. You and your crowd of vultures can high tail it to the Burger King, or better still you can take them down to your house and feed them from the load of food I saw you cart away from here before the funeral. Mama is worn out, and while y'all were lollygagging at the funeral home for the last few hours, I have been cleaning the mess that was made here last night and during lunch, and you are not going to do a repeat performance tonight."

"Now, Joan, I know there is plenty of food here for all of us, so there's no reason to be so selfish," Gladys whined. She walked over to the refrigerator and started to open the door, but Joan blocked her way.

"Aunt Glad, what part of you ain't gonna did you not understand? I will repeat myself one more time. You and your followers are not going to eat one bite in this house tonight, and neither are any of you going to spend the night here. There is a motel about a mile down the road, or they can all sleep at your place. I frankly don't give a cat's ass which you decide to do, but get the bloody hell out of Mama's house and do it now, or things will start flying and I don't mean birds."

"Come on, Aunt Glad, I don't think we're welcomed here," Flynn said. "Even the Lord his self said there would be times when we wouldn't be welcome. At them times, He said we ought to wipe our feet clean and leave. We'll find something to eat elsewhere. I'm sure He'll provide."

"Well, Flynn, I suggest you let Him do just that," Joan said. "I'm not going to, and you might as well sponge off of Him as us. With your closeness to the Almighty you should be able to bring down manna from heaven, or better still why not run up to Fish and Chip and get a small basket of catfish and pass it around among yourselves. You might even consider saving the leftovers to feed the multitude of deadbeats looking for a handout before this momentous occasion is over. Since you are so keen on obeying the Lord's commandments, I need to warn you that before you leave this place don't be wiping your feet on Mama's clean kitchen floor."

"Alright we'll go to the Burger King," Gladys whined, "but we're coming back here for breakfast before we set out for Paulding County. The family needs to be together one more time before we send Erma off for good. Since the Lord provided a way to give us this added time, we ought to make good use of it."

"If you want to come back here in the morning for a cup of coffee and a biscuit that will be fine, but don't expect more. If you want cream in your coffee or syrup on your biscuit, bring it, for we are not furnishing it."

"I never saw such a selfish attitude," Gladys grumbled. "She would let her own flesh and blood starve. I haven't had a bite since lunch, and my stomach is growling so loud I'm afraid it's going to bite me. Looks like Mr. Moody would have served us some peanuts or crackers seeing as how we had to be there so long today. Folks just don't have no manners anymore."

When Gladys and her gang were finally out of the house, I began to worry about Hoover. "I wonder what's taking him so long," I said. "I thought he would be back by now."

"Millie, you know Hoover," Leland reminded me. "When he gets to bumping his gums with Lurlene, it's no telling how long it will be before he gets back. Him and Lurlene might get all riled up, grab a shovel, and dig up Elmo tonight. Those two are mighty hotheaded, and you never know what they'll do next. Sides that, the ground is just right for digging."

"Mama, it's nearly ten o'clock," Joan said. "I wish you would go to bed. Me and Daddy will wait up for Hoov. If there is something we need to tell you tonight, I promise to wake you. That crowd will be back early in the morning, and we'll have to fix a pan of biscuits and make some coffee. Please go to bed."

I did as Joan commanded and went to bed, as I was tired. For some unknown reason, I believed the night would be different from any I had ever spent or would spend again, and I guess I wanted to get it behind me. During the night, the fierce beating of the rain on our tin roof, the loud thunder, and the brightness of the lighting went on and on as if determined to keep me awake. It reminded me of a sleepless child crying for attention. I slept and woke, slept and woke, never sure whether I was awake or asleep. I heard music. Music I had never heard before. Not the good old gospel hymns I listened to on Sunday mornings when dressing for church nor the familiar hymns I sang to myself when working around the house, but music of a different type. It was not music that comes from the radio or television. It seemed to lift my soul from my body and float me upward. I began to wonder if I was dying. Erma used to say she spent her sleepless nights reading, praying, or meditating, and there were times near the end that she mentioned hearing music that I didn't hear. With the knowledge that my mind was incapable of reading, praying, or meditating, and I could not fight this night alone, I surrendered to sleep.

Once again I dreamed that I was in the woods where I had seen Erma earlier that day, and in the distance a bright fire burning in the center of a large circle of people seemed to light up the woods. Erma sat on a stool with her hands stretched out towards the fire as if warming them. She turned her head in my direction and smiled. The people in the circle sat quietly. I did not know them, but they seemed happy. They looked at me as if inviting me to join them.

Around two o'clock in the morning, when a loud bolt of thunder woke me, I lay still allowing my mind to waken slowly. I felt as if my soul lay in a stream of cool water in the warm forest where I had visited with Erma. I had never known such peace. I felt gentle spirits breathing on me, and the shame I felt earlier about letting Erma down was no longer there. I knew I had been given a second chance to make right the wrong done to my sister. I lay in bed listening—for what I didn't know—but I knew if I listened long enough I would hear what I was supposed to hear.

I had often read that in the silence after the storm God reveals himself to others, and at that moment I hoped a revelation was being given to me. I had always believed that there is a time to be gentle and a time to be fierce, and I had been gentle throughout the entire ordeal surrounding Erma's funeral. Now I felt hands pushing on my shoulders and voices saying it's time to be fierce.

As I lay waiting to see what would happen next, I kept thinking about Erma's life. A life lived for others no matter how different it had been. Like Sophia said, Erma heard a different drummer and burned her candle at both ends, but was that so bad? I continued to remember her attempts to make right every wrong, never considering the ridicule and pain her efforts might bring her. I felt a power at work much greater than I had ever imagined. I sat up, reached to the other side of the bed, and gently shook Leland.

When I got out of bed and began to dress, I smiled at the realization that *sometimes we see and understand things more clearly in our dreams than we could ever imagine seeing or understanding when we are awake.*

CHAPTER THIRTY-TWO

Mildred Roper

The crowd that gathered at my house for breakfast the morning of Erma's scheduled burial was one with solemn faces, tired bodies, and confused minds. Most of them were in a daze from having been wakened in the early hours of the morning by thunder rumbling, fire engines roaring, and sirens blaring through the little town of Bochimville. It was as if the gods of heaven and earth were at war.

"I ain't never heard such a racket in my life," E.J. said as he sat at my kitchen table, so upset I thought he would cry. "All night long it seemed like a dozen fire trucks were under my bed squealing and squalling like a bunch of drunken hyenas. Does anybody know what caused Aunt Erm's casket to catch fire and burn down the whole funeral home?"

"All I know is what I heard from Russ Raiford who said the fire department is so stunned about the cause of the fire they are bringing in a fire marshal from Atlanta to investigate," Russell added. "The only thing they know for sure is that the fire started around the casket, but they don't know if somebody set the fire or lightning got it. Some of the noise was caused from the thunder but mostly from the fire trucks roaring in from surrounding counties. Man, what a mess. I ain't never seen such a blaze nor heard such thunder. It shook the house and scared the crap out of me. All I could think was that Aunt Erm had come back just like some folks said she would, and I kept praying if she had returned she wouldn't come in my room."

"I can't believe this happened," Gladys whined. "Erma looked so sweet in her new clothes laying there in that pretty casket Mr. Moody got especially for us. In a few more hours we would have had another service for her in Paulding County and then laid her to rest in the family graveyard. The folks up there planned to have lunch for us in the cemetery under the trees, and now all that good food is going to waste. Plus, I had to put out for a long distance call to let them know what happened. Millie, you've got to pay me for half the cost of the call. When I think that there ain't nothing to show for all we done for her and the money we spent, I just want to cry. To top it off, she probably looks like a scorched hog. Millie, you don't seem one bit upset over what happened. What is your problem? I ain't heard you ask a single question. You just walk around with that silly smile on your face."

"I understand what you're going through, Aunt Glad," Flynn said, which kept me from having to answer her. He reached over and patted her hand as he spoke. "Sometimes things happen that we don't understand, but we have to assume it's the Lord's will and keep right on living. I can't figure out for the life of me how lightning struck the casket inside the funeral home and set it on fire. Don't make no sense. Russ Raiford said the casket burned like a wood crate soaked in kerosene. Do you reckon somebody did soak the coffin in kerosene and set it on fire?"

"Stranger things have happened in this town," Leland said and smiled.

"Is that all you got to say about the situation?" Gladys asked as she hit her cane on the floor. "What is the matter with you and Millie? You don't seem to give a hoot about what happened to Erma and the funeral home. I don't understand y'all."

"Talking about kerosene," E.J. said, sniffing his nose and ignoring Gladys' tirade. "I thought I smelled some when I came up on the porch. Did anybody else smell it?"

"I didn't."

"Me neither."

"Didn't smell a thing."

"All I smell is Aunt Millie's good coffee," Hoover said as he winked at Sophia.

"I got one more thing to say," E.J. continued. "Right now, I ain't got no idea what caused the racket nor the fire, but it scared the living shit out of me, and I don't ever want to go through another night like last night. I been in storms before, but I ain't never heard thunder or seen lightning like that. And I sure as hell don't see how anything could have burned like the funeral home did with rain pouring down so hard you couldn't see your hand in front of your face."

"When I heard the thunder and observed the lightning, I simply accepted it as Mother Nature comparing her mighty power to man's puny weakness."

"Jesus, here she goes, and we ain't even had breakfast," E.J. said about his sister. "Don't she ever run down?"

"When the racket woke me up and I saw the western sky aglow," Flynn said as he pointed upward with both hands, "I knowed the Rapture had come like a thief in the night, just the way the Lord predicted it would."

"At that precise moment, Flynn, did you not wonder why you had been left behind?"

"Oh, no, Sophia, I had no doubt where I would be when the Lord separated the sheep from the goats." He smacked his lips and continued talking as he poured syrup on his biscuit and licked his fingers. "I knowed before Aunt Millie got breakfast on the table, we would see Aunt Erm standing at the back door with her pet sheep, smiling and welcoming us home with her. I felt sure that later in the morning this whole family would float upward together like astronauts on a heavenly voyage looking down on sinners left below. I just couldn't understand why the trumpets weren't blowing to welcome us to the New Jerusalem."

"Why, Flynn, honey, when I saw the skies aglow, I immediately thought you had commanded the morning to appear and caused the dawn to rise in the east, or at least you had told the daylight to spread to the ends of the earth to end the night's wickedness."

Joan shook her head and rolled her eyes. I smiled at Sophia's ability to bring from her storehouse of knowledge whatever she needed for the moment.

"Why, Flynn, old boy," Hoover taunted, "I bet you were hoping like hell that all your ex-wives were left behind to fend for themselves, now weren't you cousin? You were smacking your lips just thinking about all that lovely alimony and child support you would never have to pay. Bet that give you a real high, now didn't it?"

"For a minute there," Flynn said, ignoring Hoover's remarks, "I did think that maybe Aunt Erm had returned, but I couldn't make myself believe she would be that wicked unless she weren't saved before she passed."

"Why, Flynn, honey," Sophia said, "I'm surprised you haven't figured it out. The answer is so simple. *God moves in mysterious ways, His wonders to perform. He plants His footsteps in the sea and rides upon the storm."*

"God Almighty."

"No, little brother, William Cowper."

"What do we do now?" Gladys asked. "We can't bury her, and—"

"Aunt Glad, for your sake," Sophia interrupted, "that is probably a good thing, for I remember Aunt Erm never wanted her body placed in a cemetery. She felt they were a waste of land and every dead body should be cremated and the ashes placed in the wind to return to Mother Nature from whence they came."

"That's hogwash," Gladys snarled. "The fire department won't let nobody near the funeral home to see what's left of it much less what happened to Erma. It just ain't right to spend that kind of money on a body and not get it put away nicely. I don't care what Erma had to say about it. Like I done asked, how come y'all ain't saying nothing this morning, Millie? I guess you're happy she got burned up like she wanted to be in the first place. Guess y'all got what you wanted after all. Looks like Erma won again, and that ain't fair. I hate her."

"My, my, Aunt Glad, you are so wishy washy. Yesterday you loved Aunt Erm so much you couldn't pull yourself away from her casket, and you even fainted at her funeral. By the way, I meant to compliment you on your performance and ask if you would like to be hired out as a professional mourner. You played the part so well."

"Like always, Sophia, I have no idea what you're talking about."

"Then please allow me to go on with what I was saying, and that is, today you are whistling a different tune from yesterday. Now that vengeance has finally arrived, like we knew it would, you are angry with Aunt Erm because according to you, she has won again. But to us, she is only vindicated for the way her body was desecrated and her money wasted. A wise man who lived during Christ's time on earth said *Divine wrath is slow in vengeance, but it makes up for its tardiness by the severity of the punishment.*"

"Give us a break, will you?" E.J. begged his sister. "Jesus, we've all had a bad night. Please shut up, but while we're talking about Aunt Erm's strong will, I still want to hear what she did to get her name on a bridge."

"Well, I don't want to hear no more tales about Erma Mae, now or ever," Gladys said.

"Aunt Glad, your wishes are of little concern to us, seeing as how what you wished for in regards to Aunt Erm's funeral has turned into a colossal fiasco. If Grandfather feels up to telling the story of Aunt Erm's bridge I intend to listen. Oh, by the way, thank you for wearing a shirt and socks to the funeral, but what happened to your shoes?"

Leland giggled at Sophia's remarks to Gladys, as he crossed his ankles and arms indicating he was ready to tell the story.

"Well now," he began, "about a year after the tree episode, the commissioners approved developers' request to put culverts in Bochim Creek instead of building a bridge over it. Course culverts meant nobody could see the water from the main road, and Erma felt that was destroying the beauty of nature, so she decided to take action. Since she had been so successful with the tree episode, she announced to the board that she would sit in the creek until she froze to death if that was what it took to keep the creek from being destroyed. Springer immediately contacted the television and radio stations and the newspapers like he had when she sat in the tree, so the commissioners didn't waste time giving Erma what she demanded. They decided anything was better than all them reporters coming back to town making the folks of Bochimville look like what Erma referred to as Nature Rapers," Leland giggled.

"So is that why they named the bridge the Erma Mae Logan Bridge?"

"That's right."

"That's good. "

"While we're all here and need something to take our minds off what happened last night, Grandpa, how about explaining what the folks at the funeral home were talking about the other night regarding Aunt Erm and Springer being tried for horse rustling," E.J. said. "Would you explain that now before I have to go to work?"

"Well, I'll tell you right now—"

"NO! Aunt Glad, you will not tell us anything today, tomorrow, or ever," Sophia said as she raised her voice. "So don't go there. Continue Grandfather. We are listening."

"One cold winter when things were especially bad for farmers," Leland began his tale after taking a sip from his coffee cup. "Erma began to notice that a herd of horses on the Plantard farm were mighty skinny and seemed in need of food. Erma convinced the sheriff to go by and talk to Joe Plantard and tell him a lot of folks were concerned about his starving horses, and he'd better do something to correct the problem. Time went by and nothing changed, so Erma took matters into her own hands."

"She should have minded her own business and—"

"That's enough, Aunt Glad. Keep quiet. Go on Grandfather."

"About a mile down the road from the Plantard farm was an area with grass, weeds, and other plants horses could survive the winter on if it was available to them. It had once been a pasture with a nice flowing creek and fenced in but no longer in use.

"One night, Erma, Springer, and some of Springer's boys went out about midnight and cut the fence around Plantard's farm and herded the horses down the road to the old Glancy farm where they had also cut a big gap in the fence. They repaired the Glancy fence and went on about their business. A few weeks went by before old man Plantard missed the horses, but in the meantime the horses were looking better. We never knew how Plantard suspected it was Erma and Springer—"

"It was easy," Gladys interrupted. "They were the ones behind most of the mischief that went on in this—"

"That's enough, Aunt Glad. Silence, please."

"Well anyway," Leland continued, "Plantard swore out a warrant for Erma and Springer, and the Sheriff had to arrest them."

Leland stopped talking and wiped his forehead with a paper napkin. Then, he started chuckling.

"What's so funny, Grandpa?"

"Well, E.J., Erma, and Springer were charged with horse rustling, and it went to trial. Springer and Erma decided to be their own lawyers, and Springer notified the radio and television stations and newspapers all over the state. An animal rights organization sent a lawyer to represent Erma and Springer, but they wanted to represent themselves, so the lawyer said he would stay and advise them.

"There ain't never been nothing in the history of this town like that trial," Leland continued. "Erma brought one of the horses in the courtroom, and it pooped all over the place. The next day she brought in another one that got spooked and might near wrecked the place. Every day the courtroom was filled with animal activist groups hollering for old man Plantard's hide for neglecting the horses. Newspapers carried the story, and the TV and radio stations could hardly talk about anything else. Finally, the judge got so frustrated he dropped all charges against Erma and Springer and had Plantard arrested for animal abuse."

"Now that I've heard the story, Uncle Leland, I remember going to court, setting in the balcony, and watching the horses being brought into the courtroom. Joanie, do you remember it?"

"Now that you mention it, Hoov, I do remember. We couldn't have been over four or five at the time."

"Jeeeezus, Aunt Erm had guts," E.J. said.

"That wasn't guts. That was just being stupid and I--"

"That is enough, Aunt Glad, enough. You will not ruin our last day together. Go ahead, Grandfather, we are listening. Is there more to the story?"

"That's about it, Sophia. This whole town turned out for the trial. Maslow Moody served on the jury and offered to pay a lawyer to defend Erma and Springer and would have done so if the free one had not showed up."

"Don't see why the men—"

"Aunt Glad," Hoover said, "little cousin is right, you've had your say, and now it's time for this family to move on. I can't quote famous folks or the Bible like little cousin, but let's get on to the subject of Aunt Erm's ghost. You will have to admit that she was a strong willed woman and as long as I can remember, she requested to be cremated when she died. I guess her little old soul came back to earth last night, or better still it never left and took care of what you had cheated her out of, or should I say, tried to cheat her out of." Hoover smiled and smacked his lips. "And I might as well tell you now, Aunt Glad, payback for what has happened to Aunt Erm ain't got started yet. There are more fat ladies to sing besides you, so get ready for the concert of a lifetime."

Gladys ignored most of what Hoover said but hit her cane on the floor and raised her voice as she spoke. "Hoover, don't you start about her ghost. This stuff just happened, and it ain't got one thing to do with Erma's ghost. I don't want to hear no more about that mirror falling off the wall or that old clock stopping neither. There ain't no such thing as ghosts."

"Aunt Glad, you need to understand that many of us believe death is not an end but a new beginning, and is simply a transition into a higher state of consciousness. We believe the spirit of the deceased lingers on and is still capable of interposing in daily affairs. And if that be so, why couldn't Aunt Erm do something about the way her body had been defiled and her money stolen?"

"Hogwash. Sophia, I never for the life of me know what in tar nation you're talking about, and I wonder if anybody else does either. Erma's partly responsible for the way you are. Before you cut a tooth, she had you sitting on her lap reading to you from them gosh awful books she had stacked everywhere. By the time you turned four, she had you reciting the Bible and other stuff that most adults can't even read. The worst thing Erma did or didn't do that made me not like her was her hatred for preachers and her refusal to go to church."

"Well, Aunt Glad, let's face it, your attendance in church is rather lacking except for funerals and free food. If Aunt Erm never went to church, I personally view it as no big deal, for Jesus himself said *it is not important where you worship but how.* And as for preachers, most are an abomination and a disgrace to a civilized society, and if you need an example, just look at your own dear Virgil Jordan and nephew Flynn," Sophia grinned and motioned at Flynn with her head.

"That ain't all," Gladys whined, "Erma never even went to church to eat the Lord's Supper, and if that don't send her to hell, I don't know what will."

"Dear Aunt Glad," Sophia continued, "Aunt Erm did not believe in communion, for you see her God is not cannibalistic. In other words, her God does not require or demand blood sacrifices."

"God almighty, damn," E. J. said, as he raised his voice. "Mama," he whined to Joan, "please make her shut up. I'm so sick of her tommyrot I'm about to scream. I'll be so glad when she goes back to Athens and litters the campus with her stupid women's rights and religious rubbish and leaves us alone. We was talking about Aunt Erm's ghost, so can we please get back on the subject, but before we do, did anybody hear the panthers and wild cats screaming up around Bochim Creek last night 'bout the time we went to bed? I took it as a sign something awful was going to happen, and sure enough it did."

"Okay, little, flat-minded brother," Sophia said, as she playfully slapped E. J. on the side of his head. "We obviously don't know anything about screaming panthers and wild cats, and who said anything bad happened in the first place? It simply depends on how one interprets what happened last evening. Now, at your request, let us return to the subject of ghosts. Aunt Glad, I believe you said you do not believe in ghosts, so may I remind you that many educated, sensible, spiritual, God-fearing people believe in ghosts. For instance, when President Truman lived in the White House, he was convinced that the ghosts of Andrew Jackson and Abraham Lincoln visited him frequently."

"Sophia, I'm like E. J. and have about had enough of your foolishness. It's all hogwash, and nobody understands nothing you say about nothing."

"Now, Gladys," Leland said, "since we are on the subject of ghosts, do you remember when Hardy Stokes died and his wife give him a big expensive funeral like he told her for years not to do? The night after he was put in the ground in that fancy casket and dressed in a new suit, the quilts in his house flew off the beds, and every time they was put back they'd fly off again. For weeks they heard the old man's footsteps stomping around the house like he was madder than hell."

"Yes, Leland, I remember that. They finally had to bring in a preacher from the Catholic Church, and he circumcised the house and got rid of whatever it was. Flynn, if things start happening around here do you think you could circumcise the house like the Catholic preacher did the Stokes place?"

"I'm sure I could, Aunt Glad. I'm sure I could. With my faith as strong as a team of log pulling mules and Jeeeezus as close as my shadow, I know I can't fail."

"Thank you, Flynn, that makes me feel much better."

"Well, Flynn, old buddy, buddy," Hoover said, as he playfully slapped Flynn on the back. "I know you can't walk on water because when we were kids swimming in Florence's pond, you would have drowned if I had not pulled you out. I also know that you can't raise the dead because all that screaming and spitting you did over Aunt Erma the other night didn't make her sit up and speak. But if you can circumcise a ghost, by damn I'm going to hang around and watch. You just let me know when the big event is going to take place, and I'll sell tickets. We'll make a killing. And you can bet your one front tooth that Aunt Erm will return for the occasion. Just tell me, cousin, what kind of instrument do you plan to use?"

Everybody in the kitchen, with the exception of Gladys and Flynn, roared with laughter. I pulled a paper towel from the roll hanging beneath the cabinet and wiped the tears of laughter from my face and eyes.

The guests sat around the kitchen table a little longer eating biscuits dripping with syrup and drinking coffee while reminiscing about Erma and trying to deal with the happenings of the previous night.

Hoover and Joan left for Atlanta to see the lawyer they hoped would get Erma's money returned to us, and then slowly, one by one, the others left to pick up their lives where they had left them the day Erma died.

As soon as the fire marshals allowed me near the funeral home, I made final arrangements for the charred corpse of my sister to be laid to rest as she had requested. I was now at peace. I knew beyond a doubt that Erma, with a little help from those who loved her, had won the last and final battle with Gladys. I could hear Erma saying…*"Never avenge yourselves. Leave that to God, for She has said that She will repay those who deserve it."*

EPILOGUE

Mildred Roper

The next time the town of Bochimville assembled in as large a number as for Erma's funeral happened the day that Flynn, now known as the Rev. Oral Shockley, and Lucinda Faye Green joined hands in holy wedlock at the Rock Church that Loves Jesus.

In view of Oral's religious conversion, and a call from the Rock Church, the District Attorney's Office in Newton County felt compelled to drop all charges against him for chicken poaching.

However, the wedding was delayed when two of Flynn's three ex-wives and four of his six children, one accompanied by her parole officer, showed up to protest the wedding. The deacons held a short meeting and Deacon J.R., the church treasurer and town shyster, drew up an affidavit for each wife guaranteeing child support. The women of the church loaded the goods from the church pantry into the ex-wives cars and presented each child with a love offering from the Erma Mae Logan Feed the Hungry Fund.

No one has seen Brother Jordan since the day the deacons of the Rock Church instructed the congregation to vote to dismiss him and present a call to Oral Shockley. This decision was made the day of the exhumation of the graves of Elmo Croker and four other former residents of Bochimville.

Louella Jordan still lives in town, but Brother Jordan's name is seldom mentioned. Rumor has it that during the summer months he lives in a nudist colony somewhere in the North Georgia Mountains, and during the cold months, when he cannot run around naked, he breeds dwarf hogs in a remote section of Cobb County. There is still a warrant out for his arrest in the casket swapping charges made against him and Mr. Moody.

Gladys replaced Lucinda Faye as receptionist at the Maslow Moody memorial Mortuary that has been rebuilt since the fire. Gladys feels destiny intended for her to fill this position. In her new capacity, she is able to attend all funerals and share the county's grief and funeral meals.

Since Erma's death, I spend my days silently gloating about my accomplishments in fulfilling most of the request made by my dead sister. Of course I had a lot of help in accomplishing this, and to those who helped, I am eternally grateful. Through a judicial order, I received a large portion of money from Erma's insurance policy, and in an effort to carry out my sister's request I have distributed the money as outlined on the sheet of paper found in Erma's possessions. Once a week, and sometimes more often, with Crowie at my heels, I place a few home grown flowers near the well at the Logan home place beneath a small marker in the shape of an open book, which reads:

This well contains the earthly remains of
Erma Mae Logan
May her soul be at perfect rest

EPILOGUE

Ewell Moody

Several days following Miss Erma's funeral, the Georgia State Patrol found cause to stop and search the hearse from the Maslow Moody Memorial Mortuary, not only for exceeding the speed limit, but because the head of a mule protruded from the back window.

At the time of the search, the patrolmen uncovered what they classified as unusual items concealed in the vehicle. Among these items, and the most questionable, a Mason jar filled with gold crowns and several pieces of antique jewelry.

Some folks did not understand my hurry to leave town for a much-needed vacation immediately following exhumation orders for the graves of Elmo Croker and a few other former residents of Bochimville. However, under the circumstances I felt it too stressful on my delicate constitution to hang around.

The thought of dealing with Croker's widow when her old man was lifted from his grave lying in a pauper's box instead of the lovely mahogany casket in which he was last seen was more than my frazzled nerves could endure.

Through all of this, I have learned that good comes from every trial and tribulation, and I have finally accomplished one of my life's long wishes. I am now able to write poetry and read my books, as I so desire. Unfortunately, while engaging in these lovely activities, I am spending time in Buttsville, Georgia at the expense of the State.

My undertaking business, reconstructed several months following the mysterious fire, seems to be thriving in the capable hands of my old friend, Freddy Featherbone.

Stump Dupree, exonerated in mine and Jordan's casket swapping scheme, serves as Freddy's assistant and remains head embalmer.

Angus and Moss, also exonerated, are still employed as gravediggers. At the trial the three men simply used the Nazi defense and claimed they were just following orders from Adolph Moody.

Freddy's most profitable enterprise is the Flea Market held in the parking lot of the funeral home the first Saturday and Sunday of each month. Due to the unusual items available, it has become a profitable business venture.

What else can I say about my life except that the rest of the deeds of Ewell Delray Moody and the evils he committed are written in *The Annals of the Undertaker's History.*

So be it.

LaVergne, TN USA
08 February 2010
172379LV00004B/5/P